The Buried
Life

The Buried *Life*

Collected Stories and Prose

Wayne Luckmann

iUniverse, Inc.
Bloomington

The Buried Life
Collected Stories and Prose

iUniverse books may be ordered through booksellers or by contacting:

iUniverse
1663 Liberty Drive
Bloomington, IN 47403
www.iuniverse.com
1-800-Authors (1-800-288-4677)

Because of the dynamic nature of the Internet, any web addresses or links contained in this book may have changed since publication and may no longer be valid. The views expressed in this work are solely those of the author and do not necessarily reflect the views of the publisher, and the publisher hereby disclaims any responsibility for them.

Any people depicted in stock imagery provided by Thinkstock are models, and such images are being used for illustrative purposes only.
Certain stock imagery © Thinkstock.

ISBN: 978-1-4759-8645-7 (sc)
ISBN: 978-1-4759-8647-1 (hc)
ISBN: 978-1-4759-8646-4 (ebk)

Library of Congress Control Number: 2013907143

Printed in the United States of America

iUniverse rev. date: 04/26/2013

Contents

Sketches

The Buried Life

The weather was hot all the while my wife and I moved from California to Seattle. The sun shimmered off the dry yellow fields; the sun shone through billowing yellow dust raised by the men and machines that cut dark sweeping curves through the yellow wheat. We suffered in the dry choking heat that followed us across the mountains into the long shimmering valley with lone stands of pine and hills in haze at the horizon covered by the blue sky that opened to the sun. We suffered in the heat all the way to Seattle and the heat remained even after we found the place high on a hill beside the lake.

We moved into the empty house with bags and boxes, set what things we had in their places, and sat within the empty rooms listening to the clinking ice against the glasses of our drinks and the sound I made turning the yellow pages of the telephone directory. We looked for thrift stores to find inexpensive furniture. We had found some reasonably nice things before in California, but we had left them behind because of the limited room in the trailer that we had to pull with my old Chevy sedan. I made a list of several stores, we finished our drinks, and we left the empty house.

Seattle during our first days there was a maze even with a map. But we had somewhat learned that maze during our search for the house. So we headed out the wide white freeway dazzling in its newness; we went out across the towering freeway bridge that overlooked Lake Union.

The lake seemed a jumble of boats, ships, and cranes; trestle bridges swung up on huge concrete ends; gleaming logs floated in a jam. Beyond the lake, the hills and houses were bright in sunlight; the high thin web of bridge rose from massive concrete pillars softened by clustering trees.

One of the thrift stores was in the Ballard waterfront area, so we headed toward the sound and marveled at the sunlight off the dark blue water; we gazed in wonder at the Olympic Range patched with snow beyond the vast water dark even in the daylight.

We missed the street we wanted, turned back, then in our concentrated look for street numbers we missed the store. We saw the store as we drove past and expressed a sense of repulsion at the dismal things we saw through the dirt of the windows. So we didn't expect to find too much, but we decided to try anyway. Then after searching, we found a parking spot, climbed out into the humid heat and glaring sunlight, and headed for the two thin peeling doors. We stood aside to let an old whiskered man with worn sagging clothes pass us as we entered.

The interior of the store was dimly lit and surprisingly cool. We moved down the aisle that seemed thrust among the piles and confusion of clothes and shoes, pottery and ancient curios, strange and somewhat wondrous from another age. An ancient woman bent and wrinkled wrapped in a red sweater with a hairnet on her head and slippers on her feet shuffled out from some hidden room and came towards us down the aisle. She smiled at my wife and went around behind the piled counter

I wondered at the time on seeing the assortment of things behind the counter why they had been put there. For the shelves contained an unusual collection of ceramic shoes, pepper-mills, ceramic animals, cut glass, salt shakers, pictures, lockets, miniature portraits, book ends, ceramic cupids, mirrors, ashtrays, serving bowls, all definitely used, all obviously discarded. Then looking around at the whole store, seeing the clothes and furniture, noticing the open door and dirty broken window at the back of the store through which I could see the green leaves of trees in shadow and sunlight, I decided that everything had been placed for what I concluded was convenience.

We rummaged through the store. Several shelves of books stood against the wall; books were piled against the wall and up against the shelves until the shelves and books seemed to form a cascade. I usually would have immediately searched the shelves for what I considered treasures. For at other times in California I had found first editions of old and well kept copies that would excite me and compel me to buy. Now, however, the jumble of books held me off, so I avoided them and went toward the backroom of the store. I passed a well-dressed woman sorting carefully through old records that clacked somewhat fragilely as she slowly searched to the bottom of the pile.

As I was about to enter the backroom, a room that duplicated in its own peculiar fashion the front of the store, I heard the old woman storekeeper cackle something about going out. I turned to see her shuffle toward the door; and finally for the first time I noticed the bald man dressed in plaid flannel shirt and brown baggy pants standing among the rubble.

"Watch the store for a minute," the old lady said, head down, moving toward the door. "I won't be but a minute. Got to check on him, the poor dear. He must be suffering." The bald man stood silent with his hands in his back pockets watching the woman go out the door.

We turned in among the rubble to find a dresser we thought might do, but we decided to see if there were any better ones in the other stores on the street. We passed the bald man, his hands still in his pockets, and went out into the glaring light. We crossed the hot asphalt street to the next dim dirty store. On the way I turned to see the bent old woman slowly moving up the street beneath the burning sun.

We found nothing in the other stores so we went back across the street to the first one. The old woman hadn't returned, so we asked the bald man about the dresser. We drew him out from his place among the rubble and led him toward the backroom.

"I don't know," the man said with a rather heavy accent when we showed him the dresser. "I think maybe that's sold, but I' m not sure."

I wondered about the man's position in the store and his relationship to the old woman. I wondered how she could tell us any more than he the price of anything, for everything was piled without prices. I felt curiously uneasy because the thrift stores I had been accustomed to in California had been so orderly.

"You'll have to wait for her," the man explained. "She'll be back in a minute."

We thanked him and he went up to the front of the store. We heard him repeating his apology about not knowing prices to the woman who had been looking through the stacks of old records. Then he took his usual place among the piles of old clothing. I turned away and finally moved toward the cascade of books against the wall.

I was still selecting books when the old woman came back with an ancient looking dog under her arm. She bent to place him on the floor. "There you are, Stinker," the old woman said. The dog licked his chops and wiggled. The woman with the records stood at the counter looking at the dog.

"He must be very old," she said.

"He's not *too* old," the old woman answered. She seemed almost protesting. "Only nine. But the poor dear's got trouble with his heart—same as me. Neither of us can take the heat much anymore."

The dog looked up at the old woman and lay down beside the counter.

"That's it, Stinker," the old woman said bending toward the dog. "You rest."

The dog licked his chops again and snuffled. The stump of tail wagged slowly.

My wife went to inquire about the dresser and left me to my selection of books: I decided on a first edition of Lewis' *It Can't Happen Here*, Defoe's *Journal of the Plague Year*, Cooper's *The Prairie*. I also found a Tennyson, but I had a better copy at the house in one of the unpacked boxes.

My wife called me to decide on the dresser. I took the books and joined her and the old woman looking at the dresser surrounded by what appeared to be rubble. Then I returned to the books while my wife went to pay for the dresser.

"You should keep me away from old stores," I told her when she joined me and saw the books underneath my arm.

"I guess so," she said. But soon she was showing me a book she had found.

I smiled at her coy look. "Why don't you get it?" I insisted.

She thumbed through the book again and held it closed in her hand. I turned back to the bookcase.

I finished my random selection and began to look systematically for possible treasures I had missed. I searched behind the old discarded textbooks, behind the already discarded best sellers, behind the titles I had become familiar with searching for other books in other stores in California. Then my wife came to show me another book.

"Look at this binding," she said.

I was familiar with the binding from my purchase of one of the titles in the collection from which the book came. I was familiar with the title because I already had a copy in a box at the house in a different binding. When I told my wife, she seemed disappointed and turned away. But soon she was back with the same book.

"Look at *this*," she insisted. She handed me the book opened to the front inside cover. There I found a name in ink with a 1935 date after it. Below that name I found another name in pencil and a penciled date of 1960, and below that date the word "Love," and below the word "Love," a penciled message in what seemed like a rather crude handwriting.

"It seems strange," the message began, "that the word love should appear above this, especially on this day. But I feel that I can talk about Love. I had a love until today. He was very handsome. He had red hair and green eyes. He was a car fixer. He loved to fix cars better than anything. Maybe that's what was wrong. I think maybe he liked cars better than me. We were to be married, but now we never will."

"Isn't that something?" my wife asked when I had finished. I really didn't know what to say, but I felt the message had a poignancy because I didn't quite know the whole situation that had led to the message. How could I ever really know? The mystery, I felt, made the words of the message tender and rather touching.

"Why don't you get it?" I said (meaning the book). "Maybe I should."

"Get it if you want," I said and turned to finish my search through the rows of old discarded books: textbooks on economics, old editions of the *Standard Book of Knowledge*, old encyclopedias, old Latin grammars. Finally I was tired, so I turned, gathered the books I had chosen, and went to the old woman to ask about prices. I again could find no prices in these books whereas before in other stores in California I had always known how much a book would cost. Knowing the prices had always helped me to decide. This time I had to decide to take a chance. I was elated when the old woman decided on a standard price for each.

"They're all fiction, aren't they?" she asked.

"Yes, yes, all fiction."

"Then they're fifteen cents each."

Delighted at the price, I paid for the books in cash and took them out to the car. Then I returned for the dresser and took it out to place it in the trunk and tie down the trunk with an old piece of twine. I went around the side of the car and climbed in and started the engine. I straightened the books on the bench seat beside me. I again felt elated over my discoveries. Then I noticed that the book my wife had shown me wasn't among the pile.

"You didn't get the *Great Adventure Stories?*" I asked after she had joined me in the car. I felt astonished and oddly disappointed.

"We have a copy at home," she said. "I didn't think I should buy it just for the binding."

"Well, I probably would have bought it just for the message," I said.

I unsprung the handbrake and fought the car away from the curb.

"I guess I felt like an intruder," she continued. "I felt as if it wasn't meant for me to see."

I shrugged. Why then, I thought to myself, would someone write something so personal in the front leaf of a book?

"And besides, she ruined it."

"How do you mean, ruined it?" I was surprised at how angry I sounded.

"There was more in the back you didn't see."

"Oh really?"

Yes, she went on and on with a great deal of self-pity."

I felt disappointed."

Something about being pregnant and about the boy friend being killed or something."

"That's self-pity!" I exclaimed.

"Well, she goes on and on. She should have stopped at the first page."

I shrugged again and turned to concentrate on guiding the car along the busy streets past old faded stores, across the bridge, across the lake with boats and ships and wet and gleaming logs. I steered the car through hot and busy streets to our house that overlooked the wide blue sparkling lake.

We sat within the empty house piled with unpacked boxes glancing at the old pale dresser we had deposited then ignored. We sat within the bare rooms sipping our drinks gazing out the large bay window, gazing at the lake, the distant houses, the distant trees in the vague gray towering haze of the mountains beyond.

Hattie

Aunt Hattie, my mother's aunt, was one of our kin upon whom my father had always raised unfounded expectations. I was never sure of Hattie's relationship to Margaret, my grandmother. Hattie was "Great Aunt," so she might have been Margaret's sister, but since we had a wide network of kin, what now seems more of a clan, Hattie's position was always unclear. Just as I never was sure most of the time to whom I was related, so many of us were scattered about, or so it seemed, and I was often surprised to find I was related however distantly to someone I had been playing baseball or tag football with in the streets.

Aunt Hattie was also my godmother and would therefore according to tradition provide for me if anything happened to my parents, so everyone expected her to be my patron. Why she was chosen is perhaps more clear than when or how. She was said to have a well-to-do son, and I was led to believe that for some reason that wealth would somehow allow her to offer me gifts or opportunities which others in our vast relationship wouldn't be capable of giving. My other brothers had godparents who were as poor as we, coming as we all did from a working-class background.

Since Aunt Hattie was my godmother, I was instructed to be courteous to her because she had money—or her son supposedly did—and the suggestion was that perhaps she might leave me something when she, heaven forbid, pass on to whatever rewards she had earned.

And from time to time I even heard talk of a trust fund in my name, but we soon learned that fund never really existed. Yet I really didn't hear from Hattie or know about Hattie until about the time I was approaching graduation from grade school when Aunt Hattie suddenly appeared. My parents had me write to her, and I wrote, and to my surprise and delight Aunt Hattie came.

Since Aunt Hattie's son was rumored to be wealthy, and seeing where she lived, we assumed that she was wealthy, too. For we went to visit her once after Aunt Hattie suddenly appeared. Margaret, my mother, and I traveled to her home by bus. She lived in an area of elegant modern houses in a planned development out in the suburbs that seemed as foreign to me in its modernity as if it were in Argentina. For I saw vast sloping lawns immaculately trimmed, yellow stucco archways, red tiled roofs, and spiky shrubs that looked tropical.

And all our assumptions about Hattie's wealth were given a modicum of validity by the gifts she began giving me. For my graduation, she bought me my first new suit—dark gabardine. She bought me shoes—new leather ones—and a new, white shirt—and a new silky tie to match—one of my very own, rather than one of my father's that he allowed me to wear for any infrequent occasion that required it. How splendid I would be in my new apparel!

After graduation, I received cards from Aunt Hattie on my birthday, sometimes with a bill of small denomination that to me still seemed grand given that I was more accustomed to small change. I think I might have expected more because everyone else, especially my parents, expected more, for my parents seemed to cultivate Aunt Hattie's largess, so I eventually wondered how deliberately my parents, especially my father, had decided on Hattie as my sponsor.

But while I also received small gifts for my high school graduation, my discovery was that Aunt Hattie was not rich. Nor did I ever meet her "wealthy" son, and we found that, contrary to our persistent fantasy that Aunt Hattie was rich and therefore might bestow some wealth on me, she, too, was poor, thereby crushing my parents' (more my father's) fervent hopes.

For just as suddenly as she appeared, Aunt Hattie was gone. Soon after my graduation from high school, Hattie died under what were at the time mysterious circumstances, such events and news always suppressed, the cause uncertain. I heard rumors exchanged in hushed voices of her son being illegitimate—shocking if true at the time, and when Great Aunt Hattie died mad, whispers suggested that her madness was punishment for that sinful indiscretion of her youth.

One day after we had not heard from Hattie for awhile, someone (Margaret, I believe) found Hattie sitting at her kitchen table, the long gray hair that she had worn always twisted into an orderly braid on top her head undone, uncombed, sprawled down across her bare shoulders, her bare breasts. Margaret reported that she had found Hattie naked at the kitchen table talking to her long dead family she had left behind in the old country. She died that same day driven mad from the tumor that had grown undetected in her brain.

When Hattie died, old gossip of her wealth was resurrected, and everyone expected I might be "left something." Again, as they had been so many times before, such hopes were dashed. But long before Hattie died I had come to accept that contrary to what my father wanted to believe no treasure trove existed at the end of that rainbow. And her death signified to me that desires are seldom lived or realized, and should we try to live only according to our dreams, we may end in disappointment, if not bitterness and despair.

Pete's Smoke and Hobby Shop

When I last saw the neighborhood from the street view window of a Google map, not much seemed the same. Some of the houses were now gaily painted with bright color and complementary trim, and one house especially appeared transformed: Instead of gray siding with green trim, now the whole was a dull tan, the wood steps and rail of the front porch replaced by cement and steel, the tall front windows hidden behind a large thick bush, the green wood gate opening to the concrete walk leading to the back door beside the alley now a strip of grass enclosed in a cyclone fence. And as I moved with the directional arrow along the avenue that intersected the street where the house stood, gone now were the storefronts that I had lived with and frequented, their large windowpanes boarded and blind, so that the avenue that once appeared wide and radiant with new macadam and lined with lively windows of colorful displays now seemed a dull, narrow wasteland.

Yet these structures most likely would not seem any different to someone who had never left, someone who would never know the incidents of change that seemed to jar me: the flat I had lived for a spell vanished; the warehouse with its massive whitewashed wall and it endlessly glowing neon sign I had gazed at in all seasons and weather from the upper level of that vanished flat now a multi-pump service station and convenience store; the small upholstery store across from where I had stood waiting for a trackless trolley one time on one of the occasions of my infrequent returns, it too was gone, its front changed into a blank facade indistinguishable for all the others in both directions.

Witnessing such amorphous, anonymous structures, who would ever imagine that one had not always been used for reconditioning old furniture, that upholstery shop, too, now gone? How many times had I frequented that place (and what was it now?) when in another era it had been a smoke shop, a sweet shop, a model shop all combined into one dimly lighted narrow cell run by a man whom I had always—not unkindly—thought of as looking like a pig?

The man's paunch had usually strained the buttons of his faded flowered shirtfront where it hung over the brown leather belt; his cheeks loose, almost flapping when he spoke, he seemed to speak through his nose, his mouth puckering, while his eyelids blinked incessantly. I remember peering up at the man who had sometimes made faces in an attempt to make me laugh. I eventually came to realize that the short fat man came each day to his dim cell lined with shelves, bordered with glass cases behind which he presided, retired at times—for what purpose, I never knew until later, and I could scarcely image at the time what took place behind a faded print-cloth curtain that hung in the doorway at the rear of the cell beside the old chipped cooler into which he frequently dug within the rime-rimmed depths to fetch us ice cream bars.

Now, as I thought of it, sitting here, carried along by this magic carpet of the Internet that would take me wherever to what unforeseeable often unexpected places and events, I was amazed in recalling what part that dingy store had played in my life. How unconscious I had been the oh so many times I had gone there to buy soda and ice cream or creamsicles almost daily if I could "mooch" a dime or earn one by doing some chore, and now how utterly that place had been transformed, wiping out completely any trace of the man whom I later learned had turned to spirits and sexually explicit magazines, imbibing both behind the faded curtain: Those days seemed now so distant, leaving only a fading ghostly image of the man and the narrow shop as Google carried me forward through cyberspace.

Immediately on the corner next to Pete's, across from where I had stood waiting for the trolley, sat the green bench beneath the glowing neon sign of Tess' Tavern (it, too, now a blank facade boarded and painted over) where we gathered both day and night after we had gone to Pete's Smoke and Hobby Shop. On that green slat board bench we negotiated our next moves, or we engaged in oral contests, verbal challenges and counter challenges we won not by force of logic and reasoned argument but by the strength and insistence of our voice following and imitating our parents. And later, when we had grown into such events, from this green bench we courted the flowering young girls of the neighborhood.

To Tess' tavern, past that green bench, my grandfather Emil came frequently, and sometimes my father would come, too, and we would go with them for soda in a glass with ice and crisp salty chips, we sitting on the tall stools at the bar if it were not fully occupied, such indulgences allowed in that era. Or on occasion Emil would send me with a small-galvanized bucket for brew from the tap for which I would hand over some small coin. Here, at Tess', while the holiday feast was being prepared, the table set, the fowl roasting, the adult males would come seeking refuge from the constraining chatter of women and indulging in some beverage to slack their thirst and oil their manly discourse.

And cross corner from Tess' and directly across from what was once the trolley stop another tavern (still surprisingly open but now transformed into a hard rock bistro or cantina). This tavern along with Tess' followed the typical pattern of taverns set on opposing corners in what seemed like every other neighborhood allowing someone sufficiently wetted and invited out from one establishment to stagger cross corner while avoiding the sparse late night traffic to resume his intake of liquid and his well-oiled discussion with someone else, most likely that someone having negotiated the same somewhat sinuous path from one corner to the other.

One end of the tavern cross corner from Tess' had a doorway that led to overhead apartments. And next to this doorway a garage that housed the fulfilled youthful dream of someone who lived in the apartment overhead.

Acts of Piety

I have passed him now leaving him behind. But I can't remember his name. Perhaps it doesn't matter.

Yet I remember he had long yellow hair like silted corn. And he had visions as bright and free as his hair that was full of the sun and that he combed straight back. His approach to fulfilling his dreams was as direct:

"Your want something!" he used to command. "Go get it!"

And at other times: "Isn't this a free country?" Isn't this America? You want something, you work for it!"

Thus he proclaimed what he believed. Several grades ahead of me in school he seemed wise beyond his years, for he was more than mere talk. He acted on what he proclaimed: Quitting school to work, he saved for a car that he finally bought.

The car dazzled deep vermillion, chrome trimmed, white sidewall tires, a rich leather interior warm and fragrant from the sun, a place you would want to curl holding yourself with exquisite delight if he would only let you. Yet I always had to remain content to creep to the side, to peer through the open window at the soft sheen of the upholstery, the metal ribs, the coarse weave of the canvass top he would work down carefully exposing the interior. Then he'd climb in and drive away beneath the endless blue sky under the green umbrellas of trees above tall dark trunks, he revealed in the wide glittering street, his hair billowing capturing the sun.

So he had won this gamble, or so it seemed to me, for I was one of the envious who marveled at his success. Along with others, I watched frequently on bright Saturdays while he moved with the deliberateness and grace of a dancer or an artist. His frothing pail and hissing hose sent shimmering rivers in the gutters sluicing down the block joining the tributaries from other hoses, green coiling serpents devouring the world.

My brother, closer in age to him, would often stop by to chat. While the owner lounged carefully against the mirroring door of the washed and polished chariot, my older brother stood at a respectful distant as the traffic, the unimportant world, the universe passed by. I would listen as they exchanged utterances of insatiable, unimaginable desires. My brother was obviously, surprisingly impressed; I was simply overwhelmed and enthralled by this colossus, a living myth.

Later, recovering from loss, healing from pain, I often thought of him and his success, my visions raised by the wonder, the remembrance of that boy who had finally won his manhood. For he eventually had proven himself through his acts of piety in fulfilling his patriotic duty.

The last that I had heard of him he had returned from war a hero sent home from the valleys among the scarred hills of some distant land in a closed box.

Growing Up With the Fonz

Milwaukee during the 1950s might have been as carefree as it seemed on "Happy Days." I could never decide. For having lived the experience, I seldom watched the program, and when I look back, I realize that at the time, I was too busy growing up, going through my teens, having, perhaps, many of the same experiences seen now from a distance of several decades. So I find difficult deciding just how "happy" those days really were.

Yet, I can understand the show's popularity. First, it captured an attitude that now seems to have been prevalent at the time during what might be considered an adolescence of the American experience. And the program seemed to show an America beginning to lose its naïveté, its innocence; it showed an America growing up, learning what the world was really all about. Most of all, what I saw through the filter of my experiences, the program captured through caricature the manners and the morals of the people of the time.

And as everyone who watched during the program's long run knew the most popular character on "Happy Days" was the Fonz. He appears to have emerged with the development of the show from a typical sit-com character to one who became a cultural icon. For the character of the Fonz took over the show, dominating it, making the show his and becoming in the process a cultural hero along with all that such a status enjoys—his image, just in case you didn't notice, was everywhere.

So what needs to be decided first is just what it was about the Fonz that allowed him to emerge. What was it that continued to make him remain popular? The second move is to suggest in what ways Fonzi appears representative of actual people. By making such a move, I hope to show that the popularity of "Happy Days" indeed lay in its capturing the manners and moral of the times it attempts to portray.

To satisfy this intention, allow me to first consider other characters that developed though the 50s. Looking back now, one realizes immediately that at the time we found discerning the difference between what was real and what was ritual difficult. Now, of course, we see more readily that the character of the Fonz captures an attitude: For we took ourselves very seriously then, perhaps because we were very naïve, because we were very innocent, because we were going through a ritual of initiation and through rites of passage as individuals and as a culture even though we weren't aware we were doing so. Consider in passing what lay ahead of us during the 60s and the following decades: We had not yet experienced the pain of Vietnam, or the shock of civic and cultural leaders shot to death, or the jolt of Watergate that revealed how corruption appears to always start from the top, thus revealing to us that we were becoming a banana republic.

In contrast, during the time portrayed by "Happy Days" we had Dean, we had Brando both somewhat innocent rebels within and outside the vehicles of their films. Thus they lived the roles they portrayed so that we found difficult deciding where their film roles ended and where their actual lives began. In fact, we seemed to have resisted any attempt to make the distinction clear. In sum, they not only captured the imagination of America, they captured as well the imagination of the whole world. So we had Dean in *Rebel Without a Cause* and Brando in *The Wild One*—these titles now obviously significant when at the time they seemed merely provocative. For at the time they stirred our emotions and a yearning to be similar, or they elicited a sense of identity in that we were similarly suffering the same anguish that we instead sublimated and released only through mimicking their attitudes and manners. They elicited an empathy because both these young men, no longer boys but not yet men, seemed sacrificial. In both we saw their flaunting of the accepted morality, yet both were basically moral. We saw them flaunting the law; yet they fundamentally were more concerned with justice and fairness than those who "enforced" the law. They showed through their confrontation with some elements of society that they were representative of the paradox basic to American democracy. They were perpetually excluded because of their character, yet, at the same time, they embodied the ideals of individualism. Rejecting society, they were at the same time concerned with gaining the respect, recognition, and affection of a society that rejected them because they rejected that society.

The question then is how is the Fonz a continuation of the tradition established by Dean and Brando? How, indeed, is Fonzi representative of the attitude that seemed so prevalent at the time? Well, a couple ideas come immediately to mind that might help answer these questions. First, as I have indicated, the Fonz captured the manners and morals of a character important to the time, a characteristic exploited at the time. So we had Jimmy Dean, a young rebel without direction or purpose, the true adolescent wandering from one experience to another yet never accepting life at it happens, searching for meaning, searching for purpose, continually asking why.

Fonz, of course, was less alienated, less self-destructive, and Fonzi didn't appear to have any difficulty in establishing the certainty of his self-identity. But the Fonz had as Dean had the badge of his rebellion, the costume of the rebel: the leather jacket, the Levi's slung low, the longish hair, when at the time, the all-American image of the crew cut was more socially acceptable.

Thus, the Fonz was still representative of the young tough, and this image of the young tough is borne out by his manner. The Fonz is physical, and he was respected if not somewhat feared for his toughness. First, he was physical through the sense of an implied sexuality, his "making it" with what seemed a countless variety of girls ("women" was too mature a descriptor). He was also physical in the sense that everyone appeared to fear his anger; and he was tough in the sense that he was crafty. He was capable of solving problems others found difficult to solve, perhaps because they were more scrupulous, more squeamish about bending the law or the situation in order to satisfy their own necessities. In contrast, Fonzi appeared to have little compunction in solving problems by means or methods that were sometimes slightly questionable and perhaps at times may even have been considered illicit.

And, of course, his expressions became associated with him and ritualized and were often imitated: "A-a-a-y! or "Sit on it!" suggesting his tough mindedness.

Yet Fonzi was also sensitive: he did help his friends. He was loyal. He was respectful of those adults who showed their honest respect for him, not because they feared him, not because he was tough, but because he was Fonzi. Richie's parents, for example, admired and showed honest affection for him, and he returned their feeling in like kind.

We see, then, that The Fonz is a continuation of the rebel tradition.

The other question raised is, how is the Fonz representative of actual people growing up at the time? How is he more than just a characterization of that attitude of rebellion and also representative of the manners of American society during a given era?

To answer this question, I speak now not of Fonzi but of Blando and our growing up together in Milwaukee during the 1950s. Like the Fonz, Blando was of Italian heritage, third generation, to be exact, with dark good looks: dark wavy hair, dark almond shaped eyes, skin the color of olive oil, and already in his teens sporting that masculine shadow, a dark stubble that was always present.

Blando was also what we now refer to as macho: He, similar to Fonzi, was physical, pursuing or accepting fights at the slightest provocation, and he was built for such challenges: of medium height, he was solid with wide shoulders tapering to narrow hips, thick thighs that kept him firmly planted. And also similar to the Fonz, he was physical in the sense of moving from one "woman" to another, and we admired him because unlike the rest of us he was not naïve. Involved continually in one romance or affair after another, the outcome was always the same, and at that time his conquests were notorious, awesome, inspiring.

But in addition to these physical qualities, Blando was attractive in another way. He was, again similar to the Fonz, sensitive and in his own way loyal while upset at the disloyalty in others. So although he went from one "woman" to the next, while involved with her, he was intensely loyal.

I recall, for example, how hurt he was one night when he wasn't with us and we had picked up his current female friend bringing her along to meet him where he worked. However, instead of going directly to where he worked we had gone joyriding, his friend "unfaithful" by flirting or "making out" with the driver, an "older man" of twenty from the South. During our ride, having sufficiently imbibed one of the local famous brews, we had missed a curve, and had rolled. When we finally met him after having dealt with the required institutions of wreckers and police, we all had lied to protect him from knowing fully what had happened.

Blando was talented in ways other than with women. So his other talents attracted a following from the very beginning of his having entered our social group, and from the very beginning, I was one of the dedicated followers. He exuded sophistication in the true sense of the world: He was worldly, or so he appeared. He played an instrument as an accomplished musician. I had dabbled from time to time with one instrument after the next urged by my father who had taught himself to play several. But with Blando there was a difference. He not only played well, he played "professionally" as he was the first time I met him. A new kid in the neighborhood, he was already commanding attention by his being hired for parties at the bowling alley where I worked setting pins. His work was so much more refined. Dirty, sweaty from my work, I watched as he dazzled us with his art, skillfully and easily playing one piece after the other without hesitations or mistakes. Proud of his accomplishment, he took our applause and our praise quietly and graciously with a slight smile and a slight bow almost as if shy in being so on display. From that time on, I was a captive.

In addition to his physical presence and his talents, his material possessions overwhelmed us. Always well dressed in the latest fashion, flush and somewhat spendthrift from what he earned playing at various events, he also owned a car. His father, a short, dark, handsome man, indulged him—as did his mother, a true mamma *mia* heavy from childbearing who indulged us all eventually. She made pizza that seemed from out of this world, one of the first in the Milwaukee area who made it at all, and she created other exotic dishes that even I, a finicky eater, would devour.

His father having signed for him to buy a car, Blando set about getting it to run. In doing so, he seemed to need company, as in so many instances of what he did, and I was always willingly available. So we spent autumn evenings in the bottom of what had once been a barn, the floor gray with frost, conversing about good-only-knows-what, while he worked and I watched handing him tools, fetching parts, while we smoked, just like adults, the radio playing "Earth Angel" or some other exquisite tune of that time—Johnny Mathis just getting started—we sang along while we waited for life to pick us up and set us in the direction for which we searched.

In that car, a 41 Chevy coupe, I learned to drive chauffeuring him while he slept or while he plied his talent and spent his energy with women in the back seat. Thus I lived vicariously yearning for similar opportunities, for similar ability, my longing made more acute by the willingness, the sensuousness, the immediacy of the female while they huffed and heaved in the dark backseat.

But we spent as much time pushing that car as driving it, so eventually he went on to something more suitable, something more appropriate, something more grand: a red 48 Ford convertible with wide whitewall tires, a radio, and leather seats. The top, of course, was always down opening the world to us even in the late fall, the engine thrumming beneath the narrow polished hood, the heater turned to full blast after the weather turned brisk cooling from the mild autumn evenings when the sun went quickly leaving a deep blue twilight through which we ventured forth. Above the windshield, the universe was cold and dark. But in summer the black velvet of the night, the canopy of lush broad-leafed oak, the warm wind in our faces, the distant worlds promised us an eternity of hope, a paradise of earthly rich rewards.

I had hoped we would always be friends. So I served him at court: picking him up for school when I finally had achieved my own car, or chauffeuring for dates when he had lost his license, or when he had been infrequently grounded for reasons I never knew and scarcely imagined. And he was *always* late for dates because he was always meticulous about his appearance. I waited, watching while he shaved, a task I didn't achieve for another decade or so. I fetched his clothes, ironed his shirts, his mother complaining, refusing to do so herself, she wondering why I should. I polished his shoes. I did all these tasks willingly, paid in return by his company, by those times—now and then—when, spontaneously, he would arrive at my door "rehorsed," his red convertible revving. He was seeking company for one of his adventures, and he had chosen me.

Not too surprisingly he had moved into the grown-up world more readily, more rapidly than the rest of us. His last year of high school he worked, going to school part-time, abandoning a job he had evenings, bequeathing it to me. From that time on, we didn't see as much of each other. And after graduation when he became a laborer mucking in holes for sewers and I became an office clerk hanging around with him from time to time, I saw less and less of him until growing bored with my dead-end job, I went out to California by myself, starting college at Long

Beach, and making friends with people who showed me through their accomplishments and their attitudes and their manners that their lives were what I might someday achieve myself.

Then one day—out of nowhere—Blando was there—just like that. And when we rented an apartment together in Belmont Shores near the ocean, I had what perhaps I might have thought at one time the fulfillment of an ideal: We roamed the places I had explored alone. Leading the way, I showed him the extensive beaches, the harbor with its anchored fleet, the coffee houses, the Long Beach Pike, Hollywood and Vine at midnight, Union Station at dawn. I was acutely conscious of our being there together like that, so vastly removed, surely, from the limited world we had known and in which we had grown together as adolescents.

Most of the time, though, I was involved in study and classes. I would read to him while we ate, sharing with him my newly found knowledge and insights, just as my new friends had shared theirs with me. Blando would accept these readings demurringly without comment seeming a bit uncomfortable, a bit out of place.

So I wasn't too surprised, although saddened, when I came home one day to find him gone. Yet, at first, I was stunned: I found the note telling me that he was off south to San Diego where he had a distant relative who might help him find work cleaning vehicles at a car dealership. I now surmise that his lying around while I was so busy with schoolwork, so involved in something so foreign to him that my activity had made him restless. Then, too, perhaps my attitude and my new involvement in the world of ideas had put him off. Even though I was proud of him, showing him off to my new friends whom I considered intellectuals, they only found him quaint and politely accepted him at a distance for what he was—a somewhat lost, confused young man.

I saw him the next time when I went back home for a visit the following year. I found him there back at his old job of mucking, the job in San Diego having been somewhat brief, California a dead end. We went out together once shortly after I arrived, our evening ending at a beer joint where I became engrossed in a lengthy discussion on the nature of God with one of his former female friends. When the place closed, I found that he had gone hours before; the woman had left with her date. I walked the five miles home alone.

The last time I had any sort of contact with him I was back from the Pacific Northwest where I had finally settled, my return one of the infrequent visits I ventured over the years. That time I had traveled back to partake in the rituals of memorial for my mother's passing.

And that time the closest I came to looking him up was in the phone book. His name was there, of course, looking respectable and as solid and as distant as mine might have seemed should he have ever looked me up or had called. But he had never done either, and to be honest, neither had I, nor did I that time upon finding his name listed in the book.

Well, perhaps it might seem as if I've wandered a long way from the Fonz and from "Happy Days." O.K., I confess I have for my own purpose. Yet any of the infrequent times I watched the program, especially when I saw in later episodes Richie going off to college and Fonzi staying behind, I couldn't avoid recalling Blando and our growing up together during the 1950s. How much like the Fonz he seemed to me. Perhaps that's why I didn't watch "Happy Days" as much as I might have. Having lived the experience once was probably enough

The Man Who Loved High Places

"You ready to climb?" Wick challenged.

So we climbed—no ropes, no boots—nothing—just ourselves.

Eleven hours later we were down again from Mount Hood returning faster that we had climbed, Wick shaking with cold, laughing in a high, strained, nervous laugh. Somehow, I had been too young to be afraid. Besides, I was with Wick who seemed to know everything and had little apparent fear of anything.

So Wick was the cause of it all.

How he loved high places. He had learned to fly while still a kid, and the joy from reaching such heights stayed with him his whole life. Now it seemed that any chance he could get to soar, lifting on the wind above the clouds, he would take it. This time on the mountain he carried me along; and this time he nearly crashed and burned.

I had met Wick soon after my arrival in California just as Wick was leaving for the east to get Ann, the girl he brought back to marry. I had liked him immediately, but he was distant. I was nothing to him now. He told me so. We had no common ground for friendship. He had education: he was older. Yet he liked me, liked my spunk, my drive. Maybe someday, he offered, we would be friends. First, he advised, I had better find myself—as he had.

"You have to solo first before you really begin to learn to fly!" He was like that—direct, definite. Unformed, I stood in awe.

When Wick and Ann left on their honeymoon I became engrossed, enchanted in the wonder of the moment. I suddenly found myself in California, a place that all my young life had seemed exotic, a place that everyone I had known in the Midwest thought of as paradise. Now in the heavy heat of twilight here I was viewing the endless wide boulevards lined with tall palms, the clear blue sky before the color of the sunset thinned to neon lights, the blur of tail lights from endless lines of cars and the sweet poisonous exhaust that joined the haze lifting toward the girdered oil tanks, the slow revolving silhouette arms of chugging diesels like some gigantic insect pumping liquid eons from the dark earth. I witnessed cool mornings with gray dissipating clouds that brought the sun brightening the grass wet from morning fog. I beheld the vast ocean and breaking surf, walked the beaches, breathed in the salty air. I thought I'd never get enough of it.

Yet, I left soon after they did traveling north to Oregon to work the wheat fields. There for a while I joined Wick and Ann who had hired on at a farm in another county. We met on weekends for camping along the swift Columbia River, sleeping beneath the stars, they bundled in a double bag, I alone in my cocoon.

One Sunday I saw first hand Wick's old habit, his love of high places. We climbed the mountain—just like that. We started walking then reached the glacier where it began above the timberline. At first Ann was still with us, but we kept going leaving her behind.

"Let's go to the top!" Wick challenged.

Ann called after, protesting, claiming fatigue.

"Rest there," Wick called back facing her. "You can walk back to the lodge. We'll be right down."

Ann returned his grin with a raised eyebrow and a smile that played at her mouth, an amused expression that started in her eyes then became one of concern.

"You don't have the right equipment!"

We didn't have *any* equipment. But that slight difficulty didn't deter us.

"Shaw!" Wick exclaimed, mocking a dialect. "Who needs stuff like that? It'd just slow us down."

Then he turned to me. I was studying the sun-washed glacier, a dazzling plain that swept upward in a massive cone to the cloud-bound peak.

"You ready, old man?" Wick asked.

We climbed. Our feet sank in the soft snow soaking our shoes. We worked our legs, lifting one foot above the next, pulling ourselves up to reach them. We were soon exhausted. The sun blinded our unprotected eyes. Glaring from the snowpack, the sun sucked the water from our flesh billowing our breath. We chewed on packed snow, stopped to rest, then pulled on.

"How you doing?" Wick asked once during a pause.

"I'll make it," I insisted then started up ahead of him taking the lead. "Don't strain!" Wick yelled after. "We've got a long way to go!"

Not answering I plodded on. Then we reached a place where the glacier became the bare craggy peak thrusting up toward the whirl of windblown snow and cloud. There we stopped. We turned exhausted gazing out across the vast country extending in undulating hills, a dark green plush of trees. Curtains of mist between the hills caught the sun. We looked back down along the way we had come. We could see far below the toy-like image of the lodge. I thought of the soft carpeting of the halls, the spattering fire on the huge stone hearth, the strong savor of the drink I anticipated if we ever got down. I imagined Ann lounging in leisure waiting for us. I tried to find the rock on which we had left her sitting, but it was lost in the dazzle of the sun, the massive sweep of bright snowpack, the panorama of trees and foothills, of mist and valleys that I turned to study once again. I marveled at the beauty and serenity of the view. Then we saw the dark clouds gathering above the bright distant peaks.

"A storm!" Wick exclaimed.

I nodded speechless still struggling for breath, the rare atmosphere at that height making me gasp. I watched the distant churning clouds.

"It'll be on us soon! We've got to get down fast! We'll be caught!" "How long it take us to get here?"

"Seven hours!"

"We've got to do better than that!"

I was amazed at how calm we both were—so matter of fact. You climb for hours: you stop, get caught in a storm; you go back down. Years later I would see reports of what mountains can do to climbers by luring them, drawing them up, trapping them, never letting them go. Now I was beginning to learn, but I didn't know it then. I continued to admire the view.

Wick squinted up at the peak then back down the glacier that fanned out below. Far down the mountainside we could see the shelter we had left hours ago. Then surprising me, Wick started up toward a dark stain.

"Look at this!" he called, He began tugging at something buried in the snow. I saw him uncover a cache of tools, rusted nails, weathered boards, a nearly new Model A engine.

During the Great Depression someone had hauled these things raising them to this height to build a hut, a shelter, a refuge for those who, like us, had felt the pull, the challenge of the massive peak and had foolishly climbed to meet that challenge. Now these things lay abandoned, caught in brief sunlight, left by those descending through forest to the plain, to the ocean, to the distant thunder and the fire of war. The swift clouds darkened the sun. We started from our dream.

"We better hurry," Wick said.

I followed his lead and we chose boards, dug in the spiked jumble of nails uncovering those beneath. We drove the nails fulfilling them after their long wait fashioning the boards into a crude sled. We added a cowl and stood back admiring our invention. Then Wick turned to me.

"Well, shall we go?"

I looked at him. He looked at me.

"I guess we better," I said.

"I guess," he said.

We met each other's eyes then looked away.

"Well, let's go then," Wick said.

He stepped to the boards of the crude sled, squatted, dropped, placed himself, and grabbed the cowl shifting it to adjust the aim.

"We'll use our feet as brakes. Lean with me to help steer. We've got to keep away from *that!*" He pointed to the deep chasm some twenty yards to our left. I nodded, dropped behind him, and grabbed his waist.

"O.K.," I said.

"Let's go!"

And down we went—straight for the chasm! Wicked leaned pulling at the cowl, straining as we sailed along the chasm edge. I saw the deep abyss. We teetered until we broke free upon the steep descending plain—straight for rocks.

"Help!" Wick cried, the first time I ever had heard him use the word. We leaned and strained again. The dark volcanic clumps raced by, dropped behind bristling with jagged razored edges. Then we reached deep snow. The cowl dove in raising a wash that hit us full in the face blinding us, freezing our flesh.

"Dig in!" Wick screamed back.

I dug, my feet, my legs, my whole body shocked by the contact, the profound cold. I felt the slash and sting of ice on my face, my hands, my legs. But we raced on, our speed too great, our flesh too weak to withstand the force.

"Hang on!" Wick cried.

I felt lost. We plummeted beyond control both of us silent, our silence greater for the roar of our descent, the rush of ice and snow, the shock and jolt of the flat unyielding boards which rode the wind and snow beneath us carrying us down.

We sailed; we soared. Then suddenly the sled stopped. I followed Wick in his dive as the sled swung up behind us throwing us off. We raced on—all arms and legs, treading air, sky, trees, sun, clouds, clawing for balance, for something, for anything until we fell, we rolled, a fantastic childhood summer dream fulfilled. We tumbled gathering snow, regaining weight until we finally slowed then stopped.

We lay in heaps waiting for the sun, the sky, the slanted earth to bring us back. My lungs heaved, my blood crashed, throbbed, stilled. My spirit returned. I watched the quiet sky deep in summer blue.

Wick moaned, the sound escaping him.

"What's wrong!"

"My feet! My legs!"

I raised myself on my arm. He lay curled over his buried feet, his face raw from the ride.

"Rub them!"

"I can't! I can't move my hands!"

I struggled to him then helped him to a rock we had barely missed in our fall. Thanks to Wick I had come out better, my ride behind him somewhat sheltered. Now I bent to remove his shoes then his socks. I used my shirt to warm his feet, first holding them then gently rubbing them until the red came back and he bit his lips in silent pain. Finally he began to relax. We waited until he could rise to his feet.

"You two just come down from the top?" a man asked when we reached the shelter.

"Sure!" we somewhat boasted.

29

"You see those two crazy guys up there on that sled?"

Wick and I exchanged glances.

"Craziest thing I ever seen," the man said. "Saw it all through these." He held out the powerful binoculars. "Just a streak of snow like a large rooster tail on a speed boat. I wasn't sure at first what it was. Then these two guys just racing to beat hell! I nearly died! I don't think I'll ever see anything so funny in all my life! I'll never see the likes again! Wish I could meet those guys. See what they're like. Have to be a bit touched try something like that."

We looked back to the mountain reliving our ride. We saw the clouds break from around the peak brightening with the setting sun. We walked down the rest of the way to the lodge going in silence on heavy, weary feet.

That evening when Wick and Ann took me back to the farm on which I worked was the last time I saw them for at least ten years. I knew they would be leaving soon, their work finished. I stood in the doorway of the barn I slept in and watched them go. Then I stayed there alone gazing at the thin clear light above the dark hills deepening around the perfect constant globe that most children wish on as a star.

The Boy Who Flew Too Near
The Sun

Ann's greeting startled me. So unlike the quiet women I remembered, her wild fling into my arms took me by surprise making me feel awkward. Wick, her husband, stood behind me watching.

He had come first to greet me appearing much the same as I remembered from ten years ago: the wincing smile, the broad shoulders slightly hunched as if bracing under some burden never lifted, the wire-rimmed glasses, the crew-cut hair, the face with sharp prominent bones. He offered his hand; we exchanged the typical remarks on greeting.

Then Ann came. She had stayed behind inside to mother her two sons whom I had never seen. Wick called through the screen, and she came out in a rush throwing herself at me, exclaiming her delight seeing me again after so long. She stood back, her bright eyes beneath honey-colored hair looking me over, sizing me up.

"You haven't changed a bit," she concluded.

"Thanks," I beamed.

Yet, despite his same appearance, Wick somehow seemed different now, more so than the usual alterations I realized came from simply not having seen him in more than a decade. He had always seemed reckless seeking experiences in strange, rebellious ways fleeing from a life style

31

that seemed to him repressive. After our years apart I was amazed to see him so quiet, subdued, almost serene.

I was surprised to see him here at all, having discovered him again by accident here while I was on vacation, surprised as well to see him returned to conditions similar to those in which we had lived when I had first known him years before. Sharing the same way of life working odd jobs while attending school, we had subsisted. I had cleaned yards and houses: floors, walls, windows, sewers, garbage cans, often for little more than a meal, a sack full of fruit from the trees in the backyards I had cleaned, enough cash to keep me going until the next job. I stayed in dingy rooms at the edge of the ghetto living on dry cereal, using canned milk because it kept longer without refrigeration—all this a price of schooling while I received my real-life education by working and living, endeavors that at the time I considered noble.

Ann and Wick had helped me survive by contributing an occasional hot meal. Then he had finished his degree, had married Ann, and had moved east where he had taken his first real job teaching in a community college.

I recalled their leaving with a sense of hope that their days of want were over. Now here they were again. Something apparently had gone wrong. Yet the possibility of Wick's failure was not surprising. He had fallen short before. In fact, his whole life that I knew of seemed like a series of disasters. The despair to everyone he knew, he, himself, wondered if he would amount to anything at all. What had happened this time to bring him here in what seemed an unlikely place?

I found out after I met their sons. I saw again the dog I had run with on the sand and through the surf outside the door of their Seal Beach studio apartment when she was a pup. Now she was gross and ponderous in the California heat. Then Wick filled in the years we had been apart, and I learned what he had been through. At the moment of achieving success, he had missed it. And just as the other times, he had let the possibility of success drop from his hands.

Wick had always loved flying. In fact, his love was more of a passion. He had always wanted to soar. Everything he did seemed charged with that desire to reach, to lift on the wind gliding on vast high currents, spiraling on invisible drafts of towering air carrying him away toward the dangerous sun. His passion always got him into trouble.

He had first learned to fly before he was sixteen. When other boys were piecing together sticks to build model planes, he went after the real thing. That difference became typical for him. More important, the decision was always entirely his. So it was with flying. He had seen the tiny planes overhead feigning war. He had watched; he had saved the money he had earned in ordinary ways: cutting lawns, running errands, that sort of job. But instead of spending what he earned on model planes or on sweets he saved his money in a jar. Then one day deciding he had enough, he took his hoard, pedaled to the local airport, parked his bike—abandoning it—walked to the corrugated hanger, and demanded that he be taught how to fly.

The men had laughed. Wick had remained firm. He had stood there, a tall skinny kid with glasses. He revealed his money; they studied him then took what he held out to them. Wick's day finally came when he flew across the line of roofs, skimming the treetops, wagging his wings to the astonished, craning people in the yards below. When he returned, he had found his father waiting.

"That's the last time you do any fool thing like that!"

Wick never flew over the house again, but when he finished high school, he left. He chose a college out of state. Yet he gave into his mother's concern and his father's reluctance to let him out on his own. A half-day's drive would allow them to keep an eye on him. He could come home weekends.

But Wick didn't last long in that school. In fact, he went through a hopscotch series of colleges confirming his father's prophecy. He would never be anything worthy of his father's name. Then Wick did a stint in the service and returned to the state university where he lasted no longer than he had before. He tried to stay; he knuckled down to work, but it seemed his natural love of heights broke free. All he needed was a reason. He found that reason in the death of an international leader. Wick climbed the capitol dome to raise his homemade flag to half-mast. Someone caught him with a camera. Some one else informed authorities who questioned him. The stained enamel of the bathtub, his missing bed sheet condemned him. Suspended from school, he dropped out. He went home, a curse upon his father's house.

Soon after he left to go west. He had no hope of riches; The West just seemed more open. There at land's end where the ocean met the sky he could move free. He could range beneath that boundless sky. No one there would fetter him.

For a while he succeeded. In Oregon, he worked the wheat fields. There beneath the vast blue firmament, he dropped from ripe hills with their view of the broad swift river and the bluffs beyond before he came down among the houses of the town along the shops to the grain elevators along the riverbank where he unloaded. Once, while the shower of kernels hissed through the grating, while the belt carried the grain up into the dark void, he climbed the outside of the high concrete tube pulling himself hand over hand on the steel ladder to the cone of the roof.

Then—as always—someone yelled:

"Get down from there before you fall and break your crazy neck!"

So, of course, he climbed down.

At first they were going to throw him in jail. "Anyone as crazy as that ought to be locked up!" But his boss had intervened: A man of property, people listened. Wick had returned to the farm confined to carrying loads from the ruined fields to the barn. He left soon after the last field was cut.

He arrived in Los Angeles, moved south to Long Beach where he found a job that at first fooled him with its false sense of freedom. He rose before dawn, crept through the early morning fog, then drove a launch to anchored ships in the harbor where he climbed the sides above the vast plain of water that caught the rising flaming sun. He exchanged laundered uniforms for soiled. Returned to shore, he drove to the stifling laundry, unloaded, then left through smog-choked streets. He returned to school.

Then he found Ann.

She was unsure of him at first. He seemed too intense. She was quiet; her parents were no-nonsense people, owners of a business, a construction company. Wick seemed like an intrusion into the quiet comfort of her parent's upper-middle class home. Uncertain, Ann fled east settling on a small college in a Minnesota town. There she apparently felt safe. She busied herself helping children who were challenged.

Then one day she had found him at her door. He would have been there sooner, he explained in characteristic fashion, but he had been delayed. In a hurry, he had stowed away cramming himself into the wheel bay of a jet. He had felt them lift then drop again. Pulled from the wheel bay, blackened by a thin skin of rubber from the wheel, nearly frozen, arrested, he was lectured, the man livid with concern. He would have been dead, the man raged. Wick answered that he thought he could make it. But the man had insisted that no one made it exposed and without oxygen at thirty thousand feet; Wick should understand that. Wick had remained silent planning his next move. Released, he hitched rides, went without eating. Then, out of the blue, she saw him standing there grinning at her through the screen door of her apartment. She laughed, relaxed, gave in, stepped back, let him in.

When Wick and Ann returned from Minnesota, I came to know them closely. I became their friend, they giving me the moniker—Old Tenacity—always there: I lost consistently and quietly at early morning tennis. I took turns with them buying fresh doughnuts, hot coffee afterwards. They came to visit me from time to time in my drab room at the edge of the ghetto, the only room I could afford on a dollar-an-hour job. They would drag me out to some nearby café for a rare full meal or invite me along on some day trip in one of their antique on-its-last-gasp autos that they frequently passed onto me. They took me to their philosophy club meetings where I was introduced to Kant and Sartre and where I was overwhelmed by the seriousness of the discussion. We read together, Wick once doing the honors reading the entire translation of *Night Flight*. Finishing, he sat quiet. Ann and I watched him.

"What more could anyone say? he asked. He had sometimes considered becoming a writer. He had tried setting down a few ideas. He had tried to capture his love of flying. "After this, what's left?" he asked holding out the thin volume. "He's got it all here. There's no use anyone else trying."

"There must be something more!" I insisted. "Don't give up!" But he remained mute.

That spring, Wick received an offer to teach in Michigan. He decided to accept the offer. "I've never really considered myself a teacher," he said just before they left. "But I've done so much studying, I guess I better do something."

So I watched them go. Best man at their wedding, I saw them drive away, the old high profiled Buick, a wedding gift, lost finally in traffic. Then I turned back to the silent house to join Ann's parents who had often offered me breakfast with Ann and Wick and who had given me work during the summer. Now I shared with them the remnants of the wedding cake and helped salvage their home from beneath the debris left in the wake of their departure.

And through Ann's parents I heard of Wick again. By their account he seemed not to have changed at all. Insisting on his witnessing and attending his first child's birth at a time when such intrusion wasn't allowed, he succeeded. He handcuffed himself to Ann's arm just before she delivered. I also heard of his "success" at teaching. The apparent natural source of controversy, his students loved him and packed his classes. He made education an adventure. One time, for example, he put communism on trial. His students became so involved, some going so far as requesting an interview with Fidel Castro, the discussion throughout the community in which the college was located so heated, Wick was questioned by the F.B.I. After that interview, he stuck to flying, and when I left California, I lost contact.

From what I learned now during my accidental visit, during the time we had lost contact, Wick was offered his opportunity for success. Confined in his teaching, pressured by the addition of a second son, he, as so many other teachers, sought a career with more income. He applied to become an airline pilot, a position that would pay him three times what he made at teaching. He was accepted and was offered a contract.

They dreamed out loud about a badly needed new car, about paying off their medical expenses, about the possibility of saving for a new home, of saving for later years, of an education for their sons.

Now, instead, here Wick was completing work for his doctorate.

I wondered why he had made that choice, such a contrast to his whole life before. Why had he rejected the opportunity of fulfilling his passion for flying, especially since he had always insisted that he would never want what some referred to as a "terminal" degree anyway. Any creativity he thought he had would be smothered by that pursuit. He'd end up a "bloomin" intellectual: he'd be a spiritual zombie. He would have no part of that deadly process. He would rather live. He would seek freedom, action, adventure. He could have had all that as an airline pilot. He could have seen the world. Yet, with all those objections to a terminal degree and all the possibilities from a pilot's earnings, he was here. I marveled at his choice.

And I suddenly thought of him as Icarus. Flying too near the sun, desiring light, delighting in the beauty and glory of the air, his young wings softening failed; he had plummeted to earth a victim of his father's curse. That first Icarus was destroyed plunging to the bright sparkling sea. My friend had survived. Descending to the ground, he seemed now more like someone else. He seemed earthbound, tethered to a rock, chained there for eternity.

"What happened?" I asked.

"I couldn't do it," he admitted. I saw Ann's face fill with what appeared like the anguish from lost dreams; then her expression changed to something else, perhaps pride, certainly love.

"Better tell him," she said softly.

I turned back to Wick questioning. He grinned through his characteristic wince behind his glasses, shrugging his shoulders, sucking in his breath.

"Poor Annie," he said. Then he added. "I turned it down." Just like that.

"Tell him everything," Ann insisted quietly.

"I met a boy—a young man, really," Wick confessed. "A drop out. I picked him up one day. He was hitching rides. He was going west. He stayed with us a couple days. He made us decide.

Just like Wick. One lost boy, and in one moment he had made a decision that had affected his whole life—and Ann's.

"I'll never forget the look on his face, the sound in his voice when he told me what he had wanted, when he told me how much school had failed him. He was groping, searching, and no one cared enough to help him look. The night before he left I stood in the dark listening to him talk. No moon, no sounds, just his voice filled with longing in the black night filled with stars. After he stopped talking, I couldn't speak a word. Then he was gone."

"And with him went 25,000 a year," Ann added calmly. "Somehow I knew."

"Good ole Annie," Wick said. "She was right there with me." He reached to touch her now. "She just put her hand in mine. After that everything was all right." They were lost in each other's eyes. "I simply decided that I really wanted to teach. That meant becoming the best teacher I could be."

He didn't add that his decision also meant leaving his teaching position and committing himself to insecurity and toil for years to come while he pursued his doctorate.

"And if I were going to really help others, I needed to know as much as I could."

Just like that.

We listened to the voices of the children in the yard.

"Well," Wick said finally. "How about lunch?"

Almost time for dinner, I had spent the whole day. I had a long ways to go. "I really must get started," I said.

I rose. They followed me to the door then stood with me at my car.

"Write to us," Ann insisted. "Don't stay away so long this time."

"I won't," I promised.

I pulled away leaving them behind together on the curb. And as I left him, again returning home, driving toward clouds above the distant mountains that thrust above the desert floor, I thought of him and his final choice. Now his life seemed like a pilgrimage—an endless journey toward a distant star. And as I drove, I could almost see him rise, ascending to a bright heavenly field where I knew he would soar forever lifting on wings that would never fail.

I never saw them again. But I heard from them again one time through the Internet. One day while checking online mail in my office I was stunned by an e-mail I least expected.

"Are you the same person with your name whom we knew in Long Beach? If you are, what have you been doing for the last forty-five years?"

An attachment included a letter that apparently they sent out each year to relatives and friends reporting on the events over the previous twelve months. I read reports of illnesses and death of people I had never met. But other news reported Wicks' nearing retirement from the professorship he had held over several decades. I read of Ann's receiving a PhD. and working as an administrator. I was informed of events in the lives of people I had come to know in Long Beach. I was saddened to read of the passing of several people I had come to admire and for whom I had grown fond. But I also read of some of those I had known still active and that Wick would dine with them in the days that followed, some of those people marrying each other, unions which somewhat surprised me since I had been romantically involved with some of those noted.

I replied to the e-mail. Offering a brief survey of my previous decades I included a brief statement of my having published poetry that had been well received since I recalled the statement one or the other had made:

"Someday we'll probably ask, 'Whatever happened to that guy we knew who used to write poetry?'"

I offered to provide a full report if they should be interested and so inclined to want the details of what I had been doing over the decades since the last occasion I seen them when I had been an accidental visitor.

Then I waited for a reply.

That reply never came.

"We'll Always Have Paris"

The last time I saw Paris was on a tour of Europe by bus. I again as on previous saunterings walked everywhere, especially along the Seine. Behind the Cathedral of Notre Dame a string of children too young for school paraded in a line joined by a rope led by a woman who urged them on—in French, of course. I was reminded of Brueghel's painting of the blind leading the blind, but none of the Parisian tots stumbled or fell.

I finally saw the Muse' de Orsay and its array of cantilevered walkways and it's collection of Impressionist and modern art. For on a previous excursion, I had waited outside the Muse' while some Parisian officials negotiated heatedly to decide whether the doors would open that day since the public employees were on strike for some unclear or undeclared reason save that Paris was in its full tourist mode of the season and was therefore ripe for a strike to show the officials who was boss. After a wait of about two hours we heard the news filtering down through the gathered crowd that the Muse' would remained closed.

The woman with whom I was traveling sat on the low steps before the Muse' and wept. "I've waited my whole life to come to Paris!" She wailed through her tears. "I've waited that long to see the art, and now the place that has it is closed because of a strike!"

For the longest time afterward, I had the distinct feeling that I was somehow to blame.

I had witnessed the Louvre the previous day since it was still available and on still another occasion I had gauged the massive size of the collection by walking at a brisk pace through all the galleries, a walk that took me nearly two hours. In some galleries that seemed hidden from common view I beheld canvasses depicting mythical scenes that covered the whole massive walls. Of course, I moved swiftly past *La Giaconda* (the Mona Lisa) since I had studied it before when there wasn't a crowd of tourists who snapped flashbulb photos even though a large sign in several languages prohibited such snapshots. Fortunately, some wise Parisians had decided on covering the portrait with glass thus ensuring that anyone ignoring the sign in several languages ordering "Do Not Touch the Canvass" would not injure the pricey work.

On one occasion during another excursion I experienced the unisex toilets that from what I surmise only the Parisians appear able to accommodate for which I paid a nominal fee in French coins and in return received a supply of tissue apparently deemed sufficient for the purpose. These public commodes, however, with their polished granite floors and dark stained stalls finished with brass fittings are definitely more elegant than such depositories in the French countryside that consist of a hole in the floor and two indentations to place your feet, that is if you can find such privies, and I learned that one indication of a competent tour guide is someone who knows when and where to stop. Yet I was witness to some women who refused such an indignity and instead resolved to abide their discomfort until we arrived at more civilized accommodations.

During my unisex adventure in Paris I was oddly complacent as I was involved in basic functions that had become urgent, while in the stall beside me an attractive well-fashioned woman who had entered before me was involved in the same enterprise. We both emerged from our stalls at the same time, went to refresh our hands, drying them on paper towels dispensed to us by the attendant as part of the imposed fee, and we left going our separate ways, of course, both of us I am certain greatly relieved.

Perhaps such events are more memorable because of the conditions that define them. More frequently, however, when I'm someplace memorable or when I'm in a place I want to behold or witness at the moment I find myself in such a place, I always seem to miss the ambiance—the grandeur, the beauty, the immediacy of such a place.

So one time in Paris on the esplanade, the Hotel de Invalides on the one end, Champ d'Elysee at the other, the grand expansive lawn and gardens between, we sat to rest our bodies and our minds, having contended in silence and out loud, somehow fitting for Paris. The air was clear, the streets and boulevards fresh from the storm that had broke above us during the night, above the tiled roofs and domes of Paris while we fulfilled a romantic fantasy a la Chateaubriand, our bodies rising to climax with the storm—flashes of lightning, thunder cracking and exploding, crashing in the courtyard, echoing in our room, filling the yellow walls with quivering shadows and blue mystic light that added to the yellow and black flickering lamps of neighboring dwellings.

Here near where we languished on the grand esplanade conquering armies marched in parade, exulting in victory: Newsreels of the time capture Hitler stomping in delight to behold the Eiffel Tower, now his own phallic symbol, then returning to his bunker in Berlin. We witnessed bronze commemorative plagues near holes gouged by bullets from recurring conflicts.

Then while resting on the stone benches along the esplanade, les Champs d'Elysee on one end, l'Hospital du Invalides on the other, I witness a creature—an ant—who meanders in its typical ant manner over the broad gray plain of walkway alongside the wide sweep of grass—les Champs. I ponder, Do Parisian ants *comprend* French? Is it even conscious of my existence, some converse condition of God and man? Yet, it seems the same as all ants I have ever witnessed throughout my life, my nose to ant holes as a child, the illustrated books with tissue thin paper that displayed the secrets of those holes leading off into the dark earth, my eye to the adolescent lenspiece of the microscope magnifying the triangle of head with complex eyes and slowing waving antenna. What was it trying to tell me? Were such movements salutations, some humble petition from earthling to deity? How could I have answered? What would I have said? Does it matter now? Yet, after all those years, we meet again here—this field of dreams, illusions of grandeur, of grandiose schemes, grand presumptions all brought into sharp perspective by the small black creature that wanders on its way, meandering toward the crowded boulevard of concrete earthly realities.

From where we sat on the esplanade, we could see off in the distance the small Citroens whizzing around the obelisk at the Place de Concorde (ironically or cynically named?) where the guillotine had been set up to lop off royal heads—and then the heads of those who had started all the commotion, excitement, and terror. What must the scene have been like hearing the roar of the crowd as each head, each life dropped, the body, the arms bound behind, remained while the swelling sound rising like a wave carried on the air to this distance, the grass shimmering in the sun, the flowers radiant and fragrant, the air clear, the sky a bowl of blue and that awesome sound—a hundred thousand voices raised and roaring as one. Around us now the world was still, serene.

A similar "vision" when I went to St Germain de Pres and witnessed Les Deux Maggots and Sartre's former apartment down the nearby side street. At St. Germain, I stood beside the abbey (that I later learned had one of the great collections of classic art works and enshrined the tomb of Descartes who started all the commotion). I watched the crowds, the café, the people walking through the gathering dusk, the traffic, the street lamps and neon signs beneath the sycamore trees. I beheld the place trying to capture it, but as I watched the scene, my consciousness of the scene, the immediacy of the scene always slipped away.

I walked back to my hotel beyond Montmartre through a drenching downpour that cascaded water from the Third Empire buildings onto the wide concrete walks; the streets ran in glistening dark rivers. Above me, through tall windows in dark facades, yellow lights splayed across white plaster ceilings with rose floral designs. Water dripped from my hair and face delighting me for I was bathed in Parisian rain while walking back to Montmartre and beyond to my room.

On yet another excursion while we made our way out of the city by bus back to Le Manche to catch the hovercraft across the Channel from Calais, we experienced a Parisian standoff. At one of the many roundabouts, two vehicles entered from different places and suddenly stopped to avoid colliding. O.K., good so far. But instead of exiting, the drivers proceeded to wave at each other, both either demanding right of way or deferring passage to the other. Meanwhile, during the interval of indecision other vehicles entered and stalled behind the two blocking the way; still others stalled behind the ones already stalled until—no surprise—the circle and the streets leading to the roundabout were jammed with vehicles, including our bus. Of course, horns blared with little effect. We waited for some movement. Any movement. We saw none save for the brief appearance of two gendarmes who arrived from some unknown place, inspected the impasse, shouted some demands or directions that were drowned by the blare of horns and revving of engines, threw up their arms, waved their hands dismissing the whole affair, then turned and vanished.

Finally after forty-fives long minutes we witnessed a small movement. Some wise Parisian deferred, perhaps emulating Descartes, allowing one of the stalled vehicles to ease out of blockage. Then another inched forward and escaped until the flow became a steady stream. Thus we were released from bondage only to face another challenge:

We were *way* behind schedule in meeting the departure of the hovercraft at Calais. Our driver took charge and we flew down the divided highway at a velocity that possibly emulated that of the TGV (*tren a grande vitesse*). Approaching Calais, we saw with relief the craft waiting, the driver having called ahead to alert the staff to the reason for our delay. The bus pulled to an abrupt stop before the gangway to the dock where we piled out and ran to the craft waved through customs without inspection or having to show passports. With the vehicles and other passengers already boarded, we rushed to our seats while the engines roared to life then soared to full power lifting us above the churning water. We flew to Dover with the spume from our vessel cloaking the windows, blocking our view of the towering white cliffs.

Stories

The Jar of Coins

Even before he went with his mother to cash the insurance check at the bank, Little Felix decided that he would save the money for something later. He wasn't quite sure what he would save for. Such a decision was too important for anything definite right now. Yet, everyone asked him:

"Hey, Felix! What will you do with all that?"

And as he stood there in his usual response, in silence, his shoulders hunched, his face in a grimace, they coaxed him:

"Come on, Felix! You've got to do something with it!"

He always shook his head annoying them.

He finally decided he would have to save it. He saw himself adding the crisp green bills with their exotic portraits to the jumbled heap of coins in the large Mason jar. He grew delirious at the thought: Never had he so much money in his life.

He saved his money miserly after begging coins from anyone who smiled on him encouraging his thrift. Seeing in him an image of themselves, of their unfulfilled desires, they handed him the coins. Then how he'd move as well as he could on his mending leg to ferret out the jar of coins he buried in a place he wouldn't tell of to a soul. In its secret place, his jar was safe. His brothers always stared enviously as he carried the buried treasure back to company, to relatives, to exclamations of praise.

"What a clever boy!

"He'll be rich someday for sure!"

His joy at their attention was always soured by a stern command.

"Felix, put your jar away."

"Leave him. A penny's nothing."

"He shouldn't beg! Put it away!"

They all watched. The coin lost among the horde, the lid on, he set the jar before him on the table at which they sat. They all admired the level of the coins. Then after he was sure no one was watching he would sneak off, returning when the jar was in its place. And later when everyone had gone and he could escape his brothers' vigil, he would fetch the jar and take it to his room. There, alone behind the sturdy door, he dumped the jar on his bed. The coins piling, chimed; the bills crackled at his touch. He counted, grouping the coins before he dropped them into heavy paper tubes. The odd coins remained, left in the bottom of the jar reserved there as a start weighted by the rolls of coins. The green bills the grownups and his parents enticed him with coaxing him to exchange lined the sides. The portraits studied him through the pale green glass.

Later, when he went to the doctor for his monthly treatment, he would plead until his mother agreed to stop with him at the bank. There he would yield the orange rolls, the blue rolls, the green bills he had secured within his hand, his hand within his jacket pocket all the way. There at the bank he stretched to pass the black record book returned to him with neat figures added beneath the column of those he had received before. He followed his mother then lingering behind, absorbed, savoring the heavy feel of his gain, marveling that the coins had been transformed to paper, that paper had been transformed further into black wavy lines on the creamy page, until his mother snapped a sharp command back over her shoulder and he hurried after, protecting himself from her wrath.

Today they would go again after his brothers left for school. He stayed behind, kept home a final time. First they would go to the bank, then they would board the bus and ride across the city to the doctor. There, if the doctor thought him ready, he would have his cast removed. After their return, he would go to school, the first time in nearly a year. He anticipated all these things, going to the doctor's less, but the thought of going to the bank, the thought of having his cast removed, of finally being free from that dead weight upon his leg excited him. He thought about his return to school after such a long absence and his stomach churned.

So while his brothers ate, Felix watched as they slowly crumbled stale bread into large, ceramic mugs then sat back to let their mother pour in coffee. They added treasured sugar, precious milk. They watched the deep brown of the coffee mellow into tan. Then they leaned forward tapping down the bread, watching it stain, soften, shrink—all this a treat for them. They lingered while he restrained his eagerness to go. No amount of pleading would make his mother hurry more. "The bank won't open any sooner for you," she would say to him.

He grew angry at their slowness. He spun from the doorway and hobbled through the barren rooms of the flat, past the high windows that revealed the multitude of bricks in the wall next door, the jagged crack that marred their order, the gray light of the gangway, the barren dirt beside the walk. He hobbled into the front bedroom. There he stood on the bare wooden floor studying the brown marred dresser, the iron double bed with its painted frame scratched and chipped from their frequent moves, its faded chenille spread.

He thought of the jar in its dark safe place. He could feel its holy presence near him. The thought of it made him warm, and he held himself with joy for what would happen, what he would add to the store, his alone, secure in its place, serving him only. He would take it out, hold it now, but there wasn't time. Besides, he could sense his brothers spying from the distant room.

So he thought about the transformation taking place: The yellow check with rich black print his mother had allowed him to hold would be redeemed, replaced by those bills already coveted. Yet, there was a further transformation: His experience had changed. His pain, the jam of images of people standing over him as he lay on the asphalt road beneath the front bumper of the car that had struck him, his father coming through the crowd to take charge, his being lifted into the back seat of the car that had struck him, the gray brown interior of the car, the paddy wagon that had come to take him to the hospital, his own screams as his father and the doctor had held him down within the room of blazing lights while others reset the shattered bone, sewed up the torn tissue without giving him anything to relieve the terrible pain, all those images had mellowed with the passing of days, had become a yellow check with black lettering, and now, once he and his mother took that check to the bank, it would dissolve into those grand green bills that he would actually see, would get to touch, to hold, to have as his very own. Perhaps the pain had been redeemed.

He winced again recalling. His leg throbbed bound by the cast. That time the pain had been so great he hadn't been able to grasp it. But soon the pain had softened to the memory of a high-ceiling room with hard polished tile and walls of paneled wood sectioned by dark wood strips. Dark wooden benches faced the dark heavy railing at the front and the high raised bench above, the furled flag beside the bench, the hanging yellow tulip lamps dim in the light through tall sectioned windows along one side of the room. The stern man, gray haired with glasses in a black robe had strode to the high backed seat and made the gavel rap; then the rushing sound of people settling on the long wooden benches just like the sound of people settling at church.

He had listened to the talk among the old people: his parents, the lawyers, the black-robed judge upon the high bench. Then the judge had come down to meet him at the rail, to hold open the gate, to lead him to the high seat, to have him sit, to allow him to spin against his father's objection. Gazing down at all the faces raised to him seated on the wide seat, Felix had suddenly let his head drop back upon the curved leather, and he had spun.

From that experience came the yellow check with rich print. He had waited for the mailmen. Each day he crabbed, waiting, his mother warning him, until one day she handed him the envelope. He stood transfixed. She took it from him; he pleaded; he whined; he was slapped. Then she opened the covering, and he had smoothed the check on the kitchen table.

Now, as he stood remembering the wriggly figures of the check, he tried again to comprehend the nature of the change. The check would be redeemed for bills: those bills would have within themselves bills like those he now held in his jar. His mind worked through the concept. Then there was the bank itself. He imagined the solid gray building, the massive stone columns beside the barred doors, the cavernous interior hushed by white veined marble bright with polished brass. He saw the pink clean man, the soft, powdered women, beings who had such ponderous duties.

And he would have his part in the drama. His mother had promised him. He would reach up to press the yellow paper to the marbled shelf.

He would receive the bills, then turn, delivering them to her, and she would place the bills within her purse and snap the brass catch shut. Finally, when they got home, he would have the bills, possess them, then convey them to his hidden store. His parents had agreed that he should have the bills. They had quarreled, but they had finally agreed, and they had promised. The money was his.

"We're suppose to save it for him. We're not suppose to let it laying around. You can't let a kid have all that money to keep in a jar!"

"It won't be laying around! He'd have it hid! You know how he hides his jar. My God, if I can't find it, who can? Even my brother couldn't find it!"

During the quarrel, hearing the name, he thought of his uncle. One evening they had come home to find missing the tin in which they kept spare change for bread. The police came that night large and ponderous in their dark uniforms. He had seen their heavy deadly revolvers, their long, dark wooden clubs. He remembered his uncle's thin, sharp face between the dark uniforms of the police, his uncle's smug confession.

"O.K., but what about us?" his father had argued. "His accident wasn't cheap. Our share barely covers everything. We always lose. We were going to take care of bills!"

"We'll manage."

"All that money laying around so some kid can satisfy his greed! We can always pay him back later."

"We'll be all right."

Then his parents seemed to come to some agreement.

"So let him keep the money! I hope he loses it! I hope your brother gets it!"

"He won't lose it, will you, Felix?" the women asked, smoldering.

Felix had agreed, satisfied that in a way, for the first time, he had won. "I won't let anyone find my money!" he proclaimed.

The matter was settled, then. He would keep the bills in his jar for now.

The trolley rumbled by, waking him. He watched it slow, its iron wheels screeching as they ground to a stop. He saw the people on the seats; he heard the motor hum, then the grinding wheels as they moved. The motor gathered to a whine as the trolley passed, gathering speed in its descent, the whine fading, softened by distance.

He went with it in his mind as he would when they would travel to the bank if his brothers ever finished. He would board, sit in front, his hand tight upon the metal poles. Through the large windshield, he would watch the track sweep beneath them as they rocked, the wheels clicking gathering speed. He would watch the man work the levers. He would watch the man's foot stomp the bell. He would hear the sparks jumping from the racing pulley on the overhead wire.

He found himself staring at the houses across the way, at the wide upper porches. He followed them along to the pastor's house, then beyond to the tall barn like school, the spear pointed wrought iron fence around the schoolyard. He saw the paper cutouts, the scallops, diamonds, circles, decorating the tall windows. Beyond the school, the red brick church towered toward the overcast sky. The house next to his own cut off the rest of the street, but he could see the corner at the appliance store. He saw Mr. Henderson, the owner, in striped bibbed overalls move among the enameled stoves, the galvanized pipes, the gray propane bottles diminished by distance. Here they would board the trolley that would take them to the level of the bank. Here they would wait, Mr. Henderson chatting with them until the car rumbled to a halt, allowing them to climb, then carrying them along to the bank below

Felix turned from the window. He hobbled back through rooms bare of furniture, more expansive with emptiness. He reached the kitchen: a table, two chairs, a stove, a small refrigerator, the bare bulb above the small mirror over the sink.

"Aren't we ever going?" Felix complained.

"Hold your horses!" she commanded. The other kids howled with glee. "We'll go when I finish."

She stood fixing lunches at the sink. He watched her sweep the knife across the bread. Lard, again! His brothers ate at school because their mother went with Felix to the doctor. Felix never ate at school. Kept home, even the short walk to the school down the street too much, his teacher, Miss Peterson, a tall, precise woman with sharp, pinched features, stopped twice a week to talk with him, to help him with his work so he could keep up.

He watched as his mother turned another slice upon the first then zipped waxed paper from the roll and wrapped the sandwiches, tucking them into brown paper bags. Then she turned from the sink.

"Come on, you kids! You'll be late!"

His brothers dove into the mash of bread and coffee. They finished then straightened, pushed back their chairs, and scrambled for their coats hung behind the kitchen door. Felix, moved by their excitement, stood beside his mother who handed each a sack as they left: first, the tall one, brassy like his father, long faced, thin and dark; then, the smaller one, younger than Little Felix who stayed behind, quiet, featured like her, like Felix who stood leaning on the door frame watching as his brothers left, yelling as they leapt from the gray porch, as they raced down the gangway fleeing from the women's angry cry.

Felix and his mother left soon after. They followed the same way the other boys had gone. Turning off the light above the sink leaving the bare kitchen in the drab light through the window beside the heavy door from between buildings and underneath the gray porch of the upper flat, a mysterious place Felix had never seen, they followed the walk until it curved and fanned before the house. There they halted, startled by the brightness of the street, by the warmth of filtering sunlight through the overcast. They descended the concrete steps then turned toward the corner car stop where they would board the trolley, an extra expense made necessary by Felix's leg.

As they passed, he studied the school, the schoolyard filled with the blur of noisy children. A cluster of girls stood in the alcove formed by the massive buttress of the soaring church. He saw his friend Henry who had the same name as Little Felix's brother and father. Little Felix had always thought it odd that they should all be called the same, especially since he rarely found anyone else with his own name. In his mind the names of the three people blended. Henry absorbed in chase disappeared around the corner of the school. And Little Felix felt sad that his friend could be so involved in such activities without him being there. Little Felix felt sour at the thought that his friend seemed not to miss him at all.

Felix thought of the time he had gone to see Henry the first time Felix had visited a real farm. Little Felix had carried his lunch boarding the trolley by himself riding alone to the very end of the line beyond the houses, the dark brick of the streets near his house, the wide concrete avenue leading to the federal highway vanishing among the hills.

While Felix had visited, he had witnessed Henry's contest with a ram; the veterinarian reaming out the cow, a rubber arm disappearing into the cow's body. He had breathed in the dry smell of hay within the barn loft. He had swelled at the sight of the open fields, the slow creek lined with reeds. He had savored the surprise of his first sharp taste of fresh green pepper snapped directly from the plant.

Later, when the factories came and Felix had visited again, he had beheld the large plain of black water where the creek had flooded the fields of Henry's farm. They had constructed numerous adventures on Henry's raft. But still later, the raft sank, the fields were drained, divided, sold; then they were filled with even more factories that came now almost to the door of Henry's gray weathered house that had stood on this land so long Felix could not even begin to understand how much time the house had been there. Seeing the house crowded by factories, Felix thought about the times he had seen the bright yellow fields, the clear sky, the white new roads. Now even that farm and the weathered house were gone. He hadn't been to Henry's new place—Little Felix had no idea where his friend lived now, and Henry had never come to see him while he healed from his accident with the car.

Felix passed the school, turning his attention from these dark thoughts toward the bright expectation of their ride. He thought about the trip ahead, about his return with the bills, about his going back to school. Everyone would be surprised. He would brag to them about the bills.

The schoolyard and the clusters of children became a blur of color and movement. And as he was carried away by the trolley, Felix briefly heard the school bell, the raised shriek of girls. Then from memory he saw the race and crush of bodies queuing up in front of the wooden porch, the wide, wooden doors. He saw their journey in two ordered, wriggling lines past the tall guarding figure admonishing as they entered through the door, some turning down the dim corridor toward the windows and the cloakroom at the rear beneath the stairwell, others turning up the darkly stained stairs, climbing toward the upper classroom that held the higher grades.

Felix passed, and as he left them behind, the school, his friend, his brothers there who waved and hollered as he passed, he felt a surge of joy, a glow of warmth, a comfort in knowing he was about to find a treasure none of them would ever have. The world that lay before him like a land of dreams was filled with wonder. And as he set out to explore, he discovered in his sense of joy the importance of his world renewed.

2

The trip, as he expected, the quick descent of the car took him past things he knew so well he had digested and absorbed them so that they had become part of his being: Each place he passed held something special: The trolley rumbled past his house: He saw it whole, as something foreign, something strange. The movie house: The brick wall beside the flat where he lived became bright posters of strange ponderous beings from a world of names that held magic, from places that hung like mysteries, visions that hovered about his mind. As he passed the theater, he imagined the warm dark fragrant interior plush with seats, the hot salted popcorn heavy with oil, the people hushed in reverence beneath the silvery phantoms cast upon the huge screen. Once, he pleading, she consenting, he had returned alone to see the same picture three times, the story appealing to some unknown, unspoken need. He had impressed her with his offer to use his own money.

"Why on earth the same show?" she had asked. "Go with your brothers to the National. There's a new one there."

But he held firm, and he had won. He had run free from the house.

Beyond the theater, the place where crossing the street he had been struck. He saw again the image of the tan car looming from around the crawling truck, the driver of the car turned toward the woman at his side. Felix felt again the shock. The world once more upended, twirling as he fell—houses, trees, the pebbled asphalt street. Then the feet and legs rising from the asphalt, a circle of faces looking down at him. He heard again the strident voices arguing. He felt once more himself being lifted, his own limp weight, the heavy pain in his leg, the hoarse breathing of the man lifting him. He saw again the thin face with glasses, the same face of the man behind the wheel of the car that had struck him, the face now immense, concerned. He saw the moving lips, the eyes searching his face. Then the man's head turned toward the crowd. Felix had found himself in the back seat of the car—the bristly rug, the faces leaning in above him, faces at the windows around the car. Then there had been a cop in short summer sleeves grasping his leg.

Felix rediscovered the green interior of the police van. Then the hospital: white uniforms, glass doors that swung before him, the tiled room, the leather of the table, and once again, the blazing lights, the grim face of the doctor, his father's worried face at the table end. He felt again the pain so great, it blinded him, making him reel, so great his leg throbbed thinking about it again these many months after. They passed the place where he had fallen.

The service station: The vending machine that gave out matches for a penny with the square box dropping from neat bright stacks. The suspicious face of the station owner as Felix worked the machine and fled. Then crouching in gangways hidden by dark hulks of buildings, the sky a narrow slit above, he had stooped beside thick lime green foliage setting fire to papers, candy wrappers, stained tissue, bringing light and knowledge to his world. He thought of rats.

One day, desiring greater heat and light, he had lit a garbage can beneath the stairwell of his grandmother's flat. The paper in the can had flared then roared. He had fled amazed pacing the far alley end while the siren grew, while the men clambered with their gear. He had waited until the bright truck left. Then he had crept back to see the scorched can, the blistered paint on the stairs.

"Did you do dis ting?" his grandmother had demanded in her heavy accent from what people called 'the Old Country'. The screen door slammed behind her as she rushed out to challenge him.

He denied, but she accused. "Vhat would your father do if he knows?"

That had been enough. He had demurred; he had scuffed around in circles looking at the ground. He had thrown himself upon her mercy.

"Don't tell!" he begged as he danced in terror.

"Never again!" she warned, dismissing him. And he had hurried up the gangway toward the street. At the end of the dark passage, he had seen the twilight sky above and then the pulsing lights of the movie house.

The trolley car reached leveled track: he inspected the few storefronts with dwellings above; the myrtle hedges trimmed or ragged with black ground around the roots, the hedge roots choked with paper scraps, small scattered stones, dirty broken combs; then the area near the bank. The upholstery shop: In the window, faded drab material, naked frames of furniture hid the interior. Inside: darkness, bare dusty floors, stuffed furniture, a goosed necked lamp at the rear upon a bench. Beneath the lamp, white thinning hair, wire-rimmed glasses, piercing eyes as the old man straightened, raising his head, exposing a wrinkled face peering through the darkness as Felix had entered on a dare then had fled.

The trolley slowed passing the beauty shop he had explored alone while his father had cleaned, working one of those odd jobs his father took to help make ends meet, washing windows, cleaning floors. The quiet dominance of pink, a woman's world of hair dryer, small sinks, large mirrors, double images of colored bottles had suddenly made him aware that he was alone. He had sought the man; he had crept down to the dark basement. There in the murky light, he had seen his father filching small quantities of oily liquid from a rack of supplies. His father had let him carry the prize all the way home.

The trolley stopped allowing them to descend. Then it rumbled on through the intersection, its overhead pulley snapping blue sparks as it crossed, then disappeared.

The bank: The massive circle of a door, the high, high roof, the hush even though the voices carried rising toward the blossoms of lights hung on long chains from the ceiling. There, the promise he had been given failed. He listened to his mother and the man in the cage, the transformation of the yellow check betrayed, miscarried. He stood at her side waiting then followed as she turned away. Striding across the plain of marbled floor, she planted herself before a low counter. She waited, talked to another man, groped in her purse, showed her wallet then spun marching back to the man in the cage.

Felix began to whine reminding her of the promise. But she ignored him. Instead, she slapped down the check, turned, then held the bills before his face. His hands moved grasping at them. And there among the white veined marble, the bright brass, the solid hush of monied voices, he gazed in wonder. Then she snatched them back, folding them, burying them in her purse. He bobbed in place. His natural voice boomed. Her face became a threat, her lips tight between clenched teeth. He quieted.

"Come!" she snapped.

3

They left, then stood before the bank waiting for the bus. He felt his mother brood. He knew her anger having come to recognize her moods. Her anger now checked, she resigned herself. Yet, he realized the strain; he saw the stern countenance, the thin set lips. Then the bus came gliding. They boarded, and he, his mood affected by her mood braced himself for what he knew lay ahead scarcely realizing the trip across

57

town, not fully noticing the streets thick with stores and the side streets lined with houses, the poles and wires, the parked cars, the waiting rows of traffic at signals as the bus swept across the intersections.

So before he knew, he was hobbling up the dark stairway to the waiting room, slowly following as she swept on ahead. They were inside. The nurse bent toward him smiling. Shy, he answered. Then they lead him to the room. There, as usual, the doctor swept in, removed the cast, examined his leg. Felix felt the vibration of the saw, breathed the dusty smell of the plaster, felt then the air upon his hot cramped leg. He braced himself for the heating pad. Too hot at first, it made him whimper. They lowered it again; again it heated. He was always glad to see the treatment over. This time the doctor returned to hold the leg again, re-examining it, kneading it.

"How's it feel?" the doctor asked.

"Fine," Felix said.

"You ready to walk?"

Felix felt weak. "Sure," he said.

The doctor had promised him. Yet each time before, they had brought the bucket, the strips of cloth, the box of powder for plaster. He had watched them mix the milky liquid in the pail. He had watched them soak the cloth. Each time before, they had wrapped again; his leg had disappeared, heavy with weight. But now finally, they helped him, and he reluctantly placed himself upon his thin leg. It seemed so frail!

"Take it easy now! You won't be playing football yet!"

He limped, withdrawing his leg as it touched the floor. The floor felt bound to the building rooted to the earth. He looked down at his withered ankle and grew afraid. They encouraged him. He tried again stepping softly. He limped, the unfamiliar weight disturbing him. He faltered; he saw their scrutiny.

"Maybe we better wait," the doctor said. "There's no hurry."

Felix whined.

"Tell you what. We'll put on a lighter cast. How's that? It's small, has a metal bar to keep you off the ground. You'll be able to go anywhere."

The doctor let him keep the crutch to help him until he grew accustomed to the lighter cast.

"Take it easy, now," the doctor warned. "And come back in a month."

4

When they returned home Felix asked again if he could see the bills. This time she reluctantly consented moved perhaps by the painful memory of his leg. Opening her purse, she crouched above the contents resting the bag on her raised leg; then she straightened with the fold of bills. He ignored her, sat, and ordered them, flattening them into one exact row. He lifted each in turn and held it before him studying the strange portrait he had seen only in books at school. He marveled at the crispness of the bill so unlike the others he kept in his jar. He brought the bill to his nose, his own bouquet. Each bill he used in turn. Then he reordered them sitting back to study them again, all these his.

"We better put them away," the woman ordered.

Her voice broke his worship. He moved to get his jar favoring his leg, leaning on the crutch, conscious of the lightness of the cast beneath him. He returned with the jar beneath his free arm. Then he set the jar on the table above the bills. He studied the mix of bright coins.

"Maybe we should keep this money someplace else," the woman said.

He searched her face as she stood at the sink. He saw her lowered eyes, the thin lips. She brought her coffee to the table, she sat, she sipped. She set her cup, reached, and spun one of the bills disordering them. She picked it up; she studied it. Then for the only time he would ever remember she met his eyes; and he, for the only time in his life, stared back questioning.

"That's a lot of money," the woman said.

He nodded waiting.

"What will you do with it?"

He shrugged tipping his head toward his shoulder, twisting his body as if her question and his answer caused him pain.

"You should do something with it. Money needs to be used to be good. If you get it, you need to use it."

He squirmed.

"You've got to do something. Can't you think of anything?" She sipped her coffee peering at him over the rim of the cup.

Then his answer came, the one he had carried all along that he had hidden, afraid to offer, fearful of her mood.

"Save it," he murmured.

The silence of the house crashed down on them: The refrigerator hum, the muted traffic beyond the windows of the front bedroom, the worn workings of the clock above the doorway. Upstairs, someone moved. Beside him, she sipped. The jar of coins sat on the table. Stilled, settled, the mottled heap of coins within the jar glared; the passbook stood curled against the side.

"Put it up," his mother said quietly. And he moved quietly, slowly drawing the jar to him, curling it in his arms. He unscrewed the lid then raised the scattered bills one by one. Quietly he stacked them then folded them neatly trying not to destroy their crisp newness. Then he poked them into the jar. He returned the lid.

"Better get ready," she ordered. "It's time for school."

His stomach roiled. He winced hoping to protest. Her firm quiet manner stopped him cold.

He moved. Uncertain, his leg so frail, the crutch awkward in handling with the lighter cast, he returned the jar to its hiding place; then he went for his coat, retrieving it from behind the door where he had jammed it in his haste to possess the bills. He fastened himself within the coat then limped out the door, returning to the gray morning light.

He hobbled down the gangway to the front. There on the porch he rested braced on his one good leg, the crutch discarded against the two doors, one to his home, the other to the flat upstairs, the wooden front doors forever closed. He leaned against the gray pillar of the porch and searched the empty street, the line of houses, the empty schoolyard with its spires of fence, the buttresses of the church that rose narrowing, soaring toward the high distant cross. He hobbled down a step. Then he sat.

He studied the schoolyard remembering the distant whirl of children, some his friends who had played there. Now, the gray light on the gravel, on the concrete walk reminded him of the morning, of his trip, of his excitement and how it had failed. Cold now, the wind made him hunch and huddle on the step.

A sudden sadness washed over him. Incapable of finding the words, he pondered the feeling rising from his soul crying to him in the stillness of the morning light, the quiet of the street, the hushed world chilled by the wind. His store of images saved like coins helped him now.

One spring following the accident sitting where he sat now, the quiet warming him, a new soft breeze filling him, he had dozed in the mild sunlight alone, innocent in peace, his leg mending. Then the school bell had jarred him awake—as it jarred him now. He had listened: The first shrill yell issued from the door.

One girl had appeared from behind the corner of the school. He had seen her stand waiting gazing at the ground. Suddenly, she had bolted toward the gate as someone, a boy, had burst from behind the school. The girl had darted through the hole clanging the gate. She had come up the block moving along the line of houses across the street. He had waved as she passed, but she had ignored him turning away from him, turning at the corner going down toward Orchard Street.

He now followed in his mind as she passed the stone alleyway that lead to his grandmother's and the scorched stairs; the large white house set on a knoll with the expansive sloping lawn, the thick shrubs, the hedges, the trees, the curved walk, the surprise of rare blue rose-like flowerts he always stopped to marvel at. He left her waiting at the corner ready to cross.

He had turned back to watch the flow from behind the school, a steady broken line, one uneven certainty as they had moved through the iron gate then had spread, some leaning toward each other as they walked chatting, jostling each other as they came, passing him.

That day, there had been a slow ordered group controlled by the tall figure above them. He had watched as they had come from behind the school, down the steps, through the gate to the corner. There they had crossed, turning up toward him, coming past the tailor's, the steam from the clothes press billowing at them, they recoiling as they passed. They had reached the foot of the wooden steps and had stood there watching him, he watching them, until one girl stepped forward up the stairs handing him the bright package. He had studied them searching their faces. The long smiling face of the woman had never looked so kind. He had taken the gift, had waited while they spoke, and he had mumbled his thanks. Then the girl had turned, gone down the stairs, and he had watched as they moved away. They had receded to the corner then across the street, the woman straight as a yardstick, the children imitating, leaning to peer both ways before starting over until they reached the middle of the street where the woman had held her hands at their backs, the children then scampering to the other side where they scattered going their own way alone. The woman followed slowly then turned through the gate studying the ground, her hands in the pockets of her worn checked coat.

Now in his turn, he rose from where he dreamed of distant sunlight. He shivered in the wind. He crept down the steps, turned with his crutch, hobbled past the tailor's through the billowing steam to the corner where cautious now his lesson learned, he searched both ways before he crossed to safety beneath the towering church.

<h1 style="text-align:center">5</h1>

No one was on the playground when he arrived. He stood listening to the quiet noises in among the windy buttresses: the soft murmur of the pigeons in their cold lofty nests; the quick small movements of sparrows on the gravel of the playground; the thin traffic passing on the street. He went up the flat gray steps into the school. The door latch caught behind.

Then he stood in the emptiness of the classroom. He saw the varnished floor, the stained desks in rows bound together on slats of wood, their wrought iron legs. He saw the empty desktops, the large teacher's desk trimmed with books, softened by the green blotter. He studied the upright piano in the corner beyond the teacher's desk where he had discovered his voice and a joy in melody, where he had stood while the teacher played. Here he had won recognition and praise for his strong, pure voice.

He followed the scene displayed along the line of windows. Before his accident he had helped with other displays. The windows receded to the bookshelves at the far corner of the room. He saw through the back windows the pastor's house beyond.

He listened to the muffled blend of voices from the upstairs large room with high ceiling where the students ate lunch they had brought in bags from home. Felix could imagine his brothers there among the others. He listened to the clash and gush of voices. Then he limped to the desk at the back, the one before the bookcase in the corner opposite the door. The last desk in the room, a special place; the next seat was in the higher grades above in a room with towering windows that looked across the canopy of trees and roofs of houses. He had been allowed to ascend to that higher level from time to time to deliver something to the upper grade teacher, the delivery one of the duties that came with that last desk at the back of the room. How he aspired to rise to that higher level and remain, to be one of those older students who seemed so grand. This room in contrast seemed a burrow. And here he felt it inappropriate to his name.

Yet, this last seat that he had occupied before the accident had bestowed honor on him. This seat had given him access to the books. He had been librarian. A special duty, it held power and responsibility. It gave him freedom, more freedom than all the long months he had spent mending. When he passed out readers, he, the only one allowed to rise, would go to the cupboards along the back of the room. There he would fetch the hard bright volumes. Then he would move along the aisles handing down books that gave off fragrances. Empty handed, he returned to the corner seat while the others sat confined watching him. He enjoyed the same freedom when he collected them.

As librarian, he also earned the right to read any book he liked. Allowed to rise at almost anytime once his other work was done, he could go to the bookshelves. He could idle, leafing through the large pages bright with pictures. Yet, he had always resisted a desire to choose an easy book. He had always chosen something he sensed would win him praise.

Most often, he chose the Psalms from the Bible. He had come to know some through his singing in the church choir, the only child because of his clear, strong voice. He had searched for other books that would challenge him by the bristling crush of words. He had struggled hoping to understand. Here, they said, was knowledge.

"Can you really understand what you read?" the teacher asked.

"I can read a little," he confessed.

"Well, I guess a little learning from the Good Book is better than none. No danger in getting what you can," she had said.

Then she had gone to her desk and he had returned to the rich print upon the thin paper. Burying his cheeks in his hands, he would attack the enigma, those inscrutable signs, those unfamiliar sounds that echoed in his mind when he mouthed them. He felt encouraged by the thought that even in his trying he had gained. The attempt, so he had been led him to believe, was often better than the actual deed. Struggle was good; action was discipline. Travail was honor; the task was sufficient unto the day, his faith, any attempt however short it fell was worthy. Redeemed through suffering, won through pain, the unobtainable would be obtained; the mystery here would lead to glory there, toward the ultimate enigma, toward that mystery called God. How he wanted God! So he had searched. Yet his faith starting at the source with words on paper had met defeat. He was troubled by his failure. Faith was not enough.

"That's my place!"

A voice he knew stabbed through his dream. He stared uncomprehending. "That's my desk! Miss Peterson said it's mine now!"

Felix gaped at Henry, his friend, whom he had fought.

"Get out! Get out!" Henry cried.

Felix moved then realized his mistake. He had yielded betraying himself. Suddenly, he knew his self-deception. How could he have imagined that the place that bore so much honor would remain vacant? That seat brought such grave responsibility. Could those duties remain unfulfilled? He had been gone so long. Yet, as he yielded, as he moved, as he stood searching the indignant features of his self-righteous accuser, he sensed injustice hovering somewhere. How could he have helped being gone so long? There had been his accident.

"Since when you been librarian?" he demanded becoming defiant.

"Miss Peterson made me"

"So what? I'm back now! I was librarian first!"

"You're not now! I am now! You stay out of my place!"

Henry threw himself into the seat, hunching over the desk, hugging it, possessing it.

Felix lunged attempting to sit and force the other boy from the seat. But the crutch hindered him, and as his body jarred against the solid body of the other, Little Felix knew his weakness. His strength, conditioned through constant battle challenging this very boy he challenged now had lost resilience. The other had endured. Henry laughed realizing he had won.

Yet, Felix grabbed the desk swinging his body at the seat, swinging out again in repeated assaults. Again and again he jarred against the other boy trying to move him, to dislodge him, to regain his place—as if physical possession were enough. The other boy held on confident in victory. Then Felix stood spent, his chest heaving.

"We'll see! he threatened. We'll see!"

Then he fled hindered by his mending leg heavy beneath him, throbbing from the burden he had forced it to bear. Henry's laugh followed his flight.

Felix struggled up the stairs. He would appeal to justice. He would explain reminding her: How could he help prevent the accident? So he had crossed the street in the wrong place. He would admit that. He had confessed before. It was easy now. He hadn't seen the car. Yet, was everything his fault? He had thought he could cross before the slow truck reached him. Instead, he had found the car upon him. How could he have stopped that looming form? How could he have prevented being struck? Could he have helped himself from being dragged? Could he help his brittle bones and prevent them from breaking? So he argued as he climbed, as he fought his way up the stairs, his dead leg clunking, accusing him, mocking him.

He reached the landing. He paused, gathering for the final ascent, fighting for breath. He heard the voices in the high ceiling room. The volume swelled. Then the gathering broke, a group issuing through the monumental door.

"Felix!" the blonde girl cried. "Felix is back!" She turned to the other girls, constant companions who followed her, as always.

"Unfair! Unfair!" his spirit cried to something beyond even those raised above him. And as he sensed this new wound, he felt his anger shed, dissipated by the painful climb, confounded by this new assault. He should ignore her, brush by her to the entrance of the room where he would be safe from her guile. He recalled the group that had come to him that spring. Some within that group stood before him now. She had never come. Here, now, she hovered giving him the attention he had always sought. She had always snubbed him. He halted feeling lost.

"Hi Lori," he said spent. He rested on his crutch.

"How's your leg?" the blonde girl asked hushed, serious in noticing his cast. The other girls were silent reflecting concern.

His chest heaved. He glanced beyond her through the high windows to the thick trees moving in the chill wind. "It doesn't hurt much anymore," he said swallowing. His leg throbbed in answer.

"Boy, it must have!"

He looked down avoiding her bright blue eyes. He studied the thick cast, his naked swollen toes. His exposed toenails that seemed now like claws condemned him. "It only hurts now when I climb," he said. "When I walk a lot."

She gazed past him down the steep varnished stairs. He twisted following her gaze. He saw the steep angle of his ascent. He finally recalled his loss.

"I have to see Miss Peterson. That dumb Henry stole my seat!"

"But she gave it to him," the girl explained as if the theft was accepted.

Felix stared mute.

"You were to be gone so long," she added. The others bobbed their heads in silent agreement. He felt his weariness. "But I'm glad you're back," Lori said. The others bobbed their heads.

He searched her face. Confused and nagged by doubt he wanted to believe for one fleeting moment that she was honest. Before, he had always been deceived. "Thanks," he said. Then he heard the swell of voices as the other students rushed from the monumental room forcing those on the landing to move. He shuffled aside. The crowd stormed by sweeping her along disappearing toward the playground battlefields below. Felix climbed deserted and alone.

6

After he found the woman in the lunchroom she proclaimed what he already knew. She was kind but firm in parroting the girls who had mimicked her. "But you were to be gone so long, Felix!" the woman said. How he hated to hear her use that name now! How could he meet her accusation? Worse, she had allowed the seat to hardly cool after they had abandoned him, so they had seemed to dismiss him and to bury him.

Glum at the woman's judgment, Felix hobbled down the stairs in despair. In the classroom, he saw Henry still seated in the desk he had won stretching to peer out the window even as he tried to remain within the seat maintaining possession.

The bell rang. The pupils scrambled to form lines then filed in to take their places settling while Felix stood waiting beside the teacher's desk apart from them studying them while they inspected him. He felt exposed, vulnerable, so different from when they had enviously followed his every move as he had moved among them passing out books. Now they held him in their scrutiny glancing at his crusted leg studying his pallor eyeing the support he leaned on. They seemed awed by him. They had heard of him, had talked of him. But his lengthy absence had made him fade from their memory. Now, here he was again standing there sickly, still mending, an old myth renewed and fulfilled.

Yet, even as they watched, as they settled, Miss Peterson was at work arranging. She determined. She ordered him to the seat. He sat stunned, the others watching him, their heads rising from their books, their papers, their pencils, their varnished desks then dropping again while he found himself in front directly beneath the woman's nose. She looked down at him, her eyes large behind the wavering lenses of thick glasses. The final blow: he had to bear Henry's gloating, the other boy's presence as Henry neared coming from the back of the room distributing readers. And Felix was brought to public shame made greater by the attention he received from his leg and his return.

Through the decorated windows scenes of autumn: brilliant trees, farmer's fields both rich and bare with harvest he saw below the gray solid sky the dark hulk of the church, the cyclone fence, the gabled roofs of houses beyond the alley leading to his grandmother's.

Henry slammed a book on his desk startling him. He studied the cover opening it. The page had always fascinated him, the holy looking words, the bright pictures of boys his own age reaching joy, gaining friends, achieving adventure. All these oppressed him. Someone began to read. He tried to follow. He had read so well once. Now he felt lost. He searched for hope: The lesson wouldn't last; perhaps they would never reach him. But here, too, he failed. His name called, he heard Henry's snicker from the back of the room, reminding him of his own conceit: Henry had always been a poor reader; and Felix had always gloated over his own skill. Sometimes, Henry had won at wrestling, but Felix had always won at words Now he tried; he faltered then sat mute and flushed.

At recess, Felix moved through the doors following the others while he hobbled toward the front avoiding the clamor of the crowded back. The front always had been a place of quiet, a place he went when seeking refuge from the contrivances of ripening females, goddesses who pursued him, or from boy warriors who chased him. From the front, he could see his distant house; he could sense his mother's presence there. Now someone rushed by retreating to the battles in the rear leaving him to search the covey at the base of the church. He stood hunched and dejected. Then, suddenly, as he searched the street almost as in a dream, a distant image moved within his range, a phantom shape he recognized.

His vision directed inward; he studied the gravel of the yard, the soft stir of feathers below the soaring buttress of the church blurred by its upward sweep. The outer world swam. Then as he searched again for the wavering form that moved from behind the corner of the house his vision cleared, and he knew at last the woman in her familiar cloth coat as she passed the gray front porch, as she came down the concrete steps of the walk, as she moved past the brick movie house, past the service station, she growing smaller, diminished by distance as she descended the long slope receding to the level of the bank.

7

Felix went home with loathing, filled with disappointment and dread. When he arrived, he tried to sneak by her to the jar, but she was waiting at the sink. She spun from her peeling. She called to him. He stopped. He turned. He leaned against the doorframe watching her as she worked the knife through the yellow skin. The skin crackled. She cut through the green-ringed white core. He cowered from the sharp sting, hating what his father loved, his father demanding them in everything. Felix knew he would be forced to eat making him retch for which he would be ordered down from the table to his room where he would be punished by his hunger and his loss of rare dessert.

She went on carving. Then she turned to face him. He saw her raw weeping eyes. She used the back of her hand to wipe away her tears.

"Where you going?" she demanded, her voice quavering.

"My jar," he said.

"Can't you ever let that thing alone?"

"It's mine!"

What else could he say? Perhaps he might tell her of his day, of his humiliation and defeat. Yet, he knew he could never tell her of his true sorrow. How could he tell her that the jar and the money was his only comfort? What else could he trust? The jar, his oracle, would answer him and bring him comfort, would bring him peace.

"Go play!" she urged, she ordered, almost pleading.

"No!" he screamed, startled at his own rebellion. The shock of revolt brought with it a sweep of fear. He waited, poised, expecting her to come at him, as always; he braced himself to cringe beneath her blows. Instead, she stood dumb, shocked as he.

"No!" he screamed again thrilled at his utter release. "I want my money! I want my coins! I want my jar!" he now shrieked.

Then he spun. He clunked across the barren floor through the empty rooms. Her cry followed him rising to a wail.

He reached the bedroom. The crutch clattered to the floor. Then in the dim light of the closet beneath the dark uneven shapes of hanging clothes that held his mother's scent he groped among his mother's shoes, crawling into darkness searching behind the dusty faded boxes ageless and permanent, blinded by his fear, by his mother's shriek seeking him, her screeching muffled by the fragrant clothes as she searched for him where he groveled to retrieve the message in the jar.

He found it. He snatched up the cold glass. He heard the shift of coins as he tried the weight, lifting it, testing it as he drew it to him, hugging it, curling over it as he backed from beneath the limp shapeless things hovering above him.

He turned, and as he fled the darkness wincing from the full weight of his leg, crying out against a sharp sudden pain, he cowered beneath the looming form that held the gleaming knife, the green-ringed severed onion in her hand.

He fell and rolled hugging the jar sobbing, the coins singing following his rhythm as he rocked. Then he stopped, choking back his tears; he blinked, clearing his eyes. He set the jar on his loins.

He studied the coins that packed the sides. The distant unobstructed world beyond gleamed cloudy, limed, and without portraits. He studied the dark images of things in the room: the wavering shadows of the dresser, the dark window frame. Then he raised himself upon his arm and gazed with fascination at the world made ponderous from the double green of molded glass.

The woman stood at the door, the wet bright blade and dark handle of the knife in her limp wet hand. She waited there mourning him, crying from her pain of bitter onion.

The Middle of the String-1

[Tuesday, May 8, 1945]

The day the fighting stopped, Henry Schneider wondered what would happen to him now that the war was over. The supervisor who had sought him out before came to him again.

"Well, Kraut. What's it going to be? You decided?"

Henry looked up from his work, the chisel with which he carved the wood poised in the air. The other men in the pattern shop paused in their work then continued. Henry was conscious of their forms hunched over their benches. He knew they had been watching him, that they were watching him now. They must be listening. He heard the hiss and blast of the furnaces in the nearby foundry.

Henry shook his head. "No," he said at last. He carefully laid his chisel and turned to give the man his full attention. Henry towered above the stocky balding man.

"For Pete's sake, Schneider! What's the problem? You've had more than enough time to think it over!"

"I know," Henry demurred. "I'm just not sure."

"Not sure! Hey! I know it's a big step. But you'll come out better in the long run."

"Maybe."

"Maybe? No maybe's about it, Schneider! Think of the money!"

"Sure, the money's good."

"Hey, it's better than good. The position. Think of that. Responsibility. That's what you want, ain't it? That's what you're after? All that work for the union? Wasn't all that about position? Being responsible? Here's your chance, Henry! How far you want to go? You can get off this bench."

"I've been all right," Henry said. In fact, he liked where he was now, settled at last among the hard fixtures of the shop in which he now worked. He had gone through a lot to get here.

"Forget this, Schneider! You're stuck here if you don't take the chance! You won't go nowhere from here!"

"I've been satisfied. I got here by myself. Nobody had to help me."

That's it, he told himself. One thing he could say: he had always fought for anything he ever got—his high school shop training over the resistance of the instructor, his marriage over the objections of his father, this job after being laid off from others. No one had ever given him a thing. You had to take what you wanted! The only thing—don't give in! Don't let the bastards wear you done!

His words and thoughts were emphasized by size. A large man, Schneider seemed slender, with a long, thin face and dark wavy hair, and a dark, full mustache he sported to give himself a sense of maturity and pride. He felt he had earned it. A black Kraut, everyone called him since he wasn't fair-haired as most were on his wife's side of their German heritage. He wore the slur as a badge of honor.

"So go farther, Schneider! What you got now? Look around you!" The supervisor swept his arm toward the row of lights underneath the steel beams, toward the gray sweaty backs of the other men bent over wooden patterns and molds like the one on Henry's bench.

Henry followed the sweeping arm then came back to rest on the man's porky face: the pores, the lines, the puffy flesh. He heard the quiet tap of wooden mallets, the sudden crash of a tool tossed in among other tools within a metal box, the hot distant hiss and clang of the foundry.

"Think, Schneider!" the man urged tapping his head. What's so good about all this? What's so good about that union job? You don't even know if you'll get it. Sure, there's a chance, the same kind as you've got with what we're offering. But you don't know what's going to happen you go after that union job. This one that we've got for you is safe. You know us, Schneider. What you know about those guys? They just as likely turn on you first chance."

"You're trying to buy me off," Henry said quietly. He hadn't wanted to say that, but now that he had, he watched the man's eyes move over Henry's face.

"Think, Schneider," the man said again tapping his head. Then the man turned and stalked away. Henry watched the man's short heavy form move off stopping along the aisle of benches, bending to whisper something to the man sitting there who glanced at Henry, the man's chisel still poised in his hand.

"Kike bastard!" Henry muttered to himself.

But Henry thought. All morning, as he had for several mornings now, Henry had done little else: the offer of the foreman's job and the war's end. First one, then the other troubled him. For both really fell together. He had followed with mixed feelings the events of the last weeks, these events of the war that would culminate by drawing to a sporadic close sometime in the early afternoon of the very same day that Henry sat here pondering the effect the war would have now that it was finally over. For the past several days Henry had been compelled more and more to weigh the possibilities. Yet, he was also relieved.

He thought again about the long years of struggle, the reports in blood, reverberations of the distant thunder, echoes of gunfire, the photos he had seen—mud, fallen bodies lying along the road before snow-stark hills. Then, too, there were the letters from his wife's brother, a medical corpsman with Patton's army. Henry thought of him perhaps even now rolling through the rubble on the outskirts of Berlin. Henry thought about the letters from his wife's father in Germany pleading with them to send food—anything, but especially, if they could, cigarettes. If they could! What could Henry do even if he wanted to since he had to roll his own?

Henry thought of the struggle that they had themselves. The war had been no easier for them. They had suffered through their own deprivation. He thought of his wife and the ration book she governed with such caution, the perforated stamps, blue and classic, imposing and important that she would carefully tear from the book, reluctantly handing them over. Giving them up, she had that many less. He thought of her long almost daily treks in search of luxuries. Luxuries! Sugar? Meat? Coffee? How could these things be luxuries! He had seen the lines of refugees in the newsreels he watched some Saturdays in the dark movie house. The lines for food and goods were also here.

In later years what would he think of all this suffering now, he sitting then around the kitchen table at night, sipping strong coffee mellowed with milk, with sugar, eating hard rolls thick with real butter, those rolls bought fresh and warm from the all-night bakery he would drive to in a cherished car he would finally be able to afford, passing closed stores along the neon bright street. Now the streets were always dark, as black as empty stores, as empty as German towns reduced by bombs to rubble.

His wife still searched the paper every night for sales, for anything that was available, anything that was being sold. The next day she tramped the streets hoping she wasn't late, hoping she wouldn't arrive and find everything already gone. Arriving early, finding something still being sold, she stood in queues, waiting, waiting, clutching her purse with the precious ration book, staring at those things she knew she never could afford.

He thought of the cigarettes he made himself with the help of a small machine. He made them in scores bringing to the operation a sense of ritual: the paper filled, the lever pulled to roll the paper and the tobacco into a slender tube, the wetting of the gummed strip. Then he placed them in a factory-made tin box that he had salvaged. How long had it been since he had smoked his last real cigarette? All those luxuries had gone for the fighting men overseas. And they at home had little for themselves.

Now the war was nearly over. Maybe they could relax now. Things would be better, so Henry told himself, sitting at his bench. (He worked the chisel carefully now. Here was a real dangerous part.) The war was over. And what about his job? He thought about the returning hordes of soldiers. They would be heroes filled with tales of mud, the shock of distant cannon, of victory and conquest. And he himself had never gone. What would happen to him now? Would they have his job again, just like always? Maybe if he accepted the offer of the foreman job that would help him. He would have a job. Sure, he'd have to go back on the union, but the supervisor had been right, Henry had to grudgingly admit, the first indication he was no longer useful, he'd be gone. They'd ditch him, just like that.

The quickening of sound around him made him stop. Henry looked up from his work. The others were moving from their benches, some still placing tools. He turned back to the wood beneath his hands. He would just finish this part. Then after lunch he might complete the job itself. Henry anticipated that final sense of order. Finishing a job was always good. Seeing it finished always made him feel special. Then he could start something new. He hunched again over his work. But someone yelled.

"Hey, scab!"

Schneider whirled. Feiffer, a friend, stood in the empty aisle. "You buckin' for a raise?"

Schneider flared. "I'm union, fella!"

Lunch time, Kraut!" Feiffer accused. Then he went off between the deserted benches.

Henry arranged his equipment then followed. When he reached the locker room, he found the others already eating gathered around on benches chewing food they took from metal lunch buckets talking through their food while they splayed out the playing cards they spread among them. The men fell silent as Schneider entered. They avoided looking at him. They chewed. They snapped down the cards. They gathered them. Someone shuffled. Schneider went into the washroom. The talk resumed loud enough for him to hear almost as if they wanted him to.

"I wouldn't want no foreman's job," someone declared.

"Yeah," someone agreed. Henry recognized the voice. "You got all that worry. What else you got?"

"Nothin'" a third added. "No pay for overtime. You got to work anyway."

"No raise unless the Super gives the O.K.," another offered.

"So what have you got? Worry, that's all. Nothin' but headaches."

"Yeah. If he wants that kind of crap, he can have it. Seems strange, though, they should want *him*."

"What's strange? He helped organize. They want to get him off their back."

"You're right. That's what's strange. A guy works like hell. Takes all the flack. Then gives it up just like that for some lousy management job. He mustn't think so much about all he said about union, about sticking together."

"Maybe he'll go somewhere. He's just watching out for number one. Same as everybody."

"I know where he'll go! Out on his can! Wait, you'll see! A guy willing to sell out like that. They know they got their man. But you just let him do somethin' wrong. Let anything happen they don't like. He'll go. Just like that. You wait! You'll see!"

"Yeah. I'd rather stay where I am. I won't have that much to lose. A guy gives in like that, goes back on his words, sells out for what he thinks is better, how can he ever go back?"

"Right. One thing sure. 'How far we ever going to get?' Weren't those his words? Work like hell. Risk your neck. Some bastard sees a chance to make a few coins, he takes it. Doesn't make our job any easier if we want to stay union."

"He'll get his. Wait. One way or another, he'll pay."

One always had to pay. Schneider knew that. But it was strange now to hear them talk like they were about him. How concerned had they been before when he had taken all the risks? Now they could talk. It had been like pulling teeth. They hadn't wanted to do much of anything. They had stood around with a finger up their butt, doing nothing, when he had taken all the risks. Now they were set. They had the right last name. They had followed what he had started. They would stay because of the union. What would happen to him?

Henry went to his locker for his lunch pail. The men quieted, manipulating cards, masticating food, using their tongues to free their teeth and gums.

Schneider left. Let them talk!

He searched for his friend Feiffer in Enameling, meandering through the rows of cooling, naked forms, raw porous metal that someday would be bathtubs, sinks, toilet stools. The plant had been only recently retooled to begin making things that everyone had gone without for so long. There had been a military contract for fixtures that would be placed in the growing number of installations and housing for families with men in the military and for those returning from the war. Schneider saw the fixtures of the plant around him: the crane that carried huge black pots of molten steel to the working metal pattern he had part in making. He had carved the wooden form. They had copied it in steel. In his mind's eye he saw the huge majestic scrap crane running on the high steel beams. He thought of how it dipped into piles of half-rusted, half-glittering metal twisted and lumped that it picked up from railroad hopper cars and added to a heap then dropped it in smaller cars that carried it into the plant. He saw overhead the conveyor system that took the castings from the foundry through the blasting room then to Enameling and then the fiery ovens. Each area required a new device. How could he ever deal with each of them? Who had ever thought he could? He had so little background. Basic ability perhaps he had, but knowledge? And yet they had offered him the foreman's job. He would supervise the repair of breakdowns and the servicing of the systems. It was a step up, they had told him. He wouldn't be a supervisor—but the title wasn't that important anyway. The other guys were right. Schneider knew. All those things he passed now would be his worry.

He found Feiffer in among the castings his back against the row of forms waiting for the ovens. Feiffer glanced up at him then studied the bitten sandwich before he chomped. Schneider crouched then dropped, stretched his long legs, and opened his lunch. Around him, the plant idled: quieted machinery hummed. He heard the diminished voices of the group of men at cards. Somewhere two men, one the superintendent, were talking shop, still working. He heard the noise of his own lunch as he unfolded it. He heard Feiffer chewing. How long had they known each other? The two Krauts always ate together. Now, Feiffer seemed distant.

"How's it going?" Henry asked. "Anyone giving you trouble lately?"

"It's O.K.," Feiffer said. They don't mean it. They don't think. People just say things without knowing what they say."

"Like calling people 'scab'?"

"Just joking. See what I mean? Even I do it. Say things. Don't mean nothin' by it. Why should it bother me when people call me things?"

"Didn't sound like you were kidding."

Feiffer shrugged. He occupied himself with pouring coffee from a thermos; then he took his second sandwich. Forget it. I'm sorry," he said.

"The other guys ever say anything about me?"

"We don't talk much."

"What about you?"

"What you mean?"

"You know. About the offer."

"So?"

"What you think?"

Feiffer shrugged again. They ate in silence. "It'd be a hard choice," Feiffer said finally. "You take the job, you have to give up the union. You take the union job; you give up the job you got here. You got some time put in here."

Henry nodded. "They're really pressuring me."

"You really could? Really give one up?"

"Both good pay. Both give me a chance."

Feiffer cocked his head. "Both could make you lose."

"The war's over now," Schneider offered. "There'll be guys scramblin' for work."

Feiffer considered as he cleaned his teeth. "You're working. You're good. Why would they want some guy that's been gone for five years?"

"They'll be heroes. Me. I'm the guy that turned down their job. You think they're going to let me get away with *that*?"

"You still got the union. You worked hard for it. You give that up, you're right back where you were, taking what they give you, nothin' more."

"Sure, I risked my neck for it. What good does that do now? So I organized. They could can my butt if they want. Nothing in the law says they can't. You read it. You were there. You know. Besides the union only offered. Nothing's sure."

Feiffer agreed. "It'd be a hard choice," he said again. "I'm glad it's not mine." He closed his lunch box then rose.

"Where you going?" Henry asked.

"Finished," Feiffer said. "Thought I'd watch the guys play cards.

Schneider stared at the man. Feiffer stepped over him then started for the passageway between the rows of forms. He turned back. "Come watch us when you're through." Feiffer said.

Schneider remained mute studying the man's face.

"I hope you know what you're doing, Kraut," Feiffer said. Then he walked off, disappearing when he turned in among the unfinished fixtures.

Henry knew, all right. What did it all mean now? What did that struggle mean to anyone but him: So he had been a leader of the local union. Who had ever honored him for that? Who other than himself had even worried about it? Who even respected him now: Look how they acted now. Look how they had acted then. Who but himself thought about how he had to fight against disinterest, against fear. They *had* to work together, he had argued. How would they win anything? Did they always want to work for peanuts? Did they always want to take what management offered? When were they going to be men? When were they going to stop scraping, scrambling over each other, fighting each other for their lousy, goddamned job. He had stopped then, shaking with anger—at them, at the bosses, at himself for having lost control. Yet, slowly he had convinced them. They were risking their jobs, they had pleaded. O.K., he had agreed, but so was he. He had done so before and had lost. Over and over again, he would be last hired, first fired, his reputation following him. But he had always believed that the gamble would be worth it later. Wait, he had urged them, work together. You'll see.

Schneider's task hadn't been made any easier by the threats. He had been warned, not directly, of course: What about those problems in his former jobs? Get the reputation of a troublemaker, his chance of finding something else was slim. He had kids to think about. He had gone to see a union lawyer, had come away dejected: Nothing could stop him from organizing; nothing could stop him from being fired. Yet, he had persisted.

He recalled the clandestine meetings, the arguments, the struggles for control once the others had accepted the possibility of their success. He recalled the accusations, the suggestions by some that they would readily betray for personal gain or just for spite. Some people never had liked Schneider anyway. Then there had been the actual confrontation petitioning the company for acceptance of a union. The men had gone as a group. Schneider had led the way. He recalled the sudden change on the superintendent's face, his grabbing the desk edge as the chair shot back from under him. The man had studied them looking at each one's face acknowledging each one of them. Then he had retrieved his swivel chair and had eased himself down.

"You're behind this, Schneider," the superintendent charged. No one said a word.

"And the rest of you are going to listen to *him*!" Again the superintendent looked at each of them. "You're really going to risk your necks to follow *him*?"

"We have our rights," Schneider said.

"You have shit, fella!"

Schneider trembling with anger but with unusual control had laid the typed petition on the vast desk. He had pecked it out himself at home borrowing a machine to type it.

The superintendent stared at it where it lay.

Schneider turned with the others, moved out of the glass enclosure that overlooked the foundry, returned to work, leaving the petition where it lay. The others had followed.

"Schneider," the superintendent had said later, "You ought to be in public relations."

Henry had waited conscious of the men working there below him. The superintendent had summoned him. He had gone alone ascending the metal stairs his hard toe work shoes sounding as he climbed noticing between the open grating the men who watched as he climbed toward the glass cage office hung above the concrete plain bristling with industry. The plant manager and Henry's supervisor had been there, but they had remained silent lounging at the windows that overlooked the lines of railroad cars, the piles of crates, the monorail of the moving scrap crane. The superintendent had done the talking since it was he to whom Schneider and his followers had offered the petition.

"You've got a natural gift, Henry."

Schneider had been struck by the man's addressing him so personally. "You have the ability to sell yourself. You have the ability to sell your ideas. You really can. Why, you've sold us, hasn't he?"

The man strained back, his heavy frame twisting in the creaking chair that tipped under his weight. The plant manager had simply closed delicate eyelids opening them again to turn away gazing out over his domain. The supervisor had remained mute.

"You really are wasting yourself working at that bench. We can use you with your skills. Things are happening now that the war's over. We're talking merger with a bigger company. That happens, you'll have your chance, if you work it right. You play the game, you can get there. Think what that will mean. White shirt and tie. Money, Henry. Going places, meeting all kinds of people, even women."

Henry had caught himself becoming interested. The superintendent had sensed the wedge.

"We'll start you in maintenance. The man had said the word "maintenance" differently. Henry had tried to repeat the man's utterance to himself. He had stumbled. "There's an opening there. We'll see how you work. If you're O.K. as foreman, who knows? You can go anywhere you want from there. It'd be up to you."

Henry wondered why there was an opening in maintenance. What had happened to the guy who had been foreman?

"What's your price?" Henry had cursed himself for having asked. What made him think that they were selling or that he was buying?"

"Give up the union crap!"

Henry hadn't answered

"Think about it, Schneider."

Then the superintendent had dismissed Henry with a wave of his hand.

But as Henry had left, the superintendent called after him. "Here's your chance, Schneider. Don't screw up! Don't throw it away!" The man's voice had carried through the window of the rattling door as Henry had closed it behind him.

Yet there had been negotiations. Why should the company offer threats? Why, for that matter, should the men need a union? Hadn't they always tried to work out any differences? Why spoil their relationship by now making everything so formal: Some men, of course, had second thoughts and voiced their misgivings. The rest had backed them down. We need something definite, something binding. The company needed them. This rumor of merger meant the company was weak. Trouble now—a work stoppage, a strike—might ruin everything, might force the plant to close. Where would they be then? What good a union then? All through this talk, Schneider thought about the superintendent's offer.

Then Henry had sought information about the possibility of affiliation with the national union. He returned—surprised as anyone with an offer for him to be nominated for national office.

"The national union needs us too," Henry, more naïve than cynical, explained. "They want numbers. You see? It's like I said. There's strength in numbers. We work together, we get someplace."

"But why must it be you?" his wife had asked.

"No one knows me. The other guys are known. They need someone in the region to organize. We're going to be the first ones here, the first union here. You know what that means?"

"You'll be too much away from us," his wife had observed.

"Sure, it'll mean travel, all right. But look at the money! What I make now!"

"We manage," his wife had said. "Children need a father. Look at me; I should know."

Henry considered his wife's remarks remembering the utter sense of weariness he felt returning from his trip to Philadelphia where he had sought national affiliation: the long smoky train ride there and back; the skimpy food that never seemed to last; the drab hotel rooms. Yet, these were balanced by the brilliant newness of passing cities he had never seen before. He saw again the places charged with history. He had only read of such places. Now here he was standing where men had struggled just as he who was only beginning to fight in his own way.

Then, too, alone among the crowds, the moving, colored lights, he had thrilled with freedom. Those passing women dressed so elegantly, so exotic, those drinks he had nursed, those meals he had savored having watched others in the movies indulge in them. All these he now might have for himself. The possibilities were erotic. There would be other places: one would be Atlantic City. He saw the wide beach, the dark foaming sea, the rich hotels. There would be the convention hall with jamming voices, loudspeakers, churning smoke, just like the conventions he saw in the newsreels—well-groomed men in tailored suits making decisions. And he dressed similarly would be involved in making them.

Then he thought of his return. His bringing presents almost as if to assuage those whom he felt he had abandoned and to appease his own quilt and his own anxiety. She had left him before over something unimportant. What might she do if he went away like this more often? How passively they had welcomed him back accepting his offering: a trinket for his wife, candy for his sons. Now each time he saw the gifts, hers in the jewelry box, the sweets within the jar leeching in the pale light from the large picture window beside the table where he sat each day after work sipping coffee watching smoke curl from the cigarette he had so carefully rolled himself. At those quiet times he thought about the distant city, so strange, so far away, so vast he felt the loneliness that he had sensed, the futility that he had never actually admitted to himself until he had seen his passive wife, his indifferent sons, the pale light from the window on the white enamel of the table where he sat. Nothing was ever free. No one ever had freedom. Sure, he might gain. What? Money? Power? Responsibility? Perhaps. What would he lose?

Then that same afternoon as he worked and as he reflected on these things the war ended. And he, too, despite his problems, his dilemma, perhaps because of it, felt the growing excitement. He, too, felt the pressure of the intensity with which the others followed the cries from men who rushed through bearing the news.

"It's over! They've surrendered! The Germans have surrendered!" Those cries that rose above the jar and clash and hiss of machines vanished among the heavy struts and beams that closed in their world.

Schneider tried to keep working, but he finally gave up amid the chaos of the jubilation, and he put away his tools arranging them as always in precise order then locking the chest of drawers that sat beneath the bench upon which he worked. He started for the washroom jostled by the men who seemed to flee from him. He washed using the large circular wash trough, changed clothes hanging them neatly within the metal locker from which he took his empty lunch pail. He suddenly felt foreign, more than he had recently: the loud laughter, the shouts and exclamations of joy echoing off the tile walls and the smooth concrete floor as the men washed then changed clothes were alien to him.

And as he left, the others surged around him in a group, passing him, moving on ahead, tossing back remarks that seemed directed toward him, laughing among themselves as they disappeared. Henry moved alone watching them disperse across the freight yard. He climbed the weathered stairs that led from the cindered yard to the red brick cobbled street. Then he waited for the bus.

He would stop at Laynie's, he decided. A beer or two, the quiet—if there would be any quiet now—the dim lighting of the tavern where he had stopped now and then would allow him to relax. He could use that quiet now, could use the sense of peace, more so than other days. Then, as in other days, he would walk the short distance to his flat, would climb the stairs, would sit at the table beside the large window sipping coffee enjoying the rich flavors of milk and sugar that he would add today in celebration. He would light a cigarette and add that flavor to the pleasure of his sweetened coffee while he listened to the news of the war's end, the reports of celebration. Maybe, if he were lucky, the woman directly across the way would come home, enter her bedroom, undress completely, slip on her silk robe, all this without drawing the blind. Schneider's loins surged at the vision of naked thighs and hips and breasts.

The trackless trolley glided to a stop, hissed open, and took him up and in jolting him against the polished pole as it bounced and swayed across the redbrick roadway of the bridge that took him down into the interior of the rejoicing city happy with tears for the war's end.

2

The day the fighting stopped, Felix, Henry Schneider's youngest son, cut into the shadow of the walk between the gray slat board houses and ran to the rear screen door. He peered toward the fenced backyard, and he was glad when he saw his brother wasn't there, glad that maybe he had beaten his brother home. Then he yanked open the door and started up the spiral stairwell scrambling toward the kitchen. The screen door slammed to behind him. He stopped; he braced himself. He had failed again.

"Felix Schneider!" the woman's voice warned from above. "You go back and close that door until you can close it quiet!"

Felix complained, but he went back down the spiral again. At the door, he opened and closed the screen, counting loudly. Then he eased the screen door closed behind him and stood at the foot of the stairs lifting his face to where the tan walls began their spiral.

"Ten times, Ma!"

"All right," the woman's voice called. "Don't you slam it again!" Felix resolved with hope then started up the stairs.

He found her waiting at the top alone. She handed him a pale blue envelope. A letter! And he thrilled at the victory. Each day since he himself had written he had hurried home from school leaving his friends ditching his older brother hoping a letter had come. Now, at last, it was here. He took it from her then threw himself on the kitchen chair by the table beside the large picture window that looked out at the flat across the way. He checked himself, shot up straight, stared at her. She wagged a finger but went back to her kettle, her half-conscious stirring as she listened to the soft murmur of the radio listening for news about the war's end.

Felix carefully unsealed the envelope then flattened the thin tissue paper on the table. He read by the large window beside where he sat. He struggled to decipher the fine hand printing. Then he finally gave up disappointed at his inability to read alone. He slid from his chair and crept to her.

"Ma?"

She went on stirring.

"Can you read this for me?"

He waited afraid to ask again. Then she surprised him: She wiped her hands on her apron, smoothed the apron, and took the letter. He hugged the refrigerator while she read.

The letter was brief: an apology for not writing sooner, an explanation that the war and duties kept his uncle busy. His uncle thanked him for his letters and hoped that the fighting would be over so that his uncle could return home. That was all. His mother handed him the thin sheet of paper. Felix took it from her and returned to the chair by the window. Then he sat and studied his uncle's fine print.

The letter should have said more, Felix decided. He had waited so long. Now he wished he could see his uncle. Felix liked the man who looked so much like his mother, reflecting the same fine sharp features, the same hair that held a touch of fire. Felix liked the man better than any of his other uncles. The man had gone away to war. The last time Felix had seen the man there had been a party one summer long ago. That day, mild and bright, the sun flashed from windows, from speckles in the granite blocks of the alleyway beside his old basement flat where Grandma Waldner now lived above. That day long ago his uncle was in a tan uniform and there had been a strange girl whom everyone said was his uncle's wife. Felix though her pretty, so he liked her right away. He liked her heart-shaped face, her long dark hair that caught the sunlight. She wore glasses, too, but so did Grandma Waldner, so Felix hadn't minded that the girl had married his uncle.

His uncle had left that same afternoon. Felix had run to him promising that he would write if his uncle would write back. But his uncle only had smiled his thin smile and had left without saying anything. The girl, his uncle's wife, started to cry, kissing his uncle again and again, clinging to his uncle's neck. Grandma Waldner cried, too. Almost everyone seemed to be crying. Felix had wanted to cry, but he didn't want anyone to see him, especially not his brother. "What a sissy!" His brother would tease. So Felix had smiled and he had squinted against the sunlight dancing from the granite blocks of the alley in which they all stood saying good-bye. Felix always squinted against any bright light, so no one, he felt sure, had seen him cry.

After his uncle had gone, Felix had been given an extra large piece of chocolate cake. He had wolfed it down, and no one had scolded him for eating so fast. So he had asked for more, and he had been surprised to be given more. Everyone laughed and marveled and remarked at his appetite for cake. Afterward, at any party, he would gorge himself to make them laugh. Then his father upset that Felix drew such attention for such behavior had issued a stern warning. Now Felix always squirmed in place longing for cake anytime there was a party.

He had forgotten his promise to write his uncle. Then one day a letter came addressed to him! Excited, he had begged for them to read the letter. He had whined; he was finally cracked. Then they had read him the letter.

He had been glad to hear his uncle talk. He had wanted to write back right away, and he was surprised when they agreed to help him. But then his brother who looked like Pa, wanted to write too. He and his brother Sonny had quarreled over who should write first.

"You always have to do everything I do!" Felix had cried. "I'm the oldest!" Sonny proclaimed.

His mother scolded threatening them both. Sonny stood grinning as he always did making Felix angry as he always did until Felix flung himself at the older boy. His father had grabbed him then beat him with a paddle his father had fashioned and shaped especially for such tasks. Then while Felix sat on the sofa in the other room both his flesh and spirit smarting they had helped Sonny write his letter first.

Yet, eventually Felix felt that he had won: He continued to write even though his brother had stopped. Felix liked to write. Writing was like talking. He liked the tissue envelope with all the numbers of his uncle's address Felix printed himself. Best of all, he liked his name on the envelope that came to him from overseas where Ma and Grandma Waldner had come from. His uncle had come from there as did his aunt Erika although no one talked about Aunt Erika or when they did they spoke about her only in whispers. But Felix liked her anyway despite what others said. She gave him things that he never got from others. Yet he had never told her or anyone how much he liked her. In fact, he had never told his uncle how much he liked him. Maybe some day he would do that.

But now he would answer this letter right away. He turned from the large window above the shaded passageway between the wood sided flats. "Can I write, Ma?"

She stood mute, her eyes nearly closed. He asked again.

"Felix!" she warned. "I'm trying to hear the news!"

"Aw, nuts!" Felix whined. He threw himself against the chair.

The woman reached him in two strides. His arm caught most of the blow, but it still hurt and he howled.

"Shut up!" she ordered. He bawled.

"Just you wait 'til your father gets home!"

Felix thought then of the hard sting of the wood. He thought, too, of his recent punishments. None, he decided now, had really been fair. They hadn't been his fault. A newly varnished doorjamb his father had recently finished; he had been called to supper. He had hurried, had stepped, had slipped on the wet varnish. He had landed right beside his father's chair. Another time, the freshly painted bedroom. "One finger print!" His father had warned, "Both of you get it!" Soon enough, Sonny fell against the wall with both hands. They were lined up; then they were beaten, first one, then the other. But Sonny never cried. He simply rubbed himself grimacing at his father in arrogant submission. His father, angered, had turned to the younger boy. Felix had screamed begging his father to stop. Afterward they were sent to bed without supper. He saw again the dim twilight of his room that day, felt again the gnawing hunger, lived again the stinging smart of his beaten flesh.

"I'm sorry, Ma," he said.

"You damn well better be!"

"You gonna tell?"

She didn't answer and went on stirring.

"Please, please don't tell!"

"Go meet your father," she commanded quietly.

He scampered ignoring the cry that followed him. He used the front hallway because it was quicker and he wouldn't have to worry about letting the screen door slam to. Going down the straight stairway painted like the other with dark brown baseboards, dark steps with black rubber matting, tan glistening walls with the dark brown row of fleur-de-lis his father had painted decorating the stairwell, Felix descended now to the glass door with the frosted oval pane that slowly closed behind him by itself.

3

Schneider changed busses at the cemetery. He waited as usual with his back to the wrought iron fence. Each time he looked up the boulevard toward where he anticipated the bus, he was conscious of the white headstones, the granite markers, the red marble monuments. Through the tall laurel shrubs softening the black rods of the fence he saw the graves, the trimmed ripe lawn between. Once for a time he had tended that lawn working at the only job he could get. He had considered himself lucky. Others had looked and had left discouraged. So many out of work, he felt fortunate to labor in the clear morning sunlight, the day still cool, the grass wet and pungent sticking to the whirling blades as he trimmed between the graves. Henry thought about that job each time he waited where he now stood.

He looked again up the boulevard to where the distant traffic crossed. He searched for the image of a diesel bus that would grow, become real, loom, slow, stop, then carry him the rest of the way home.

Those first hard years: his marriage, his children, his trouble finding work. He had thought all that finally behind him. He never had learned, it seemed. For here he was with the same old problem springing up again forcing itself upon him destroying his peace disturbing his thought as he waited for the bus to take him home.

Schneider had married young, perhaps, as some suggested, to escape his father's house. Perhaps, as some suggested, he had fled into bondage. He had met the girl when both of them were little more than kids. Schneider had worked in his aunt' store, a sweet shop. Henry saw again the black metal chairs with wire backs, the marble tables, the glass case filled with trays of sweets, the jars above with candy wrapped in rainbow-colored paper, the red wooden counter topped with polished stone. The girl had come in with a friend or her sister. Henry had been immediately attracted to her. He wondered now what had it been that had made him so interested. Perhaps that she came every day. In time, he came to know her: they had talked, she shy and reticent at first, he open and bold. Then as their talks became longer, no one else seemed there, while his aunt, a thin unhappy woman determined to succeed despite her alcoholic husband was always there behind the stirring curtain warning him of those who had come wanting sweets.

Eventually the store closed, the bitter woman deserted by her husband finally admitting defeat. Henry continued to see the girl. They became serious. They talked about marriage even though both were so young. They petted. And Henry, over-stimulated, reacting in his blood to the restraint and deprivation of his father's barren life, his mother's cold indifferent response, pressed, coaxed, persuaded, finally won. Henry went boldly to his father.

"I'm getting married!" Henry had announced.

"Like hell you are!"

"I have to." Henry insisted quietly.

His father had looked stunned; he had searched his son's face.

"I'm not kidding," Henry had said.

"That's nothing to kid about," his father had said, his eyes questioning.

Henry had met his father's scrutiny. He studied his father's hard features, the silvering hair, the stern countenance. What was it in his father's searching look: Was that man afraid? Of whom? Of what?

"You're too young," his father finally said. "You know the way things are. How you going to pay rent, put food on the table? And you'll have a family to support. Where you going to get a job that will pay you enough to do all that?"

"We'll manage," Henry said. "We love each other."

"Love each other! You can't eat love! Love won't pay the doctor bills!"

"We'll manage," Henry said. "We're getting married."

"The hell you say! You don't have too. You can get things fixed."

"What you mean 'get things fixed'"

"I thought you knew all about those things. You knew enough to get her in trouble!"

"She's not 'in trouble'! We're getting married! Besides, what would happen if Liz got pregnant? The word finally uttered exploded into the room. "Would you want her to do something about 'it'?

"That's different. She would never let that happen. And if it did, I'd throw her out of the house!"

"You really would, wouldn't you! Your own daughter! Well you can throw me out as well!"

"So leave why don't you! But as long as you live in this house, I say what goes!"

"Then I guess I have to leave!"

Henry had fled the house followed by his father's angry cry of prophecy: He would never give his consent, would never sign the papers. Henry would fail.

But Henry and the girl were married anyway. Henry had gone to his mother, and after the woman's initial shock, she readily agreed to sign for Henry to protect the family from disgrace. Yet, the bitterness of his father's curse and his father's refusal to attend the wedding followed him after Henry and the girl moved in with her mother.

Henry reflected on that bitterness. Why had it been so deep, so prolonged, renewed and prolonged by every incident that brought Henry in confrontation with his father? The bitterness had never been resolved, eating at them both, neither relenting, not even when his father suddenly became ill, suffered through a rapid but terrible decline, and finally died. There had been no reconciliation, and now the bitterness lingered like a bad taste of bile or a sour churning gut every time he found himself pondering. How had his life and his marriage been determined by his father's curse?

The bus slowing to a stop woke Henry from his reverie. He stepped back to avoid the collapsing door. He climbed the steps, showed his bus pass, then swayed along the aisle toward the empty seat in back as the bus moved from the stop. Henry saw again the black iron fence, the laurel shrubbery, the bristling chaos of gravestones, all receding now, growing small as the bus crept out into traffic and gained momentum.

Had his whole life been shaped, molded, defined by his father's brooding presence? So Schneider had rebelled. How much was his life affected now? He thought about the dilemma he faced. How had his father anything to do with that?

So he had married young and against his father's admonitions. Now as they moved through the intersection, Henry looked up the cross street toward his aunt's house where they had held the wedding. Now at home on his dresser stood a photograph in which neither he or the girl seemed happy. He looked thin in a borrowed suit too short for his legs, the coat sleeves riding up his thin arms. She looked heavier already filling with the child she carried. His aunt hovered at their backs before her white frame house. Her yappy dog worried their feet.

He had left his father's house living with her mother and her step-father before he could establish them in their own one-room basement dwelling from which they peered at rumbling traffic overhead, their sole entertainment, save for the radio, a hand-me-down wedding gift which played continuously just at the level of hearing. Then he had found the cemetery job that at least had been something, and after that he hadn't had to ask help from anybody.

His mother had visited them from time to time bringing preserves, offering money. At first, Henry had refused, too proud (too "bull-headed" some would charge); then he had relented. He took only the food for his wife because he knew that gift came from his mother. The money, an accusation, an insult, he let lay untouched. The money could have come from his father, or his mother had squirreled it, and she most likely needed it as much as they. His mother retrieving the money left, and Henry, feeling triumphant, had playfully waltzed his awkward pregnant wife making her laugh. Then he had relished the sweet preserves with fresh hard rolls he had gone to buy.

He discovered soon that he had married problems: His wife's family. She, too, had wanted to escape. But they had simply followed bringing with them the realities of the very things she had fled. Her stepfather, an itinerant house painter, was usually more drunk than sober. One brother an habitual thief already jailed, released, confined again, released again now prowled defended by his mother, an indulgent heavy woman who borrowed from her daughter, always insisting that the loan was only temporary, just until her man got work.

Henry laughed now to himself recalling that lurching man swaying up the stairs grizzly from a two-day growth of beard on sharp features smelling of paint and alcohol adding to the mix of turpentine and spirits the reek of large white onions he ate like apples. How long had that man ever worked? How often had he ever found it? And when he did, how much of the pay went for booze? Yet, the girl's mother had always insisted she would pay them back once things were better.

His wife's sister was a tease. Uncontrolled, she roamed, sought excitement, sneaking out at night, answering the low calls of lusty boys beneath her window. Henry thinking of the girl dwelled on the implications of her acts savoring the stir of her suggested sexuality. If only . . . If what? He crushed the thought from his mind. And yet—his wife should be more like her sister! No! What use in wanting something more? He had made his choice. He had a family. Wasn't that what he had wanted? The other girl would never change. She would always roam. He was better off with less excitement. The other would be a one-time deal, little more, if it might happen. He was all right, he decided. Any dissatisfaction was his own damn fault. If he needed work, he should have kept his nose clean, his mouth shut. No one had ever asked him to get involved. The problems he had were his alone of his own making.

Considering his wife's passiveness, he realized she had always been that way. Still, he had been attracted to her. Now she was his wife, but she had brought her family. They weren't his fault or his responsibility. Thank god her family didn't actually live with them. Bad enough they were always there, especially her other brother, the quiet one who looked so much like her. Well, he was gone. Finishing school, never finding steady work, he had been one of the first to enlist when the war in Europe had been dumped on them by the start of war in the Pacific. Yet, Henry sensed that somehow the boy was always there. The letters that she got she always passed to him allowing him to read them. Before that, the brother's constant presence, his quietness, his thin smile, so much like hers, as if he were at the same time resigned while guarding some secret. The brother and his wife spoke German conversing softly with each other excluding him, exceeding his scant knowledge. He had always flared, had always wanted to insist they speak American, that they weren't in Germany anymore, that people would single them out, give them grief because of what the Nazis were doing in Europe. But he had always checked himself.

He had compensated for her passiveness and for her interests that seemed to him to have drawn them apart. He had found distractions by becoming interested in sports. He had played a little basketball in high school. His height had won him attention, and the coach had invited him to try out for the team. Then he had found trouble there, too; practice time had cut into study time and the time he spent working in his aunt's shop. His father had growled about how little money Henry was able to pay for his room and board. So Henry had quit the team to catch up on his schoolwork and graduate; he had started working more hours; he had met the girl. Married, he took up basketball again playing for the church league. That hadn't been any high school game, he decided. If he thought about it, he could say it was almost professional. True, they never got any money for playing. But the idea was the same. They played as if they were really professional, really being paid.

He had enjoyed the evening practice sessions: the clash of voices in the gym, the light upon the polished floor; the clash of bodies and the good feeling that came from his exertion, from the sense of his strength, from the praise for his ability as he time after time sent the ball cleanly through the hoop; the hot showers afterward; the clean feeling of the cold night; the sweet snack and steaming coffee afterward for which he and the others would stop when they would relive the moments they had just shared; the one cigarette he allowed himself while in training, the flavor richer from the sacrifice. His participation had helped him avoid dealing with her family.

Then one day he had returned from practice to find her gone. He had searched for her, cool in his anger, finding her—of all places—at his father's house. His mother had confronted him, her round face accusing him, her eyes angry behind her glittering spectacles, her ponderous breasts heaving beneath the flowered linen dress, her short heavy frame blocking his way to the round oak table at which his wife sat sipping coffee smoking a store-bought cigarette. Henry had sensed his father's presence in the darkness of the front parlor beyond the kitchen light that flowed from linoleum and gleamed from enameled walls then edged the flowered carpeting and the dark sheen of the dining room table.

After negotiations, he and his wife had compromised: He had given up basketball. She had returned to him serving him before she served her brother.

Thinking about his wife's quiet brother and where the young man was with the troops in Europe, now in Germany from where the young man had first come while still a boy, Schneider felt guilty. He tried to be fair. He considered the brother's milk route his only job before he had enlisted. That job hadn't lasted long, but one morning Henry had gone with him, accepting the young man's invitation. Why had he gone? Henry wondered now. Perhaps to respect the brother's attempt at friendship? Yet, how vividly Henry recalled the early morning still dark with stars, the cold metallic smell of the truck wet from ice, the glass bottles in wire and wooden crates, the bottles singing as the truck swayed. Then in the gathering light softening the night becoming dawn dimming the stars save for one bright globe that gleamed in the clear dawn, they had raced across the brick-paved streets between low dark structures crowded with long unloading trucks that dropped behind as they sped along toward the bright soaring towers, the black girders crisscrossing the storage tanks above the curving railroad tracks that cut through asphalt. They had swept along the shining water of the quiet river then raced empty toward the expectation of warm yellow lights, fresh yeasty doughnuts, strong black coffee. And after they had indulged themselves with pungent tubes of rich tobacco that morning Henry had felt strangely fulfilled.

The kid was all right, Schneider decided, better than the other—the thief. The kid was just quiet—that was all, as passive as his wife. Schneider remembered the one time he had questioned the young man.

"How's the milk route going?" Henry had asked.

"It's not." the young man had said, his mouth in that thin strange smile Henry often saw on his wife.

"You'll find something else," Henry had consoled.

"Sure."

But after that the kid hadn't seem to try, at least not like Schneider would. Any time he didn't have a job, he had looked. He had found something. He was always willing to work. He was responsible. He had his pride. He wanted nothing gratis. He would earn his living. He would pay his own way, pay for his wife, for his family, now that it was under way.

Yet, why should the kid's manner bother him? So the kid had always come to sit and to softly talk in German to his sister. And Henry noted again how his wife had prepared things for her brother—sweet breads, *kuchens* that seemed luxuries. But didn't Henry get to share? He, too, enjoyed the aroma as he had entered, sweet spice and strong coffee, then later his cigarette. He had offered one to the kid. Now the kid had grown to manhood and had gone to war. Where was he now, Henry wondered? Berlin probably, returning to the place of his birth.

The brother had married just before he had left for Europe. Schneider recalled how surprised all of them had been. Who would have thought the kid had even been interested?

"I might not make it back," the kid had offered, and they all had sobered.

"You should have let us know about all this!" the young man's mother had wailed.

The kid had only smiled that thin smile. Schneider discovered later that his wife had known everything all along.

Schneider thought now of the brother's wife whom they hadn't known of and whom they hadn't met until that day the kid had gone off to war. Henry saw the woman's dark hair, her pale features, her body.

Where was she? No one saw her much. She kept to herself, it seemed, caring for her child, a girl. Again Henry mused, who would have thought the kid had it in him? He had never even seemed interested in girls. And now he was married and had a child? Now and then Schneider's wife went to visit the young woman, but he had discovered little from those visits, except that her brother's little girl was blonde and healthy.

Thinking about the little girl, Henry sobered now, reflecting on his own daughter, reminded of death. How would he ever be able to live with how she died? Remembering her now renewed the pain. His eyes blurred the high frame houses set against each other behind the trim lawns they now passed, his vision turned inward toward the image and the vivid recollection of her short terrible life and of her dying. How could he ever live with that? He saw her as he knew her, so small, so defenseless, he had been almost afraid to touch her. Henry thought again about the brother's child. Now, again, as he did so often on remembering, he wondered why his child had died while the other had lived.

The bus lurched to a stop waking him. He hurried from his seat, descended through the stairway to the street before the door hissed closed and the bus fouled him as it churned away in a spray of noxious cloud. Then Henry stood exposed. Traffic flowed crossing before him. Stoplights changed from green to yellow to red to green to yellow to red. Noises swirled around him; traffic roared by. The brick buildings of stores rose above him toward the tangled wires beneath the scattering clouds.

4

Felix looked up the street for the trolley car his father sometimes took. One waited at the stoplight on Twenty-seventh, four blocks away. Felix scanned the grated rail guard, the large round spotlight, the square windows bordered by dark varnished wood and the black domed roof diminished now like all the stores he knew from here to there: Tess's Corner Tavern on Twenty-fourth where his Grandpa Schneider used to stop, where sometimes Felix himself had gone carrying a pail to buy his grandpa beer. On Twenty-fifth the National Tea Company with its green front and gold letters across the plate glass windows. His grandmother shopped there frequently, and sometimes he went with her, wandering among the maze of pungent boxes and spicy cans, the bins of fruit and vegetables to the enameled cases of the meat counter. On Twenty-sixth the delicatessen with its high concrete stairs he climbed beside his parents, waiting while they bought boiled ham and potato salad for Sunday supper; the bakery on Twenty-seventh he knew from its good hard rolls, its *kuchens*, as his Grandma Schneider called them, from the warm good smells that filled him each time he entered. Kitty-corner from the bakery beside the waiting trolley car, he saw the spacious grounds of the nunnery, the gray granite blocks of the building, the wrought iron fence that surrounded it. Beyond the nunnery, the bricked street reached asphalt; the trolley tracks curved and disappeared up Thirty-seventh running to where his great aunt lived. He gazed at the distant crest of hill, the blue sky above, the high towering clouds above the hill that curved and dropped toward the suburbs and the new stucco houses, the tan brick apartments, the wide new concrete streets, the wide spaces between the building and the homes, the empty lots with trees and grass, and finally the open fields. He rarely saw these things, so when he ventured there that far, he was filled with wonder. Here, where he spent his timeless days, when he crossed the alleyway, he was a stranger in a strange land.

He heard the trolley car start then gather speed. The engine whine rose; the hemisphere ballooned; the varnished wood, dulled and softened by the haze of sunlight and distance deepened to a shiny burnt orange as the trolley grew, loomed before him rumbling, its bell clanging, until the car slowed, the huge iron wheels screeching to a stop in front of him, making him cover his ears, he shivering from the noise. Then the massive car rumbled away, descending the long gradual incline that went down to the level of the valley now buried beneath asphalt streets whose signs commemorated the names of men. His father had not stepped down from the car.

He rose from the step and started up the block toward Laynie's. His father almost always stopped there after work for a beer, most often not riding the trolley, walking instead from Twenty-seventh, stopping at the drugstore, then coming down the half block past Schmidt's small, box-like green grocery, until he reached Laynie's, two dozen strides from his flat, avoiding Tess's where Felix's grandfather used to stop, even though it was on the way.

Felix reached Laynie's. He peered across the concrete stoop through the open door to the long dark polished wooden bar. He saw the men sitting on the high stools, their feet on the metal rungs, their arms before them on the bar edge, their drinks before them. He studied the sunlight off the rows of bottles behind the bar before the huge mirror, the bottles doubled by their reflection. Above the bottles, the mirrored image of the open door, the shaded sunlight of the street and the trees leafing out in green. Opposite the bar the dark table area, save for the soft glow of colored lights of the jukebox and the sunlight gleaming from the chromed legs of the tables, the light from the doorway shimmering on the sallow face of the thick-legged woman cupping her drink as she stared out the doorway at the passing boy.

Felix reached the green grocery and turned, saw Schmidt, the round-faced, bald man studying the scale, whisking a bag from the tray. The man saw Felix and waved. Felix grinned at being recognized and waved, turned back, passing again the open door of the tavern, peering in again to make sure his father wasn't there among the line of men who sat along the bar. He saw again the dark area and the colored lights. Now he heard the throb of music; he breathed in the warm thick smell of beer, wet wood, billowing tobacco smoke. He went back to the prison of his porch to wait.

He looked down the avenue toward Twenty-second Street to the movie house and the filling station where he had been struck by a car and dragged while trying to run across the avenue in front of traffic. He studied the two storied flat next to the brick wall of the movie house where he had lived while his shattered leg had mended.

Then they had moved here where he now lived, and he wondered why they had moved since he and his brother were always in trouble for the noise they made in their upper flat and the landlord's family living below. Both he and his brother had suffered for that noise, and he recalled the loud discussions rising from below between his father and the landlord that resulted as always with Felix and his brother being punished.

Felix forced himself to recall more pleasant events: Sometimes in the evening when his father worked late shifts, Felix and his older brother went with his mother to the class she took to become a US citizen and thus display her patriotism. The class was held in the same public school his mother had attended and where Felix had more recently entered the world through schooling by way of kindergarten. Mrs. Klein, his mother's teacher, hadn't minded Felix and his brother sitting in her class, and during the holidays, the class celebrated the Christmas season with songs and cookies and punch made with soda. Felix had thought the punch in a large cut glass bowl an unexpected, elegant addition. Several class sessions before the party, Felix and his brother had been set to work making paper chains of appropriate colors to decorate the classroom. So while Felix worked at making paper chains, he had listened to Mrs. Klein lead the class through a quick tour of United States history and a slower necessary guide through the intricacies of US government that Felix, along with most of the class, found perplexing. But listening to her, Felix could tell from her unaccented, correct English that Mrs. Klein was a proper lady with education.

Then one time surprising and exciting him, Mrs. Klein came to his house for dinner. Everyone thought the occasion quite special to have such an elegant lady visit their home, and to celebrate the occasion, Felix had been coaxed to dance as Felix always did whenever he could while his father played his red concertina with ivory button keys. But that time Felix was shy and reluctant at first to be on such display for such a guest of honor until he saw in her delighted expression what he took as approval. Then as always, as he moved through steps he invented in response, the music took over, and he had abandoned himself to the rhythm of the dance. His older brother who as always thought Felix was just showing off stood watching in glum silence.

Felix woke himself from his daydream and rose from the porch steps to look up the avenue searching in anticipation for his father who had not stepped down from the trolley. Where was he? Felix fussed. Would he ever get here? And there were so many things beginning now that the war which had taken away his uncle was coming to an end right at that very moment. Felix stood waiting and watching the growing events.

5

Schneider pushed through the crowds past the slowly flowing traffic, the busy stores: the liquor store crammed with rows of bottles, the cocktail lounge opposite, tiled and modern that he never entered; the bakery, its windows filled with twisted piles of shaped, sugared, jellied sweets; the five and dime, a riot of color. Then he reached the trees, the houses, the intermittent stores along the way.

He found Layne's tavern jammed with people standing two deep along the bar. The tables opposite the bar along the walls were filled. He saw the flushed faces of the people embalmed in smoke. Sullen with disappointment, he turned back down the concrete stairs. He moved toward home.

Felix saw him then. Turning from his study of the crowd that had gathered, he saw the tall man, the long, thin face and dark, wavy hair so unlike his own. He saw the dark full mustache the man would later shave away. Felix rose from the porch stoop and ran to him then turned and hurried by the man's side, taking the lunch pail, wrestling it out of the man's hand, lagging behind to settle it in his grip.

"Guess what I got today!" Felix cried. But Schneider ignored him, his long legs carrying him to the porch. Felix caught up to him at the door as Schneider bent to read the paper at the neighbor's door. He snatched up the paper, scanning it.

"I got a letter from Uncle!" Felix proclaimed.

Schneider dropped the paper and went in through the door with oval glass panel. Felix followed. Schneider climbed the stairs calling out as he ascended. The woman came to meet him stretching up for his expected kiss. Felix lounged in the doorway.

"You heard."

"I've listened all day."

"It's almost over," Henry said.

He went by her to the kitchen.

"It's hard to believe it's true," she said, following.

"It's true all right," Henry said. "Just a matter of time. The generals on both sides are getting together. They're meeting right now. All they have to do is sign. Just a piece of paper. After that—it's finished!"

Henry seated himself at the table beside the large window. She poured him coffee. He blew on it, sipped it, set it to cool. Then he recalled his promise to himself, and he rose, went to the cupboard, then to the fridge. He returned, sat again, helped himself to a spoonful of sugar then added the milk. He noticed her studying the milk can, the spilled grains of sugar on the red check oil cloth. She brushed up the spoils, letting them sprinkle into her cup.

"Go ahead, have some!" Schneider urged. "Take lots!"

She shook her head. He knew she was thinking of the tan ration book with its blue perforated stamps for sugar and flour, the long queues. She had been turned away so often: "There's a war on!" people told her, as if she didn't know. Sometimes even Schmidt who went out of his way to supply the neighborhood with scarce items would wrinkle his bald brow and shrug. "What more can we do?"

The war had been too long. The thrift she had learned while still a child when they had arrived from the old country had been reinforced by the prolonged hardship. She had learned well: the insistent, constant gnawing hunger lingering through the week, sometimes eased by heavy lard spread on coarse bread, the lard gritty with salt and burnt debris saved from every meager dripping until the week's end. Then her stepfather lurched home loaded with brown paper sacks, staggering in the whiskey reek that made her gasp. His clothing spattered with paint, stained with thinner poisoned the air and made her retch. But from the brown sacks came glistening liver, striped bacon to fry it in, new potatoes, rich soft bread, and rare butter. She and her sister and her brothers had lingered around the kitchen waiting, sickened by the pain from the rich aromas of frying food. Then they ate, wolfing their meal while her stepfather sat with heavy lids watching them eat, crunching on a large white onion.

"It's over now!" Schneider insisted, breaking into her reverie.

"Almost," she corrected quietly. She studied the milk and sugar. Guenther will be home," she added softly.

Bitter with remembrance, he turned from her gazing through the window to the blank roof of the house across the way. Above the roof, he saw the steeple of the church soar toward the clearing sky. He thought of how he could see it from the hillcrest that dropped him from open country. He remembered how he could hear the sound of its bell softened by distance carrying to him where he stood gazing at the silhouette against the fading light as he dropped to where the steeple rose above the crowded streets.

He reached to the radio by the window ledge. He toyed with the dial, listening to the sweep of sound, the blare of music, the clash of voices. He paused at a station he knew then adjusted the volume so that the sound dwelled at a murmur. He waited for the news, waiting with the same resignation he had mustered when he had sat here before while he had shook in a jar soft butter from cream skimmed from the top of bottled milk.

So the war was finally over. Once again the realization of its end brought him both joy and worry. Again he was confronted by the question: What would happen to him now? Because of the war, he had finally found a place where he felt settled, where he at last had found some security. Each day working at his bench, the chisel in his hand, he had found in his work a sense of skill, a sense of pride, even while he had also found doubt. For even though he considered his work artful, even though he worked with care and craftsmanship, he had remained dissatisfied. In some ways, the job he had now was better, more rewarding, perhaps, than any he had ever had before. Still, how much had his choice been managed? How much had he been compelled? By what? By whom? His father's prophesy? His own reaction? His youthful rebellion? How much was he a product of his father's house?

He had always wanted to be a maker of fine wood products, and for a long time he had never really thought of anything else. But he hadn't done well in the technical high school that he had been urged by his father to attend so that he would learn a trade, and he readily admitted to anyone his not having done well, even when looking for work. He reasoned, however, that his poor record at school was due to his *always* having worked. By working he escaped that gray haired man who always fought him, but as usual his father had contended with him about his wanting to craft fine wood products or to work in carpentry: "How many jobs were there doing that?" His father had challenged. Henry needed something steady, something more secure.

But Henry had always wanted to work with wood because he liked to see and touch the smooth surface and the dark grain as the wood took shaped beneath his hands. How marvelous to start with a raw rough plank then fashion it into something beautiful, something lasting if it were cared for. Prepared, fashioned, caressed, molded into shape, that raw wood through his skilled efforts might produce a chest of drawers, an elegant table or cabinet made with special designs similar to those he saw in museums, furnishings existing from another age. He always marveled at the workmanship, the design, the sturdy, lasting quality. He imagined the patient work, the fashioning, the finishing, until finally a product just like the museum piece he had witnessed before him. If only he could create something similar, something as glorious.

But he had never come close to achieving what he wanted. He had applied for enrollment in a cabinetmaking class in tech school, but he had been refused. There had been too many students better than he, and the teacher, always had something in for him.

"Schneider," the teacher had said, "You're too darned independent! You're too much of a hothead! I don't want you around! I don't want to have to keep fighting you!"

These words came back at him each time Schneider took their paper salvage to the junk man across from his old school. Felix always went with him. Then they would see the dark heavy brick, the dirty thin crisscrossing wires covering the windows while Henry and the boy had stood upon the spongy dirt-caked boards among the piles of towering refuse watching the junk men thump bundled paper onto the rusty scales.

And one time he and his sons had attended a football game at his old school where he witnessed the purple and white jerseys of the players, the large empty stand gradually filled, the stadium lights on the hard green turf, the dark night beyond the stadium walls, the steaming breath in the chill night, the band music, the shouting crowd, the slap and clash of players during the game, and then afterwards the large expanse of concrete wall, the iron railings, the long row of lighted towering oaks that edged the stadium top, the fading lights as he and his sons receded along the dark side street past rows of cars, hearing behind them the final muffled roar of the crowd. He had gone to that game perhaps to redeem a time when he had dreams and ambitions and possibilities but was unable to indulge himself in such activities. He had only been reminded of his unfulfilled dream, and he had never gone again.

Unable to get into the cabinetmaking class, he had taken patternmaking instead. His father, a patternmaker all his working life, had been pleased, and Henry had, indeed, found some satisfaction. Patternmaking, he had developed the habit of telling himself, involved nearly the same process as cabinetmaking: the design of a gear, a tool, a valve slowly took shape, transforming raw wood into flowing curves; then the pattern was transformed into metal. Here, too, was beauty in the glowing, blistering heat, the sparks, the splattering spill of the molten metal, the sour sweating men in dark goggles and soiled bandannas. Through them his design was made durable.

Yet, in various ways the tech school teacher's words always seemed to come back at him: One time he had argued with the supervisor about a design. Another time, he had revealed himself as a union man. He was labeled as a troublemaker and agitator.

"You're a good man, Schneider, a good worker. But you never know enough to keep your nose clean and your mouth shut!"

Before the war he had wandered from job to job, working for a while as a gardener in a cemetery then as a mover's helper. He had done odd jobs—painting, hauling. When the war broke out, the others went to fight. Married, having children, he remained to finally find a job at patternmaking. He had found it good to work with wood again. And the regular pay, despite the war and rationing, had allowed them to have things they never had.

He crushed the cigarette in the ashtray, souvenir of his trip to the national convention. He shoved back the chair and rose. The woman watched him sensing his mood. She remained silent sitting with lowered lids, thin lips, while he slid past her, past the boy who whirled aside from the doorway as his father fled. Schneider's footsteps echoed in the hallway. His voice echoed back to them. "I'll be at Laynie's!" Then they heard the slowly closing door as the latch caught in the high hollow of the empty hallway.

6

When the boy followed, his mother's warning cautioned him. He lingered on the porch, uncertain of his father's mood. He watched the developing excitement, the growing celebration. The tension after the long years of war, after the mounting suspense with each victory, especially in the final weeks, spilled in relief and spread throughout the city:

He watched a man light fireworks with a cigarette, exploding them beneath the creeping, honking cars, beneath the rumbling iron wheels of the trolley. He watched the startled, laughing people in the cars and in the trolley. He saw the cars back up in an unusual long line at the stoplight crowding the street. Older boys meandered through the waiting traffic then back to the sidewalk on the other side. A soldier followed obviously drunk staggering in the street between the cars, shouting at the drivers who stared at him, shouting at the others in the cars who laughed at him. The soldier wheeled across the street toward two young women who scampered from his reach as he lunged at them. They laughed as they hurried up the sidewalk out of his reach. Then the soldier collapsed against the white brick warehouse. Two men in the storage office came out to look at the soldier slumped against the wall. One of the men shook his head as he returned to the office. The other man tried to help the soldier to his feet, but the soldier waved him off, labored to his feet, then weaved away. The man stood looking after before he went back into the office.

Felix thought again about his father and remembered his mother's warning. He crept through the deepening shadows past the cindered lot between the buildings to the concrete stairway of the tavern.

The crowd had thinned, but men still lined the high stools; women were clustered at the tables opposite. Schneider sat at the bar at the end near the yellow wall near the brown doorway leading to the living quarters at the rear of the building. Schneider sat hunched, his long hands playing with the package of factory-made cigarettes he had bought almost immediately upon ordering the glass of beer, the shot of whiskey. He paid for the drinks with the worn, creased bill garnered until now within his wallet. He used some of the change, walking to the machine, shoving in the coins, waiting until the coins dropped, yanking on the knob that spit the green package with red circle to the tray. He tore away the corner of the package while returning to his stool. The others along the bar eyed him. He forced out the cigarettes by beating the package on his fist. Then he offered one to Laynie who lounged nearby expectant.

"Go 'head!" Schneider insisted. "War's almost over!"

Laynie reached with his thick hairy arm, the others along the bar following his movements. Laynie stood leaning his huge body against the shelves behind the bar that held the rows of colored bottles along the mirror. The two men sucked in enjoying the luxury of rich tobacco, conscious of the soft murmur of the radio beneath the drone of the voices in the bar.

Then Felix crept into the light of the doorway. Laynie waved: Schneider had been generous with his smokes; Laynie no longer worried about the kid coming in alone. Laynie called out, and Henry looked toward the doorway. Felix cowered, but Henry waived to him. Felix climbed the stairs then crept through the dimness imbued with soft color from the jukebox lights and the rows of colored bottles along the mirror behind the bar. He crept through the curling smoke that swirled before him as he passed along the heavy forms hulked on stools at the bar. Henry slipped from his stool signaling the boy to take his place.

Felix climbed, grasping the bar for help. He settled, his legs dangling, his hands holding the rounded edge of the bar, steadying himself upon the high seat. Through his thin pants he felt the warmth his father had left. He looked along the row of men following the staggered line of glasses, the bottles, the elbows, the rigid fingers holding hand rolled cigarettes. He peered along the bar to where the bar curved before the broad window with painted, backward letters. Through the late summer trees beyond the houses across the avenue he saw his Grandma Schneider's house. He saw the distant hordes of flowers blooming in the yard. He saw the woman's heavy movements, small now, as she bent stiff-legged, the printed linen dress draping from her haunches exposing shapeless legs embalmed in coarse tan stockings.

"Soda for the kid!" Schneider ordered. He turned from gazing through the window.

"Sure," Laynie said. He bent his huge body, reached toward the cooler, unlatching it, reaching in, then slamming it, turning back again to pour orange drink over glistening ice in a glass. Felix watched the man's watery, pouched eyes, his heavy sagging face. He studied the gray thinning hair. "Here you are," Laynie said. He took the ten cent piece from the change on the bar grasping the coin between thick thumb and sausage finger. He turned to lay the coin beside the register. Felix sipped delighting in the fruity sweetness of the orange iced drink.

"Well, what you think?' Laynie asked. He leaned on the shelving, his head cocked toward the radio. He watched the street, the shaded sidewalk, the sunlight lancing through the open door. He smoked, holding in his breath, savoring the heady richness.

"Who knows?" Schneider said, reluctant to talk.

"Well, let me tell you, I know one thing. It's been a while since I've had one of these." He straightened, nursed the butt then reluctantly crushed it under foot.

"Have another," Henry said. He tamped out others from the full pack offering Laynie the jutting tube end.

"No! No!" Laynie protested. "You haven't had any more than me! Save them for yourself!"

"Go *'head!*" Schneider ordered. "It's time we started thinking of ourselves for a change. Sometimes I think those military guys had everything."

"I don't know," Laynie said. He hesitated then took the cigarette offered him. He used a matchbook he dug from the wrinkled pocket of his shirt dark with sweat. "They've had a tough fight."

"Laynie's right!" the man on the next stool joined in. Felix turned to look at the man. The other men along the bar banked, facing them. "The war's been no picnic for them!"

"It's been no easier for us!" Schneider insisted. "Sometimes I think it's been harder here. We've had to do without. Everything we gave up they got!"

"Schneider's right!" someone added. "Lots of times that kind of stuff is wasted. They dump it, or else the officers get it, sell it under the table. The dogface men hardly get to see the stuff."

"Yeah," another added from the curved end of the bar. "I've heard of guys getting hold of the stuff—just like you said—sell it on the Black Market—some guys get rich!"

"While we go without!"

"Yeah! Yeah! But that don't mean it happened all the time. Our boys still had a tough row. Those Germans were mean ones. They almost had us on the ropes!"

"Right! Just look at what our guys have gone through. Let me tell *you*, they gave up plenty—five, six years, some of them. What most of us her give up? We stayed home, working overtime because the other guys were gone, because there's not enough men here. We got jobs because other guys gave up the good part of their lives, got killed even, while we make coins we sometimes can't even use. How you like to give up that, fella?"

"It's over now! I've done my share!"

"Me, too! I got a brother in!"

"No! No! I mean what we done by ourselves. What we done without. Most of us have someone in. Some of us have lost guys."

"I couldn't go myself. I've been glad enough to do without."

"Right. So what if some guy takes advantage? That's war! He's just smart! He's just watching out for number one, same as us!"

"And most of the guys still had a hell of a time slogging it. We all gave something, but I'm glad I stayed here!"

"Well," Laynie said. "It's sure going to be nice to get some better booze than what I've had to dish out."

Schneider nodded, sipping at his glass. "That's what I mean. Why should they get anything better? I haven't been able to buy anything but weak beer, while those guys use our stuff to hustle: first Frenchies, now Freuleins!"

"You'd do the same, fella!"

"If he had the chance!"

"Who'd want him?"

"Not even his wife!"

"I believe it!"

"Yeah!"

Stung by their remarks, Schneider smoldered, sucking at his beer that foamed his mustache.

"Yeah!" a new voice hawked.

Heads along the bar spun toward the door. There in the darkness against the streaming sunlight, the drunken soldier swayed through the doorway, then lurched toward the bar. Now Felix saw the loose black tie, the matted hair, the raw red-streaked eyes. "Yeah!" he parroted. Then he stopped, teetering while his eyes swept the bar. Someone stepped from his stool, making room; another did the same.

"Here's a 'Joe' now!" someone called. "Come one in, guy!"

The soldier studied them, his mouth slack, his face limp. Then he understood. He grinned, straightened, swaying back, then stumbled forward to the bar grasping the rounded edge to hold himself.

"Sit!" he ordered. "I'm all right! I'll stand." He leaned between the men at the bar, looking up at Laynie who watched him. "Set 'em up!" the soldier shouted. "Let's all have one! Let's all drink to the good old U.S. of A!" He stumbled, grabbing at the barstool. Then jolting onto the seat, he slapped the bar. "Set 'em up!" he shouted again.

Laynie strolled down behind the bar. "Whoa, fella!" Laynie said trying to laugh. The other men, his friends, watched him. "Looks like you've had plenty of celebrating."

"Not enough!" the soldier cried. "Not nearly enough. Got to salute all those poor dumb Dogfeet."

"They've certainly done it, though," someone agreed.

The other men nodded.

"You bet," the soldier insisted. "Ain't nobody going to stop me from saluting them!" He bent over the bar eyeing Laynie. He swayed trying to focus on the worried face of the man who studied him. "*You* trying to stop me, fella?"

Laynie stood mute studying the man. The others shifted uneasily on their seats. The soldier stood back, twisting unsteadily, reconnoitering the bar and the dark table area opposite. "Got to drink to them," he mumbled. "Cause *we* showed 'em!" he muttered. His eyes swept the men, the windows, the ceiling, the bottles, then he gazed down along the bar to where small Felix sat in the dim light away from the door and the cool shadows of the street. The soldier shouted at the boy. "I guess we've shown those Krauts! Hey, kid?"

Schneider bolted the remainder of his beer and turned. "Let's go, Felix!"

Felix suddenly remembered his half-finished drink. He saw it there before him on the bar wasted now by his distraction. He mourned the loss as he slipped from the barstool, his feet loud against the floor from the drop. He trailed his father toward the door.

"Hey!" the soldier challenged. He swayed away from the bar.

Schneider stopped. He searched the soldier's square features, the flushed face, the set muscles of the jaw, the taut muscles of the arm where the soldier had rolled the tan starched shirt cuff.

"Where you goin'?" the soldier growled. "I'm buyin' you a drink!" Nearly as tall as Schneider, he stood teetering, blocking the way. "Here's the money," he added. He bent, fumbling for the tan pocket. "Let's have one!" he offered. "The kid too!" He bent toward the boy. Felix saw the bristles on the sharp chin, the ruined eyes. "How about some chips?" he breathed making Felix draw back. Then the man rocked upright swiveling from the waist toward Laynie. "Hey! Give the kid some chips!"

"Stuff your chips!" Schneider growled. "He don't want none!"

"Come on, Schneider!" someone complained. "The guy's only trying to be nice! He's celebrating for Chris' sake!"

"Schneider!" the soldier shouted. His face twisted slowly into an expression of disgust. "S'matter! You another Kraut?"

"Up yours!" Schneider said, brushing past the teetering man. "Felix! Come!" he ordered.

"Hold on, Kraut! the soldier hollered. He grabbed at Schneider. "What outfit you been in? Where you fight?"

Schneider stopped, studying the man, seething.

"A Kraut!" the soldier hissed finally. He poked at Schneider's chest. "Where's you swastika! Where's your goddam' iron cross!"

Schneider brushed away the accusing finger, the taut accusing hand. Then one of the others came off the stool taking the soldier by the arm.

"Easy, fella," the man coaxed.

The soldier shrugged him off.

"He's got kids," someone offered. "They wouldn't take him."

"Shut up!" Schneider bellowed. "I've fought! Right here, I've fought! He searched the faces watching him.

The soldier laughed in Schneider's face. "A god-damn 4-F!" he sneered.

Schneider swung catching the man off-guard, catching them all by surprise. Felix heard the squash of bone on flesh, the sharp cries of the other men as the soldier stumbled from the bar. One lunged to catch the soldier flailing back toward the broad window with the painted letters. A stool clattered to the floor. A glass fell and shattered. Laynie hit the radio, twisting at the volume knob.

A blast of noise—horns, whistles, sirens, the shrill hysteria of screaming crowds. "WAR'S OVER! WAR'S OVER!" Someone screamed. A boy with newspapers bolted in shouting headlines as he came, "OVER! IT'S OVER! GERMANS KNOCKED OVER!"

Schneider shot past him through the yawning door, dropping to the concrete walk. Felix slowly followed filled with awe as he moved through the cooling day, the sun lower, the shadows lengthening. He followed filled with excitement from the bar, shaken by the swell of sound, the spilling tension as they plowed their way, his father storming ahead past stalled vehicles that crept through unaccustomed crowds wandering in the roadway where people were laughing, shrieking, staggering beneath a load of troubled joy.

7

Felix found his father recovering on the porch. The man stood before the door leading to their upper flat his head against the oval glass his back to the noise and loud confusion of the street. Felix lingered on the walk before the stairs. Then Henry turned. He grasped the porch pillar supporting the roof. He leaned and watched the celebration. Then he sat, his arms draped across his high knees, and Felix crept beside him. The man and the boy sat and watched the boys with fireworks. They watched the traffic, the people in the cars, the crowds that ambled past exclaiming about the war's end.

The cacophony increased as Henry and Felix watched: exploding fireworks, shouts, blatant car horns all joined until the sound became a fracturing of noise, a jar, a blend and splay of sharp reports raised against the open sky. To this a bass brought variation: above the din coming to them from the river and docks, the deep bellow of a ship answered then in turn by screeching tugs. A third voice introduced a factory whistle, this one close by from the valley beyond the full trees of the park four blocks away. Another whistle joined the first, smaller from distance.

Henry cocked his head searching the deepening sky. That distant piping seemed familiar. Yes, he was certain now. Who in the factory where he worked had courage enough to blow that whistle? A man next door came out and blew a new year's horn then went back in again without comment. Henry's eyes focused dropping from the clouds to the high cross upon the steeple of the church.

Henry moved, straightening his legs across the stoop to the walk. He shoved away rising toward the celebration, turning from the tavern sign, moving now past the neighboring house, past the appliance store on the corner, across the tree-lined side street and over the wide concrete walk before the sweep of stairs that rose to meet the massive wooden doors, the towering brick of the church, the soaring steeple reaching toward the deep sky, bluer now with scattered clouds touched with light above the high aspiring cross.

Henry turned up the stairway climbing the low stairs by twos, by threes, reaching the door, the huge brass handles, tugging on them, the door unyielding, then turning away to survey the street below. He quickly descended going around the side beneath the line of stained glass windows of biblical scenes. He found the small door at the rear, tried the knob, then beat upon the ribbed paneling of the door. He listened, studying the boy who waited with him looking up at him in wonder. He beat again. Then they heard footsteps, the unlatching lock, the quick crack of the door and then the sallow face beneath the gray tweed cap.

"Yaah?" Emil asked.

"It's over!" Schneider said.

"Yaah?"

"The war! It's over! Hear that!" Henry swept his arm toward the quiet empty side street beneath trees with young new leaves. The noise and commotion of the thoroughfare seemed distant.

"So?"

"The war's over." Schneider said. "People are celebrating. They're making all that noise. We should ring the bell."

Emil seemed startled. "The bell?"

"Sure. We should ring it. You can hear it for miles."

Emil shook his head.

"Come on!" Schneider demanded before Emil could speak. "We've got to hurry! We can be the first one!"

Emil stared at him as if Henry were insane. "The first one?"

Schneider moved toward the crack of the opened door that Emil filled.

"Just let me in. I'll ring it!"

"You can't do that," Emil said. He held the door closed blocking Schneider's way.

"Why not, for Chris' sake!"

"Don't take the name in vain," Emil admonished. "You not ring bell because not now is service. The bell, she's rung at service. I know. I ring two, three times a day. At German service, at funerals, for a wedding maybe once or twice."

"But this is special, for Chris' .... The war's over!"

"What does Pastor Carson say?" Emil asked.

"What's he got to do with it?"

"He should say," Emil said.

"Oh, for crying out loud!" Schneider moaned. He dropped his head shaking it then looked up again at Emil in the crack of the door. "O.K. I'll talk to Carson."

"Yaah. You do dat."

Schneider faced the paneling of the latching door. Then he spun. He hurried back along the arching windows, the noise growing as they reached the avenue. He cut beneath the towering church front, past the stairs, past the peppered graveled schoolyard screened by wrought iron fence spiked like the steeple, past the yellow slatted school high and barn-like nestling yet dwarfed by the massive church. Felix hurried to keep up, his bad leg aching.

They reached the rectory. Schneider bolted up onto the concrete porch. He jabbed the button. The lace curtain hung quiet on the beveled glass door. He jabbed the button again, holding it this time, hearing the faint bell within. Then a dark shape loomed behind the curtain; the lace was held aside; the door opened and the short thick man revealed himself in white shirtsleeves and tie and gray suit pants, a finger in the leather bound book to mark his place. His dark eyes searched knowing them but questioning behind wire-rimmed glasses. His forehead furrowed beneath the black straight hair smoothed back upon his head.

Schneider answered the man's eyes then told the pastor what he wanted. The man studied the concrete of the porch. He shook his head when Schneider finished.

"Come on!" Schneider insisted impatiently. "We've got to! That bell can be heard for miles. We should ring it!" He thought again of how the sound of the bell had reached him as he had seen the distant tower soaring dark against the deepening sky.

Then as the three of them, the two men, the one tall and slender, the other short and thick, and the small boy beside them stood there on the porch, they heard from far away a tolling bell, somehow still and strange, as the pure sound rose above the streets and canyons, above the screech and pipe and tweedle of whistles, the blasts from ships raised toward the sky. On the streets below, the crowds stopped to listen while the bell pealed a still, pure sound.

A trolley rumbled to the corner stop and stayed. People leaned out to listen to the bell then returned to shouting. A soldier in the trolley was shoved out from the crowd hanging in the open door. A young woman clung to him; then others in the street grabbed him and held him high passing him back then shoving him again into the trolley. Now more whistles joined the others while the distant bell went on tolling. People walking in the street were laughing, shouting, walking behind the trolley that crept away from the stop carrying the soldier who now rode up front beside the driver.

"You see?" Schneider said. "You hear that? The bell?

But the pastor was adamant. "No," he said, shaking his head. "It wouldn't be proper. It would be out of place."

"The war's over!" Schneider shouted above the honking, the whistles, the deep boom of harbor ships. "Just listen to that! Look at that!" He swept his arm toward the people in the streets, toward the people in the cars and in the trolley waving to the two men and the boy on the porch. "We should be part of that!"

"Let others act according to their conscience," the pastor said. "We act according to what's proper and due respect."

"But we've got the tallest steeple, the largest, clearest bell! Let's use it for Chris' sake—to *show* respect—for those who fought and won that we might worship, for those who fought and died that we might live!"

The pastor searched Henry's face with his fierce eyes, then turned to search beyond the brick columns of the porch to the street, to the people, to the world gone mad with joy and relief. "O.K.," he said finally. "Wait here. I'll be right back." Then he went in through the beveled glass door leaving Henry and the boy on the porch gazing out at the moving celebration.

The pastor returned still in his shirtsleeves but without the book. He held a key before him as he descended the concrete porch steps, and Henry and the boy followed him as they returned to the small door at the rear of the church. The pastor hurried in opening the door, and they went down into the dark basement Felix knew so well from the bright Bible pictures at Sunday School, from the gaudy costumes, the glaring lights and dim yellow faces of the audience during school plays, from the wondrous jumble of games and booths and long tables piled with food for the church bazaar.

Now they hurried past the dim pillars, the upturned chairs piled in darkness. Now they reached a stairwell mounting behind the altar. Felix amazed paused to inspect this unsuspected place then hurried after the men through the hushed church, up the wide carpeted center aisle between the long wooden seats beneath the high ribbed vaults, then underneath the undulant sweep of the balcony.

They found Emil at the front of the church vacuuming the carpeting beneath the balcony. He turned surprised when they approached. He shut down the vacuum, nodded to the pastor lifting his tweed cap revealing his smooth bald head.

"I'm sorry they bother you," Emil said. "He want to ring the bell." He scowled at Henry then looked back to the shorter man. "I told him no. But he say he want to ring the bell. That we should ring the bell. I send him to you." He glared defensively at Schneider.

"You did right, Emil," the pastor soothed.

Felix listened to the hushed echo of the voices off the soaring vault
of the nave. He heard the muffled cries of the crowd beyond the huge
heavy doors that they stood before. He wanted to yell to hear his voice
echo in the hollow. Instead, he followed as the men climbed the stairs to
the balcony where he always sat because it was so high and because it was
where he sang in the choir. He followed up the stairs past the tall pipes of
the organ against the wall of the balcony then up into the steeple where
he had never been. The plastered walls gave way to wood then turned
to naked brick; the varnished stairs gave way to steel treadles suspended
from the brick, open stairs through which he could see down—straight
down—into the dark pit from which they had climbed, ascending until
the walls spun as he followed the men up the twisting open stairs.

They climbed through a small door into a hollow room. A thick
rope hung dead within the center of the room. The room had no ceiling,
disappearing through grating lost in the early darkness of the steeple
closer to the night. Above the grating, as they strained back to peer
hanging back their heads, they could just make out the huge shape of the
great bell.

Emil looked at the men questioning with his eyes. Felix thought that
Emil having the same name as his grandfather who was dead seemed
odd. Then Felix saw him there, tall and thin and old, with a thin pointed
sunken face hairless and sagging. He saw Emil who came each day for
every service passing Felix sometimes in the cold clear mornings to climb
those stairs they had just climbed to pull and hang upon the rope and
send the peal across the city dispersing the pure vibrant toll that rose in
strokes toward heaven.

"You want I ring?" he asked. He looked from one man to the other.

"No," Schneider said. "Let me." He took the rope in his hand. "Show
me how."

"Yaah," Emil said. "You do like this." He placed his hands, curling
them, grabbing the air. He pulled down. "Then you let go." They
followed as his head went back, his hands uncurled. "You don't let go,
she drag you up. She burn your hands." He stepped back straightening.
"Remember," he warned again.

"Sure, sure," Henry said, impatient to begin. He heard the street
noise below ascending. He heard the lone distant bell. At least they were
still second. Then he grabbed the thick rope reaching high. He pulled,

startled at the weight, surprised by the resistance, by the heavy woven strands of the rope, by the shock of his own weight upon the rope end.

"Too high!" Emil warned. "So high, you waste!"

Annoyed, Schneider twisted toward the man then grabbed the rope again pulling at it. This time the bell, reluctant still, sluggish, cold, ponderous, clanged. The sound was feeble. Yet the sound quivered through the hollow of the room stirring the boy who grew afraid.

"No!" Emil called. "You must do like this!" Then before Henry could prevent him, Emil stepped to the rope, grabbed and pulled, stepping back to let the rope slither up. This time the bell gathering pitch and melody boomed and echoed in the concrete hollow. Schneider fumed with failure.

"Here! Take these!" Emil shouted above the sound of the bell. From a shelf, he snatched heavy leather gloves offering them to the man. But Schneider refused. He shook his head and grabbed for the rope.

"You better!" Emil yelled. "Your hands! You burn! I know!" He held out his thin, callused hands for them to see.

Henry pulled the rope then quickly took a glove and pulled again and slipped on the second glove and pulled, released, then pulled again. Now the bell, roused from its cold heavy stillness swung and pitched and thundered sound against the brick, the steel, the pliant quivering flesh, stirring it, stirring all—steel—brick—flesh—filling them with sound.

"I'm going!" the pastor yelled. "Emil can lock up when you're through!"

Both men twisted toward him nodding then straightened toward the rope. Felix watched the pastor disappear through the darkness of the low doorway leading to the steeple well. Then he turned to watch as his father gathered all his bitter strength against the slithering dancing rope.

Schneider rang the bell until the sweat stood out on his forehead. Schneider rang the bell until the sweat ran down stinging his eyes. Schneider range the bell until a wet circle of sweat spread out upon his back and underneath his arms.

Watching the tall slender man, seeing him tire, Emil came to stand beside the rope. But Schneider shook him off. Emil stood back and waited. Then Henry realized his waning strength. He stepped back, and Emil took the rope.

Emil gathered to the task knowing it, knowing the bell, knowing each tone, each voice. Each time he pulled, the sound changed qualities, changed pitch, changed voice, until the changes seemed like melody. Yet the sound maintained through each swing, through its return gathered, while Emil range the bell, his thin body moving with the sound, bending and straightening with the movement of the rope.

Felix watched. Henry watched. Both marveled at the strength despite the thinness of the man. Schneider was envious, but he thrilled to see the man work the rope as he, himself, leaning against the quivering brick wall breathing hard wiped the sweat from his face.

Emil rang the bell until the sweet sound rang out across the city from the high tower. Emil rang the bell until the people shouting and laughing down in the streets became aware of the bell. They stopped, leaned back, gazed up toward the high steeple that soared above them from the street. Emil rang the bell until the sweet sound reached to the white distant towers, to the red distant steeples shocking them into life until slowly, eventually they, too, pealed out their mellow individual answers to the insistent vibrant purity of the bell that Emil rang.

When Emil motioned to him, Schneider came and took the rope and pulled, and the bell reached down to fill the hollow of the room where the boy stood against the quivering wall, reached down to fill the boy with fear, reached down to fill the boy with joy and wonder for the sound of the bell as he watched his father pulling on the rope.

Henry tired. His tall body sagged; his breathing came hard and fast and deep. He motioned for Emil, but Emil heaved, wrung wet from his turn at the rope.

"We've got to keep it going!" Schneider hissed.

Emil winced, unable to speak, shaking his head. Henry pulled on the rope a final time before he let it go. They watched the rope dance in the air as it rose with the swinging bell. Then as the bell began to die, as the rope descended, they heard again the change, remembering the sound they had brought to the bell. The two men turned to the boy, their eyes holding what they could not speak. Felix suddenly felt afraid. He didn't want the rope. The rope was thick with coarse heavy strands. The rope was welded to the sound that shook him. But the men looked at him telling him again with their eyes about the bell and about how they were tired.

Felix stepped to the center of the room. He watched the rope snake and dance. Then he reached high on the rope and pulled. The rope came toward him fast, faster than he had thought it would, startling him. Then the rope rose again so suddenly that he forgot what Emil had said about releasing it. The rope carried him, lifting him until he dangled above the floor. Then his own weight pulled on him and he slipped, his hands burning as he slid down along the rope dropping to the floor. The rope descended then slithered as it rose again. Felix curled his hands against his pain, crying out, his cry drowned by the thunder of the bell. He saw his father watching him, and Felix reached again for the rope. Felix pulled with his whole strength, pulled against his smarting hands that stung and burned from the rope. The rope came back at him fast, but this time he released it in time, and then as the rope rose, he heard the sound above him; he felt the sound along the rope as he reached and pulled and reached and pulled again, until Emil came, rested now, and took the rope.

Felix stood against the wall curling his hands blowing on them as he watched the man and the rope and heard the bell that filled the room, the bell that rang within him, filling him, ringing out alone above the city, above the distant towers and steeples silent now, the whistles from the factories, the deep bellows from the ships all quieting one by one as the people in the streets disappeared one by one, going home to prepare for the night.

Emil sensed the quiet. He released the rope, stepped back, stood heaving, motioning for Schneider to rest. The rope wriggled and snaked and leaped as it rose, came down, then rose again. The three of them turned then left inching down the dark tower filled with the dying bell, going down to the dark hushed hollow of the church.

Emil let them out the heavy front doors. They went down the wide steps to the sidewalk where they stopped hanging their heads back to look up at the steeple, the bell still ringing in their heads as they turned and saw the yellow street lamps, the flashing colored sign of the movie house down the street. Someone waited in the quiet at the trolley stop on the opposite corner. Cars moved by unhindered now.

The men shook hands. "You did good," Emil acknowledged, but Schneider only nodded, turning now to cross the side street past the dark appliance store past the neighboring house to the gray warped porch.

8

His father sent him up alone, but before he went through the door with the oval glass pane, Felix lingered watching as his father moved up the street, his shoulders slightly stooped, his gait slightly listing as his father made his way past the cindered lot then up the concrete stoop beneath the sign of Laynie's bar.

When Henry returned, he found the boy still on the porch. He ushered the boy up before him, the boy surprised that he had not been admonished for lingering on the porch and the night now full upon them. Henry took the boy up to their flat and washed the boy's hands. Felix whimpered. Henry spread ointment on the burns. Then they ate alone, the woman sitting across from them silent, the older boy lounging in the doorway sweeping from the man to the boy with questioning eyes, amazed and strangely still.

"We rang the bell," Henry said. Neither the woman nor the older boy dared ask more.

When the two finished eating, the woman cleared the table, the boys were sent to bed, and Henry went to sponge himself and change clothes. Then he was ready in loose shirt and slacks. He went to the boys' bedroom. He stood in the doorway, a huge dark shape against the kitchen light. He told them where he and their mother would be, that they need not worry, that they were old enough now to mind themselves, and that he and their mother would be back soon. Then Henry stooped to peer through the blue dimness beneath the upper bunk where the older boy lay. Felix saw the face in shadow above him.

"You O.K.?" Henry asked.

"I'm O.K."

"Good boy," Henry said.

Felix again saw his father's huge image in the light of the doorway. Then he heard them leave. He heard the heavy door closing and latching itself. He lay in the answering silence, in the dark haze beneath the bulge of the upper bunk listening to the quiet until the noise of jubilation stilled by the sunset rose again among the gaudy lights. He lay in the darkened room ignoring the whispered questions of the other boy who finally cried, the whimpering changing to a deep easy breathing as the other boy finally slept while Felix listened to the last long rumble of the trolley slowing, screeching to a halt, then rumbling on.

The night remained. And as the sounds of jubilation dwelled, dwindling again, Felix heard the distant music of the concertina marble red with ivory button keys, his father's only legacy, rise with the mellowed voices raised in peaceful song from Laynie's bar to where he lay within the shadows of the room above the dark subsiding streets. He curled his hands turning on his side to face the wall for which he had once been punished; then he sunk toward stirring dreams and a final quiet sleep before the dawn.

The Middle of the String-2

[January, nine years later]

Henry Schneider was asleep when the phone call intruded his erotic dream bringing him fully awake. Two o'clock in the morning, he knew the nature of the call, who the caller, and the reason for the call at two o'clock. Henry threw back the covers and rose naked in the chill of the house, the heat from the oil furnace set low to ward off the cold of the season. He went to the wall phone in the kitchen and uncradled the receiver.

"Yeah?"

"Schneider?"

"Who else?"

"We've got problems."

"Who doesn't?" Henry asked. "And nobody else can handle them?"

"Well, yeah. We're working on them, but we will need someone to authorize and check what we've done and sign for the work."

"And I'm the only one that can authorize, check, and sign, right?"

"Well, yeah. You're the boss."

"Don't I know it," Henry said. "O.K.," Henry sighed. "Give me half an hour to dress and drive in."

"Sure," the caller said.

"And keep working."

"Sure, we'll do that."

"Good." Then he recradled the receiver and returned to the bedroom. His wife was awake in the dark. He began to dress.

"Again?" she asked.

"What else?"

"Three times this month."

"Yeah."

"Won't it ever end?"

"Probably not. Try to sleep."

"Maybe. But I worry about you. You work too hard. And it's so early and so dark and you have to drive all that way."

"It's not that far."

"But then you'll have to work your day shift too."

"As always."

He finished dressing, went to the bed, leaned to kiss his wife, then turned to go. "Try to sleep," he said again and left the bedroom making his way to the door of the enclosed windowed porch leading to the gravel driveway and his cold car that was at least new, one small benefit of what he often referred to as his lofty position. He climbed in, started the car, and let it idle with the heater turned to high. Then he climbed back out and used the handy scraper to clear the windows of frost, climbed back in, put the car in reverse and backed out of the pea gravel driveway lined with young cedar. Then he put the car in drive and headed through the short warren of streets to the straight road that led him to the state highway that would take him down into the city and the factory where he worked.

The routine drive to the factory was uneventful, but all the familiar places and scenes Henry passed appeared more vivid and strange because of the dark and the stillness of the scene since most everything, including taverns were closed. He passed beneath the circles of streetlamps on the asphalt pavement as he followed the guidelines in the center and along side the roadway that was heaped with dirty snow. He stopped at all the expected signals along the way and waited for the green light. Not another vehicle in sight, he wondered why he had to sit and wait for the signal to change, but he waited; then he went on when the light went from bright red to bright green. He again entered darkness after the brief oasis of light, now passing the dark houses with dark fences, dark trees, dark lawns despite the frozen snow covering them. But eventually, as he knew he would, he reached more lights and sparse traffic once he reached the edge of the city.

Then he came upon the bridge paved with red brick left over from a former era and then the entrance to the factory and the cindered lot with the parked cars of the nightshift. He pulled into the spot reserved for him against the towering brick building it, too, dating from the previous century. Before he turned off his headlights he noted again the sign on the factory wall that designated the spot with the title of his position. Who would have thought? Henry wondered as he heaved himself from the car and locked the door. After all he had endured was this privileged spot one of the few returns he had gained in exchange for what he had invested?

As he walked across the cinders of the lot shivering from the cold, he glanced up at the light in the row of windows at the top of the building. He heard the all-too-familiar clash and hiss of the foundry. He entered the building passing the overhead crane that lifted scrap metal to dump them in cars that would take the scrap metal into the foundry to be melted and cast into bathroom fixtures. The crane cab was dark, and the crane suspended on a huge rusted rail hung silent. Inside, the heat from the foundry and from the ovens that baked the powder on the castings into enamel was a welcome relief after the frigid early morning air.

What was he doing here this early in the day when at one time he would have been sleeping in the warm comfort of his bed beside his wife? So much more than the trip he had just made into this place that sometimes felt like Hell itself, had his journey been worth the challenges he had faced and what now appeared to be the sacrifices he had endured? He shrugged off such morose thoughts as he meandered his way through the various departments that he knew all too well from his years of servicing them while working as foreman of maintenance: the foundry that appeared not fully functioning, most likely the source of the problem that had led to the earlier call as it was most frequently. Then he passed through Enameling and the raw castings waiting to be finished and those already coated with enamel powder ready to be baked; then he reached the patternmaking department where he had worked for a decade at a task that he had enjoyed to some degree because he had worked with wood to produce the patterns that would be cast in steel and then used to produce the fixtures he had seen standing on end as he had gone through Enameling.

His mind, always busy, again brooded on his acceptance that he had never advanced any further despite the promises that he had been given when he was first offered the position he now held. Again he dispelled the thoughts. Too early in the day to begin such second-guessing when before him he had the task for which he had been summoned as well as his full shift of hours after he had resolved the current problems.

He reached the locker room. Opening his locker, he set his lunch pail inside, took out the coveralls, and pulled them on over his clothing. He would need the extra layer despite the heat from both the foundry and Enameling while he made his way through the open spaces between departments, the cold in his passing seemingly more so because of the changes in temperature. Then he turned to his work heading back to the foundry to find the man who had called and to learn of the problem that appeared so urgent it had brought Henry from his warm bed and sleeping wife. Where would it end?

2

During his regular shift after he had resolved the problems for which he had been summoned, Henry received a summons from the supervisor by way of messenger requesting that Henry come see him at his earliest convenience. That the word "request" was used made Henry wonder what was this about with such formal sounding wording. Henry went to see the supervisor when he had a break and when his crew was eating lunch. He usually ate when he could, and then he would often wolf his food.

He climbed the steel stairs to the glassed-in office that overlooked the pattern shop where he had spent so many years turning raw wood into finely crafted patterns that he was always proud to display, the closest he had come to fulfilling his dream of becoming a craftsman of fine furnishings: cabinets, tables, chairs, chests. And he had fashioned some of these for his home as gifts to his wife, one a large chest of cedar wood with brass fittings he had fashioned with care. The chest was always proudly displayed in a prominent place wherever he lived and often used as a seat for his sons when he entertained visitors.

He reached the office, the same one to which he had climbed years ago with others who now worked under his direction as foreman when he had organized the workers to form a union and to petition management to recognize their affiliation with a national organization. The same supervisor who had been there when Henry had placed the petition on the superintendent's desk was there now when Henry entered. That same supervisor had also made him the offer that he at first had found difficult to accept and then he eventually had found difficult to refuse—his current position as foreman.

"Well, here's Henry now," the supervisor said. He rose to come to Henry and offered his handshake. Henry took the man's greeting then inspected the man attired in suit and tie and polished shoes while Henry stood at the door in his coveralls and hard toed boots scuffed and worn from use. "Come in! Come in!" The supervisor ordered. "Have a seat!"

But Henry told the man that he preferred to stand.

"Sure. Suit yourself," the man conceded.

"You wanted to see me?"

"Well, Henry, it's about where we all might be going."

We? Henry thought. He was always curious when someone included him when no one had asked him and no one else was around. He waited.

"Well, you certainly have heard the talk about where we might be going."

There was that "we" again.

"You know. The company?"

"Sure. I've heard that we've been having problems."

"Yes. Well, that's why we wanted to have a talk with you."

"Well," Henry said. "What do I have to do with company problems?"

"You're one of us, now, Henry. How long you been with us now?"

"Eighteen years, going on nineteen, first in patternmaking, now as foreman of maintenance. Why? You probably already know all that."

"True, Henry. Just checking. Well, Henry, as foreman now you're part of management. You make decisions every day that directly influence the health of the company."

"But now the company's sick. So I just do my job trying to keep this old pile of bricks running. The problems I hear about seem to be about money."

"Right, Henry.

"Well, I've never been that good dealing with problems about money. Otherwise I'd be better off than I am. So what am I supposed to be doing to help the company with its money problems?

"You're one of us now, Henry. Most likely you've heard talk of our merging with another company, a larger one that's been very successful."

"So I've heard. How likely is that merger? What happens then?"

"Well, what it would mean is that we would most likely reduce our work force here and focus on turning out just a few of the products we now handle—smaller ones that are less costly to make and would sell more. The larger items that we now make would be taken over by the larger company that has several different locations where each place has a few selected items to manufacture."

"O.K. I understand that. What does all that business about merger have to do with me?"

The man pushed back in his chair, rose, and went to stand at the window overlooking the storage lot for empty surplus garbage wagons that had once been pulled by teams of horses through the brick paved alleyways of the city. He turned to study Henry.

"Henry, I know you're someone who always wants to come directly to the point."

That might help, Henry thought.

"Our merger means that reduction in force would include some positions in mid-management."

"You mean like foreman."

"Yes."

"Which most likely means my job."

"Yes."

"But what about what you said when you first offered me the job almost nine years ago. You told me that if I—as you put it—'gave up the union crap' and took the offer of becoming foreman of maintenance that I'd be better off, that I'd have a secure job."

"I never said that, Henry. If you recall, that was the superintendent. Well, Henry, times change."

"Don't I know it," Henry conceded. "So what's the deal? Why talk to me when I don't have any real say in what happens?"

"But you do, Henry. That's why we wanted to talk to you. We want to recognize and honor your loyalty and dedication by trying to help you keep your position."

"How? What do I have to do with it? You make the decisions."

"Well, Henry, we have another offer."

"Another offer."

"Yes. Well, with the likelihood of merger and the certainty of reduction in force, we might be able to salvage some positions through relocation."

"You mean moving."

"Yes."

"And you would want me to relocate."

"Yes."

"Boy! I had better think on that for a while. I'd have to talk to my wife. Moving? That'd be a big change."

"Sure it would, Henry. But you'd have the chance to advance."

"How so?"

"Supervisor."

"Really! That's what you promised the last time when you offered me the foreman job. 'Give up the union crap,' you said—O.K.—the superintendent said. Start with the foreman job then move up to supervisor. I'm still foreman; you're still supervisor. Not too much has changed. How likely is it I'd get to be supervisor?"

"Very likely. We've already talked to the management of what will become the parent company. They're looking for qualified people to fill positions they've had trouble filling. Of course, we told them about you and your qualifications and your dedication and leadership abilities. We even told them about your former union activities that you readily gave up to accept a management position. They were interested. They've agreed to consider you for a supervisory position in one of their locations, one where you'd know the operations because they're similar to ones we have here."

"But they're only considering."

"Of course. And of course they would want to meet you and discuss your resume and your career goals.

Career goals? Henry thought.

"But with our encouragement," the supervisor continued. "They'll most certainly concede to our requests."

"Requests. So what happens if I don't agree? Seems to me that all that you've said is iffy."

"To put it bluntly, Henry. You don't relocate, you very likely will be part of a reduction in force."

"I'd be laid off."

"Right."

Henry stood mute. He surveyed the face of the man who silently returned his inspection.

"Well, Henry. You most likely want to have a bite to eat and you'll want to think things over before you decide. Why don't you talk to your wife? Let us know as soon as you can."

"Sure."

"We're ready to move on this, Henry. We don't have a lot of time."

"Sure. I understand."

"Good talking to you again, Henry."

Henry turned to go.

"Get back to us soon, Henry."

Henry left the office closing the glass door behind him. He went back down the steel stairs peering through the openings at the benches idle during the lunch break that was just ending while he made his way past the returning workers as he headed toward his locker. He would at least have some coffee, have a smoke. He didn't feel much like eating, not after what he had been through again. He'd grab a bite later if he had time when his appetite returned. Now he thought about the work ahead, about what he had just been through, and he wondered how he might tell his wife. Telling her might be the hardest part of what he had to do.

3

When he finally told her by taking his typical approach and, as the supervisor had noted, coming directly to the point, she remained mute. She stood at the stove cutting meat and vegetables into a pot while Henry sat at the table with a cup of coffee and a cigarette. He studied her quiet movements and her expressionless face, her lids lowered while she worked, her thin lips set.

"What do you think?"

"What you want to do?"

"I haven't decided. I thought I'd ask what you thought first."

126

"I haven't had much time to think."

"I know. But what's your gut feeling."

"What you just told me, what they want you to do is scary."

"Sure, it would be a big step."

"How could we manage something like that?"

"Well, the company would help with moving."

"But where they're asking you to go seems so big and so strange."

"Sure, but we'd manage. Look how you did when you came here."

"I was just a young girl then. Coming here was so exciting. And I had people here I knew and who I lived with and who helped me. We wouldn't know anyone where they want you to go."

"We'd meet people. We'd manage. What they're offering would mean we'd have things we've never had. We could buy a house. I've read that houses out there are big and they're built so that people can afford them.

"We have a house here."

"So we can have a better one there—a bigger one."

"Why we need a bigger house? You talk as if you really want to go."

"I want most to keep my job! And I'd be working at a level I never thought possible! I'd be a supervisor! Maybe I might even eventually become superintendent! Think what that would mean!" He paused in reflecting on the audacity of his own vision. "After all our years of struggle, we deserve something more!"

"But look how hard you work now. All hours of the day and night you get called. You work too hard. You'll work even harder."

"I know. But what I'd be paid would make up for all the hours and the responsibility."

"So you want to go."

"What you think?"

She again stood mute.

"O.K., he said with a sigh of resignation. He had suspected her response. "Think about it."

She nodded. "What about the boys?" she said finally.

"What about them?" Henry asked.

"You should ask them."

"What about? Sonny is out on his own now. He's met someone he wants to marry. And he's got a job that he likes and he'll probably stay at. He won't want to go."

"But what about Felix?"

"Felix will be on his own soon enough. He'll be graduating high school this year in June. He'll be looking for work. He certainly will want a job that will take him further than what he does now. Working weekends on a chicken farm isn't much of a career."

"But he might want to come along. Everybody talks about such a place they want you to move. He likes travel and adventure. I bet he'd like to go."

"O.K., I'll talk to him when I get a chance, but what about you? No matter what Felix might want to do or even Sonny, you're the one who would have to move. You're the one who has to decide."

"I'm just not sure. This is all so quick. I have to talk to people. See what they think."

"Who? Your mother?"

She remained silent. Henry knew that's what she meant. She always talked to her mother and her brother and her sister if she could ever get them to stop long enough to listen when she had to decide on something important, her brother always working to support his always growing family and her sister always moving, running around, changing husbands. And he knew how her brother and sister would respond if she asked them. Her brother would say nothing or just quietly agree with Henry that the deal might be a good one. Her sister would at first be indifferent but then she would encourage them to take the offer. Go for it! Her sister would exclaim. "You ask me, I'd go in a flash!" And her mother at first would express concern, perhaps regret her daughter's moving so far away, but then she would resign herself to her daughter's departure as just another part of life, thus turning the problem back to his wife. He decided he couldn't wait for her survey of her family's judgment.

"Look," he said. "If I don't agree to relocate, I might lose my job."

"So you lost jobs before," she countered. He was surprised at her uncharacteristic blunt response. "You've always found work."

"O.K., but maybe not now. I'm a lot further down the road than I was when everybody was out of work and I was willing to take any job I could get."

"But you're still young, and now you've got special skills."

"So you don't want me to take it?"

"I just don't know. I'm not sure. Just give me time to think."

"O.K.," he conceded. He rose and went into the front room to watch TV.

She turned to set the table for the evening meal.

4

Henry couldn't sleep, perhaps because he expected the phone call that always seemed to come just as he finally slept deeply or just as he had released his anxieties by means of his wife's warm yielding body. But now he worried that Felix had not returned home at the expected time. Where was he? Henry wondered. What trouble had he gotten himself into this time? He rose and went to the wall phone in the kitchen next to the sink.

"I know it's late," Henry said when his wife's brother answered. "I'm sorry, but Felix isn't home yet. I figured you might know where he is."

"It's O.K." his brother-in-law said. "We're still up with some of the kids. I don't know for sure where he is, but I remember Felix telling me this morning about a swim meet he had this evening after school but that he would try to meet me before I left my night job."

"So he didn't meet you?"

"No. I waited as long as I thought he would come. That was well after ten. He didn't show, so I left."

"O.K. Thanks," Henry said and hung up. Then he returned to the bedroom. His wife stirred in the dark.

"Felix didn't meet your brother for the ride home."

"Where might he be then?"

"I don't know. Neither does your brother. I'll go look for him. It's snowing and it's already covered the driveway."

"Be careful in such weather," she said.

"I will."

Then having finished dressing for the conditions, he leaned to offer her his lips that she accepted. Then he went to the door and into the heavily falling snow. He went to his new blue and white Chevy, unlocked the door, climbed in, started the engine, then let it idle with the heater set on high while he climbed out and used the brush to sweep the accumulated snow from the windows and headlamps. He climbed back in, placed the lever in reverse, and backed along the driveway to the road that already had begun to fill with snow. Henry was thankful that he had a new, reliable vehicle and that it had snow tires that would allow him to navigate roads with heavy accumulations. He turned toward the drive along the lake that would take him to the country road leading to the small city ten miles distant. He wondered what he might find at his first and most demanding obstacle: A long rather steep grade that led up to the state highway. If he made that grade, he expected to have little difficulty other than finding where his son might be this late at night and in this increasingly challenging weather. He did not bother turning on the radio, nor did he take the trouble to light a cigarette that he felt he could use right now. The green glow of the dash lights, the warm air from the heater, the quiet steady efficient sound of the engine allowed him to relax and focus on the worsening condition of the road and the increasing snowfall. He drove on enjoying to some small degree the quiet beauty of the snow in the dark night.

He watched both sides of the road, but he expected that Felix would most likely be on the opposite side of the road trying to thumb a ride if any should appear, and Henry knew that possibility was slight since he had not met any vehicles after he had passed the crest of the hill at the state highway.

Then halfway to the small city where Felix attended high school and his brother-in-law worked Henry saw a bent figure trudging along the road—not along the side, but in the middle of the lane. He slowed. He stopped. He rolled down the window part way letting in blowing snow. The figure bent toward the open window.

"You need a ride?" Henry asked quietly and relieved.

"I could use one!" Felix cried through his tears. Then Henry watched through the sweeping wipers as his son crept around through the deep snow to the side door that Henry leaned to open. Felix climbed in. "Thanks," Felix said with a deep sigh.

"You're lucky I couldn't sleep," Henry said. Then he slowly turned the car around and directed it toward home.

They stomped up the porch steps shaking off the snow and sweeping it from the porch. Inside, they took off their shoes on the mat before the door and let them set so the snow could melt. The kitchen light was on, and they could smell the rich aroma of freshly perked coffee. Felix's mother stood in the kitchen wrapped in a robe. Felix went into the living room and stood before the oil stove while Henry went to embrace his wife. Warming his hands, Felix felt the heat from the stove begin to warm the rest of him. He felt his feet begin to warm and with the returning warmth he began to feel the pain of his reviving flesh. He started to pace hoping that movement would help warm his frozen flesh and restore warmth to his limbs and body. As he paced he avoided looking at his father who sat at the table sipping coffee and enjoying a long-delayed smoke. Felix's mother had returned to bed.

Henry sat at the kitchen table sipping coffee watching Felix pace the living room carpet waiting for his feet and hands to thaw and warm from the freezing cold they had endured.

5

Felix missed his ride with his uncle after he had competed in a swim meet. He was pleased that he had won his event and had broken a school record surprising himself and everyone else. He recalled his indifference while he swam lap after lap at the same time he could hear the cries of encouragement of team members and the few spectators who took an interest in swimming.

Soft snow had been falling off and on all evening, and unlike the previous snow fall, that first one during which he had stood with her and then had watched as she had been whisked away by the "college man," this time he saw the snow shower as lovely: how it hushed the streets, coated sidewalks, filtered through the street lamps in bright swirling streams against the black night he saw above the towering cornices of nineteenth century buildings of the city center.

Earlier in the late afternoon he had stepped into a café that appealed to him because it was located on the edge of the business district and therefore seemed somewhat hidden. Here he would have a light meal before walking back up to school to prepare himself for his event. He had sat in one of the few booths with high wood sides, the one he chose close to the door allowing him to inspect the movements of the man behind the counter who was the cook and waiter and from where Felix could watch the three men who were spaced along stools at the low counter. He ordered and waited for his food while he sipped his drink. Then the door beside him opened; the small bell tinkled; someone entered bringing cold air and snow. The cook greeted the person who had entered as if he knew the person well. Felix recognized the voice that returned the greeting.

The women who had entered shook off her coat, hung it on a hook by the next booth, and slipped into the seat. Able to see over the wall of his booth Felix recognized the young woman who met his eyes but did not respond to his inspection. She was his Senior English teacher. Why was she here? Felix wondered. The cook came to take her order then went back to his grill. He returned to serve Felix his food then stopped at the next booth.

"So what you up to this weekend?" the cook asked her. He leaned against the edge of the booth beside her coat then leaned in toward her.

She informed the cook that she was going on a trip with a friend.

"Hey, that's great," the cook had said. "Too bad I can't go with you. I wish I had the time."

Felix paused in his chewing. The young women met his gaze then looked down.

"I'm sure you'll have a great time," the cook said. "You've earned it." Then he went back to his grill.

Felix finished eating. He rose and went to pay for his meal and without looking at her went out into the falling snow leaving her behind. He walked back to school considering what he had heard and witnessed. He thought about seeing her in class during the school week. She was a new teacher just out of college, and his class was one of the first she had taught. He had been moved to her class when the one he had been assigned had been over enrolled. He was glad for the change. The teacher of the other class had been teaching for years and rumored to be strict and traditional. And that teacher was a man. This new teacher was young, pretty, petite, and dressed in a fashion that was closer to that of her students. Sometimes that dress—short, pleated skirt that molded to her shape; satin blouse that clung—seemed provocative—at least to Felix who began to fantasize while he watched her move around the classroom, while she drew near him distributing class materials then stood beside him, her hip right next to him where he sat. He could breathe in her fragrance.

She was also somewhat provocative in her teaching: While leading the class in studying literature she had students try writing poetry imitating the style of poets whom they were studying. Felix was excited about the assignment because he had written what he considered poetry and he had already done what she required. So he reviewed some of what he had written and submitted it to fulfill the assignment. Others in the class were less than thrilled at having to write poetry. But one or two in class knew about Felix's writing and had considered him a bit strange for always keeping to himself and, of all things, writing poetry, but now they alerted others and several had solicited Felix for help and he was excited by the sudden attention after being shunned as weird and then becoming instead a hero.

Felix ended by writing poems for most of the others in the class who submitted the work as their own. The young teacher had read some of the poems to the class and Felix was thrilled to hear his poems read and praised. He was disappointed, however, because she had read none that he had submitted under his own name, ones he thought better than those he had written for others. Yet, he received some encouragement when she asked to see him after class, and when he lingered allowing the classroom to empty he was stirred by being alone with her, she sitting at her desk, he standing beside the desk while she praised him for his poems that she said were well written, some even mature, and she had asked to see more. He at first was excited about the possibility and he had promised her that he would show her a collection of what he considered his best. But he had as yet not kept his promise, and he wasn't sure now whether he would.

After the swim meet that ended later than expected, he had quickly showered, quickly dried, quickly dressed and had hurried down to the Five Points hoping that his uncle had not yet left his part-time job. But when Felix reached the bank on one corner of the intersecting five streets he saw opposite on another point only the dim glow of the nightlight over the lunch counter where his uncle worked.

So Felix turned and started walking the ten miles home hoping to hitch a ride along the way. But as he reached what he knew were the city limits, few cars had passed him, and those that did turned off into a driveway or side street. Then as he trudged along, snow began to fall more heavily covering the roads and blowing into drifts as he reached the area of dark homes beyond the city limits. He had walked this way during summer and had enjoyed the walk despite the distance. But now the night was black and bitter cold. He had no hat, no gloves, no boots having expected to ride home with his uncle in a warm car.

His father met him halfway. By the time his father came upon him walking in the dark, he was frozen. Slipping on the concrete road where earlier traffic had packed the snow polishing it to a slick sheet, he had fallen twice, had struggled to his feet, and in utter despair, his body racked with sobs, he had found himself calling out into the whirling storm for his father. A minute or two later, he saw the headlights of the only car he had seen since having left the city an hour or more ago. When the car stopped, in the headlights that caught the streaming snow, he recognized the chrome grille of his father's blue and white Chevy.

The window rolled down slowly against the swirling storm.

"You need a ride?" his father asked through the partially opened window.

"I could use one!" Felix cried with pain and relief. He crept to the side door through the falling snow caught in the headlights and climbed in.

Then as his father carefully maneuvered the car around on the treacherous road heading the hood through the storm toward home, the warmth from the car heater made Felix begin to feel how cold he had been. And on the slow way along the snow-thick road, as Felix explained what had happened he became suddenly aware that while the words spilled from his mouth he had fulfilled his father's prophecy: his going out for the swim team and being out on school nights would eventually lead to trouble. Felix had always been trouble, one damning incident after another, and now this. Yet, his father said nothing, save, "You're lucky I couldn't sleep."

Home, his father sat at the kitchen table sipping coffee, indulging in a cigarette he had denied himself during his search for Felix, while Felix walked the precious living room carpet reserved only for company, his movements helping to relieve the pain of heat and blood returning to his thawing flesh.

6

The day that Henry Schneider learned that his job had ended, the sun shone brightly, a natural expected condition that contrasted sharply with Henry's and his friend Feiffer's sense of sudden loss. In his pay envelope he found a folded sheet along with his check. He withdrew the sheet, unfolded it, and although he didn't want to read it, he thought he knew what the sheet would tell him, so he read.

The memo was addressed to him personally informing him that his position had been eliminated because of reduction in forces. He read that he would receive severance pay commensurate with the position he held before its elimination. He read a statement praising and thanking him for his years of dedication but that present economic circumstances required the action stated in the memo. The memo was signed by the director who had been president before the merger of his company with the larger corporation that had bought him out.

Henry noted wryly that this time no supervisor asked him to come discuss possible alternatives. Henry replaced the sheet in the envelope and looked up to survey the factory that had been so long a part of his life. Feiffer stood nearby with his pay envelope and a sheet of paper in his hand.

"So you got it too." Henry observed.

Feiffer nodded. His long time friend had warned Henry of the possibilities while Schneider had been considering the earlier offer that had given him the choice between continuing his union activities and possibly working for the union at the national level and his giving up those activities and possibilities in exchange for moving to the position he had held until today. Henry was silently grateful that his friend had not confronted him with "I told you so." Now Feiffer had also been issued a letter informing him that he too would be considered surplus.

So just as they had worked together all these years, they now would leave together. They decided to celebrate by having a beer. Henry suggested a place down the street from the factory. He knew the place from when he had bowled there in a league. They parked their cars and walked together into the tavern section of the bowling alley. Most of the lanes were dark. Two lanes on the end were lighted and being used by members of an afternoon league who were practicing. Henry and Feiffer sat at the bar and ordered. Then they sat sipping from their glass of tap beer studying the bowlers on the open lanes and listening to the sound of balls hitting the alley then rolling, then the shock of pins scattering and falling into the pit, and the sound of the machines resetting the pins.

"So what now?" Feiffer ask.

Henry shrugged. "What you think you might do?"

"What? You mean work? Not much. I've had enough—at least for a while. I'll rest and play it as it lays. I've got my cottage at the lake. I'll just enjoy myself. Do a little fishing. Just take it easy."

"You got a nice place," Henry said. He remembered the summer some years back that Feiffer had offered Henry and his family use of the lake cottage during Henry's summer vacation. "All of us really enjoyed the time we stayed there. I've never see the kids so happy. They were always busy doing something. Rowing on the lake. Fishing day and night. They wore themselves out. Slept like logs."

"Yeah, we like the place too. So I'll use it until I get tired of doing nothing. Maybe I'll use what I got for severance to start a business."

"Really? What kind of business?"

"Don't know right now. Maybe something to do with fishing. I'll just wait to see what happens. So what about you?"

"Well, we have a piece of property in Florida. Maybe we'll check that out. See what it's like."

"You mean you might live there?"

"Maybe. We'll see."

"Then how come you didn't take what they offered about your relocating?"

"Wife put the kibosh on that. Too far away from her family. Too big a place. Wouldn't know anybody. So how could I accept that offer?"

"And if Florida don't work?"

Henry shrugged. "I guess I'll look for something here."

"Doing?"

"What else? Must be some place that needs a patternmaker."

"No union work?"

"I'll pay dues. Let someone else do the talking. I've learned."

Feiffer nodded. "So I guess it's time," he said.

"I guess."

The two men finished their beers then slid from their stools and filed out into the bright sunlight even brighter after the dim interior of the bowling alley. They strolled toward their cars.

"Keep in touch," Feiffer offered. "You got my number."

"Sure," Henry said. Then he offered his hand. Feiffer grasped Henry's hand. The two men studied each other.

"Thanks," Henry said.

"What for?" Feiffer asked.

"For being here."

Feiffer gripped Henry's hand. "You too." Then he withdrew his hand and turned toward his car unlocking it. He looked at Henry again and lowered himself to the seat and started the car. Henry watched as Feiffer pulled away glancing back one last time. Henry watched him drive off. Then he turned to his own new blue and white Chevy waiting to take him home. To what, Henry wasn't sure.

7

"Well, you know what to do," the supervisor said. "You've had years of experience."

Henry nodded. He knew all right, and he knew how many years he had labored at this task.

"I'll leave you to your work," the supervisor said.

He placed a hand on Henry's shoulder as if he understood why Henry was here; then he went off toward his glassed-in office similar to the one that Henry had worked under for too many days, except that this one was on the factory floor and was not as lofty.

Then Henry turned to the folded design sheet on the bench, spread it before him, studied it, and turned to his toolbox.

How long ago had he last used it?

He thought about the intervening years ending with the latest disaster: his travel to Florida pulling a small trailer behind the blue and white Chevy that now was not as new. There in Florida he and his wife had surveyed the property he had bought on speculation similar to the piece in Arizona that had turned out to be a scam by wealthy investors and lost to foreclosure. In Florida, hoping to find a place where they might build and settle, he and his wife had stared in disbelief at the stagnant fetid waters of the swamp that was supposedly their property. And while they stood dismayed and angry, hosts of insects that seemed huge swarmed around them tormenting them. Henry and his wife had fled back north to a place where they at least knew what deceptions awaited them.

Opening now his toolbox Henry inspected the neat array of tools he had always used, each tool in its appropriate designated place. Here, at last, was something he knew was certain. Then he chose a chisel that he lifted from its resting place and held it firmly in his hand. And as he bent to begin his task, he suddenly felt at peace with a still, small sense of joy at being in a place he knew he belonged.

137

A Clear, Descending Light-1

[Early Autumn]

Felix was in one of his favorite places when he heard his father call his name. Sprawled across the sidewalk between the house and the heavy green picket fence that ran along the brick alleyway, he lay with his face close to the sun-bleached eroded concrete walk beside the foundation of dark brown cinder blocks, his head upon his arms. He watched the scurrying of the small red ants he had studied in books he had walked to get from the library on Eleventh Street. His head rested on his arms as he studied the sudden appearances and disappearances, the frequent crossing of paths that seemed almost meanderings until two met with antenna waving; he followed the comings and goings from the mysterious darkness of the hole surrounded by the ring of fine yellow dirt. He lay upon the sidewalk gazing at the busy activity of the small mound beneath the multi-colored rose garden. He watched the amazing transport of heavy burdens, the explorations, the long, orderly lines that disappeared among the dimness of the roses. One ant strayed wandering to the foothills of his fingers then labored up his hand climbing the long ascent among the fine down of his forearm.

He lay upon the walk under the warm autumn sun watching the anthill until he heard his father's voice calling him from the front of the house. Felix scrambled to his feet. Reminded by the faint stir upon his arm, he gently blew the ant from his arm and turned and went though the gate to the front yard.

His father stood on the high steep porch beside Felix's uncle. The men were so absorbed in talk they only absently noticed the boy who came to the bottom of the gray porch steps and squinted up at the two men standing just outside the door. His father, tall with dark hair and eyes and light rimmed spectacles, still held open the screen door in the act of closing it, more concerned with making his point to the shorter slightly built man beside him than with closing the door.

"You think they'd help you if you didn't have rights by way of contract?" He insisted. But he didn't wait for an answer, and the other man wouldn't have responded anyway. Instead, he continued to study the traffic crossing the intersection at the corner.

"Hell, no!" The larger man continued. "I've had to fight for anything I've ever got. And it won't be any different for you. It's a little better now since they've got a contract where I work. But it won't get better for a long time yet. Maybe it never will. I'm just glad I don't have to deal with all that anymore."

The large man's demanding voice grew louder, more insistent so that someone listening and not knowing him would think the man angry. But he became so involved and carried away by what to him was the unimpeachable rightness of his views that he wasn't aware of the loudness and tone of his words until someone would advise him to calm down.

The tall man had been thinner once, referred to then as slim or lanky with a long thin face that was handsome and youthful. Yet even now the heaviness and thick muscled corpulence that would affect him later was beginning to fill out the face and soften and sag the belly.

The smaller man by his side was only shorter in comparison, and seeing the two men together, Felix could readily notice again the fine sharp features of the smaller man that reminded Felix of his mother who had many of the same features, the same chestnut hair that settled into soft waves when combed and the same resigned quiet nature that Felix's mother used to accept the larger man's insistence and growing anger that now as usual caught him up and stopped him floundering in his own frustration at not finding the right words. He paused attempting to sort and clarify his thoughts and control his ideas. Then as he paused he noticed Felix squinting up at him with his mouth pulled into a characteristic grimace.

"You want me, Dad?" Felix asked.

"You want to come with?" his father asked, his frustration and anger now subdued.

"Sure," Felix said always eager to go along anywhere especially when he would be going with his uncle. "Where we going?"

"Your uncle has to go into the doctor's to have his fingers checked."

Felix looked at his uncle's bandaged hand. A joiner had sliced his uncle's fingers on one hand to bloody stumps. Felix winced and cringed imagining his uncle's pain when he had lost his finger tips in the whirring steel blade of the joiner.

Felix remembered now that someone had taken his uncle to the hospital while someone else had gathered the severed finger tips taking them to his uncle's house and burying them beneath the soft moist earth of the backyard soil to wait for the time—according to belief—when the fingers tips would be rejoined and the fingers made whole again.

The two men moved toward his uncle's car, a new two-door, pale green '47 Studebaker parked at the curb. Felix entered first pushing back the front seat and settling himself in back. He lounged in the comfort of the softness and newness of the headliner and the embracing curve of the back window that swept around him allowing him to see in any direction at a glance. He marveled at the difference between this his uncle's newer more modern car and his father's older taller one.

His father climbed into the driver's seat pleased at the chance to drive the new machine, but then he recalled the purpose of their trip that reminded him of his interrupted discourse on the porch.

"Now see what I mean?" He began as he moved the car away from the curb, his question half lost through the open window as he turned to scan the street and the two-storied flats that rose above tall elms thick with summer leaves.

"What a bunch of bull to have somebody go eighteen miles to see a doctor when there's fifty doctors practically right next door."

Felix sat on the soft throne of the back seat and watched his house recede behind him. Then he saw his friend Ronnie's house and then the apartments where one of his great aunts lived. Seeing the apartments, Felix recalled how another friend had been hurt while the apartments were being built. His friend had backed through a hole open to the cellar of one building plunging and catching his jaw and tearing his neck and jaw upon the ledge as he fell. Someone had brought a ladder to help his friend out, and someone else had called an ambulance. Felix recalled his friend lying in the ambulance that took him away.

Now as they passed, Felix saw the completed apartments finished with redbrick. But when he visited his aunt whose apartment was filled with new soft furniture and quaint frilliness Felix always recalled his friend's accident and the odors of new bare boards and wet cement when the apartments were being built.

Thinking about his friend and about his aunt, Felix didn't hear his uncle's answer to the question Felix's father had raised. Yet he knew they would have to travel eighteen miles to the small city were his uncle worked because the company doctor's office was there. And Felix heard his father curse the insensitive arbitrary requirements of employers. But then Felix saw that they had turned onto the wide thoroughfare that would take them out of the city.

Felix knew well this part of the city that was his neighborhood and helped define his existence. But now from his backseat with the sweep of rear window what he saw took on a different appearance became renewed and the source of inspection. He saw streets that he alone or with friends often took to the large park just a block away, and he and his friends often changed routes depending upon their intended activity or their intended destination. One street would lead him to the railroad yards and the billowing clouds of steam from the thunderous engines that shook and jarred him with their massive weight and their blasting out shrill piercing shrieks that always carried to his house waking him in the night. He would stand above on the viaduct and view the long lines of boxcars on the maze of crisscrossing steel tracks, the boxcars with white lettering displaying names and places that seemed exotic. That same street led him past the sunken gardens to what he called the Flower House where he strolled beneath dusty panes of glass over graveled paths in a warm humid atmosphere of ferns and palm trees and orchids then over bridges crossing quiet ponds with tiny gaping fish.

Another street led to the Lagoon with its green murky water where he and his friends sometimes fished—or tried to without ever any success with their homemade hooks and dried bread for bait. Then the path led him to the redbrick boathouse with arches and dark interior that grew cool in summer from the concrete floor, dark in winter with their skate blades scoring the wooden floor placed over the concrete for the skaters to come in for snacks and hot drinks.

Another street led to the playground from which they followed their own wandering path to the ball diamond then past that along a packed dirt path bordered by thick bushes to the poker chip factory where sometimes among the discard pile they found chips of several colors, white, red, blue, that were nearly unblemished and that they would carry home as treasures to store in cluttered boxes in dusty attics.

A third street led them through the park to the high green hill with a "real" log cabin preserved from the time the first pioneers settled the area. From the roof of the cabin he could gaze at the center of the city with its the tall buildings and distant spires and a blue gray haze among them and the bright billowing clouds above.

They passed the movie theater where he went to movies sometimes if his neighborhood theater had films he had already seen. The one he passed now was bigger than the one in his neighborhood, this one with a balcony and huge vaulted lobbies that reminded him of the movies houses downtown that he rarely attended.

Now he saw the long row of residential houses that marked the way out of the city. He knew these houses too because he had come this way in summer to the State Fair. And this was also the way to his cousin's house, so as he passed the street on which his cousin lived he searched to see whether his cousin might be playing on the front walkway. Then seeing the walkway empty he imagined the dark wood hallway with its long flight of thickly carpeted stairs that curved at the top before the door.

He imagined the dark stained wood interior, the large front bedroom with the row of high windows overlooking the metal porch on which he and his cousin seldom sat.

He saw the living room between the front bedroom and the dining room, the high ceilings of all the rooms, the dark wood square archways and the dark wood pillars separating the living room from the dining room. He imagined the large thick-legged dining table, the high windows along the side revealing the upper story of the flat next door, the dark stained wood of the sideboard and cabinets that covered the wall separating the dining room from the kitchen, the large mirror between the cabinets. He saw the doorway leading from the dining room to the two other bedrooms separated by the tiled bathroom.

He saw finally the kitchen all in white: baseboards, doorframes, appliances, sink, table, and tablecloth. At that table he sometimes sat with his cousin, his aunt, his grandmother tasting the exotic food that they prepared and that he would never have at home.

They passed the State Fair grounds, the fair closed now and silent. He recalled the summer fun, the rides and heat, the juicy hot dogs, the frothy root beer, the wonders of the side shows in colored tents, the strong odors of animals, the huge horses and their droppings, the milling crowds of people throughout the fairgrounds.

He noticed then that they had left the city behind and had entered a landscape that he only knew vaguely because he had seldom traveled this way, so this way held his interest most.

The occasions on which he had come this way were summer trips to various lakes that lay beyond the city. Each trip had taken him to a lake new to him, so the roads they took seemed different and they always renewed in him a sense of wonder.

Felix sat in the middle of the back seat watching both sides of the road so that he wouldn't miss anything. Occasionally he looked back through the curve of the rear window to watch the road recede and grow smaller behind him. Or he would look past the heads of the two men in front beyond the hood to the countryside ahead that seemed to race to meet them, the road devoured beneath the wheels then dropping vanquished behind.

They reached the crest of a high hill that descended in a long gradual slope. They viewed the landscape before them, the blue green of the gentle rounded hills bright beneath sunlight, the various colors of late summer leaves: clumps of yellow, red, and orange and groups of brown among the remaining green.

The long shining road stretched before them as they descended into a countryside that appeared new, and as they descended the long slope they saw the glimmer and haze off the buildings of the town that lay in the valley at the bottom of the long slope. But when they reached the bottom, the road began to curve and then wind so the town was lost from view. The road took them through stands of trees along the way stretching across the undulating landscape to the high hills.

Then as they turned through curves, Felix could catch glimpses of the towers and turrets of the city, flashes of sunlight from buildings that were lost again among the trees. But suddenly as the road curved again they were descending again, and finally the trees thinned and separated into clusters revealing houses. Felix was surprised to see the houses he had viewed as glimmering whiteness dissolve into old gabled houses and stark new structures, and he was even more surprised to see the houses so richly colored with yellow, pink, and red brick, so different from the endless variety of gray slat board flats in his own neighborhood.

The streets became wider. They passed a yellow and red filling station among the green of trees and bushes. Felix saw a car parked at one of the pumps, a man standing holding the hose to the car watching the meter whirl. They passed a large old gabled house with porch and twisting pillars and wrought iron grating on the roof. A sign stood before the house: "The Spa—mud baths, massages, and beauty aids."

They came to used car lots, the sun flashing and sparkling off the vehicles, then railroad tracks and cross arms, the station yellow and brown, a green baggage car beside a sloping platform beside the station. They came upon more old and towering gabled houses and then they reached the rows of wide vast storefronts on both sides of the street with people walking and looking at the merchandise displayed behind the windows.

Felix looked through the open doors of stores to the interiors under the high dark ceilings and the round golden lights dim against the bright late summer day outside.

They passed rows of cars along the curb with meters that Felix had never seen. Then they slowed, came to an empty space of asphalt, pulled into that space, and stopped. His father shut down the engine to a soft murmur before shutting it down completely leaving stillness until the thump against the door handle swung wide the door across the pavement before the storefront. They climbed out, stood, stretched, shut and locked the car doors, his father handing his uncle the keys, then turned toward the center of the city.

They walked until they came to an intersection of five arterials that lead through five parts of the city from five roads that came from five parts of the rolling country that stretched beyond the city. They stopped and turned to face each other forming a small cluster among the passing crowd of people and the moving press of traffic between the tall buildings and vast paned storefronts. The two men stood above the boy looking down at him watching him as they asked their questions, the people moving past glancing at the men and the boy, then moving along with the crowd.

"Look, Felix," his father said. "We're going over to the doctor's office over there." His father looked and pointed toward a large building with a rounded front that fit into one of the five points of the intersection.

"You can come along, or you can stay here and look around. How about it?"

"I'll look around," Felix said calmly although he was trying to control the surge of excitement at the prospect of his being on his own in this wonderland of a place he didn't know. His first thought had been to go along with his father and uncle, but then he considered the mysterious interiors of stores, mysteries that needed solving.

He wanted to see them up close, to be there and look out from inside to the sunlight and see the ghost of the pale green car he had ridden in pass by him on the street.

His father and uncle watched him while they stood at the intersection waiting for the light to change allowing them to cross.

"You better meet us over there," his father directed.

He nodded toward the large gray round imposing front of the bank across from the building that they were going to.

Felix nodded in agreement. "How long you going to be?"

His father looked at Felix's uncle.

"About an hour," his uncle said.

Felix nodded again and watched the traffic and passing people then stayed behind following them along the row of storefronts having decided already which store he wanted to first explore before the others.

"O.K." his father said. "We'll meet you in an hour by the bank. There's a clock over there, so you'll know." He nodded toward the clock above the jewelry store on the intersection opposite the bank. "Don't get lost."

"I won't get lost."

His father and uncle studied him then turned into the crowd and waited for the light then crossed the street to the curved front building his father had pointed to. Felix watched as they entered the building. Then he turned toward what surrounded him waiting for him to explore.

Felix remained at the corner of the five point intersection inspecting the tall rounded fronts of buildings, many of them made from the same peculiar design: large fitted blocks of stone that bulged into half of a tower before they ended beneath the sky. Felix studied them comparing them to the tall buildings of glass and concrete, many of them square that dominated the center of the city that he always viewed from the roof of the log cabin.

He walked back along the sidewalk toward the car and stopped before the large glass panes and wood framed doorway of the five and ten cent store. He watched people moving through the doorway, their side view reflected in the angled window before they reached the sidewalk and turned into the crowd.

Felix stepped through the doorway and stood beside the white enamel scale just inside the doorway and scanned the interior. How many times had he seen a store similar to this one and had explored those stores with his older brother and a friend? Here he saw again the bright red framework above the windows, the bold lettering and numbers. Yet this store appeared different from the other stores he had come to know and that had become part of him. Why were they different when what he saw seemed the same?

The lunch counter had the round vinyl covered stools, the pie and cake cases on the counter, the colored posters of food on the wall behind the counter, the waitresses in pale green uniforms with white collars and pockets, the row of people bunched together on the stools joined by a heavy woman settling onto an empty stool, a young man in white shirt and dark tie spinning from a stool and the stool quickly filled by a person waiting in the row of people waiting behind those seated. Here, too, were the same high dark wood counters with green glass partitions separating the colored yarn, the bright spools of thread, the strings of costume jewelry, here the red print cards on the partitions, the same dark wood floors that sounded under the many feet. Here the same mingling of voices, footfalls, cash registers, and the monotonous chiming bell.

But as Felix started down the aisle past green hanging plants and tanks of fish, past tools and china, he noticed the aisle was wider, the dark wood of the floor lighter, more bare. Then as he moved toward a stairway that ran the whole width of the store and he descended toward the doorway and window fronts at this end of the store, he found himself in shade on a street different than the one from which he had entered.

Before him in the bright sun a movie theater, a department store with a name he didn't recognize, a shaded alley way, a restaurant, and the building his father and his uncle had gone into. He turned up the sidewalk toward the intersection and reached the place where the two sides of glass came together.

Felix crossed the intersection following the course his father and uncle had taken passing the dark wood frame of the jewelry store, the ruby brightness of the sign hung in the wide glass window, the dim interior from which riches sparkled and gleamed, but when he reached the other point of intersection, he turned aside from the doorway that exposed the wide flight of wooden stairs that led above to the doctor's office his uncle went to and instead made his way along the gray granite front of the building past a market with a green front and bins of colored fruit and pungent vegetables beside the doorway. He glanced inside at the rows of food and saw the bald-pated man behind a low counter leaning toward the heavy women in a limp cloth coat as he filled a bag with what she had bought: the meat wrapped in white paper, carrots with their green fernlike tops, the round gray and purple turnips.

Felix moved along the street to the bridge across the river that flowed through the heart of the city from the rolling country side, flowed past grassy parks that had been planted along the riverbanks near the outskirts then reaching the city center confined by high concrete walls until it flowed beneath the bridge on which Felix stood then beneath the roadway and finally flowing free between the steep earthen banks beyond the bridge and then the sloping banks before it again reached the rolling country on the other side.

Felix turned up the narrow side street lined with narrow wooden buildings that clung to the top of the steep riverbanks. Then he came to a green park with towering trees of dark rough trunks shedding red and yellow leaves upon the grass beneath. Felix wandered through the park viewing buildings at the edge of the park and the moving traffic and the flicker and throb of neon signs faded thin against the afternoon sunlight.

Felix walked beneath the tall trees watching the movements outside the park until he came to a high mound bordered by a cyclone fence.

He walked slowly around the mound impressed by its height and its size.

He stared through the crosswire squares of the fence at the flow of earth and grass that swelled at the center and rose above the fence toward the thick underside of green and yellow leaves of trees that grew outside the fence. Then he read the plague attached to the fence that told him of the mounds beginning. Felix stood gazing at the burial mound amazed that the huge pile of earth before him contained the bones and beads and baskets of people who had lived here before there was any city here or anywhere, things that he had seen often in the museum he went to at home. Then his mind turning now toward the mystery before him, the conic towers, the brightly colored shingles intermingled with the canopy of fully leafed trees, the gray stone surface of the building nearby faded as the mound became part of the primeval forest it once had been.

He stood transfixed imagining the mound as part of a village, the nearby building, the fence, the city outside the park gone, the park and mound now a part of the forest that grew dense across the vast rolling countryside he had seen on the way into the city. Then as he searched inward and as he became lost in his own wondrous time he could see the village hushed at night and the movements of women and children before the curling smoke of fires. Then he saw the slow dignified movements of the serious men huge to him in their redness and wildness as they brought someone to the mound, perhaps a boy his age, bringing with them colored beads and bright bronze ornaments to adorn the body wrapped in furs that left the face uncovered. He stood gazing at the mound until the harsh sounds of traffic, a blaring horn followed by screaming tires tore the veil and dropped him back through time to where he stood beneath the tall leafy trees before the fence and the mound.

Felix turned slowly from the mound. He approached the grey building of huge blocks of rough granite. Viewing it and reading the lettering above the double glass doors he discovered that the building was a library with the same design of a rounded room on each side of the straight entrance just as the one he walked to at home on Eleventh Street to retrieve books on nature, especially those on ants. Dare he explore this familiar but strange structure?

He climbed the stairs, pulled on the large door handle, then pulled back the heavy door. He entered the foyer before two more doors of glass paneling and dark wood frames, just like his library at home.

To the right and left where two concrete stairways leading down into dank dark passageways, one descending to Women, the other to Men this, too, the same as at his home library. He moved up the low stairs before the two doors, pulled on the handle of one and stood before the tall large arc of wooden counter behind which a women, how old, he couldn't guess, stood guard. She inspected him above the rim of her dark framed glasses.

"May I help you, young man?"

He was startled: Not many people called him 'young man'.

He shook his head. "This is just like the library at home that I go to get books on ants."

"Really? And where is that?"

He stated his address from memory.

"That's quite a ways," she said. "And why are you so far from home?

"My uncle had to come see his doctor. He works at the lumberyard by the river. He got his fingers cut off by a machine."

"Really? Well, how might I help you?"

He shook his head again shyly. "Just looking," he said. Then he turned and went back out the inner door and then the heavy door he had to push against with his shoulder to open it, just like at home.

He went out of the park using the asphalt path then moved down the gradual slope of the street to where the older rounded buildings began again and where he found himself at the intersection in front of the bank his father had pointed out to him.

Felix found the door to the bank open. He watched people hurry in then reappear standing before the door while they deposited money in their purse or pocket then moved off into the clusters of people at the intersection. Felix stood before the open door of the bank gazing within at the long dark counters with their high brass cages and the serious looking people behind the cages carefully tallying the flow of bills that slid across the smooth marble counter. Felix stared at the round thick door with its shining fixtures standing open before the huge hole that allowed access to the vault.

His concentration broke when he heard the sound of coins hitting the polished granite floor. He rushed to find the coins as they rolled in arcs then whirled flat to the floor. A man stood turning slowly searching the floor. Felix offered the man the coins he had retrieved.

"I think that's all," Felix said. "That's all I found."

"Thank you," the man said. "What a good boy." Then the man started for the open door leaving a coin in Felix's hand. Felix studied the coin, looked up to find the man, then suddenly spied one last coin resting on the colored tiles of the large mosaic just inside the door. Felix called to the man who had quickly moved in among the people at the intersection.

Felix hurried to retrieve the coin and run after the man. But then he saw the large profile formed from small squares of stone. Felix studied the profile following the lines of the stones that formed the large nose, the many different colors of the feathers, the gleam of the tiled dark eyes, then the more perfectly formed lettering of the bank's name that sounded Indian when he spoke the name to himself.

Felix turned and went out to the corner searching for the man who had lost the coin then drew back to the side of the bank when Felix couldn't find him. Felix climbed on a high step between two of the black granite pillars supporting the bank entrance. He ran his hand over the hard polished surface noting the grains of the stone. Then he turned to watch the passing scene.

The afternoon had been heavy and hot with sunlight flashing off the large store windows and off the cars that swept by in the heat, the people in the cars squinting against the sunlight fanning themselves with their hands. Then Felix suddenly noticed clouds coming from the west having been carried across the vast grasslands and rolling hills of the countryside.

The gathering clouds suddenly shut out the sun and cooled the city.

Felix noticed the change and relaxed his squint. A slight breeze blew cooling him, and as he stood between the tall pillars of the bank, he noted the change enjoying the coolness while watching people come and go to and from the bank moving easier now, more relaxed in the still warm but cooler air.

Then from what seemed far away Felix heard a sound he couldn't identify, the sound at first a murmur then growing until it became a rumble echoing within the hollow between the buildings. Felix wondered at the sound not knowing what it could be. He scanned the street searching for the source while the sound grew until he heard what seemed a multitude of babbling voices and a multitude of feet marching out of step broken and chaotic yet blending to make the noise rise about the sound of traffic.

Suddenly the sound broke around him until he clung to one of the bank pillars. And then they came around the corner of the building mostly in pairs, some in larger groups of three or four, unruly clumps that crowded others off the walkway. But some came alone following cautiously behind the others. Felix saw that all carried books as they came through the now cloudy humid afternoon. Some glanced at Felix standing between the pillars of the bank now his sanctuary. Felix stared wide-eyed, mouth open as they passed until the flow became a dazzling blur.

Grown accustomed to the flow, Felix began to study those passing. He inspected the changing shapes of bodies, the colors and cuts of hair. He saw the young women some passing in groups chattering while strolling in a strange gait that appeared to him more of a wiggle. He saw couples, the girl held at the waist, the boy ignoring the whole world to watch the moving smiling lips of the girl. Then the flow thinned until only occasionally some came carrying books so that Felix waited curious to see if any more would pass. And with the flow diminished to a scattering of one or two, the sound of the flow gone, the world seemed to have stopped so that Felix no longer noticed the streaming traffic and flow of people but was lost reflecting on what he had just witnessed.

And just as suddenly at that moment in the gray overcast a place opened and a slanting ray of sunlight shone on the brick roadway of the side street next to him down which the sound and flow of people had descended.

Felix marveled at the flashing brilliance of the polished car and then the stream of sunlight that caught tiny globes of matter and whirled them in a long slow gyre that made them glow. The slow spiraling dust glowed golden in one long ray of clear, descending light that struck the vast window of the jewelry store and sent back the light to Felix's eyes. Felix beheld the gyre of light in dazzled wonder.

Then the gray clouds closed again and Felix felt himself slump in the coolness and the calm after the flowing sound of the crowd and the single ray of descending sunlight. The gray clouds shut off the light then broke and scattered lined with white against the rich blueness of the open sky.

When the two men came across to the corner, they found Felix waiting between the black granite pillars of the bank watching the flow of traffic and parade of people, his head moving slowly from side to side surveying the passing scene. Felix had watched them negotiate the five points of the intersection first crossing directly then laterally, finally arriving at the point on which the bank was located. Felix jumped from the stoop where he had held his post then walked with them to where his father had parked the car.

Felix waited while his uncle opened the car then handed the keys to Felix's father.

Felix climbed into the heat and stuffiness of his place in the back seat. His uncle seated himself while Felix's father went to the driver's side, unlocked the door, climbed in, started the car then eased it out into the flow of traffic when he saw the chance.

They went down through the intersection, and Felix from his vantage point through the curved rear window looked back to where he had stood between the pillars of the bank and saw an image of himself watching the receding car in which he rode.

His father turned the car up a side street passing the narrow wood houses along the riverbank then turned again, and they passed the green shaded park with the gray stone building and the burial mound beneath the canopy of leaves.

Then they finally reached the street that led them out to the rolling hills thick with trees outside the city. They passed again the large Victorian houses, rumbled over the railroad tracks then passed the railroad station, The Spa offering mud baths, then out beyond the houses to the curve that straightened to the long stretch of rolling countryside and trees yielding their colored leaves.

They moved toward the long hill that would take them above the valley before they descended again into the grids of narrow pavements, the wood or asphalt sided gray two-story flats, the stores and signs that Felix knew so well, the spare closed spaces of greenery, and the people in closed vehicles congregating, crowding, going homeward moving slowly through thinning sunlight and the waning day that dimmed toward twilight.

A Clear, Descending Light-2

[Late autumn, almost winter]

Coming out of the locker room feeling fresh and taut after recovering from near exhaustion, he let the heavy door wing back to latch itself closing off the heavy ambience of steam, wet bodies, damp towels, and slippery concrete from wet feet. Before the door had fully closed, a shouting voice and the sound of the thrumming diving board had echoed from the pool. The door closed, he moved into the brown tiled hallway. He noticed the scratched tiles, the swirls of scuffed polish before he raised his head to view the line of brown metal lockers set in the yellow plaster walls and saw her standing waiting at the end of the wall of lockers.

He had thought of her all during practice while he swam what always seemed like endless laps up and down the pool. He had felt something in him stir thinking of her. He had thought of her smile and he had felt a secret sensual joy. Some considered her heavy, but he thought she held a beauty of her own that was hard to discern. She wasn't over weight, but she was fuller and heavier that most of those of her age. So he might have thought at first meeting her, but then he had seen the contrast of her light complexion and dark hair cut short in the latest style that perhaps accentuated her full figure. He had especially noted her eyes with their contrast of dark pupil and blue gray iris that gave her eyes a wild quality, a gleam of freedom or even sensuality that had made other boys seek her out, court her, pursue her despite her more than petite size. Her personality, perhaps reflected in her eyes, also helped her.

She was winning in her own way, confident and friendly and somewhat aggressive in her establishing friendships. He eventually had been overwhelmed by her overtures to him during study period. Then he had been humbled when he discovered that her movements were something of a game that she played with others as well. He had been reluctant to continue her game. Yet she had enticed him back when she had noticed the open and naïve manner in which he had responded to her first overtures and, of course his reluctance to respond again became a challenge she was eager to meet.

He had approached her shyly while they lined the hallway waiting as those of the previous hour had filed out and the next hour students filed in and took their assigned places. He learned, however, the main reason she had displayed interest in him was that he sat behind her and that she had decided to make him interested because of his hesitancy or caution or distance, or just because she enjoyed the game that helped overcome the feeling of being imprisoned. Then her notes began, she delivering them over her shoulder, those notes always in purple ink on blue paper with the dot on the i in the shape of a heart followed by the spoken invitation through the bright smile, another of her assets, and the vibrant laughing eyes.

Then at the homecoming football game that he had come to with a newly made friend, she had smiled and invited him, and he had sat with her throughout the game that they mostly ignored, he also ignoring his new friend who was always cool to him afterwards. After the game he had walked with her back to the school toward the gym and the sounds of the school dance, they laughing at how little of the game they had noticed.

At the dance, while at first they watched the couples in socks on the gym floor from beneath the oval indoor track hung from the walls, she had coaxed him with her typical gentle persuasion to try the dance floor. And he in his typical manner had been reluctant even though he had danced often at various celebrations or at neighborhood parties. But that dancing was more traditional and with people whom he knew well since they were family or relatives. So he was hesitant to dance with this female he didn't know well and to whom he was attracted in a way he had never felt with the other people with whom he had danced. Then she had accepted an invitation to dance from a city boy whom she had know most of her life having attended the same elementary school. He had blanched and felt weak while she danced with other boys so that he finally had followed her onto the floor and held her in his arms acutely aware of her nearness and her body as thy moved awkwardly at first due to his clumsy movements as they came out from under the overhead track then out onto the floor beneath the soft colored lights, the soft glow of lights at the exits, the shadowy faces of people looking down from the railing of the oval track above.

While they moved around the floor in what was more sliding than dancing, he feeling odd in his stockings, he noticed the stags (those without partners) and the stragglers aimlessly lounging at the borders of the dance floor, some gathered laughing, some seemingly envious watching the members of the dance band, or some sitting in the bleachers usually pulled out for basketball games but now serving as a refuge for those who only watched.

He remembered with some chagrin his being one of the watchers refuged in the bleachers during previous dances. Then he had wandered about the bleachers somewhat disinterested in the dance because he didn't know the kind of dance he saw, because he didn't know anyone with whom to dance, and because he lacked the courage to impose his socially unskilled self on some unsuspecting female. But most of all he was at the dance only watching because he had to wait for the school bus that waited for the dance to end before it set off on its usual route but now at night.

So he had moved from the bleachers through the crowds to the groups along the edge of the dance floor, then out through the green walled concrete basement to the stairs, the street, the crowd of parked cars on the gym class playgrounds, the people staggered among the cars, then waiting alone along the line of black and yellow buses that waited for the last dance to end.

The street lamp had shone down on the whole scene: The dark bare trees, the yellow tan brick of the school, the glimmer of light off the parked cars and buses, the black iron railing around the meager patch of grass that passed for lawn along the walls of the building, the litter of notebook paper and paper cups, the people listening to the music through the open windows at the top of the gym, then the last dance ending and the people streaming out as couples or in groups, the couples still clinging to each other, the crowds and movement beneath the street lamp, the waiting at the black iron railing. Finally the pale green interior of the bus, the darker green of the vinyl bench seats, the last look through the windows, and then the bus moving away from the curb into the night.

After that night of the homecoming game, he had sought her, and he found again that she had simply thought of him as another prize because he was different. Shy and strangely honest in his manner she saw that he never tried to present himself as something other than who he was. So he differed from the others whom she had strung along and who had pursued her: He was a "country boy" from a small town ten miles distant. The others whom she knew and ran with were from the city just as she was, and they displayed, as she did, what they took as sophistication by their fashionable dress, their stylish hair, and their socializing with only those whom they deemed worthy of their association, meaning only those from the city, dismissing anyone who did not meet their criteria as "hicks" or "retards."

And when he decided that she was a flirt and a tease and held himself back, she turned to him in earnest attracted now because he had become a prize to be won and because in her pursuit the others who had sought her lost interest. So in effect she had committed herself to winning this one boy, and the others took her move as a sign of possible frustration or rejection on their part and thus sought elsewhere for release.

She smiled at him now as he came from the pool locker room and then turned with him as they went down the hallway of brown metal lockers in yellow plaster walls.

Outside the day was cold and gray. Late autumn: the first snow was expected soon. The light was already fading, the day growing dark in the early afternoon.

Turning the corner, they headed toward the Five Points intersection three blocks away. Cars wumped past them on the cobbled brick roadway sending them blue exhaust fumes that choked them as they walked.

The air with the darkening of the light was quickly becoming chilly and Felix already felt cold around his ears from the lingering wetness of the pool and shower.

"You should dry yourself better," she suggested as she had done often enough before.

Felix just shrugged in resignation with his hands in the pockets of his leather jacket, a prize possession that he had saved for because everyone who aspired to be noticed wore one, and, of course, she had approved his purchase by helping him select the one he now wore. Besides, his hair had to be wet to comb in what was considered the latest style that she, of course, approved, so he accepted the stiffness of his hair and the chill that came as a result of the wet hair.

They walked in silence, their relationship now having reduced to subtle signs and small unseen brief touching after their first initial revelations in seemingly endless words about what their lives had been before they met, she, of course, taking the lead and then drawing him out. Yet even now he was discovering new aspects of her life that surprised him and would always surprise him as long as he knew her, so in the end he would realize how little he had known her, if he had known her at all.

They passed Library Park. The asphalt pathways that led to the granite block building were gray now strewn with leaves from the dark trees now bare that recently had been vibrant with a display of autumn leaves: orange, brown, red, and yellow. The leaves lay in piles on the hardened earth, the grass dead and flat. Only a short time past all had been a rich deep green: trees full and heavy with summer leaves, the thick grass soft and sweet with fragrance when cut. Now the dry brittle leaves whirled and skittered across the ground and walkways blown by wind from the cold gray sky that matched the gray of the building and the cyclone fence that surrounded the mound just beyond the library building.

Felix recalled again as he always did the first time he had seen the park, the mound, and the building. That time had been late summer nearly autumn. The weather had been heavy, hot and humid, the park still filled with rich growth when he, just a boy, had come and stood before the mound amazed at its existence. He had read the plague fastened to the fence and had then gone off to meet his father and uncle who had left him alone to wander as he pleased exploring this place that at the time was new to him. Even now walking her in weather that was nearly winter cold and deadened, he recalled the wonder and the richness of that day. How he had imagined the mound opening, spilling before him the beauty of the world free from granite building, asphalt walkways, gold steel cyclone fence.

He had never told anyone about that day he had first wandered into the park. He had come to the city for the first time with his father and uncle and he had been allowed to wander by himself while his uncle went to have his severed fingers examined, treated, and rebandaged. He had never even told the girl beside him although they had sat on benches in the park beneath the canopy of trees watching the flow of cars and buses and the stream of students. How could he tell anyone? They would all laugh and think him odd or worse, and he knew that she would too.

The red light at the corner of the park stopped them. The brittle leaves scraped and rustled across the road. Crushed leaves powdered the gutter and the street with a soft brown. Green light. He touched the girl's arm and they moved across the street. The gray pavement beyond the park and stoplight marked the city center. A drive-in restaurant, one of the first in the city, always filled because of the novelty with narrow Formica counter, low vinyl covered stools with chrome trim, tables with plastic tops along the large windows, boxes along the counter that accepted coins for the jukebox against a wall.

He had been with her to this gathering place when it was surprisingly quiet. The lights on during the day were warm against the darkening sky, the traffic moving by outside unheard, yellow headlights dulled, traffic lights bright in color. That time had been one of the first he had eaten away from home on his own, and he thought that the occasion somewhat special because she had been with him.

Across from where they walked descending the gradual slope that ended at the Five Points intersection, a movie theater, the marquee already lit, the rows of bulbs flashing in streams, the young woman in the ticket booth whom he knew from attending the same class, a couple going into the lobby, an arm crooked replacing a wallet, the tickets torn, the stubs returned. Here, too, he had been with her sitting close in the warm darkness heavy with the scent of people and popcorn pressing toward her own ripe fragrances. Or he had come alone after practice while waiting for a ride home with his uncle, he tired of wandering the narrow stone-paved streets, tired of peering in through large paned windows reflecting the image of himself and the street behind him, tired of the gray granite buildings, the cars lined before meters, the flow of people passing glancing at him, tired of the odors of merchandise: the tire store, the bakery, the flower shop. So he had turned beneath the bright streaming lights of the theater and entered the dark warmth broken only by the dull light of confectionary stand and the heavy scent and quiet movements of people. Then he had groped through the dark toward a vacant seat before the bright blue vastness of the screen.

But now he passed with her on the walkway opposite the flashing line of bulbs and the girl in the glass cage staring vacantly out at the darkening street on which they passed.

Some stores were closing, and as they passed, he saw the darkened store fronts, the small light within revealing someone bent over the day's receipts glancing up as the couple passed then returning to the receipts. Felix peering through the darkness noted his own image, his arm extended, his hand upon the small of her back noticing the slow sway of her body as she walked beside him.

More stores: the old department store so old it seemed as from another era aging further as they passed: the dark wood, the bare wooden floor between high dark wood counters, wooden floors that sounded hollow beneath infrequent footsteps; the idle help dressed in spotless suit and undisturbed tie stood leaning on a stiff extended arm, the other arm upon the hip, a polished shoe on the point of the toe behind the crossed leg as the person watched people pass before ineffective open doors.

They reached the Five Points where each of five roads came from rolling hills, grasslands, forest, farmlands, lakes to where their point ended before the dark polished pillars of the bank.

They waited for the light. He had been here before so many times he couldn't tally them. She, too, had been here many more times most likely because she had lived here in the city all her life. But the first time he had been here had been what seemed now long ago. He would have difficulty explaining what he had experienced that time because what happened seemed now so circumstantial and so distant in that bright warm late summer afternoon when he had stood between the dark pillars of the bank staring at a single ray of sunlight that had broken through the covering of clouds and filled the street with a glowing gyre. He had stood at that very spot they were passing now, and he had heard what was then a wondrous noise, a murmur that had become a sound of mingled voices far away then growing as the sound echoed off the tall buildings and in the hollow of the street between. The sound had grown to that of a multitude of feet marching out of step. He had stood gazing at the ray of light listening to the growing sound then stared wide-eyed at the horde that came down the sloping street to the point of the bank.

He had marveled at their size, at the beauty of the older girls, all of them radiating an aura while they had passed.

Now here he was again years later—how many he refused to guess—standing waiting for the stoplight to change, he in the exact same spot where he had stood, and suddenly he saw a brief ghostly image of himself as a young boy between the pillars gazing at him as he stood waiting for the changing light. How enthralled he had been by the sound of the voices and the multitude of feet, the sight of sunlight off the hair and brightly colored clothing in the warm summer afternoon. Now here he was cold and dumb concerned only with her and his present situation. He wondered what the talk of those people had been about. He vaguely recalled expressions on the faces and in the gestures of the arms and head and movements of the body. But he had been ignorant of what any of it meant. Perhaps he now knew more.

The traffic light changed. They moved through half a circle of the compass pausing at one point on a small island of building and sidewalk then starting off again until they reached the awning of the old granite stone building with tall windows then turned and stood against the stone front watching the day grow dark.

The lights within the stores behind the large windows began to glow and brighten. Neon signs hung in the windows deepened in color. The interiors of stores evolved from behind the mirror of their reflections: counters appeared. People moved within the stores becoming apparent.

He moved to keep off the gathering cold stuffing his hands in his jacket pockets, burrowing his neck and shifting his weight from foot to foot. She hunched as well and turned toward him looking up from under her lashes offering an expression of innocence and sensuousness that always moved him.

"You don't have to wait," she said quietly. "The bus will be here soon."

"I'm all right," he said.

Then with the stillness broken he was able to finally express his concern. "Why do you have to go? Why don't you stay?" he asked almost pleading.

Her beguiling expression left her face. She assumed an air of indulgent patience. "Mom expects me home right after school. And I'm already late," she said.

"When will I see you again?" he asked. "I need to see you."

"We've been over all this," she said becoming petulant. You're so busy with your swim team and I have my club activities. There just isn't time for us to spend together. And Mom thinks you're too serious. She thinks we need more space and more time for other people."

"I don't need other people."

"Well, I do."

"I need you!" he said.

She moved away from him stepping out around him going down the front of the building. She went as far as the driveway between the building and a small grocery. There she crept into the shelter of the driveway and turned toward him as he followed as she knew he would. She looked past him at the street and flow of traffic ignoring him as if to punish him, for what, he didn't know. He bent his head toward the sidewalk. Tears came to his eyes. She glanced at him then turned. She laid her hand on his arm. "Don't cy," she said assuming again her indulgent voice. "Not about me."

He shook his head then turned further into the doorway of the grocery fighting for control. He suddenly was aware of where he was and his awareness made he wonder why he was crying. He tried to understand the sick feeling that came over him when he understood what was happening. Why should it matter? But then he insisted to himself that it did matter, that he was losing something that had become a dream. Later he would wonder if his sadness from the event came from his awareness that he couldn't always if ever control the conditions of his life and that those conditions would never again be the same as those when he was a child standing between the pillars of the bank opposite from where he now stood. Or perhaps his sadness came from his sense of loss after having had something and then having to accept that he would never have it again.

He understood finally that he didn't have an answer to any of his questions and that finally he really didn't care. Now what only mattered was his sense of loss at this time, in this place. Nothing else existed. Nothing else need exist.

He stood beside her in the doorway waiting for he knew not what. He wondered why he was waiting. What was there to wait for? He could wait just as readily at his uncle's car or where his uncle worked where it was warm or wait in the café at the corner where he could have something to eat or something to drink. He told himself that he later would do just that and watch as she passed whenever she came to wait for her bus. Or he would stand beside the trees along the dark river waiting for his ride watching her pass seeing her talking passing him by without noticing him or not acknowledging him if she did notice. And he wouldn't care.

The snow that began to fall was unnoticeable at first. Single flakes fell on coats and hair melting immediately. Then as the flakes increased, people proclaimed the first snow, paused in their movements, looked up in wonder then went on, some continuing to exclaim their renewed thrill at seeing the snow.

Felix and she huddled in the doorway of the storefront watching the increasing snowfall, the melting flakes wetting the sidewalk and caught now in headlights of cars that hissed over snow wet streets. Then falling more heavily and steadily, the snow obscured the colored neon lights and large glass panes of storefronts.

Felix stood dazed. He wished he could thrill to the first snow as he always had since he was a child. But this situation and his sadness only blinded him, made him numb and unaware. He wondered what she was thinking. She appeared expectant, moved by the snow, the soft beauty that muffled sounds. But to Felix the sounds seemed to roar and brake through the sheet of falling flakes.

A bus dusted with snow squished through the mushy gutter. The door hissed open letting out yellow light, heavy heated air of wet clothes and wet vinyl seats and wet aisle with sand. The cold outside the bus rushed in and met the young man swinging down from the stairs. The door hissed closed behind him. He stood squinting through the thick fall of snow, pulled at his colored stocking cap, and started up the street where he paused, came back, and saw the couple huddled in the doorway. He came in out of the snow. They moved back into the hollow to allow room for him.

"Hi!" he said speaking to the girl ignoring Felix, only briefly glancing at him and then only with an air of condescension.

"Hi, yourself!" she said. Her face brightened. She smiled her most dashing smile at the young man who had crowded in out of the snow.

"I stopped by your house," the young man said. "Your mother said you hadn't gotten home yet perhaps because of the snow. So I thought I'd come escort you home"

"That's sweet!," she said.

She continued to smile forgetting Felix who stood next to her watching the couple exchange smiles, he obviously excluded and suddenly understanding what the young man's arrival meant for him. He felt even more hopeless. He felt powerless to change the course of events that were now directing his life. He felt an utter sense of loss. Now there were no consoling adults. Here was his life, and he felt compelled to find meaning however feeble his efforts. He fought against his despair knowing he would lose. He felt as if events were going past and beyond him, that the comfort he had felt in the contact of human flesh and mind was ebbing and leaving him with the despair he fought while he watched the couple press upon each other ignoring him, the young man domineering, the girl submissive, almost coy in her response, so unlike what Felix had witnessed before. Felix felt sick inside. He stared in bitter disappointment at the moving traffic muffled by the snowfall, headlights piercing the falling flakes, exhaust curling up around the headlights of the cars behind as the they halted waiting for the traffic light to change.

Another bus pulled up through the thickened slush. The door hissed open issuing the yellow light, the green interior, the people peering out windows. The couple moved from the doorway leaving Felix alone. She glanced back once with a questioning look, moved to offer one final gesture but was pulled away by the young man who moved her toward the bus. The bus door closed. Felix saw her in the yellow light within the bus. The bus pulled away from the curb. Felix watched as she started back toward the rear of the bus walking toward him as she moved away on the bus. Then the outline of the bus blended into the curtain of falling snow. The red and amber moving lights glowed small above the shorter vehicles that crowded around the bus. The bus inched through the traffic toward the bridge then across the river and toward the bend in the road that finally hid it from his view.

He stood in snowfall huddled in his prized leather coat. Snow swirled into the doorway. He watched the moving figures in the heavy snowfall in the fading light. He watched the slowly moving traffic. The snowfall thickened sounds: dull, wet slap of windshield rubber blades; the roar and searing sound of engines revved from idle. The snowfall thickened movements: dark shapes moving past him, people bent and huddled treading cautiously without boots through the mush of snow that piled upon the walkway; the creeping cars, red glow of taillights, white blaze of headlights that caught the curtain of flakes; huddled figures in cars peering out through the windshield at the long line of slowly moving traffic.

He moved. He turned and started up the street the same way the bus had gone. He moved along the line of stalled cars ignoring them now. He came to a dark green front of a restaurant, large gold lettering framed in black upon the window, warm yellow light that streamed through the snowfall illuminating the mush on the sidewalk.

He reached darkness leaving the stores and lights behind and came to the bridge. The dark river swept between the banks dusted white by snow then beneath the bridge. He scooped snow from the railing and dropped it in the swirling water that swept it away beneath the bridge; then he went across the bridge and turned in across wood planks that led between the stacks of lumber dusted and wet from the snow.

He reached the car piled with snow and found it locked then stood by the cold railing along the river watching the dark water and the splay of colored lights and blaze of white lights through the snow. The world was quiet as he stood against the cold iron railing between dark trunks of trees, the branches heavy with snow.

He waited in the darkness until his uncle came. The doors unlocked, they entered. He felt wetter and more chilled within the dry cold interior. The engine whirred, choked, and then fired. The windshield wiper swept an arc of snow. They left the lumberyard moving slowly into the line of traffic.

Neither spoke until Felix climbed out in front of his home and they exchanged only a brief farewell. Now both sat heavy with their own thoughts while they moved slowly in the line of cars through the ruined snowfall of the city until the traffic eased then thinned and they gathered some speed heading for the dark soft virgin snow that lay upon the empty country road.

A Clear, Descending Light-3

[Late spring decades later]

Why had he returned? He stood now in the lobby of the old brick building, old even in his time when he had spent what had seemed like endless days here. The building seemed ancient now. No longer used for the purpose it had been built, used now for storage of old broken furniture, discarded items that some penny-foolish soul had clung to, the school building was now little more than a warehouse of stored relics that crowded out the vanished movements of vibrant bodies, deadened the ghostly echoes of clashing voices celebrating life, and left a yellow brick shell. He stood draped in a long unseasonable coat over equally unseasonable clothing among the dusty discards and debris looking both ways down the high old hallways. A stillness descended, hovered in the air: a scrape of chair leg on a wooden floor somewhere, a door closing, the latch slowly catching, a voice hung upon the silence, all these stilled by the very stillness, a disembodied voice in muted answer rose and gathered, suspended in the hollow. The stillness in the thick air between the stacked tan boxes and dusty furniture took up the sounds of traffic on the street outside: the rapid wump, wump, wump of car tires on the brick cobbles of the street, the cobbles relics of a vanished era, echoing the clop of hoof beat. Why had the cobbles never been paved? Why had they never been smoothed with black glaring asphalt sending back summer heat?

The high rounded windows above the stairwell still revealed the ancient oak trees, the branches stirring in the soft spring breeze, the new leaves moving in a whirl, caught in sunlight, settling, stirring, casting a dark shadow through the windows in the stairwell.

Homeport, he thought not knowing exactly why. Perhaps, just maybe, he could relax now. Even at the thought, as curious as it seemed, he felt his tension letting down. And he realized suddenly how uptight he had been. Why? The events of the previous few days? And he had thought that those events hadn't mattered. He had followed along unthinking through the ritual, the celebration of a memorial for a life passing. So it had been his mother? He had loved her in his fashion, but they had never been close, not since she had expelled him from her womb.

"Can I help you?" The voice was that of a woman, an older woman, perhaps not quite the age of his mother whose wake and encrypting he had recently attended.

The woman's voice disrupting his reverie made him turn among the pile of cardboard storage boxes. He searched her aging features. Did he know this wrinkled face before him? Who was this woman, rouged and powdered, clinging to a passing era, just as he was changing even now as he was passing. Did he know her? Had he? Did she know him? Probably not. No matter.

"Just looking," he said. I used to go here once. Some years ago. Before they built the new one."

"Oh, yes, I see," the woman said.

He watched her wrinkled mouth work as she spoke. Did she see? What? An aging man catching her in years?

"I won't be long," he said. In fact, he told himself, I've seen enough. He was ready to leave. He looked around at the piles of cartons. "It certainly has changed," he said finally.

"Yes," the woman said. "It's been this ways for some time."

"I imagine," he said. He turned toward the wide stairwell and the squares of glass panels in the large double door. "I'll let you get back to your work."

"Yes," the woman said. Her wrinkled red mouth worked. "Nice to see you again."

When had she seen him last? Never, probably. And if she had, she would most likely have forgotten. Surely she did not remember him from when he had moved through these halls when they were mackerel crowded and he a fresh-faced youth. Could she have recognized him? He would be pleased to think so. But already she was turning toward her own life, moving toward the dark framework of the frosted paned door with bold black lettering that still told the world that this was the building office. He nodded to her trying to reassure her as she glanced one final time before disappearing, her shadow fading from the yellow frosted paneling.

He started down the stairwell, the polished granite stairs ground to a concave hollow by the thousands of shoe soles that had scraped over them through the five decades or more that the building had been used as a school. Numbness gripped him. What had he really seen? Nothing. He had allowed himself to be frightened off by an old woman who hadn't really cared if he had been here. What did it matter to her? He stopped, turned back up the shoe worn stairs.

He walked the halls searching. The long banks of lockers mostly gone, discarded where? Why did any remain? He could still hear the ghostly clash of metal doors, the distant clang of combination lock banging to rest on locker doors. Here now within a space allowed by a break in the bank of lockers, the school's book storeroom. How nervous but important he had felt standing in the line that had snaked back along the corridor, he inching forward, shy behind the stylish, boisterous city girls flirting with the stylish city boys, he finally receiving his assigned texts that first year he had attended here. And, of course, in this line he had first seen her as she had approached through the crowded hallway boisterous and self-assured, unlike he who was not assured of anything, especially himself.

Continuing past the shut door of what had been the book store, he reached the study hall where he had spent two periods with different seats adding to his self-conscious confusion when some city kid purposely took the wrong seat raising a commotion settled finally by the teacher-monitor's commands that had only increased the turmoil. The tall windows covered with cross-wire screens to ward off flying objects from PE classes still made the room seem like a prison. He had thought so even then.

The long rows of varnished desks bolted to wooden rails were gone. Yet he could see the spot where he had sat. He saw the image of that city girl he had witnessed in the hallway now in the desk before him, soft, warm, sending up rich fragrant essences of powder and cologne. She had snubbed him at first as a country hick; then as the days passed in their slow procession, she had turned toward him more and more to ask for his help with her school work that he found easy, their heads together, her face, ripe lips, dark lashes, bright blue eyes so close he had thrilled before the study hall monitor looked up from his desk on the raised stage in front.

Now the stage remained barren, empty of the desk at which the man had sat, his hair graying, hound jowls hanging, his always blood-webbed eyes searching through puffy lids. Later, the man had been his physics teacher as well, a recollection that brought to mind precise experiments the man had led them through instructing them by means of physical laws on how to drive dangerously and live to tell the tale. Where now that wise wreck of a man? Dead most likely. He had heard about the man and a sudden rupturing of the heart. In the stillness, he was suddenly aware of the quiet throbbing pulse at his temple.

He had come to know that young girl in study hall—perhaps too well. Their lives had become inextricably, perhaps inexplicably bound. How boisterous she, how quiet he staring, watching, inspecting, self-conscious of his nascent stirrings, his nascent urge. They had talked too much bringing warning stares from the man raised upon the stage. What had that man gone through? He, too, now returned had taught for a while at the same level. "We probably killed him," he confessed to himself now.

More recollections of the girl came crowding. So many filled his mind: The football game. Her silent potent invitation, a mere look that had said it all; then he on the seat beside her and she so close. The sudden quilt he had felt then, and that he felt even now:

He had come to the game with a new friend, a boy he had in most of his classes. He had been to dinner at the boy's home. Even now he saw the way they had gone from the school to the boy's house: streets lined with trees, the houses elegant becoming spare, scattered, and then the free, unbroken landscape of hills and pasture, ditches, streams, some fences that they had to climb, grazing horses, too; then the tract of new houses, one of the first in the area. He had marveled at the newness of the houses and their modernity. Anything modern impressed him, he admitted, even now. The new friend had just moved from Colorado. Bright in both math and science, he had worn clear-rimmed glasses and quietly stated that he was going into nuclear physics. Where was he now? Had he succeeded to his dream?

Sitting beside the girl, he had lost interest in the game, despite his new friend. Then he and the girl had walked back through the darkened streets following the others to the school to the gymnasium softened by small yellow lights and dance music. They had stood on the balcony of the in-door track watching the others stream onto the floor and begin to move to the music. She had coaxed and teased him to follow her down to the crush of bodies on the floor below. He had thrilled to her touch, her closeness, her soft fullness, her close movements along with his. That for the longest time was the closest they ever came to having sex.

He turned now and sought the hallway then sought the hidden door he found still there, then crept through and stood upon the oval hung against the wall below the steel beams of the gym. How many times had he been here? How many times had he run this track, circling endlessly, shaping his body, breaking it, challenging it? He heard the ghostly echo of pounding feet. He saw again the ghostly images of a host of boys running (he included) still running, running throughout eternity, damned ghosts avoiding now the barrier stacks of dusty boxes crowding the oval that hung beneath the steel rafters above the wooden floor below. For what mortal sin had they been condemned to such an endless circular pursuit? He thought of Dante's *Inferno*.

He recalled his father's friend who years before had run upon an oval track similar to this one; he had won races, too, nearly won the city title, or so the friend would boast sitting at their kitchen table, cards held before him near his chest, cigar smoke circling toward the ceiling, beer glass half empty to his right, his middle-aged body sagging to a paunch.

Now the single echo of a closing door, of footsteps, someone's clearing throat, a hollow voice. He searched the wire windows, the light and trees and houses and green leaves beyond.

"Are you still *here?*" the working wrinkled mouth accused, challenging him. She stood with head back looking up at him peering down at her lost in the cavern of the gymnasium floor.

"Just leaving," he said.

He turned and fled seeking warm sunlight. Again the concave granite steps, the green walls, the high rounded windows, then the iron railing he had sat on bordering the bright lawn that he often had lounged on. Bright black paint caught the soft spring sunlight and rippled beneath his hand as he fled down the stairs to the walk, to the street lined with ancient, rough-barked trees. He slowed. He searched the street and the scabrous dark branches of the vaulted trees, the new green leaves that caught the sunlight arched across the cobbled street shading the sidewalk in a soft green glow. Passing cars broke the patterned sunlight, cars rippling underneath the shadowed glowing light sending flashes from the red brick roadway, cars moving underneath the high vault of leaves passing toward the open square of park and the buildings beyond where the city center began. He watched the cars, the sleek gleaming metal, the dark sheen of windows mirroring the trees and the sunlight. Tires rumpled over the red cobbled roadway in their passing. He turned and followed.

The tunneled canopy beneath the trees spread and soared over the freshening green lawn of the square. In the center, the granite building, old even at the time he had first seen it. A Carnegie library very much like the one he had visited while a boy seeking books by Hugh Lofting about Dr Doolittle who could talk to animals or his seeking books about insects and ants, especially ants, wondrously thick books with tissue thin pages and a multitude of images. How impressed he had been on visiting that first library and now this one of almost exact design, both buildings formidable, almost sanctified. He had marveled at the people passing in through the dark wood doors. He wondered now if such buildings were raised to retain such childish awe as he had then. Were such buildings to impress the child, to intimidate that child, discourage the budding pride, subdue the sense of growing strength and of individual purpose?

The asphalt path crossed through the park. He followed to the center, stood looking down the path beneath the cathedral of trees to where it broke beneath the bright grass. A dark, iron hitching post, relic of the past, then the high sloping lawn leading to the dark wood of ancient houses, so old any whispers of mortality had faded, human odors so intermingled they had been lost in a heavy dreariness of years.

A sigh heaved from his chest in relief from the thought that had slowed his breathing to a shallow movement. He stood upon the center of the walk, a well-dressed man those passing glanced at then openly inspected, turning their heads as their bodies moved forward, glancing backward from a distance some paces down the walkway that led out from underneath the trees to the safety of the city. Then as he lost the image of himself standing there in the center of the asphalt cross for all to witness, he inspected the round granite front of the library—Victorian, ornate Carnegie, glass door in its wooden frame, white globes upon black iron pillars.

How many times had he climbed those concrete stairs, the granite stairs within the doors, past the ivory statues, past the large curved varnished oak circulation desk, past the side rooms—the dark reference room with dark wooden tables, dark heavy volumes in endless, towering rows, then the sunny children's room, rainbow colors of the books upon the shelves, bright posters, bright sunlight through the cross-ribbed windows, down the dim aisles lit from above by flowered globes of light, down past the multitudes of time-faded books to the cubicle with high windows that overlooked the field hockey court, the high wire fence that separated the wooden houses from the park and the small band shell.

He had sat in one cubicle or another, watched the day change from sunlight becoming deep blue before it became black, the dim globes among the darkened book stacks glowing dull yellow, neon lights from the stores and building beyond the park deepening in color in vivid contrast to the blue of gathering night.

During lunch periods or waiting for swim practice after his last class, he had stood unseen at the tall curved window of the cubicle watching the raptured circle of faces following the silent heat flushed features of the two boys stripped to undershirts who had moved in a primal dance on the crush of orange and yellow leaves upon the grass, circling, watching, jabbing, lashing out, rushing in to flay, to pound, then breaking back, feinting, inching in again. He had witnessed the heavy breathing, the blood above the eye, the bloody teeth, the stringy, sweat-soaked hair. Then some adult had come to separate the combatants, pushing through the circle that had broke and scattered before the loud angry words, the outer edges of the circle having slunk away, glancing back, pausing in flight before the mass of mingling bodies broke before the righteous anger, words more mighty than fists. He had stood apart at the tall curved window watching the two boys heaving breathless, arms hanging, head hung, listening to the indignant voice berating. Shirts were put back on; books retrieved from beside the tree trunk where they had been dropped; crushed leaves remained upon the trampled, littered lawn. He had later learned that the fight had been fought over a few pennies, or the theft of affections, over a slur, a curse, over a challenge, or simply from the pure love of fighting. Love always found a way.

He had returned to Shakespeare's sonnets, to Shelley and Keats, the Song of Solomon, the Book of Job, books on human reproduction with drawings of male and female genitalia that he had lingered on, books on astronomy with black plate images of vast white eternity. His mind had raced away filled with numb awe, agape, amazed and ultimately filled with an inexplicable fear. Recalling all this, he thought of Pascal.

Then a stir within, a heaviness that had moved him from the wooden seat back down the aisles past the curved desk, the ivory statues, down the granite stairs, this time turning aside down the narrow stairway to the damp, dank cellar of ribbed ceramic, dark gray concrete, odors of wet urine, of mold, and dark green walls that had always made him shiver, made him shiver now, remembering.

The shiver brought him up to sunlight, to warmth beneath the vault of trees, the gray curved front, the glass doors, the wooden frames, the round white globes on dark iron pillars. He turned toward the woven wire fence galvanized gray, the plaque. Here he was again. How many more times would he come here? Why was he here now? Why would he come again? Where then the design? What he saw instead was coincidence. How odd those unanticipated happenings that had *taken place* when he had been just a boy and then later an adolescent. Both times he had been thrust into the same location almost by accident:

The first time was an unexpected day trip with his father and uncle.

The second time he attended the high school here that had been the only secondary school available, was also the county seat, and he lived in a town outside the city. An added twist had been that he had moved to that county town with his father, mother, and brother because they had been evicted from the house they lived in when he had made that first day trip. Yet another tenuous connection had been through his having visited the city to display his exhibit for a science fair held in the gymnasium of the high school. While tending his display, he had been fascinated by the building because of its structure and age. And during a break, he had wandered down to the square he had come to know as Library Park where he had studied again the library so much like the one he had frequented as a boy and then had stood again outside the cross-wired steel fence gazing at the cone-shaped burial mound. Both the school and the park with its library and mound had moved him to choose the school here rather than one in the metropolitan from which he had been forced to move. But he had rationalized his choice by claiming that the school was more academically rigorous than any metropolitan school. What he had really said was "it's a tougher school." And he also had said somewhat snobbishly that he preferred the challenge.

This time, however, he had been deliberate in seeking this place. But why deliberate?

The burial mound surrounded by fence rose up before him green with ripening grass, patched with shade and sunlight through the rich leafy covering of the dark trees. But nothing happened this time, not like that first time. No splitting earth now that spilled the bones, the colored beads and baskets. No vision of the smoke of village cook fires, the muffled sounds of forest voices, forest footsteps. He remembered—he could at least remember—but that was all past. Nothing now appeared, nothing would happen. He knew that now finally. He turned from the mound. The path of asphalt, once a earthen forest path led him toward the warm open sunlight off the buildings. He felt suddenly cold and bitter. What was he finally leaving behind?

Coming out of the park, he stood upon the pavement waiting for the signal. He gazed down the gradual incline toward the busy five-point intersection at the bottom. He searched for a sign among the flow of people, the quick movements, the intermingling color of hair and light spring clothes. He searched the whirl and clash of traffic, the crisscrossing cars, of engines, gears, and rising blue exhaust; he saw the sunlight filling the street between the yellow buildings. Yellow? He couldn't remember them as yellow!

The light changed. He started down the incline searching for a sign. The storefronts, how had they changed? How could he tell? He had only vaguely been aware the many times that he had ambled down this hill consumed by what he had thought was love but had only been unsatisfied lust. What was there left now after all these years? What feeling did he have now after the changes through which he had survived? Only vaguely did he recall the stores and neon signs and store fronts, the smaller ones anyway, for there was the department store with its wide panes of glass, the displays that seemed to show no change. He could recall only the style of clothes then. These displays he saw now were *a la mode*, changing as style had changed. There were other changes. The dark wooden frames (had they ever been new) were gone. Bright metal framed the windows. Wood interiors were gone. Worn wooden stairs that hollowed with footsteps, wooden floors worn bare and yellow as the stairway, the high dark counters, all were gone. Wide banners on the windows proclaimed a remodeling sale. Here, then, was change, but what of these smaller window fronts. The angle of sunlight on the pavement, the street in shade that lichened the buildings and the dark storefronts: the thin black band that squared the window, the large black lettering, the dim pale green interior, the slant of sunlight on the wall, the window display, the white doily, the vase, the roses. Had he ever seen these here before? Where else might he have seen them?

Move on—the incline compelled his movement. Where was he going? Why, for what, was he searching? He heard his footsteps, saw the shaded concrete, the sheen of storefronts, the brick and block that rose above him and then the sky, the vault of blue.

The bottom of the incline lay ahead, that intersection of the five points where the roadways from the rolling hills and countryside met at this place in the round fronts of buildings on opposing sides, the points of buildings at the islands, the two streets that intersected, and his, the third, tangent to both. He thought of his second year geometry class and the tiny woman teacher who appeared ancient with her wrinkled face, her hands seemingly larger because of her small size, her thin arms that revealed the bones and veins, the twisted fingers as she held the stick of chalk while she led them through proofs. Yet, despite her patience, he had not done well struggling to prove Euclid's axioms. He had asked for help from his uncle supposedly good at math, but even then he had struggled. He had been relieved to pass the class.

He came down the tangent past the jewelry store with huge rounded windows that caught the light and the images of busy intersection and cast them back blue and distorted. The windows of the jewelry store were framed by dark wood that made the store always seem dark even in the bright sunlight of midsummer. He passed beneath the octagonal metal clock set upon a high ribbed metal pole. Here it was then, the clock he had remembered in other places, distant places—Gas town in Vancouver, B.C.—where he had remembered without remembering exactly. There had only been a vague fleeting image.

Here he was, then. Why? What changes had he sought? No! What permanence did he seek? What did he notice now? He searched. The same gray rounded buildings meeting him, his search finding the same silent inscrutable fronts. Existing before he had, they still existed, would exist even after he was only a fleeting recollection. In whose mind? So he brooded, for he had observed the full moon and once had a similar thought—the moon—lovely goddess—had existed long, long, before he or any of those whom he had lived with had met, had loved, had quarreled with, had abandoned for someone else or for some always vanishing dream—would exist long, long after he and all the others were gone back into the void. Now before him the same wide panes of glass that sheered and flattened the island points: Walgreen's glass doors with plastic handles, glass cases, green lunch counter and the vinyl chrome trimmed stools where he had sat with her, with others, had waited for his uncle and the ride home, now that place was abandoned and unlit leaving empty shelves, the black and white checked floor dusty and strewn with kibble, the lunch counter and stools gone.

The signal changed from red to green but he remained, turned aside, and crossed the cobbled narrow street that he had followed to this point here and now. He noted the ice cream parlor on one of the five points. That store had once been a clothing store for women. When and why had that other store closed? When had this one opened? On a whim, despite the chill of the day, he crossed and entered. A young woman was alone. About the same age as those whom he had pursued decades ago, her greeting was cheery. He admired her young, lovely face, her long blond hair set in a ponytail. He surveyed the flavors in the showcase. He ordered then studied her young lithe form in tight jeans as she bent to scoop out his flavors into a paper cup, the jeans worn thin and pale where she sat. Oh, to be so young and attractive! Then taking the paper cup and plastic spoon he went to sit at a table that mimicked those of similar stores in another era, one perhaps in which his father had worked when about the age of the young appealing woman who had served him. While he ate from his paper cup watching her move about the store in her lithe body and tight jeans, she coming near him straightening chairs so near that he could breathe in her youthful scent, he recalled again the young women of his time as she now chatted with him gaily since he was the only one in the store, her closeness, her fragrance, and her youth slightly erotic. Then, as always, a young man about her age entered and greeted her as if he knew her well, and she chatted with her friend while ignoring him until he finished his dish, rose, deposited the paper cup in the disposal canister, thanked her, she off handedly returning his remark, and he left.

He moved toward the round black pillars and the swell of speckled gray stone that loomed above him as he crossed the street to the bank. Here were changes, then. Glass doors now instead of brown wood and brass bars gleaming golden. The counters and cages gone and instead one long low plastic covered separation instead of high wire cages with dark wood paneling and gold bars that hid the tellers, guardians to him then, hoarders of the wealth that he had then only really begun to appreciate. Now the lowness, unobtrusive counter exposed the smiling, pleasant looking women behind. But were these changes? Hadn't all this come about when he had still been here? Perhaps, he guessed. But one thing remained: The mosaic in the floor, the colored stone, the image of a First American, the letters spelling out the indigenous sounding name of the noble edifice that he could now pronounce readily. He heard the clink of a coin. He started; he searched, just as he had those years ago. But now, as always, he found no stray treasure. And the light seemed different now. How different? Artificial. Florescent. The old interior had been dim and broken by the rays of sunlight slanting through the gold leafed windows—or so he recalled.

He turned; he stood between the pillars where he had stood that day now so long ago those pillars he had seen then and that he now imagined seemed unreal and that boy he had been not really him. He briefly inspected the smooth speckled pillars as if somehow they would help redeem that long ago time; then he turned to search the five points.

Whom did he know here now? That youth whom he had met by accident, had never seen before, and thankfully never saw again? He had been alone then having been abandoned by her who had yielded to the gallant courtship of a college man. So he had gone to an afternoon movie while waiting for the ride home with his uncle who was working a second job at Walgreen's as a fry cook after finishing his day at the lumber yard.

He and the youth had left the movie theater at the same time. The young man had begun speaking to him, but he hadn't understood any of what the youth had uttered and couldn't remember now. Yet he had followed that strange young man through various places, the youth babbling a continuous stream of incomprehensible words, they ending finally on top the building of the jewelry store above the doctor's office his uncle had gone to that day long ago. They had gone through a door to the overhead apartments that had been surprisingly unlocked. Then the strange young man had climbed the black steel ladder to the trapdoor that allowed them access to the roof, and he had followed.

The bitter, cloudless night had been even colder on the high open roof that was caked with ice and dirty frozen snow. Then another surprise, shocking really, when the youth had begun picking up chucks of ice and frozen snow, going to the front of the roof where it curved above the rounded front of the building, and tossing them over the side to the street below. Stunned at the boy's indifference to what might happen to anyone below, he had told the boy that the boy was crazy and that he was leaving. Then he had fled descending to the street below, dodging the plummeting chucks that the youth had continued to hurl at him while continuing to laugh.

Would anyone remember him, he who stood here wondering? Why would he expect such recognition? Had he anticipated someone emerging from the steady flow of pedestrians, someone who would call his name, remark at his return, wonder at his having changed so little despite the interval of years. He glanced at this reflection in the plate glass window of the bank. There it was again, always startling him. So that's how he looked now to others. The letters broke his image. How had he changed? How much? Would he meet anyone he knew? Would they know him? What would he do? Stand awkward and uncomfortable hoping that the meeting wouldn't last? That the person wouldn't feel compelled to invite him for a drink, a meal, most likely an unexpected, unwanted mutually bitter experience for both?

Whom else did he remember besides that crazy youth he would never forget? Where were any of them now? He searched the intersection hoping and dreading. The flow of traffic, the changes in the pitch of engines, mufflers, gears; the storefronts still unchanged. How could he know if they had changed, the buildings remained the same: the restaurant, pink stucco front, the two odd narrow off-set doors, the neon sign, the hint of tall wooden booths and wooden kitchen doors through the lettering on the window. People moved within, a man waited at the counter, another at the cash register fumbling through his pockets, paying, leaving, pausing outside the door, replacing the billfold, then turning and stepping in among the flow of people moving up the street. Did he know the man? No, but he watched the man move up the street past the candy store, the white blocked building with the hemispheres for windows, the small red fronted grocery store where he had stood with her that late fall afternoon when she had abandoned him and he had remained when she had left on the city bus with "the older college man" who had suddenly arrived during the snowstorm to gallantly escort her home. He studied the green front of the other restaurant that he remembered more in nighttime when the neon of the window had darkened and bathed the sidewalk in a rosy light that cut the darkness; the auto store; the department store, both gone now; here, then was a change; and then the white ringed fence, the public parking lot where the man turned aside and vanished. Then the bridge and the swiftly flowing river always dark always flowing, from where to where, he would never know.

He returned his search to the intersection. This time he searched the corner he had stood at before crossing, examined the high-pillared clock, the round windows of the jewelry store, the thin neon letters in the window, the dim interior, the sheen and flash of gems and jewelry. He stopped his search at the window top, the rounded window with its dark wood frame, the high clock, the cobbled street, the gray corner of the bank in front of which he now stood, all stopped him, made him tilt his head in wonder. What was it? No, rather, *where* was it? He scanned the sky. No clear, descending light broke through the clouds. For now there were no clouds. Now if the light should come, perhaps bathing him again in its splendid gyre of substance and debris, would he see it; would he understand its deep illumination?

Who needed clouds? He stood in sunlight now. He stood and watched the bright glimmer of sunlight off the buildings, the bright whirl of colors, the flash of shining autos, paint and glass and chrome. He caught the bright flash of color from the clothing of the people moving through the five points of the intersection, the pale faces above the bright clothing. He stood and watched the colors move from sidewalk to dark asphalt, across the traffic stripes, in front of waiting autos, to the opposite sidewalk. He stood and searched the intersection; then he searched his memory to recall again that light that had broke through clouds. But again now there was no light; now there were no clouds.

He gave up and shook his mind from the fog that had made him stare so hard that a young boy passing had gazed enraptured at the aging man staring into space, gazed even while he passed so that his head turned as he passed even while he moved past the man so that the boy turned and he walked backward looking at the man before he turned toward his own world among the windows of the stores, the colors, the odors and aromas and fragrances, and the radiant sunlight of the street.

He broke from his haze and watched the boy move up the street wandering from metered car to mirrored window, stepping over the sidewalk cracks deliberately avoided; he watched the stops to search the windows, the sudden starts, the near collisions with pedestrians, the boy always unscathed; he watched the boy until the boy had turned a corner. Then he turned from his own darkening wall, around his own corner, the corner of the bank, and started up the incline past old remembered stores dim in memory, dim with time, dim with the quiet sunlight off the shaded street. He went back up the hill. The stone blocks and black pillars of the bank receded behind him.

He stopped at the intersection at the top; he glanced down the narrow side streets taking in for one last time quaint brick buildings, the old stone buildings from another time more lost than his own. He crossed the street, came to the lush green park with its trees and their rough dark trunks; the mound, the dull gray fence, the round library front, the high rounded windows, the globes of light on black iron pillars. He reached the yellow brick school, the black iron railings, the pale green grass, and the empty window of the rooms that he had filled with his life.

He rushed up the walk, through the doors, down the corridor before anyone might hear the door relatching. He sought the passage tunnel from the older yellow building to what had been the new annex now dated as well. He recalled dreams in which he had searched through such a passageway with yellow walls hoping in his dream to find a way out. But those dreams had only led him down twisting brown vinyl stairs to another endless corridor much like those he moved through now in dim light over dirty brown vinyl tile to the yellow steel door.

He pulled on the handle, surprised but relieved when he found that the door came open. He entered the locker room. Here still the gray brown concrete floor, the brown lockers scarred and bruised and bent. He went along the narrow passage to the pool that was drained now, of course. He stood at the edge of the tiled depression, the deep end sloping to the shallow where he had helped some hesitant younger kids learn how to float. He gazed at the black lane stripes along the bottom that he had viewed so often through the haze of blue water while swimming lap upon what seemed endless lap often thinking of her; he noted the depth markers along the side and the alcoves that once held benches on which he had rested during practice.

He turned, went back to the locker, stopped, then suddenly removed his coat, his shoes and socks, his shirt and trousers, his t-shirt and boxers so that he stood naked on the cold concrete floor among the lockers, his warm loins stirring when he thought of the young woman in her tight seat-worn jeans who had served him ice cream. He walked to the line of tiled showers. He twisted the handle. Nothing. What had he expected? He stood in the silence. He saw himself standing in this exact same place decades before listening to and gazing at the trickle of water down the floor drain while he studied the wet tiles imagining himself decades in the future standing where he now stood. Well, he had at least accomplished that.

But was that why he had come? To accomplish only this? Had he come in search of lost times in a sudden vague attempt to redeem those times? How redeem them? Why? Would being here again standing naked and alone in place he had once felt so full of life and hope and promise ease the sense of failure, the intimation that most of what he had done, especially with people, had ended in disappointment if not disaster, that he had fallen short in achieving what he had aspired to? And what did all this searching, all these dark, troubling thoughts, have to do with his mother's passing? If only he had told her just once his true, deep feeling? He suppressed a sudden sob that choked him threatening to overwhelm his self-control. And what if she—just once—had truly responded to what he might have confessed? Too late again, as always. And he suddenly recalled a comment he had overheard made by a colleague: "He never finishes anything!" So it goes, he conceded. Was he now finished, at least here, now, in this place that had always haunted him?

He woke from his séance. He went back to where his discarded clothes lay heaped on the concrete floor. He dressed. He left.

Outside the day was as it had been, as it always would be here, in this place as it had been before time itself, before anyone had been here to notice, long before those who now lay as hollow residue beneath the mound in the nearby park, gift of Carnegie, the supreme puritan capitalist. A mild warm breeze, the soft sun bringing for a fleeting moment how the world as it had been and had looked once, alive, fresh, and pure. He walked the short distance to the car gazing at the sunlight as it played among the stirring leaves of the ancient trees that had been here when he had first seen them and that were here now and would remain if they never troubled any civic minded soul who would campaign to have the trees chain sawed, the street widened, the redbrick roadway covered with asphalt icing.

He thought of Libby the young man still more adolescent than adult who had amused everyone and attracted needed attention by cruising the streets surrounding the school in a used and battered hearse always hesitant to start and always willingly filled with vibrant pubescent bodies who helped push start the moribund vehicle.

Libby had died of leukemia the day of graduation, the report of his death arriving and announced to those gathered and graduating during the ceremony celebrating the end of one phase of their lives and launching them into another phase still unknown while Libby's had ended his unfulfilled. The news coming in the soft early June night beneath the stars, of course, brought pause before the onset of ritual festivities.

He thought of Carmona a short, dark, intense Latino youth who had pursued him for reasons he never had understood, Carmona fighting everyone and anyone in an instance, some of those fights that he had witnessed through the curved window of the library. That lad's life, too, had ended before launching into a new era, not in a used and battered hearse but in a crushed car one rainy night the same night, according to reports by companions, that he had lost his virginity, he most likely crying to the Blessed Mother when he could no longer hold back the compelling urge and he had let go, his seed that held a coiled legacy of ancient sorrow and gory sacrifice bursting into the blood gorged womb.

He reached the car, climbed in, and started the engine. He sat for a while looking through the windshield at the sunlight off the hood of the car and the shimmer of sunlight among the stirring leaves of those eternal trees that lined the brick paved street. He sat for a while looking down through that green vault of trees that seemed more a tunnel to the vast blueness of the sky above the Nineteenth Century buildings clustered at the five point intersection where he had stood as a boy between the black pillars of the bank those decades ago.

Then he engaged the gears, swung the car around in a U-turn, and drove away without looking back.

One Morning Sure

When he returned—not to see her or the child—but to visit Ward and the woman his friend had eventually married, one of the first events mentioned in talking about old times they had shared had to do with Marnie.

"Oh? How is she?" Claude asked.

They were eating breakfast on his first morning there. He watched Dee move around the kitchen bringing food to the table. He had been surprised to see that Ward had married her. Of all those his friend had know she had seemed the most unlikely choice. A slight girl with not much of a figure, she wore dark-rimmed glasses that made her seem owlish. Yet before Claude had left, she had come around regularly to where Ward and he lived to clean up for them by doing the dishes, buying food for them from time to time when they were low on funds that weren't too abundant at any time. She cooked for them as well, so he guessed that her persistence had finally won out. Now a strange smile came to her thin face when he asked about Marnie.

Oh, she's fine," Dee said. "She had her baby."

Claude at first ignored her remark and leaned over to fork up the last of his eggs. "I'd imagine so," he said finally. He pushed away his plate. "It's been three years. What she have?"

"A girl," Dee said.

"That long?" Ward asked. Ward lit a cigarette and offered Claude the pack, but he refused having given them up. "That long," Ward said again shaking his head.

Claude had first seen Marnie from time to time moving in and out of the same group in which he had first met Ward. Their meeting was characteristic, for everyone in that group seemed to wander in and out around each other—sort of like the searching characters in one of the plays they were continually producing.

He had come to know the group rather casually, so he never really considered himself a part of that milieu. He had known one of them from his hometown, a tall, horsey girl with big teeth and large, protruding eyes who had told him quite dramatically but softly about the West Coast, Southern California to be more precise, and how she was going out there to become an actress. So when he had arrived in the same area after having spent time in Eastern Oregon, he had looked her up.

Then he had moved in with Ward whom he had met at several of the cast parties. An intense, powerfully build man, Ward's reddish hair, his gray hard eyes, and boxer's nose didn't make him a pretty boy. He admitted that. So instead of going after the lead in plays, he committed himself to character parts by means of which he aspired to steal the show. Others who were well known, some even in films as featured actors, had made it on the basis of that technique. So Ward thought that he would too. Ward had always been involved in some aspect of theater, and Claude and he had lived together as casually as they had met. They had gone their separate ways most of the time, had avoided each other most of time, had respected the other's privacy when one of them had overnight quests.

Ward had entertained a great deal, and Claude had always found difficult shutting out the muffled urgent sounds in the quiet darkness of their one bedroom apartment with him using the sofa for a bed to accommodate Ward's entertaining his frequent sleepovers. The next morning was always a bit strange because Ward and his guest would emerge from the bedroom laughing and friendly, greeting Claude who had risen early and had moved about the room quietly so as not to disturb them from their needed sleep after their heated endeavors. Then they would all go to breakfast at some nearby café. Claude never could help feeling odd talking calmly and intellectually to a woman sitting across from him whom he had heard crying out in passion the night before. One had smiled at him from across the table, and he had hated himself a little for wanting her. All these moves, however, were taken quite casually. The cast parties were the same way, and that's where Claude had met Marnie.

"She still living with her parents?" he asked.

"You still interested, fella?" Ward teased.

"Forget it. Curious, that's all."

Ward wagged his stubby finger. "Remember the last time."

"O.K. O.K." Claude said. He felt himself getting angry, but he checked himself. Ward sensed his mood and quieted. They drank their coffee, and Ward smoked.

"What she name it?" Claude offered trying to make up for his silly anger. Dee told him and he repeated the name to himself adding his surname. "Not bad," he said.

"I don't know why you ever let her do it," Dee said.

He couldn't answer her.

"Have you seen her?" Ward asked.

Claude shook his head. "Maybe I should drop around."

"Ward!" Dee said. "Don't start things!"

"What the hell!" Ward said. "He ought to see his own kid."

Claude looked at both of them amazed. What was all this about? He wondered. "What she doing now?" he asked. Something was happening between them he couldn't understand. He didn't want them fighting about something he had done, especially now when he had found out that they weren't getting along too well lately.

"She's working. She's a supervisor now."

"Really? Where she live? He saw her hesitate then look at Ward, her dark eyes startled behind her glasses. Ward shrugged as if to say, "Who's starting it now?"

"Next door."

"Really!" Claude exclaimed. He heard a child cry.

"Nicky," Dee said relieved, and she left to take care of her son.

Claude saw Marnie that night. Ward and he dropped into Roy's place for a beer or two. He was glad to see the bar still going and that most of the same people he had known were still there. Marnie was sitting at the bar talking to Roy. They were quite a complement. She was light, almost pale compared to Roy, her long blond hair fine. She seemed voluptuous, a little heavy, her body soft. In contrast, Roy was lithe and dark. She was attractive in her own way, but she seemed slow, most likely from the way she spoke, always hesitant before she said something. But Roy broke immediately into a wide grin. Claude was glad that Roy remembered him. Roy offered Claude the same long dark hand.

Roy had bought the place shortly before Claude had left. Near where Ward and Claude used to live together, they had found the place easy for them to stroll down to in the evening for a couple of beers. They had found that going to Roy's was unique because most of Roy's customers as Roy himself were black. Claude and Ward hadn't considered themselves liberal or anything close. They simply liked Roy who had from time to time been part of the group in which Ward and Marnie circulated. A tall man with a long face that displayed his bones, heavy lips and perfect teeth, he often used his features to mime the black stage stereotype. And through Roy's mediations, they had come to know and enjoy the people they had met there.

At times the tension admittedly became high, especially after Ward's group began coming to Roy's. Some of them hadn't liked the attention that the women received from Roy's other customers, and the situation really got tight when the women responded openly to the attention they received. But Roy usually kept control by cracking jokes and playing the clown, and Jim, the enormous cook, helped with his friendliness and his strength.

The reaction of Ward's group had seemed strange in a way because they really hadn't appeared to care about anything except themselves and the importance of the part they would be acting in their next production. So they formed a small closed company in a small world of their own making. Coming together without touching, meeting only out of mutual self-interest in hopes that what they were doing together might lead to something bigger, they rehearsed then performed. After the run of the play, they held the traditional cast party that frequently turned into a bacchanal after everyone had imbibed sufficiently. Then they again began wandering in all directions, turning up again, meeting in the most accidental places: a cloistered café, a speedy car wash where they exchanged reports about their successes in acting as well as their flops. Only incidentally did they talk about their offstage, everyday lives. Their stage lives bound them and gave them purpose and identity. So they talked only about their stage lives when they met.

Sometimes they seemed more like characters, people with no real personalities of their own because they were always acting—so it appeared to Claude. One, for example, became the Sewer Man after a character in a play by Giraudoux. He had played the part as a cartoon character emphasizing his already enormous bulk by wearing a too-small derby, bibbed overalls, and rubber boots. After his "fantastic" success, he was always the Sewer Man. Another was the Rebel, a slight angular lad who slouched around in red windbreaker and jeans always scowling, eternally misunderstood. A third was The Ingénue with long blood hair wrenched back in a ponytail accentuating her gaunt face. She talked continually about her game of Lover Roulette, but the others referred to her behind her back as Old Bevel Heels. And, of course, there was Marnie.

"You remember Marnie, don't you?" Roy asked.

Claude turned to her. That slight wry smile of hers played at the corners of her succulent mouth. "Yes," he said. How could he forget? "How are you?" He asked acknowledging her.

"Fine," was all she said never one for talking.

Claude ordered beers all around. Roy came from behind the bar, and they went to an empty booth by the window. Ward wandered off to mingle, and Claude sat across from Marnie and Roy. For some reason, Claude kept noticing the red glow from the sign in the window reflected off the peeling walls, the dark wood of the booth, the brown bottles, and the wet rings on the tabletop. A scratched record still crooned the blues above the low voices, the same record he had heard the one time he had Marnie alone.

It had rained that night. Perhaps the wet rings on the table made him think of heavy rain, one of those Southern California rains that heaves to downpour then settles to a steady drench that drips in globes from thick flowering bushes soaking the abundant plants, beading then dropping to the spongy grass in the rain-steeped night. That night the rain in a way had been responsible for his taking Marnie home.

That night when Ward and he had arrived at the party they shook themselves from their coats, went to the kitchen with their bottle then carried their drinks back to the crowd in the low front room. Marnie had come with Roy. Claude had squelched the feeling that had troubled him at the time. It was Roy, he told himself, the joker wild of the group. He went to greet Roy. He had nodded to Marnie. She had given Claude that mild smile, and as he talked with Roy, she had moved away to join the others. Then Claude, as usual, had wandered alone on the outside of the groups who were, of course, exchanging reports of their acting. Having a drink when his glass was empty, pouring one for someone else, lighting a cigarette for someone, he noticed Marnie's movements from time to time as she rose to walk to the kitchen then return. She always held his eyes before she turned away. Once she came in when he was in the kitchen, so he filled her glass. She thanked him quietly and left. He had watched her go then had followed her. She was Roy's he had told himself.

But later as he sat in a stuffed chair relaxing, lightheaded from the drinks, enjoying himself by watching the groups wind up, their talk becoming louder, more excited until the room had filled with a babble that had become a drone, she had stood before him looking down at him slumped in the chair.

"Why don't you join us?" she had asked. She had sounded drunk.

"I'm fine," he had said.

"All by yourself," she had said. "You look like you need someone to talk to."

"I'm all right."

"I'll talk to you," she had offered. Then she was in his lap draping her legs over his. "How's this?" she had asked. Her thighs, her fragrance, the warm scent of her flesh and her hair surprised him.

"I think you've had a bit too much," he said. He offered to take her drink.

"Uh, uh," she said. "I'm fine. I just thought I'd keep you company,"

"What about Roy?"

"Roy can take care of himself."

Claude had searched the room. Roy was in a corner looming over the newest member of the group, a small girl, pert and stacked that Claude was hot for. Roy grinned down at her, his long arms wide, flailing when he leered, laughing, always playing the clown. The girl seemed overwhelmed. Claude turned back to the softness on his lap, her lips, her pale skin.

"I think I need a drink," he said.

She moved off of him allowing him up. They went into the kitchen but found the bottle empty. So Claude searched for Ward, and Ward had peeled off money from a wad, held it up folded without turning from his drink or his audience. The reddish-haired hand that held the money and the folded bill itself simply became props and pointers to dramatize a statement.

Claude found the bedroom to extract his coat excusing himself for some reason to the couple stirring in the dark oblivious to his creeping form. He headed toward the door, came back for Ward's keys, then finally reached the fresh wet air outside. The rain had paused. Marnie was waiting for him at the gate.

The headlights of the car swept the heavy growth, the darkness between the yellow circles on the wet asphalt, the dark houses, the rain-soaked lawns, the rain heavy bushes. Then they came suddenly into the dazzle of neon and florescent street lamps, headlights, traffic signs, arc lights that swept the belly of the clouds. The bright interior of the liquor store was a paradise of booze in colored bottles. Then back they roared through the neon glow that edged the darkness, back across the slippery yellow circles that seemed like stage lights.

They heard the party as they came up the stairs into the doorway of the house camouflaged by flowering shrubs then hit the heat of the pastel room with swirling smoke, the clash and battle of voices, of gesturing arms and studied expressions. He deposited his coat in the dark bedroom, this time ignoring the couple that rustled apart then closed again as he left. He carried the bottle to the kitchen, cracked the seal, and poured a drink. He handed it to her then poured one for himself.

She stood in the doorway still fresh and sharp from the air and the wetness outside. He watched her sip her drink devouring her with his eyes. She peered at him above the rim of her glass then set her glass on the counter, set his beside hers, and waited. They came together. He searched her with his lips, his hands, his thighs, then broke away and calmed, reached for his drink, and studied her.

"What next?" he had asked.

Her penciled brow went up. A gleam flickered in her eyes.

"Let me take you home."

"Maybe," she offered.

And after that things seemed to fall right. He pressed her the remainder of the evening, and she seem to come around. Then the crowd diminished, Roy disappeared, and the evening had settled to a stale, dull end. When they were ready to leave, he asked again, but she laughed a strange, nervous laugh, and backed away. Ward teased. So she came with them to the car, and they drove through the dark early morning streets to their apartment. There she became coy. Claude became angry. Ward laughed and started up to the apartment.

"I'll take the couch tonight," he said then turned. "Don't make me miss a good night's sleep," he added before he disappeared into the darkness of the courtyard. When they finally followed creeping through the dark apartment to the bedroom they heard Ward's steady snore.

She spent a long time in the bathroom. He waited naked beneath the sheet watching the crack of yellow light from underneath the bathroom door. He listened to her movements, dozed, then came awake to find the place dark and her beside him. She was silent for a long time, and when he first didn't touch her allowing her to get used to him, she called to him, her voice sounding loud in the stillness, sounding scared. She stammered.

"You can't tell me this is your first time," he said.

"Well, not like this."

"Don't worry," he said.

"I don't know," she hedged, but then he turned toward her. He stroked her loose breasts, her soft belly, her thighs. She quieted, relaxed, so he raised himself, coaxed himself between her thighs, and he lost himself in her yielding flesh.

And that was all. He would swear to it. So help him, the next thing he knew, she was heaving him off, and he had simply settled back to sleep. When he woke, she was gone, and Ward was wandering in tossed and rumpled squinting beneath heavy puffed lids searching.

"Well, how'd it go? Where is she?

"I don't know. I fell asleep."

Ward went into hysterics wrinkling his face, the heel of his hand against his forehead. "Fell asleep!"

"Don't rub it in," Claude said. He flipped back the cover sheet, rose, and went into the bathroom.

"Looks like you did something, fella," Ward called.

Claude looked back at the stained sheet. "Forget it," he said.

And they did. They went to breakfast. Ward took back the bedroom and when Ward went to bed after changing the sheet, Claude heard him chuckle to himself before he fell asleep.

The next time Claude saw Marnie, Ward and he were hanging out letting the light in the room grow dark as the sunset reddened the sky to a flame behind the black shapes of the palm trees outside the windows.

They shared a bottle while Ward talked about acting, which really meant he talked about himself. So Ward was talking, Claude was listening while they drank. Then the doorbell rang and Ward ran down the stairs in bare feet. He came back slowly, quietly resuming his lazy sprawl on the couch.

"Someone wants to see you," Ward said. Claude could almost see the gleam of amusement in Ward's gray eyes. Ward was beginning a mustache that flourished red, and he played with it running his stubby fingers over it, smoothing it while his fiery eyebrows arched.

Then she just appeared around the edge of the door as if she had swung in on a pivot. Claude remained silent watching her heavy form silhouetted in the golden light of the hallway. "Can I see you for a minute?" she asked softly. She peered in searching for him.

"Why not? Help yourself."

"I mean alone. Is there someplace we could talk alone?"

Claude could sense Ward's amusement plainly now from across the room. "What's the secret? There's nothing you can't talk about with Ward here."

"Please," she urged.

So they drove along the ocean in Ward's car then turned back, returned to the apartment, parked. They sat in the darkness watching the throb of the neon sign from the bar, the glow and change of traffic signals, the few people beneath the bare bulb chain of lights of the used car lot, the intermittent traffic. He listened to the noises in the night. What she told him made everything seem unreal. He sat there in the plush darkness of the car and tried to make himself grasp what was happening. The whole situation seemed too weird.

"Are you sure?" he asked again.

"Positive," she answered again softly.

"But my god! I fell asleep!"

She was silent and coy.

"I can't believe it."

"It's true," she insisted quietly.

They talked for some time not really settling anything, and he sat wondering how he would find a way out of all this that had begun so casually. Her position was clear. She refused to try to do anything. Her faith forbid it. She had told him that right off even though he hadn't suggested anything. Yet when she also insisted, however gently, that he was obligated to do something, he grew angry.

"What do you need?" he asked sharply. "Money?"

"I don't need money," she said in her quiet way.

"Then what *do* you want?"

She had remained silent. He tried to read her thoughts, and he decided he understood. He flatly refused. He had things to do, he insisted, places to go. He remembered a line of poetry he often threw out to convince people how serious he was about his ambitions, and suddenly he realized that he sounded the same as the other poseurs of the group in which she circulated. But he flatly refused what he thought she intended. He couldn't be tied down.

He had offered his help. Beyond that he refused to go. No, she had insisted, for now, she simply wanted to use his name. Her request was hard for him to believe. Yet relieved that was all she wanted he readily agreed. Then finally she had left, and he had crept up the stairs to the apartment searching for a drink.

Ward's cigarette glowed in the dark. "Congratulations."

Claude had said nothing and had gone to bed leaving Ward to the couch where he sat.

Someone always let him know how she was doing. She worked for a while, but she had to quit. He felt badly about her losing her job, he imagining that she was sneered at because of her condition and she not wed. Then he had found out that she wore a ring and went by his name.

Toward the end when she had gone home to her parents, he began to consider leaving—not because of this business regarding her condition—but because he was beginning to feel restless. Things seemed to be coming to an end for him here. His few friends had married, had found jobs out of state, and had hooked up rented trailers behind questionably reliable cars that they eased out into the flow of traffic. He had watched them leave standing on the curb beside a palm tree; he saw the quick flash of traffic closing up the brief hole that had opened to take them in. He had left the city himself soon after, and in the continuing events of his new life, he had forgotten about her.

Now here he was again talking to Roy. And again here was Marnie who as usual said nothing. She let Roy and him talk. He told Roy about the Northwest, about how much of a blue laws state the place was offering opportunities to exploit the *de facto* prohibition. He also noted the active theater scene that also offered possibilities. Roy expressed interest.

"Hey, man!" Roy exclaimed. "We ought to work something out."

"We might be able to."

"That'd be great, man!"

"It would," he agreed.

"You know . . ." Roy began.

Claude waited for him to find the words. Roy clowned drawing on his cigarette, exhaling through his teeth, a black-faced Bogart.

"I ought to give you something. You could check things out. Who knows, we might be able to help each other."

"I'll give you my address," Claude offered. "You could come up. I'll look things over and let you know. I'd be glad to do it."

"Sure," Roy insisted. "I'd be sort of like a silent partner."

The possibilities seemed promising. "O.K.," Claude said. "I'll see what I can do."

"Do that, man," Roy said.

Then some of the rest of the old crowd came in, and Claude had to greet everyone and tell them how he was doing. They stayed for a beer then all of them decided they should head down to George's near the beach. Before they left carrying Claude along, Roy offered Claude his hand. "Don't forget me," Roy said.

"I won't," Claude said and followed the others out into the night. Marnie went along.

Claude was surprised to see how large George's new place really was. The old one had been small. He recalled the night it had rained: Ward and he had kept back the flood of water and sandy mud that had washed in the back door with one of the typical downpours. They had mopped and bailed while George, a small wiry Greek, ran in and out of the back making espressos, fetching sweet pastries for his customers at small tables in dim yellow lighting.

George's new place was large, crowded, elaborate, bright, and located in a swanky resort area. There was even a small group of musicians and a black singer with an operatic articulate voice whom Claude recognized. And there, of course, was small George who pretended to remember Claude and then excused himself from further talk and trotted off to his cash register.

They ordered over the applause of the crowd around them as the singer finished and came over to their table. Marnie introduced him. The singer took Claude's hand searching his face then pulling out a chair from another table, chatting briefly with the people there then turning back. Ward went of to talk to George; Marnie and the singer went into a close huddle across the table, and Claude was forced to look around the room at the assortment of mixed couples at the other tables.

Claude was glad when they left, the singer offering the typical "nice meeting you," Marnie only offering her typical slight smile. Ward came to fetch him and they weaved their way through the billows of smoke, the drone of voices, the crowd of tables and legs, and reached the thrill of salty ocean air. They drove home in silence, bid each other a quiet goodnight, and went to bed.

The next morning Claude woke to find everyone still asleep. The house quiet, the baby played by himself in his crib. Claude tried to read but gave it up when he found himself re-reading the same page twice. He grew restless with sitting around waiting. So he dressed and crept down the stairs. He walked the empty streets witnessing again the tarred squares of the concrete roadways, the stores with iron gates across the doors, the tall palm trees, the bright hazy heavy sky. Everything appeared the same. He stopped for coffee at a corner stand then turned back toward Ward's place. He paused before the court of apartments next door.

Why bother? He wondered. He recalled Ward and Dee's discussion of the morning before. Now he was bored. What had he to lose? And he was curious. He turned up the walk into the court, found Marnie's name by the mailboxes in the archway at the courtyard entrance, then went down the walkway searching for her door.

When he found it, he knocked: the panes of the glass door rattled. He heard stirring within. He rapped again. The gaudy flowered curtain of the door swung back from the bottom, and a small girl with brown skin stared out at him with the brightest blue eyes he had ever seen. The curtain dropped, and he knocked again.

"Who is it?" a sleepy voice he recognized as Marnie's asked.

He called in his name.

"I'm still in bed," she answered. "Could you come back later?" Her pleasant manner surprised him, a contrast to her apparent indifference of the night before.

"Sure. Sorry to wake you."

"I'll see you later, O.K.?" she invited.

Claude strolled the few steps back to Ward's place. Everyone was still in bed, so he went back downstairs to the concrete steps. He sat and watched traffic.

Then someone came out of the court where Marne lived. The man didn't see Claude. He was too busy adjusting his sunglasses, lighting his cigarette Bogart-style gripping it in his perfect teeth. And Claude didn't recognize the man until the man's long face and hands, the lithe rhythm of his body as he strolled to the car told Claude who the man was. At first Claude was going to call to the man, but then a certain rainy night suddenly came back at him, and he just watched as the man climbed into the car and drove away beneath the sun that pierced the early morning haze and hanging clouds and bathed the street and palms in bright glowing light.

Praise Her in the Gates

The traffic through the parkway on that Sunday, the first really warm day of the year, was slow. At times it stalled. So as they neared the exit, he could tell that she was troubled about their being there like that, exposed. Conspicuous in the high, open carriage, they were subjected to the curious stares and the impolite intrusions of everyone they chugged by. Their engine chortled loudly inviting inspection. Some, kids mostly, yelled at them, pointing at them, calling them out to others while they chased after as the relic passed through the wide streets, as they neared the park, as they passed beneath the latticing of new leaves, the vaulting trees above the narrow roadway. They slowed behind the line of sleek modern cars. Now they stopped, their bodies quivering with the horseless carriage.

He saw that she was disturbed, perhaps by the motion of the machine, perhaps by the place where they found themselves now, although she tried not to show it.

"Sorry you came?" he wondered now out loud hoping to relieve the tension. But she was silent, her face a study, a blank. She gazed ahead raised where they were above the line of low modern vehicles that crept before them as they slowly followed.

Now sitting conspicuous in the high open carriage, she appeared self-conscious, irritated, obviously trying not to show her emotions, and he hadn't counted on their being caught there in the gateway to the park stalled among a gawking crowd. He should have known.

But he worried more about the car. He considered the section of town, the ghetto they were approaching, however slowly. Why, he wondered, did parkways always seem to lead to ghettos? He saw ahead, suggested now through the trees, the distant blighted beginning, the houses with asphalt sidings, their window frames bled of color, the slow decay, those stained, crumbling buildings, some abandoned, some boarded, others charred, all were testimony to previous summers and their perennial madness. That area had always been trouble. He knew the razed plains of scattered rubble, the heaps of brick, the sharded glass, and the scarred wasteland between.

He admitted then that they should have come another way. Had they done so, they could have swept down the long fast hill giving them a view of thick leaves and of luxurious homes, the crushed foil glittering of blue water, then they would have moved quickly through the park the other way. Now the traffic on the other side passed freely. The long low modern cars rushed by. The occupants stared. A car of black men slowed then passed eyeing her. He saw their quick, knowing inspection. He glanced at her; he saw her expression. He blanched; he flushed. "Sons-a-bitches!" he cursed muttering to himself. Then he crept forward with the old rare auto carrying her along.

He listened to the engine as it rattled in the vibrating hood. What would he do if it stalled? Could he start it again? The vehicle was so old. He had tried to learn it well enough while he had worked on it. Yet, here where they found themselves, anything could happen, and he would lose it all, everything that had led them here to this moment: this relic he had refurbished, this traffic line they crawled in stalled. He suddenly tried to see it all again—the years before the relic and their beginning. That sequence dealt with, looked at squarely had helped him as he had worked on this machine, would surely help him now.

They had quarreled about his purchase of the relic as they did about everything now.

"You paid how much for that!" she screamed.

Surveying it again, he had to admit, if only to himself, that she was right. He had paid too much, but of course he would never confess to having done so, certainly not to her.

"It's something I wanted!" He defended. "It's something I had to do for myself, just this once. You should understand that. Isn't that what you always say?"

He saw her blanch at the charge. Then her face contorted in anger and she appeared about to cry. "Don't start bringing up old dirt. That's not fair!"

"Fair! Who in hell cares if it's fair? All's fair, they say."

"And who in hell are *they*? I say we can't afford it!"

"Well, I've paid my dues," he said suddenly quiet. "I've earned it. I need that relic. And I'm going to have it.

So he began, perhaps like everything else in his life, this, too, somewhat of an accident. He had been looking for something, and he had just happened to come across the notice. Just as impulsively, he had found himself on the long fast trip alone to where he first saw it. There within the musty barn the prairie sunlight pierced as he entered, as he helped heave back the creaking door, he had gazed at the crumbling hulk yellowed with dust. He had come all the way to see that. And the price! "You want how much for that? Ridiculous!"

The man, typical prairie farmer in bibbed overalls and hard-toed boots, had only shrugged. "You come all the way to see that. Be a shame you went back home empty-handed."

And he admitted that he had loved it at first sight, as if it suddenly filled a void and satisfied a hunger that no food, however exquisitely prepared—her special talent—could satisfy. So just as he had found himself driving there, he found himself driving home pulling a rented trailer carrying the relic behind. And she, not surprisingly, had objected to his purchase.

"What in the world?"

"I wanted it," he defended.

"But what will you do with it?"

"What you mean, what will I do? Restore it. It will be worth it. I think of it as a good investment. It'll give me a good return. Wait. You'll see. Let me at it. I'll make it into something beautiful. People will beg me to give them a ride. Someone will beg me to sell it to them."

"That! You must be kidding. When will you find the time?"

"I'll find the time. I need that car. I'll work on it weekends and evenings. I certainly can't let my attention to it distract me from doing my day job.

"And you'll just take time from me again," she complained "Just like always. What about me? What about my needs? What am I suppose to do while you're playing with that?"

"Playing! What about your friends?" Then he saw that his tone appeared to have warned her, making her wary.

"What about them? she asked cautiously.

He remained silent watching her, turning to inspect the relic.

"Don't!" she pleaded. "Don't start again. I don't want friends. I have no friends. You know that. Look what happened last time. You saved me when I made a big mistake."

She closed in on him becoming affectionate. But he stiffened and stepped away.

"Sure," he said. "All we've been through together. What would you expect?"

"I need you." She insisted. "That thing will take too much from both of us. What will I do?"

"You'll find something," he said. "You always do. What about all your social commitments?" And then he turned toward the relic leaving her to heaven or to her friends or to her social commitments—whichever came first.

So he began. He started in autumn when the days were still warm, the leaves still full upon the trees just beginning to yellow. He started soon after they had returned from their trip together in an attempt at reconciliation after her most recent affair. Now he felt the impact of that trip, and he grieved to think that they would never have that contact however brief again.

They both had shared the experience at first until their conflicts returned. The trouble began in North Dakota over wine: He had ordered; the waiter had searched and had returned apologetic. Offered a substitute, he had been gracious and condescending in accepting it, and she had taken him on.

"You always make such an issue out of everything!"

"Who's making an issue? I'm paying for this."

"We don't always need wine," she had said. He had looked at her amazed. Then she had added, "Maybe we shouldn't have come."

"Now's a fine time to think of that. Too late now, isn't it? Well, we're here. Shut up and enjoy yourself!"

His voice having grown loud, probably from one too many drinks before dinner, the others around them in the low close room with a décor suggesting a speakeasy were quietly watching. He had challenged the white tablecloths, the red plush of the walls, the fixtures reflecting that of a former era. He had ended by staring down the silent spectators finally taking on some old wattled bitch, some hick, so he had thought, sinfully indulgent in creating excuses for the weekend and her orgy of repentance.

Then in the dawn the stifling humid heat had broken with the storm that had passed over them in the night waking him to soft cleansing rain sending up fragrances of earth and mold. The land, the dawn, the sweet rain he had viewed standing at the open door to their stifling room had made him conscious of her there in bed, and he suddenly had wanted her, wanting to reach for her, to touch, forgive, to ask forgiveness. Instead, when he had stretched beside her, she had turned away as always. Then they both had brooded in the gray early light, its evanescence like some brooding presence, like the turbulent, blue-black sky, the rain-fresh quiet, the sleeping town they left behind as they rose through the liberating curve of concrete overpass to reach the crest beneath gangrene-gray clouds. And then the land had opened before him thrilling him with the dual silver undulations of the ribboned highway that furled through quilted cultivated land, a patchwork of ripening and checkered fallow that suddenly furrowed toward the bent horizon. He had seen the island farms: the red barn, the windmill, the white balloon-frame house, all a galaxy of habitation that caught the streaming shards of gathering light. Seeing all that, he had felt again his bitterness, his brain dull and heavy with the residue of toxins from the previous night. Then he had followed the silver undulations of the road that had fled before them leading them back to their lives, their problems, and their quarrels.

The autumn days were still warm when he began his restoration, the leaves still full upon the trees just beginning to yellow. The air of the rented garage in which he worked was heavy with stale dust and heat in the warm evenings before he stopped, having lingered, before he finally trudged home to eat whatever he could find. Then the light he worked by as the days grew shorter, the nights descending faster, narrowed to a patch upon the sidewalk outside the garage door.

He ignored the curious inspections, the swiveling heads as people passed. Some occasionally stopped, black kids mostly. He answered their questions—to tersely, perhaps, his tone of voice driving them away. But he praised himself for his restraint and self-control.

Then as the weather chilled, the trees slowly falling bare, the days becoming overcast and gray, he closed the doors upon himself and his work. He remained alone, the door cracked just enough for air, the concrete bitter cold, sparkling with frost, grinding beneath the soles of his fur-lined boots whenever he moved, his breath billowing. The air that crept into the garage warmed, enriched by the sooty kerosene stove over which he rubbed his red curled hands. He eventually brought his dinner in a sack from a drive-in on his way from his office. And as he ate munching his food, sipping the still warm coffee, he studied the silent metal noticing the places where it gleamed dully, the dust having been accidently rubbed away. He studied the scattered parts that still needed refurbishing.

And while he ate or while he worked, while he stomped and paced within the frosted garage, while he endured the cold restoring the hulk, that garage his cell, his holy martyrdom he sometimes thought about his trip to get the relic that sat silently before him. And when he recalled that trip he wondered why that more than a long day's journey appealed to him still.

Then he recalled the time that now seemed long ago when he had stayed behind. That time a friend he had idolized, perhaps had even loved, had gone off with someone else searching for a similar vintage vehicle in some lost prairie barn. Returned dark and healthy from the prairie sun and pumped with excitement the friend had reported on his venture, his dark eyes rich with white. The two travelers had shared with each other, reminding each other of the pleasures they had experienced: the accommodating whore within the plush hotel. The drunks they had brawled with and vanquished outside blaring, reeking, smoke-filled bars. And he who had stayed behind stood listening, awed, envious, alone, grieving silently for his lost hope. Of what, he could never admit or speak.

Was that it? He wondered now. Pure insanity, the whole business, the notion of restoring an old relic like the one on which he labored. Still, the perversity appealed to him. Even more perverse: the idea of going all that way to get it. And, of course, there had been her objection. Perhaps that was why he had decided in the first place having needed something to get his mind away from what had happened between them, getting even, perhaps, for what she had done. So he had forced himself to take on this task. And doing it seemed to have worked.

For by spring when he swung back the door again, the relic had changed. The air of the garage heavy now with paint mingled with the mild swarming air outside. He walked streets glistening from soft rain beside wet stick-limbed trees thickening with buds in the soft new wind. In the evenings, he went to a local café where he ate alone, paid in silence, returned alone to the slowly restoring relic.

She again of course reacted. At first just annoyed, she would drop a sullen comment now and then regarding the time he lavished on that thing. Then as he worked, pleasant to her now and then, she would grow furious, chiding him, reminding him of his inattention before and its consequences, of what she had sought to replace his absence. What had he expected?

Wasn't he afraid of being so inattentive? she had charged. Wasn't that the problem in the first place? Maybe that's why he had never reached her when others could. What had he expected her to do? Was she supposed to wait until he was good and ready to bring her what she needed to be completely filled and satisfied so that her yelling from passion would make the neighbors ask who was being killed!

In response, he fled again leaving her to do what she would. Yet as he reached the closed door, the dusty ribs of the window, the opaque dirty glass confronted him. Now a mirror, it chided him. Things could have been otherwise. He had to admit that finally. Their relationship had always suffered from the extended times away from her due to his employment, even after their marriage, he having given up his dream, even after they had settled, had even come to enjoy each other. For there had been a few good times, he admitted. They had been able to talk almost as friends. They had searched the City where they had lived together. They had explored each other. He recalled how she had responded at first, crying out the pet name she had labeled him with as she had soared toward climax surprising her and satisfying him. She had always been so warm and loving afterwards. Then having discovered that she had conceived but having miscarried, she for no clear reason had blamed him. After that, each time he touched her, reaching for her, she had never been the same in her response: she had submitted to his carnal needs out of obligation rather than mutual desire.

Thinking of those first years he then recalled the various menial jobs he had held during their struggle, the long hours of tedium doing mindless, routine tasks he had learned to execute competently the first day. Then each evening while he worked he had gazed out at the darkening sky and the light reddening toward black. The bright perfect globe in the twilight had always made him wonder where he might be bound. Now he knew.

He recalled the kids he had tried to befriend while working those mindless tasks. No matter where he worked they started coming. He had let them hang around even though one owner had warned him: "Watch out they don't steal you blind. You'll have to cover the loss." But he had ignored the claim and had come to know them through their lives, their hopes, and their desires. Interested, he had enjoyed their spontaneity and their attention even though he had finally held them off. He could only go so far.

Two he especially remembered. Half brothers, the one round-faced with coarse oily skin, coarse woolly hair; the other fine-boned, delicate with smooth dark skin and large almond-shaped eyes, often came as a pair. The older round-faced boy laughed at everything; the other smaller thinner one seldom smiled. The one was boisterous, the other quiet. The younger one often came alone. Suddenly there he was with his dark serious eyes watching. What had happened to them he had always wondered. And, as usual, he had found out about one almost by accident with troubling results.

He had returned one time to the neighborhood where they had lived, his return more by chance, like everything else, this time on one of his frequent business trips. He had driven through the area out of some strange compulsion to see the area again, almost as if he were reaffirming the basis and the purpose of his work, of his life, and of all those intervening years that had led him to the moment of his return. He found, of course, that the place where he had worked had changed. Now shut and boarded, time and circumstance had distilled it to a wasted hulk. Yet it still remained a constant reassuring him. Of what, he couldn't say.

Then he suddenly had seen the older boy, larger now of course, an adolescent, run across the street directly in his path causing him to brake. He had wanted to shout, to stop, to talk, to restore those years during which they had been lost to each other. He had passed; he had waved in greeting. In response, the boy's eyes and features held instead of recognition, instead of laughter, a dull smoldering hate. And he had driven on shaken and afraid.

Now as he worked alone in the garage, he tried to estimate how long ago all that had been, both his working there and his return. His estimate in turn made him aware of what they had been through since then, he and the woman, she whom he not realized he hardly knew despite the years together. Those years together bound in struggle rolled away behind. What they had wanted together, he could never really decide. Now it didn't seem to matter.

Then one day she confronted him in his lair, coming directly to the garage, tracking him down. "Well, so I've found you at last!"

"Been here all along," he said.

"Too long," she replied. "So this is what I've been replaced by!" She stomped around the machine, her heels ringing as if they were striking steel. "Very nice," she admitted. "Did it do what you wanted it to do?"

"I think so."

"I'm glad for you. I'm very glad."

"So am I."

Then. "I'm leaving you. I want out."

"No," he said quietly but firmly. "You can have anything you want, anything else, but not that."

"Why not, for god's sake? I don't want anything else. Nothing else works."

"What about your friends?"

"To hell with my friends. Always my friends. I don't have any friends. They're not friends; they're users. You know that. They use me; and I feel soiled.

"I'm glad to hear you say that. I appreciate your admission. But you can't have out."

"I'll leave. I'll sue.

"Go ahead. I'll fight. And I will be as dirty and as despicable as I can learn how to be. No more nice guy. I'll drag out your well-soiled lingerie. And everyone will see what you truly are. Then where will your precious social standing be, your precious moral character that everyone has praised you for? You'll have nothing. You will be nothing. You will feel worse than nothing. Trust me."

"You . . . You . . . I can't think of anything dirty enough to call you."

"Don't bother. It doesn't matter. You'd be right. You can't have out."

"But why not? What do we have? We have nothing together anymore."

"I have my pain. I have my hurt. And I want you to enjoy it with me. We can at least share that. What I only have now is the satisfaction of seeing you low; and I have this," he said indicating the relic. "Restoring it has helped me. It's helped me live through all the crap and my admission that I was wrong about you, about us, that my whole life with you was wrong from the start, my giving into you, of thinking that I loved you when I knew I shouldn't have or didn't, when I should have done what I had wanted to do for myself even before we got involved. But you played your card then, didn't you? You gave me your ultimatum: 'What about me?' you asked."

And as he spoke, he saw again the place where they had the exchange: a lot strewn with rubble from demolished buildings they had to avoid while parking for free thus avoiding what seemed at the time like an exorbitant expense. 'Make a commitment or I leave!' you threatened. "You weren't going to wait. Well, now I have things the way I want them. Leave if you dare. I'll worry you to death. I mean it. Trust me.

"You really do mean it. You hate me that much. I see that you do."

"Better than indifference. My feeling allows me to know that I'm alive. Call it rage. Call it revenge. Call it self-inflicted punishment for all my faults and all my wasted years. Call it anything you want. You can't have out."

They searched each other's eyes for the first time in years.

"O.K.," she said taking a deep breath. "You win. For now. But don't expect me to be discreet about my friends."

"You never have been discreet anyway. The way you huddled with them when they arrived. Your preparing meals you knew they would enjoy. You think I was so naïve or so stupid not to notice? Anyway, what does it matter now? Nothing can touch me. Not anymore. Not even you."

He studied her as she searched his face and his eyes again. Then she turned, starting for the door."

"Hey!" he called. She stopped, her back to him. "The weather's warm. This beauty's almost ready. How about a ride?"

She spun to face him. He grinned at her.

"You really mean that, don't you?'

"Sure."

"Some other time," she said then left.

He returned to work on the relic satisfied in a small way that he had exacted some return for his years of investment to her. Then as the relic neared completion, his success, his sense of control made him magnanimous. So when he gauged the next opportunity, he had a proposal for her even more startling than the invitation for a ride. And it, too, seemed almost perverse. A trip. Not just a joy ride. A real bonifide trip.

"We haven't been anywhere together in years," he said to her on proposing his idea.

"You think you can get me to do anything you want, don't you? Besides, how can we afford the expense with all that you spend on that thing? And how can you even suggest such an idea after all you said? Why would you want to go anywhere with me when you hate me so?"

"But I also love you," he said perversely. "Perhaps now more than ever. I have capacity enough and feeling enough now for both. How about it? Who knows, maybe we can even get it on again."

He saw her hesitate, and he took her hesitation as an indication that she didn't reject his idea out of hand. So he plunged to the advantage.

"Come on! Where shall we go?"

"I don't know," she said totally confounded.

"I do." he offered.

"Where?"

"You know—The City—San Francisco by the Bay," he exclaimed.

So they went.

Once having agreed, both threw themselves into the hopeful spirit of the event. Both became excited hoping for a good time. After all, they had shared such times before. They could even agree on how to meet the expense: their savings or a bit of their investments since they now had a sufficient number that repaid them adequately. And had they separated, let alone divorced, that store of possibilities would mean little anyway.

Once there, they revisited all the places they had been before, places special to them away from the crush and the promotion of the tourist attractions, places they had discovered and had frequented when they had lived there early in their lives while attending classes, when neither were yet a success, that outcome in the distant future, but when both had been full of hope and ambition.

Now here they were again. And as they walked, and as they drove enjoying the famous hills, the famous residential areas of Victorian houses, the multitude of famous views, the bright clear weather that he claimed he had ordered for the occasion, he boasting of his influence, his direct line, then crooning the Tony Bennett tune, they both reflected on where they had been and the place where they found themselves now returned, at least some of what they had hoped fulfilled.

Yet the changes in the City were startling. Gone those comfortable six-table Chinese places where they had shared plates of food eating leisurely, often spending most of the evening talking while the typical Bay Area downpour streamed down the walls of windows that closed them in dry and cozy with comfort when they could afford little else, familiar at last with the family who owned the place, who served them, who always stopped to chat. And there had also been the museums that they came to haunt, the small movie houses that offered art films. These had been some of the good times.

But reflecting on those former times, having perhaps indulged a bit too much in vintage wine, he became sullen then morose. Near the end of the first week they were involved in a minor traffic incident. He became enraged; she withdrew; and they gave up, cut short their stay, and returned home early.

He resumed work on the relic bringing to it all the disappointment it could bear and bringing it finally to completion. All that remained were the final touches, the careful buffing and detailing. He would finish by late spring he determined. And as he worked, his concentration and his attention allowed him once more to dissipate the bitterness their recent trip had renewed. He even began again to suggest to her joining him once he was finished and when the weather was warm enough to launch the inaugural drive. But she refused withdrawing into her own activities that had become more dear since he had threatened to destroy them and her. He found that he returned more frequently to their empty condo.

Late spring: the relic sat complete. He sat looking at it. He studied it wanting to share it, wanting suddenly to share it with her, unhappy knowing he couldn't. But the warming weather offered other possibilities:

the good times he would have going for rides even alone. Maybe he'd join a car club where he would meet new people. Yet, for a reason he couldn't provide, he wished he could talk her into going.

Instead, she startled him this time. She asked again for him to let her go since she was leaving anyway, that she had met someone with whom she could finally and truly be friends as they had been once perhaps. He was in turn shocked, crushed, angered. And as the old resentment flared, he threatened her again.

"I'll destroy you. I'll take your career." Yet even as he uttered the words he sensed the hollowness of his threats. For this time he saw that she refused to be afraid. Instead, she withdrew leaving him alone with the relic.

At last on the first really warm day, he rolled it out. He nodded to the people in the neighborhood of the garage who had been noting the progress of his work as they had passed. Now as they gathered to admire what he had accomplished, he accepted their remarks quietly. Again, encouraged by the refurbished relic's reception by others, he invited her again.

"It means a lot to me. You should be there with me. You have to be there with me." He insisted quietly.

Her response indicated that she didn't understand. Or perhaps she did. "You feel you haven't really won unless I go along with you," she offered.

"Something like that," he admitted. "Look, I'll compromise. I'll offer you a deal. You come along; I'll seriously consider what you've been asking for. I promise."

"Really!" she asked. I don't believe you! That's too easy! You won't do what you say!"

"I will. Trust me."

"You're telling me that you'd really consider letting me go just because I agree to go with you in the lousy thing? There must be a catch."

"No catch. But you'll have to do more than just agree. And if you join me in the grand inaugural ride, my considering what you want will be my way of admitting I was wrong, I guess, admitting I could never control you or keep you or destroy you. Doing so would mean destroying everything I felt of value in what we once had. And I'd hate myself for allowing me to act that way."

He watched her as she studied him for a long moment, and when he openly and steadily returned her gaze, he surmised that she was beginning to believe him. Finally she agreed to go.

Then he briefly caught her up in his almost childlike delight of her acceptance and, of course, at his accomplishment in restoring the antique for which he had paid so dearly.

""Look at it! Lousy thing, indeed! It's beautiful—just like you!"

He noted how she demurred at his remark, apparently not knowing how to take what might seem like an off-handed compliment. But she seemed to enjoy his small renewal of affection, however brief, however suspect because of what he had promised in exchange.

So here they were now still caught in the slow file through the park.

Yes, he thought, acceptance had been the start. Now their years together should matter more. A couple of incidents of indiscretion in all those years shouldn't have ruined everything. And, he admittedly had indulged himself in what to him had been just innocent encounters of affection that she had seen as flagrant as if they had involved sex. But then he admitted his wishfulness. Those years were never really enough; in truth they had never been enough.

But for a while he had tried by accepting her friends, helping her by serving before dinner drinks then the gourmet dishes with full accompaniments along with the exquisite wine he had selected for the occasion followed by the rich desserts a final flourish he had helped her prepare and finally by the thick complementary cordials and strong coffee. Such feasts always brought satiated gasps along with expressions of delight almost indecent.

"How did she always know their favorite dish?" he had asked somewhat innocently.

"I have my ways," she had said somewhat smugly, her answer bringing laughter and remarks at his expense:

"Hey, man, better watch it, baby! A woman starts cooking a man's favorite dish where's she getting her seasoning?"

He, of course, had smiled hearing calmly all that was said, accepting it. He had congratulated himself at first on being fair, by supporting her, by being gracious to those whom she had introduced into their lives, into his home, his sanctuary, even if most of them were of ethnic origin. He had often wondered where she had found most of them. They seemed to come from everywhere in all shapes and colors. One had even been a pimp.

"Variety is the spice," she had teased, her quip bringing more laughter.

"The family of man," he had countered. Then he had added to himself sotto voice: "Such acceptance and understanding you wouldn't have even if you had slept with them in the same bed." Yet some of those at the table had studied him upon his remark.

And all the while he had felt self-assured, pious in his trust that he could always make up to her for any remark at the end after everyone had left, after they relaxed with nightcaps reviewing the evening, its success, the usual disappointment from her having sought something from the guests that had escaped her.

Then later waking from libidinous dreams of dark sultry women, of dark phallic men, moved by the whisper of the rain-soaked dawn, he had turned to her, reached for her in his need while she had stirred in her sleep, had woke, resisted. And he, as always giving up, had been left alone unfulfilled.

The traffic moved again inching them forward. Then it stopped and suddenly the traffic troubled him. His anger flared. Her latest affair came back at him overwhelming him. He fumed. He burned. He cursed himself, cursed her. And he had thought that he had finally forced it down, digested it. He laughed bitterly to himself. She turned; she studied his face. He studied hers; he saw her worried eyes, as if those of a dying quarry.

"What's wrong?" she asked.

"Nothing!"

She remained silent turning again to the line of traffic ahead that bound them in a chain holding them equally from behind trapping them.

"You can never let it go, can you?" she said finally.

"Why should I? Can you?"

"Please, not here."

His anger churned. "Please, not here!" he mimicked.

"Try to understand!"

"Oh, I understand all right!"

"You don't! Weren't you ever curious?"

He thought about the round-faced boy. He saw the image of that stride frozen now in time always there another constant as the boy crossed before him to the other curb. He had been curious then. And what about the time he had almost reached to touch the inert form of his boyhood friend, the boy whom he had idolized. The smooth olive oil colored skin over hard muscle had made him wonder. Then his friend had shifted in his sleep. And he had snatched back the offending hand, that time, too, his curiosity repressed.

"You certainly have, haven't you? he blurted.

"Yes, I guess I have," she answered quite still.

He spun toward her. Again her countenance, part joy, part reverie, part satisfaction destroyed him. She held an innocence and a beauty he found hard to reach, impossible to bear. Her expression, as always, made him wild.

"In my own home!" he accused.

"It was never a home," she answered calmly.

"Take them in! Accept them! Try to be their friend! They turn on you! Just like that!"

"It was as much my fault as anyone's"

"Yes, I know. You were curious."

She remained silent. The traffic moved. He fought the relic into gear. They lurched forward. The engine died. He cursed, set the controls, scrambled from the vehicle, his anger diverted now directed toward the machine. Ahead, the line continued. A plain of asphalt opened before them. Behind, they blared. He turned toward them. He saw the indignant faces. He wondered what they expected, if they couldn't see. He cranked. The line sent up a blast of noise. The engine caught. He scrambled up. The thing chortled jerking them forward toward the halted queue. The others revved and chased them.

The yell startled him. He whirled. He saw the bright laughing teeth, the eyes in contrast to the dark gleaming skin as the pack of boys came along the grass beside the roadway ducking beneath low limbs of new leaves.

"How 'bout a ride?" one boy called. Already he had disappeared behind the high carriage back. Already he saw the dark fingers, the light nails, the palms curl and grab the edge.

"Stay off!" he shouted. But the boy was already up on the tire leaning now toward the hollow of the carriage with its plush restored upholstery.

Another boy raced along the side grabbing, skipping, heaving up onto the running board beside the woman who turned toward the boy then drew back.

"Give me a ride! the boy yelled in her face.

"Get off, you little bastard! he screamed.

The boy's expression sunk. His dark large eyes swept the man's contorted face. Then he leaned back, dropping off behind.

"Get out!" he screamed at the boy settled in the back. He turned to swing at the boy, but the boy scrambled then jumped.

"They expect everything, don't they!"

"You're always so nasty! They're only kids!"

"Wait, they'll grow big! They'll want something more!"

"God, you're so mean!"

"Stick it!" he hissed.

Then someone yelled. He spun.

"Hey, mother!" the call came again. And there among the bushes beside the relic he saw them gather. He saw the cocked arm. "Catch this, mother!" The stone arced but missed. The others stooped, straightened, threw all in one swift set. They stooped, straightened, threw again until the stones rained.

Then they finally found their mark. The woman took the first shock upon the flesh around her mouth. He saw her eyelids slowly close as she accepted, her hand going slowly to her wound.

"Black bastards!" he screamed. He ducked the deluge of stones, yanked at the handbrake, set the spark, then scrambled cursing through his teeth as he grabbed a wrench ready at hand beside him. He yelled; he leapt, racing toward the bushes, pounding toward them as they scattered. He lost them.

He stood there raging, searching, cursing until he heard the sound against the quivering tin. He spun engorged cursing her, cursing them, cursing himself. Then he charged shouting, racing toward the pack that had reappeared across the road.

There among the bushes at the gateway to the park they gathered; they stooped and straightened and threw. Transfixed, he stood planted to the soil, the grass, the scattering pollen. He saw the dark parabolas of stone that showered and drummed the relic. Their rocks, like ancient messengers, rose, arced, fell again, plummeting. They struck the woman with dull insistent shocks that slowly bent her toward the wasted seat.

A Bearer of Gifts

"You'll like it here," Mrs. C, the manager, insisted. She had just shown us the empty apartment on the top floor. "Wait, you'll find out. We share things. Sharing makes living here so much nicer. We're all so friendly."

We reached the ground floor landing. "I'm sure you'll like living here," she said, again not letting us respond. Yet we had already decided. M the woman with whom I currently lived turned to me in delight after we had wandered through the place.

A corner apartment, it filled with sun through tall bay windows. We marveled at the view of the bristling city, the flat valley beyond that we had fled, M having given up her former life to live with me. The building throughout was wonderfully maintained: well-kept carpeting throughout, soft lights, "And we have a security door that shuts by itself and locks. No need to concern yourselves about any of the trouble we've been having lately. We lock the doors at six o'clock even in summer. You'll never have to worry."

We went back to Mrs. C's suite to sign a rental agreement and place a deposit. The assortment of odds and ends made the place seem as if it were annexed to a second hand store, a curious contrast to the rest of the building. "You'll appreciate the appliances. They're excellent. Well cared for. It's difficult to find a place like this anymore. Folks seem to like it here. We rarely have vacancies. Only when someone—you know—passes.

"It's like a residential hotel, "M remarked.

"Yes, that's it exactly. Everything so convenient. No one disturbs anyone else. No intruders or solicitors; no one gets in unless you invite them. There's mostly older people here. In fact, you're the first young ones we've had in some time. It's quiet. Nice atmosphere. So friendly."

"And it has a double oven," M said. "We can make bread!"

"You bake," Mrs. C said.

"He does," M explained. "He makes marvelous loaves. I can't do anywhere near doing what he does."

"Actually, I just knead. She does the rest."

"Of course," Mrs. C said.

"We'll have to christen the place," I announced. "Old World Dark . . ."

"Amiga Elena!" M corrected. "His invention," she explained.

"You're right," I agreed. "As soon as we've settled."

"Then you've decided to stay with us?" The older woman asked.

"Yes, of course. We'll take it!"

M exchanged open smiles with Mrs. C.

We moved in that weekend, and we immediately discovered our first mistake. Actually, we had two problems, but they were contingent. First, the house we had lived in was large; the one bedroom apartment we were moving to had not nearly the room.

"Where will we put all this stuff!" I wondered out loud.

"We'll manage," M said from the galley kitchen. I realized she had overheard me. I went to lean in the doorway. She was surrounded by boxes that nestled her legs. She clung to her possessions, her remnants, garnering them, unlike the children she had given up to live with me. I tried to resign myself for her.

"They'll never fit," I said quietly.

"They will!" M insisted. "We'll put the buffet in the hall, the trunks along the living room wall. We can use them to store things. They're old. They're probably worth a lot. I've had them for a long time."

"Something simply has to go!"

Then I thought about our second oversight. A top-floor apartment with no elevator, the only way of reaching it was by using carpeted stairways. All the debris of both our former lives to which we both had clung we had to pack up by foot four floors. Actually, I did most of the packing. After the first few loads, M's old, always unexplained ailment re-appeared. So while she stayed above unpacking recovering her strength, I labored up what seemed like the endless flights of stairs.

My frequent trips quickly revealed the friendliness of the place. As I trudged up feeling like Sisyphus, I passed several of the other residents. They smiled and greeted me.

"Still at it," one remarked. I didn't answer. I just smiled and nodded thus saving my breath for the climb.

"It's a job, isn't it?" a heavy older woman said. She stepped aside to let me by. "You go ahead," she said. She stopped at the landing wheezing. "I'll just be in your way."

I nodded wheezing in turn and trudged on.

"I know what's it's like," another stated. "I just moved in myself two years ago. I probably won't ever move again."

I plodded past nodding with understanding.

"Some of the tenants have lived here twenty years," Mrs. C, the manager, had told me." Now I thought I knew why. Yet carrying the big things, I discovered what made people want to stay. For suddenly I had help. As I struggled, wondering how I would ever get the load up the stairs, someone always appeared. On their way up coming home from an errand, they would silently stoop to grab the other end then help me carry it up.

"We've got the whole building in on this," I remarked to M on one of my trips. The other resident and I chuckled out of breath. Then as I placed the item, I turned to thank him, but he was already gone vanishing behind one of the numerous blank doors. Sometimes I heard someone's weight on the stairs descending. Most of the time they simply disappeared as quietly and as swiftly as they had appeared.

Then the quantity of things we had and the frequency and number of the trips began to annoy me especially when I arrived on one trip to find M engrossed in one of my books she had happened upon distracted from her task of putting things away.

"Let's get rid of some of the garbage before we bring it up," I insisted.

"You're right," she said finally yielding to my demand.

And later after we had settled, I found myself carrying things back down to the storage locker in the basement.

"How's it going?" Mrs. C asked when I met her in the basement on one of my trips.

"Well, we're in," I said. "Now we have to put things away if we can find room for them. We'll probably spend the next six months sorting things out and bringing most everything back down."

"It's a job all right," Mrs. C consoled. "But if there's anything you no longer want, why just leave it in the cage here at the end." She sidled along beside me.

"Yes, I know. You told me."

"Did I? Well, you can put them there. If no one wants them we'll have a social service group come for them. I leave things all the time. So do others. We share things that way."

"Great idea," I said. "I'll remember that."

On another trip I met her again.

"Still at it."

"It never ends," I exclaimed.

"You're certainly unloading a lot of nice things."

"We can't use them."

"That's a shame," she said eyeing the load in my arms.'

"They're not much good."

"Well, you just leave them there. I'm sure someone will pick them up."

"They're welcome to them."

I opened the cage that held the boxes I had placed there on previous trips.

"Oh my!" Mrs. C remarked. "Preserves!" She lifted a jar from one of the boxes. The rich contents sucked away from the sides. "Are they still good?"

"Sure they're good. Nothing wrong with them. The jar's only a little dusty from being stored so long, that's all."

Mrs. C studied my face. "Well, if they're still good.

"Just a few rust spots on the cap. We can't use them."

"Maybe I'll just take these for myself. She started searching through the boxes in the cage.

"We don't have room for them, and we never seem to use them," I said.

But she was lost in her search. "Such nice things! Such a shame to waste them. I love music! And I'll just place some of the books on the hall table. Someone will use them I'm sure."

On my next down to the cage I discovered that the things I had discarded were gone. Only the empty boxes remained.

Finally we were in; we were settled; we could begin enjoying the view, the quiet, and the plush security of our new apartment. Near Easter we considered the possibility of bread. We had made it before for this occasion. Now the event was almost a tradition. A Greek recipe, the bread was more like cake. Baked as one loaf in a pail, it rose above the sides while it bloomed so that the finished bread looked almost like a huge mushroom. This time, the size made us hesitate. We were only two. Before, we had help. Now the circumstances of our lives left us alone together. The freedom we enjoyed now had its consequences, its responsibilities, it limitations.

"What will we do with it all?" M asked. "There's so much."

"That is a problem," I agreed.

"We didn't have that problem before."

"True."

"We'd be eating at it for months."

"We could freeze it."

"It would lose its flavor. It would go stale. We'd have to eat it all ourselves and we'd get fat."

"I guess we'll have to forget about it this year."

"There must be something we can do," M said clinging to the past.

We studied the photos of the loaf. So lifelike, it reminded us of the sweet rich flavor, the cake-like texture with nuts, dried fruit, a hard sugary crust. Behind us, the steam heat radiator spit at us sending small thin vapors into the room.

"I know," M said finally. "We'll share it."

"We've always shared it," I pointed out. "We're out of all that. There's no going back."

"Of course not," M insisted. "I didn't mean *that*."

"Then what *do* you mean? Share it? With whom?"

"With the others," she said flinging wide her arms.

"Others?"

"We'll give everyone here a surprise. It'll be friendly. We'll leave a slice at each door. The outside doors are locked at night, aren't they? We can leave everyone a piece then. We'll be the Easter Rabbit. We'll get to have some without having too much. And we'll have the enjoyment of making it as well as having others share and enjoy it with us. We'll be the artists. We'll have an audience, and they'll be able to eat our work of art!"

I was caught up by her excitement. I hugged her. "You know, at times you're absolutely brilliant."

"Thank you," she said coyly in playful smugness.

"When do we start?"

"At your pleasure, sir," she said indicating the cupboard that held the staples.

"After you." I said bowing her before me as I followed.

Our surprise was almost discovered. The warm aroma of baking bread filled the building sending everyone into paroxysms of ecstasy. Emerging from behind locked doors, they discussed the event in the halls. We heard them on the stairs as we climbed, their voices as sharp as old crones.

"What a marvelous smell!" one remarked. "Smells like bread."

"A very sweet bread. Whose is it?"

"I'm not sure. It's coming from the top floor."

"I wish I were young enough to bake again. It's been so long."

"I know what you mean. I'd do the same, but who would I bake for. Just me now. I figure, why bother."

"You're right," the other agreed as we reached their landing. Both turned to watch us as we passed not returning my greeting. Their clucking resumed after we passed.

That night we spread our Easter cheer. The loaf was beautiful. A golden delicate crust, a fine texture, destroying it by cutting into it seemed almost a crime. But after it cooled, we sawed out the first large slice for ourselves. We ate it as if it were dessert accompanying it with a chilled Sauterne, the slight fruity flavor of the wine a fine complement to the cake-like bread. Then we set out on our pilgrimage to spread our contributions at the individual shrines, leaving a slice at every station. The carpeted halls were still; the perpetual light arrested our reflections in the window of the fire escape. We heard the hushed stir behind blank doors. Then, our task complete, we crept back home to divide the last large piece, increasing the enjoyment of our feast because we had shared with others. We went to bed exhausted, satisfied with having spent the day fulfilled.

The next day the place was in an uproar. I walked into it coming down to meet the day dressed for my morning walk. M stayed behind languishing in the lassitude of our early morning love, a celebration. Our pagan rhythm and her spontaneous cries had proclaimed the new season of life.

Several had gathered to discuss something. Mrs. C was among them. Morning," I said. "What's the problem?"

"Someone left bread at all the doors last night."

"Oh?" I asked. I felt that revealing the source of my gift would destroy the spirit of giving.

"Yes. Seems everyone got some."

"Well," one of the other old women broke in, "you won't catch me eating it."

"Me neither," another agreed.

"Why in the world not?" I asked.

"Who knows what's in it?"

"I won't even touch it!"

I was stunned. Then as I searched the halls wondering how my good deed had fouled, I saw the undisturbed phalanx of gifts lined where we had left them at each door. The rainbow colors of the tissue we had used to wrap the offerings made my spirit sink.

"I'm sure it's all right. What could be wrong with it?"

"You never know these days. Lots of strange dreadful things happening. It could be anything."

"Oh, come now. Would someone want to do something to all of us? It seems like a nice gesture. Why, it's Easter," I proclaimed. I already felt guilty for having to defend what I had thought of as my good deed.

"Well, did you get a piece?" one accused. She seemed suspicious.

"Yes, of course," I admitted telling the truth. The piece I had for breakfast began to sour in my stomach. "And I ate it too. It was excellent."

"Then someone must have broke in!"

"To leave bread?"

"With something in it!"

"Maybe it's a former tenant who had a key made. We had some trouble once. Not everyone we've had has been as friendly as we are. We had to ask them to move."

"Maybe it's just a nice gift. It still could be someone in the building."

"Who? You're the only one young enough to handle it. The rest of us are old. We don't have the strength.

I searched their faces seeing them for the first time. They seemed like hags.

"Nor the money!" one of them added. "Bread like that, even home baked costs money. I barely scrape by now. You wouldn't catch me baking bread, least not leaving any for others to chomp their gums on!"

"Look!" I cried in desperation. "I'll try a piece." I went to the nearest door. Snatching up the piece, I ate it greedily attempting to prove its wholesomeness.

"That's only one. What about the others? You could have kept that one clean for yourself to show us!"

"You're all ridiculous!" I cried. But they only glared at me. I fled through the door that led me to the noisesome street. The door latched behind me.

Soon after, the door was locked even during the day. I had always been annoyed at the door being locked. Six o'clock, the day still bright with sunlight, the door was latched. I had to fumble for my keys groping around bundles trying to work the key into the lock at the same time I had to twist the knob. And when the door finally gave way I stumbled through knocking against the door as it swung back at me blocking my way. Now finding the same situation during the day annoyed me even more. I complained to M.

"How come the door's always locked?"

"They've had trouble."

"Trouble? The business about the bread? My god, they're paranoid!"

"The bread might have had something to do with it. But there have been other incidents. Someone's pension check was missing from the mailbox."

"How in the world could they know that?"

"I don't know!" M said exasperated. "Ask them!"

"Not a chance of that happening. They'd only accuse me!"

"Well, did you?"

"Did what?

"Take the check? Poison the bread?"

"Look, don't you start!" I felt myself getting angry. She sensed my mood. She came to me. Her touch calmed me.

"Maybe we should move," she soothed. "It's never going to be the same here anymore."

"Move!" I shouted flaring again. "Not on your life! We've just moved in. And you know who's going to have to move all this crap back down all those stairs!"

She broke away from my arms and went to the window. My anger flared more.

"O.K., you move; you go yourself!

She ignored my rant.

"The hell with them! Someone should have poisoned them! Serve them right, the old bats!"

M turned to face me. "You're being childish," she said quietly. Her manner made me aware of the truth of what she said.

"You're right," I said. "I guess I'm reacting to that business about the bread. How could we have been so wrong?"

"We couldn't know. And when you think of it, you can't really blame them. What would you do if you found food on your doorstep? It's just not done."

"You're right, again," I admitted.

"Maybe we should try something else."

"No, thanks. Once is enough."

"But what if we used a different approach? This time we'll take it to someone specific."

"That would be admitting to the other time. Then they'd probably accuse me of stealing the check—and anything else that's happened lately."

"You could simply present it as an apology for your behavior the other day."

"That would be admitting that I was wrong or at fault. I didn't do anything criminal. They're the ones who are suspicious."

"They're old," M suggested. "They're afraid."

I considered. "Well, I guess we should try something. Living here in this atmosphere is certainly not good."

"If we don't do something, we might just as well move.

"All right," I conceded with a sigh. "We'll try something."

"Good boy!" she said. She went to the cupboard. She began setting out the ingredients for bread.

The return from our mission of friendliness was ignominious.

"Got any other bright ideas?" I asked.

"I thought it would work."

"Do me a favor. Leave the thinking to someone else."

She grimaced at my remark and retreated to her window and the view of the valley where she once lived with her kids. I thought of what we had just been through. The Bear, as he was referred to by all the other residents, snarled, snapped, slammed the door in our faces, leaving us with our warm fresh loaf a dead weight in my supplicating hands. Now it sat on the counter growing stale while we sulked licking our wounds.

"There must be something we can do," M said coming away from the window.

"If there is, I don't know what it might be. I've had it! I give up! We've got two choices now. Live here and keep quiet—or move.

"Which one do you prefer?"

"Well, I sure as hell don't feel like hauling all your stuff back down again."

"Some of these things are yours!

"Not much."

She sulked. I let her.

"Well, if we stay here, we better try to do something," she said.

"We've tried. Let's forget the whole thing. It'll pass. We'll survive."

"But it's so silly and sad."

"O.K., but we tried. How far did we get? If you think of something better, do it yourself. I'm through."

She thought for some time. I went off to read leaving her to muse by herself. When I found out about her decision I was surprised.

"What's this?" I asked. I offered her the slice of bread I had found on our doorstep. "This some kind of joke? Well, I'm not amused."

Her eyes grew large, her expression one of disbelief. "How strange," she said.

"Come on!" I demanded. "You don't have to play games with me!"

"I don't know what you're talking about," she said.

"They're everywhere," I explained. "There's a piece at almost every door."

"I don't understand," she said wrinkling her brow.

"Look," I said. I led her to the hallway. There along the corridor at each door was a napkin and a slice of bread. "You don't ever give up, do you?"

"I really had nothing to do with it," she insisted.

"Then who did?"

"I have no idea, but whoever did had more success. Some pieces are gone."

Just then we heard a commotion behind one of the doors. The door burst open and the old man referred to as Bear staggered into the hallway. "They're going to poison us all!" he howled. Then suddenly he pitched forward to the carpeting, his gross body a dead weight.

Screams, raised arms, loud voices! We struggled to carry Bear's sagging body back into the room from which he came. There on the table half-finished was the slice of bread beside an open jar of old preserves with a slightly rusted lid.

I waited for the bell. Then I answered the door.

"We'd like you to answer some questions." the man said.

"Certainly. Anything you like." I sensed M listening from the living room.

"I understand that you've been baking bread."

"That's right," I said. "We have nothing to hide. We have."

"I'm told you also pass it around."

"We tried but failed, and we didn't the last time."

"You want to explain why you tried giving out bread?"

Once I thought of it, my reason seemed strange. "We thought it'd be nice to share. We wanted to be friendly, that's all."

"Poisoning someone is a strange way of being friendly."

"We had nothing to do with it. Besides, how do you know he's been poisoned? It could be anything. They're all old here, anyway. I've seen that guy wheezing up the stairs practically having a coronary by the time he got to the top. Why don't you find out what's wrong with him? Maybe it has something to do with the preserves. They were old. We threw them out."

"Lady next door says you offered the old guy bread."

"We did, but he didn't take it. When we saw no one wanted what we offered, we gave up."

"Get your coat," he ordered.

"What for?"

"We'd like to ask you more questions downtown."

"But, my god, I didn't do anything!"

"We'd like you to come along quietly without resisting."

"This is insane," I cried.

"Calm down," M soothed coming up from behind. "Everything's going to be all right. We'll get you out of this."

"Get me out? Out of what? I didn't do anything!"

"We'll get a lawyer."

"Lawyer! I don't need a lawyer. Why do I need a lawyer?"

"Come along quietly," the man ordered.

"Sure, sure," I agreed. I searched the room, the sky outside the windows, the maze of streets, the crowd of buildings of the city, then the valley beyond.

"Go along," M coaxed. "I'll call Lane." (He had helped her get her freedom. He also had appeared overly friendly toward her, and she hadn't seemed to mind.) "He'll get you out in no time if I ask him."

"I don't see why I have to go at all."

"Come along," the man said.

"I'll call Lane and be right down."

"We can phone him from wherever he's taking me."

"No. You go. "I'll straighten things out here. What if they find out about us?" "That won't help you," she whispered. "I can stop and see the kids," she said out loud.

"And leave me sitting?"

"I won't be long."

"I'll need a ride back."

"Of course, she said. "I'll take the car."

"Sure."

"And I'll need some cash," she said. "Lane will most likely want something, and I'll need money if you have to stay."

"Stay! But I'm going to be right out!" I insisted.

"Well, just in case," she said. "Just give me a blank check." She went for my coat and my checkbook.

"Thanks," I said defeated. I shrugged on the coat, handed her a signed check, then turned to the man waiting. He followed me out into the hallway and then down four flights of carpeted stairways.

"Don't forget this!" M called catching up to us as we descended the stairs to a lower floor. She dropped the load from the landing above. I caught her gift of bread with my bare hands.

One by One We Drop Away

The day before his birthday Tomaso slept late. When he woke, he rose and dressed and came out to the kitchen for his coffee and cigarette. Then he went for his daily walk along the river descending the long stairs past the place where the young couple had sat, they perhaps just out of their teens, he going past them down to the water's edge to the lingering hard dirty late winter snow on the river bank still bright and stark against the dark cold deep water.

He walked along the river watching the boats, gazing across the water to the empty hills that rose before the buildings of the city began again. He went along the riverbank until he came to the dirty yellow slat board shed. A heavy discharge of smoke billowed dark contamination from the chimney.

Tomaso watched the smoke he knew came from the pot-bellied coal stove. He imagined the one dimly heated room with its lone bare yellow lamp. Tomaso knew all the old men who sat around the stove smoking cigarettes or chewing snuff then spitting into a pot of congested brown-orange slime of cigarette butts and shredded tobacco, burnt matches and spittle. Tomaso had stopped many times on his walks along the river. Sometime he even had sat in on a hand or two of cards. Sometimes, he, too, had added to the pot of slime. Even now as he walked beside the river he could imagine the dog-eared playing cards soiled from being held so many times. Yet, the pictures and markings

225

were still bright, the cards still gave off a faint scent of plastic. He could imagine the sound of the cards being mixed and shuffled, snapped down on the round dark table. He could see the quiet playing out of the cards placed down in the center of the table or spread in a dramatic show. He could see the dimness of the room; taste the churning smoke from pipes, cigars, and the pot-bellied stove. He could sense the heavy darkness of the air, the heavy odor of tobacco, and of old bodies sometimes slightly incontinent. He could image the glow of the stove and the heavy air from its heat and smoke.

Tomaso sensed these events, imagined them, and knew them as he stood on the riverbank beside the dark water. Then he saw directly the sunlight off the rippling foil of water, the sunlight dull and meager through the gray unbroken clouds. Tomaso studied the red clinkers and dark fused cinders of the path on which he stood. Held up upon the sides of the cinders, suspended across the vast chasms between them, he saw the shed against the darkness of the path and the bright snow. He turned slowly taking care not to fall and plunge into the chasms between the cinders. He went back along the river to the long flight of stairs that climbed the bluff leading him toward home.

Tomaso had decided to remarry one mild spring day while walking alone beside the dark river. He had decided while studying the bare black trees and their dormant green buds swelling at the tips of black twigs. He had turned away from the trees, away from the river. He had seen the young couple, the girl upon the young man's lap, as they sat upon the stone steps leading up the bluff away from the river.

Tomaso had seen the young couple watching him bundled in his heavy topcoat climbing slowly toward them up the stairs one careful step at a time. He was aware of how he must appear to them with his bald round head and the great blue veins beneath the smooth skin. His lively dark eyes greeted them. His fingers twisted with age as he had taken his hand from his coat pocket reached for the young man's shoulder and lay his hand on the young man's shoulder as he passed. The young couple had smiled at Tomaso and then had turned toward each other as Tomaso passed. Tomaso wondered as he made his way toward home whether the couple ever would remember and talk about that old man they had seen that day on the steps leading up the bluff from the dark river wondering whatever had happened to him.

Seeing the couple, Tomaso had told himself of Margaret's kindness. He had told himself of the soft comfort in her bulk. He admitted that perhaps she reminded him just a little of Beatrice, his first wife. Poor Beatrice! He had said to himself while signing across his chest. He hoped she had rested in peace and was now in Paradise.

So the young couple had made him wonder: Why shouldn't he marry again. He had been alone long enough. His children could now easily care for themselves. What was to stop him? Before he had never really found anyone to take Beatrice's place. Who could ever be quite like his angel? So he had never really looked. Now, however, he had decided it was time.

He had met Margaret at a friendship club, a club for older people. Tomaso had always felt somehow out of place. The sight of these older people, some of them apparently feeble, others quivering from age, had made him uneasy. They all seemed banded together out of desperation. He wasn't desperate, and he wondered why he had even thought of coming. Yet, once he had met Margaret who clearly appeared neither feeble nor desperate, Tomaso had accepted the others. So after meeting Margaret he had gone often to that place. Each time he would search for her avoiding the old ones who always clustered together. Then he would spend the whole evening by her side telling her about his family, about the old days in Italy. And when the accordion band played a lively number, he would lead her out onto the dance floor carrying her along with his strange hopping that passed for dance. He would shout, too, enjoying the music and the movement, and everyone would laugh; then he would clap and shout when the music ended. Margaret accepted his display of energy quietly and with pleasure, for she felt her own particular kind of joy at his attention.

But as he walked going to see her that day after his walk by the river, he reminded himself that he would be Margaret's third husband should she finally accept his proposal. As far as he was concerned he would be her best since she had told him about her former life. Her life before had been one reason he decided to marry her. Surely he could give her more than what she had before. For Margaret in telling of her first husband, the father of her large son, revealed how she had left him in Germany when he had decided along with so many others to follow the burning torches and blazing flags with twisted crosses. She had told him how she had seen the coming plague of suffering and loss so that she had gathered her small child, how she had packed her shabby bags, and had left for an unknown life in America.

Tomaso also knew that her second husband had been a house painter, an angular man who drank heavily and who brought to their marriage five stepchildren. Tomaso was told that during this marriage she never counted on more than one good meal a week when her husband staggering home dull with whisky and reeking from paint and alcohol swayed as he placed the paper sack upon the table, swayed backward sweeping his arms with satisfaction as he pushed the spattered paint cap back up his head. She had told Tomaso how they had eaten heartily that meal. The rest of the week they ate stale bread dressed with lard saved from the one good meal of the week.

Tomaso recalled sitting quietly while Margaret told him how her second husband slowly died. She had remained at his side through his long agony. She had borne his cries of anger and of fear as the disease consumed his organs until his mind was drowned in pain. She had stood by his coffin as his children came to view him finally lying in peace.

Tomaso thought that in contrast Margaret surely was struck by his difference. She had not hesitated long when he had come to her excited in his usual way to ask her to consider marrying him. He had decided, just like that, and she had accepted his suggestion without hesitation.

Then her tall heavy son visiting her with his family had come to tower over him, smiling down at him, shaking his hand, the son's wife and children welcoming Tomaso to their family. Tomaso had been wild from the acceptance. They must go soon, Tomaso had insisted, They must get the license to marry. So he and Margaret had gone to the towering city hall, underneath the huge thick arches, though the massive heavy doors, into the dim interior. Then they were sent to doctors assigned to them by the Department of Public Health—Senior Citizens. Tomaso had objected to the examination. Why the need for an examination. "Look at me! Look at her! Don't we look healthy? They had hushed him quickly with their threat: No examination—no marriage license.

Tomaso relived that examination for a long time. How could he ever forget? He still felt embarrassed recalling the young nurse handing him the small jar with his name printed on the label, she asking for a sample, and he finally understanding what she requested. He recalled, too, the doctor asking him questions about his love life. Whose business was it other than Tomaso's? And then there was that funny feeling when the doctor had inspected his private parts and the young nurse right there outside the thin screen writing down everything the doctor told her.

Then at last the examination had ended, and they had left accompanied by the echoes of their voices off the high vaulted ceiling of the city hall and by the echo of the huge door closing. Their feet had scraped and sounded on the polished granite floor as Tomaso had led Margaret from the dimness beneath the great curved arches into the sunlight.

They had gone home to wait for examination results. That was the law. Tomaso had been upset. What a bother! Once he had decided to do this thing—to marry again, he had wanted it done quickly with as little delay and as little trouble as possible. For once he had made his move to marry again he realized again the pain of losing Beatrice. He had suddenly recalled the loneliness and the long years alone. True, yes very true, he told himself, he had his children and now grandchild. But, still, alone at night, his body, his spirit longed for the comfort of soft bulk beside him. But because some law said that they could only marry after waiting for results of their examinations, he had resigned himself to what seemed like an unbearable wait.

He had spent time visiting Margaret and talking to her son when her son was visiting, drinking with them, making them laugh at his stories of his boyhood in the old country. Margaret's son liked Tomaso. He could tell when the son had accepted his embrace. Stiff with size and from breeding, Margaret's son had been startled at Tomaso's offering him a kiss on leaving. Tomaso had first offered his hand; then he had offered his lips. The son had accepted, reluctantly at first. But because Tomaso was honest and open in his affection and because he was fun to be with, because, after all, he was soon to be his stepfather, the son finally had accepted Tomaso's embrace.

So Margaret's son had helped Tomaso in what had seemed to be the longest days he had ever known. But the good dark beer had helped to pass the time, and he had brought his dry blood-red wine. Both the beer and wine had loosened everyone's tongue as well as their spirits. As a result, everyone thought that this marriage was, indeed, a fortunate event for bringing together two such fine families. They all thought ahead to the many fine times that such a union would bring. They all thought of how they would look back and recall Tomaso's anxious wait to remarry. Someday they would laugh and tip their glasses of dark beer and Tomaso's red wine and declare how fortunate to have someone as much fun as Tomaso as part of their family despite the differences. He was amusing. He made them laugh. Sometimes Margaret would laugh until she cried.

Then Tomaso had received that phone call from the doctor's office.

He was still in bed in his room directly off the kitchen that was his family's daily gathering place, but he lay awake staring at the paint-covered cracks in the ceiling thinking of what might be ahead now that he had decided to take a wife. His unmarried daughter Lisa called through the door.

"Papa?" she asked. "It's the doctor's office!"

"The doctor!" He exclaimed. He threw back the covers and swung his legs over the side of the bed. But he had moved too fast again. He stood grasping the bedstead until the dizziness passed. Then not bothering about a robe or about slippers, he hurried through the door. His daughter frowned at his bare feet.

"Papa!" she commanded.

"Yes, yes," he said. "But we can't keep the doctor waiting."

She sighed, signed herself, and shrugged rolling her eyes to the ceiling for comfort and support. Tomaso had hurried to the phone to answer.

"Mr. Tomasino?" The woman's voice at the other end seemed pleasant enough.

"Si! Yes, that's me," Tomaso said.

"You had a physical examination with us recently."

"Yes. Yes. That's right. Last week."

"Yes. Well, the doctor would like to see you about it," the woman said.

"Sure," Tomaso agreed. "But what's the trouble?"

"I think you'd better come down here as soon as you can," the woman said.

"Sure, sure," Tomas said then was silent, and the woman on the other end was silent too, and Tomaso listened to the silence on the line."

"Mr. Tomasino, if you're able to come down today, the doctor will talk to you then. We have an opening this afternoon at one o'clock. Can you make that?"

"Yes," Tomaso said. "I'll be down right away. Thank you for calling."

Tomaso hung the receiver on the hook. He turned to see the anxious face of his daughter. What would he do with Lisa? Almost thirty now, still unmarried, and he about to take another wife. Everyone urged her to find a man. Lisa only became self-conscious.

"What's the matter, Papa?" she asked. Her dark eyes had scanned his face looking for some sign.

"I don't know," Tomaso admitted. "Something about the examination I had last week. I must go to see the doctor."

"Something's wrong, Papa!"

"No, no," Tomaso insisted. "It's only something they forgot."

"Don't *lie* to me, Papa!"

"Who's lying? I don't know. The woman said 'come soon.' I'm going right away."

"You never take care of yourself," his daughter scolded. "You never let us take care of you." Her voice indicated her fear. "Look at you now!" She cried. "Look how you are! No wonder something's wrong!"

"Who said something's wrong?' He waved his hands at her. "The woman said to come, that's all, so what can be wrong? I'm going now. I'll find out. I'll tell you. I promise. You'll see. Nothing's wrong."

Then he kissed her and patted her hand and turned toward his bedroom. He closed the door behind him. He turned to dress.

When Tomaso returned, his daughter was waiting for him, her dark eyes large and searching. Tomaso could see that she wanted him to speak, but when he entered, he only met her eyes. Then he went past her to the kitchen.

She followed then waited while he removed his topcoat, while he went to hang it in the closet of his bedroom, while he returned running his hand over his hairless head, rubbing his hands against the chill of the early spring day.

He poured himself coffee from a pot that always seemed to be ready. He seated himself at the table. He lit a cigarette. Lisa didn't protest. She sat across from him waiting, knowing that when he was ready he would tell her. He cleared his throat.

Of course, he had told Lisa the truth. He wondered now why he had ever done so. What good had it done? But he had promised even though he knew he should have kept quiet. He should have just gone ahead with his plan to marry Margaret without revealing anything to anyone. Then he would live as best he could as long as he could.

Poor Lisa! How she had tried not to show her feelings. And she had managed somehow. She left the room finally, but she had managed. She had tried to remain there. He had realized how much she had wanted to help him. But he had ended by helping her, comforting her, assuring her. Perhaps his attitude of resignation had made her leave.

He didn't intend to be resigned. His resignation was more from shock. He simply tried to deal with what he had learned. She had left the room. He remained staring out the window not seeing anything trying to grasp the reality of what he had been told. Yes, what was happening was real. Yes, he had expected a time like this sometime in his life. He had never considered that such a moment would trouble him. Problems about one's being or not being were always something that he would accept later when they occurred.

Before, he had always expected it would happen suddenly, perhaps violently. Like everyone, his life had its share of trouble: His childhood in the old country. There had been the wars. He had survived those. He had survived marriage. He had survived many in his family, including Beatrice, his wife. Now, having survived this long, he had looked forward to settling down with Margaret, slowly dropping toward senility then that long dreamless sleep. But along the way—along the way—oh, how he had expected to shine and enjoy those good years before him. Now, he had this—something inside consuming him, devouring his life. He felt caged. He felt bitter. After everything—this—only this: Pain, loneliness, a slow decay, the same as Margaret's second husband.

He went for a long walk along the river; he went to see the priest; he went to see Margaret; he went to his local tavern; he finally returned home. Along the river, he had seen the dirty yellow shed with its stove, its pot of brown orange slime, and its endless card game. Such was the purpose of life? The priest had tried to help, but he could only offer what Tomaso already now accepted on faith and only turned the problem back to Tomaso who understood at once that the problem was his alone as it was for everyone, no matter how they might express their concern and sympathy. Seeing Margaret, he, of course, considered telling her what he had learned from the doctor, but then his fear of her having sensed something wrong because of his unexpected visit and that she would no longer want to marry him if he told her what he had learned so saddened him that he quickly left, his sudden departure surprising her again.

He should have never told Lisa. Perhaps he feared that Lisa might accidentally, perhaps even intentionally, tell someone else, perhaps she might tell Margaret because he knew that Lisa didn't approve of Margaret marrying Tomaso, and her revealing his condition to Margaret could be one way of preventing them from marrying. For he recalled again Margaret's second husband and what she had said: Never again would she want to see something like what she had witnessed in her husband's slow demise.

Yet he also wanted to believe that no matter how much Lisa disapproved of his marrying anyone, she was still a loving daughter and would eventually accept what he so obviously wanted. Besides, had he committed Lisa to secrecy? Why should he have kept it secret? But he realized now that had he not even told Lisa he would have made the situation easier for everyone. They wouldn't have treated him any differently. He suddenly would be gone. They would be shocked, but they would recover.

Of course, his recalling what Margaret had told him about her former husband had been the reason for his deciding not to say anything to her of what he had learned. Yet if he did tell her and she no longer wanted to marry him, as he expected, he wouldn't blame her really, but perhaps he could offer her substitutes. He was well enough off, reasonably so. He had worked hard, saved consistently, invested wisely, lived prudently. And whatever he had would be hers. She would be secure then if not happy. And along the way she would help him without her knowing. But what would be her response once his condition eventually became apparent? So he was saddened when he could not bring himself to reveal to her the truth.

The dim tavern he had gone to after visiting Margaret was empty. As usual, Ricci, his friend, had been behind the bar. Tomaso had wondered what had happened to his other friends whom he had frequently met there to exchange banter in Italian. Ricci had asked about Tomaso's health. Suddenly the dimness of the bar, the bitter odors had annoyed him and made him feel ill. He left his glass unfinished.

He wandered back along the gaily-colored storefronts that issued a rich mixture of aromas along with colors and sounds of the old country as people in doorways talked and greeted him, he returning their greetings in kind. He wandered back along the high old house fronts he remembered as new. He walked beside the thick towering trees that lined the street. He had seen some of those trees as saplings. Now they stood enduring. But like everything else, how long would they remain? He had seen cutting crews. He recalled the wild erratic snarl of the chainsaw, the white core wood that still smelled ripe. Thank God the house when he returned was quiet.

Even to Tomaso when he returned home, the house appeared just like any of the others along the street of similar houses: two story flats with slat board siding built in the early years he had lived in the area. Wooden stairs leading up to the high wood front porch beside the bank of tall windows along the front wall opening to the street and the small plot of grass. Beside the house a slight incline of two concrete tracks separated by a strip of grass or packed black dirt led to a small area of concrete before the small garage large enough for one vehicle but typically used more for storage than for sheltering an auto.

As he entered, he knew without noticing the interior that was also similar to those of other houses throughout the city: Tomaso knew from having lived here so many years the dark stained wood interior, the large front room with the row of tall windows overlooking the small patch of grass and the street. He knew the living room and the high ceilings of all the rooms, the dark wood square archways and dark wood pillars separating the living room from the dining room. He knew the large thick-legged dining table, the three tall windows along the sidewall opening to the driveway and a view of the similar flat next door.

He knew the dark stained wood of the tall sideboard with the glass front cabinets that covered the wall separating the dining room from the kitchen, the large mirror between the cabinets and the framed photographs above the mirror, some bled with time. He knew the doorway to the left of the sideboard that led from the dining room to the two other bedrooms separated by the tiled bathroom.

He moved through the dining room to the doorway right of the sideboard opening to the expansive kitchen with a high ceiling, everything of one color—white: baseboards, doorframes, appliances, sink, table, and tablecloth where at that table he sat for meals with one or more members of his family enjoying the hearty food that one or both his daughters prepared always reminding him of his youth in Italy.

A large picture window on the sidewall of the kitchen allowed him a view of the driveway and small concrete area before the garage and the small plot of black earth between the house and driveway. Through this window he could also view the small fenced yard and the pillared back porch of the house across the driveway with a door the same as Tomaso's that opened to the kitchen.

Off the kitchen beside the large ceramic sink with washboard counter a small room with toilet and sink, and immediately before the small room another larger room with high ceiling that had space enough for a double bed, a dresser, and chair. A small closet opened in the wall opposite the bed. From this room Tomaso could venture forth to survey or join his family and to where he could retire seeking sanctuary.

Yet as soon as he arrived home and removed his coat, while hanging it in its usual place in the closet of his room, he thought of that young couple he had seen that day as they huddled on the steps leading down to the river. He thought of the birthday celebration for him tomorrow with his whole family around him. And again he thought of his visit to Margaret.

When he had gone to see her earlier, he had asked Margaret again to join him and his family for his birthday celebration. She, again, had refused. No, she insisted, it was his day; he should spend it alone with his family. Her refusal had made him want to tell her what he had learned from the doctor. Then she would refuse to marry him. Why not, he had decided, resign himself to defeat? He had been alone this long. Why not a little longer? Then he would be gone and she and all of them could go on with their lives. Still, he had insisted on her presence.

"You should be there," he had told her. He stood in his coat still buttoned against the spring chill.

"I tell you, no!" she, in turn, insisted.

"You should be part of the family!" he cried.

"I will be soon, won't I? she asked. "There will many times more that I will be there with your family for your birthdays."

"Margaret!" Tomaso cried stung by her assurance.

Then he stood silent. How could he begin? What could he say? What could he tell her now? That he needed her more than ever? Was that enough? And she most likely would ask why. What then would he say? He would tell her what he had learned?

He felt tired now. What would he feel when everyone would be watching him as if they were waiting? He would be tired of everyone treating him as if he were fragile. He wanted something else. He wanted peace and acceptance. Was that too much to ask? She would help to distract them. They would all be so busy getting used to her being there, of her living there, she would disrupt the pattern of their remorse and disrupt the gloom that would settle upon them. She would be a blessed intruder.

"Help me, Margaret!" he had wanted to plead, but again he kept silent.

He had seen her study him searching his face as if she had read his thoughts. What had she seen? His face thinning, growing gaunt, the large blue veins already becoming more prominent, the ridges of the skull more sharply defined? He understood that she knew such signs well. She had witnessed it before. She had told him it always took longer than one thought.

He had turned from her then and wandered to the window then turned back sullen and bitter. "I better go."

"But you've only just come," she said.

"I shouldn't be here. I should be home. They're waiting dinner for me. And tomorrow? My birthday? Guess what? We are going to have a cake. My god, I need a cake! They have candles, too. Candles—just like a kid! One for every year! We'll probably burn down the house if we light them all!"

He buttoned his coat around his neck against the spring chill. He moved to embrace her.

"Ciao, Margaret! he said. Then he turned toward the door.

"Auf Wiedersehen!" she replied. "Happy birthday!"

"Grazie! he said then left.

"Guido! Lisa cried with joy. "Papa! Guido's home!"

Guido had snuck in the back door as he had always done while living there.

Then in the brief spell before the others came, Lisa, surprised and delighted, clung to him while her brother swept her off her feet whirling her around the kitchen in his arms. At the stove, Maria, Tomaso's older daughter, laughed then lah lahed a tarantella, accompanying them by waving her large spoon.

"How's my favorite girl?" Guido asked wooing her as always, stopping their dance, standing back, still holding her.

"You say that to all your women," Lisa countered.

"My favorite girl," he insisted releasing her from his arms.

She studied his dark handsome features, the dark wavy hair, the large dark eyes, all these features a mirror of her own. Both of them reflections of the their mother, Tomaso's Beatrice.

"I'm fine, now that you're here." She yielded, smiling, finally releasing him.

He went to Maria quietly greeting her with a kiss on the cheek. She smiled patting his face.

Then the others rambled in from the other room where they had been absorbed in a TV sport event of a local team. Gruff, heavy Bruno, Maria's husband, came, his loud rasping voice, his bald pate, his thick hairy arms with huge hands and sausage fingers, his hairy knuckles that he offered now with his quick embrace. Frankie Boy followed all arms and legs and loose lingering adolescence, his lean face flamed and pocked with acne. Then finally, the Old Man, Tomaso who seemed gnome-like, his dwarf-like body, his large bald head with its great blue veins showing through the taut skin at the edges of the skull, his muscular arms, his large, knurled hands. The others stepped aside to let him through.

"Guido." Tomaso acknowledged quietly.

His son stooped to return his kiss and his embrace.

"What's the occasion?" The old man's eyes bored into his son from behind his glasses.

"Occasion!" Guido countered. "It's your birthday tomorrow, Papa. I came to see you."

"Too long you've been away." Tomaso growled.

"You're right," Guido admitted. "I was passing through town. We have an engagement here. I thought I'd better stop to come see you, especially since it's your birthday tomorrow. You're not getting any younger." He exchanged glances with the others over his father's bald dome of head.

"Hey!" Tomaso yelled. "Watch what you say in my house! Who you think's getting old? Not me!"

"No, not you, Papa." Then. "You been to the doctor lately?"

"Who told?" Tomaso searched the faces of the others. Lisa turned away toward the stove. "It's nothing," Tomaso insisted following Lisa's movements. "Just a checkup, that's all. A man of my age has to be a little careful. Suppose I decide to marry again? I'd need to know I'm still strong." *Capisce?*

"Married! Who'd marry you?" Guido joked, but the others didn't laughed. Then they seemed to scatter, Bruno going for the jug of wine, tall Frankie Boy draping his arms over the top of the refrigerator studying everyone's moves. Maria retreated to the alcove of the sink and cupboards. Lisa at the sink washed dishes. The two men, father and son, were left alone facing each other in the desert of the checkered tile kitchen floor. The high old ceiling of the old house soared above them filled with billowing from steaming pots. Tomaso glanced at them then turned to his son.

"You don't know her since you've been gone so long," Tomaso said. We already have license to marry."

"You're kidding!"

"I don't joke about such things."

The silence was deadly. Then Tomaso turned toward the stove.

"Lisa!"

"What, Papa?"

"Don't 'what Papa' me! How come Guido's here?"

"Hey, look," Guide broke in. "Can't I ever come to see my Old Man for his birthday?"

"Don't call me that."

"Wow, Papa! Why you so touchy? Look, we're stopping over for a couple of performances. I was so close, I thought I'd have a chance to see you."

"It's about time. You stay away always too long."

"I've been busy, Papa. I've finally made it! I've got what I've always dreamed of. You should be happy for me, Papa!"

"Fine. We're happy for you." He scanned the faces of the others watching. "So you got success. But no time to see your own family."

"I shouldn't be here now, but I was so close, how could I pass up the chance. I have to get back soon for tonight's performance but I wanted to see everybody."

"Sure. You come. You go. Hello. Goodbye. That's all!" Tomaso complained.

Hey!" Bruno shouted them down returning with the wine. "He's here. Let's enjoy him while we can!"

He handed Tomaso and Guido a coblet from the tab and filled them, then filled his own. He set the jug of wine beside the table pushed against the large window that looked out at the gray slating of the flat across the driveway. "Your health!" he said. He quaffed the wine.

"*Salute!*" the others chorused sullenly.

When the meal was finally ready Lisa called. Tomaso went in before the others. He sat alone at the table toying with the utensils set beside the plates on the fresh tablecloth. The knife and fork touched each other then clinked against the plate. Tomaso sat in the corner between the wall and table next to the large window that overlooked the driveway hidden from the overcast. Tomaso sat with his hands holding his head, another cigarette smoking between the fingers of one hand. He listened to the chatter of the women at the stove across the kitchen. He looked up to watch his son and son-in-law engrossed in the game they were watching on TV. The blue light of the TV reflected from their dark eyes.

Guido sensed Tomaso's gaze. He turned and met his father's searching eyes; then he turned again to his own interest.

The women bustled in the kitchen passing each other as they carried food from the stove to the sink then as they brought food steaming to the table then as they returned to the stove or sink. Before Tomaso they seat a large oval platter of glistening pasta. He waited. Then Lisa called a second time, and the others finally appeared.

Good looking Guido, the dancer and ladies' man, waltzed in. Bruno, coarse, heavy, thick, lumbered in after. Guido grabbed Lisa, spinning her, waltzing her again around the kitchen. Lisa gasped with delight.

"Lisa's finally got a man!" Bruno exclaimed. His deep gruff voice betrayed his kindness.

"Oh, baby!" Guido panted. "Be mine. Make me the happiest of men!"

Plain dark thin Lisa laughed throwing back her head letting herself be swept along by Guido's sure deft movements, "Don't tease!" she cried.

"Me tease?" "You're just too pure."

"You watch it, girl. You'll get something yet!" Bruno joked.

Maria howled with shocked glee and feigned offense.

"Enough!" Tomaso snapped.

They quieted. They rustled to their chairs and seated themselves at the table in their accustomed places.

Bruno took the glasses passed to him. He filled the glasses from the large gurgling jug then passed them back. Bruno set the jug beside the chair on the side where the table sat along the wall under the large window that looked out upon the concrete driveway bordered by barren black earth that Tomaso's grandchild dug in leaving hollows. Tomaso studied the gray overlapping slats of the neighboring house. Tomaso sipped at his wine. The women finally took their places sliding in their chairs to the table. Then they called again for Frankie Boy, already adult but still living at home, and Frankie came thin and tall with a long face, dark hair, and dark eyes just like the others. Frankie came with fluid movements collapsing loosely onto his chair muttering to himself, expressing himself with limp movements of his hands and arms. Frankie settled himself in his own peculiar fashion pulling his chair up to the table, swaying before he quieted then signed himself joining the family in prayer for blessing of the food. Lisa stood with folded hands while Tomaso prayed then signed himself on finishing. The others followed. Then Tomaso reached for the platter of pasta, and Lisa turned toward the stove.

By the time he had finished his second large glass of wine, Tomaso had mellowed. He sat back in his chair watching while the others served themselves pasta and chicken from the large platters, bread from the basket. Then they ate while joking, laughing, and chattering so that the high hollow room was filled with the sound of their communion.

Lisa was seated next to her father quietly studying him, eating slowly as she always did while the others wolfed their food.

"Eat, Papa," she urged quietly.

"Sure. Sure," Tomas said. "I'm not so hungry now."

"You hardly eat anything anymore."

"I eat enough," he insisted.

Then she was quiet again enjoying the few moments her father was still. "It's your day tomorrow," she said finally. "What do you want for your birthday?"

Tomaso shrugged. "I don't need anything."

"You must want something."

"Nothing!" he insisted.

"Guido," Lisa pleaded. "Help me! Papa says he doesn't want anything for his birthday tomorrow."

Guido turned from his talking with the others. "Come on, Papa! You need something."

"I want Margaret here!" Tomaso demanded.

The others studied him with mixed expressions: Lisa grim, Guido puzzled, Maria, Bruno, and Frankie Boy curious.

"Sure!" Tomaso said. "You asked. Why you ask if you don't like?"

"You want her here?"

"Why not? It's my birthday! I'm still here! This is still my house! If I say what I want, that's what I want!"

"I don't know if that's a good idea, Papa."

"Then go!"

"Hey! Hey! You two!" Bruno shouted. "Let's eat in peace."

"Hush now," Maria soothed. "We'll work it out so that Papa has what he wants."

"What's the big deal?" Frankie Boy asked. "If that's what he wants for his birthday?"

"Suppose I marry?" Tomaso asked. "What then? You'll leave?"

"She won't have you, Papa."

"She will. You'll see. What then?"

But Lisa remained silent.

"Let's eat," Guido offered. "How about more wine?"

The others settled again and resumed their eating. They drank more wine.

"I've noticed something," Guido said. "There seems to be more fighting now. How come?"

"She starts it!" Tomaso snarled. "My own daughter. Ask her!"

Tomaso was aware of his family around him at the table. He saw the heaps of food; he quaffed the strong dry wine. He heard the loud abandoned laughter as the others ate. Tomaso thought about his old decaying body. How had it grown so old? He fought his feelings. Yet, tears welled in his eyes. The laughter hushed. Tomaso's grandchild Little Tom ran in late shouting. He stopped short halted by the sudden silence and by Bruno, his father, pulling him to his side.

"I'm sorry," Tomaso said. "I'm very sorry." He wiped his eyes with his napkin; he blew his nose; he stared back at his family watching him.

The women looked down into their laps. Bruno slowly shook his head struggling for words.

"Come on, Pa. You'll outlive us all," he said. He toyed with the food on his plate. Lisa rose setting her lips, pushing back her chair. She went to turn on the flame beneath the coffee.

Tomaso saw that he had soured their mood. He poured himself wine, drank it down, and poured himself more.

"Don't drink so much, Papa!" That was Lisa as always.

He ignored her. He began to sing as he always did when there was unnatural stillness at the table. Silence was for funerals he had said often. So now he sang songs from his boyhood in Italy. Thus he lost himself in remembrance and in the warmth of wine. He filled their glasses. Then they finally joined him in his song.

The next day on his birthday Tomaso indulged himself by sleeping late. When he woke, he rose and dressed and came out to the kitchen for his coffee and cigarette. Then he went for his usual walk down the steps of the steep bluff and along the river until he reached the yellow shed with billowing black smoke. There he turned and went back to the steps that took him up the bluff.

When Tomaso reached home, he hung his coat in its place then turned and wandered through the rooms of the house wringing warmth into his thin cold hands. He rubbed until the knuckles went white against the tendons and the veins. The house felt tingling warm after the cold. The women were in the kitchen. They gossiped while they cooked. They helped each other, and the chatter and the gossip helped them in their work. Tomaso felt alienated and alone. He wandered to the front room. Bruno, little Tomaso, Maria's child, and Frankie Boy, were watching spring training baseball on TV.

"Sit down, Pa!" Bruno invited. "It's a good game."

Frankie Boy offered Tomaso his seat.

"No. Sit! I'm fine."

He moved again. He stopped by the sideboard set against the wall of the dining room. A mirror hung above the drawers between the glass cases of dishware. Tomaso studied himself in the mirror. He saw again that dome of baldhead with the great blue veins. Then he looked above the mirror to the picture of the young man in sailor's uniform. The young man had thick wavy hair and a thick black mustache. In some ways, the young man in the photo reminded him of Guido. But Guido was thinner and had some of the features of Beatrice, Tomaso's first wife.

Tomaso turned from the photograph of his younger self and wandered into the kitchen. He poured himself coffee and lit a cigarette from someone's pack on the kitchen table.

"Papa!" Lisa scolded. "You're smoking too much!"

Tomaso shrugged. As if his smoking too much mattered now. He rose and left the room. The women stood hushed.

Tomaso approached the two men watching TV.

"We should go get Margaret," he said.

"You'll think she'll come?" Frankie Boy asked.

"She will if you two and Little Tom ask her. How can she refuse?

"It's worth a try," Bruno said. "If that's what you want."

"That's what I want."

Bruno and Frankie rose and went for their coats. Little Tom went for his coat in his bedroom. Then he made a side trip to the kitchen.

"We're going to get Grandpa's girlfriend," he informed the women who stopped in their work, Maria glancing at Lisa who stood mute at the stove.

Then Little Tom joined the men as they left through the front door.

Guido arrived while Bruno and Frankie Boy along with Little Tom took Tomaso to fetch Margaret. They were determined to bring her back to celebrate Tomaso's birthday despite her having insisted that Tomaso should dine alone with his family on his day. Maria was off in some other part of the house.

Lisa and Guido hugged each other again until she finally began to relax, her dark head of hair worn Madonna style resting on his chest. Then he stepped back holding her by the shoulders at arms length, searching her dark eyes and her features so much like his own.

"Now what's all this about Papa?" he asked aloud.

"He wants to get married."

"So he said. So what? You know him. If he's made up his mind."

"But he's old, Guido!"

"Better not let him hear you say that," he teased.

"Oh, Guido, be serious! Just this one time!"

He held her hand again, "Sure, Sweet. For you, anything."

"What will we do?"

"It's not that bad, his marrying, is it?"

"But it is. He's sick, Guido. He's dying!"

Guido sat back in his chair to study her anxious face, her frightened eyes. "You're serious," he said.

"Of course I'm serious. Would I lie or joke about something like that? He told me just after he saw the doctor. They found something, took some tests, called him back. I was here. I answered the phone. I don't know. I can't remember what it is I was so upset when he told me, and he didn't fully understand what they told him. But it's bad. I know that."

Guido searched her eyes then turned from her and went to the window. Between the house and the driveway, the black earth he had dug in as a child lay barren and stark, pocked with hollows from children's games, pebbled with small white stones that seemed like bones.

"And he still wants to get married."

"Yes. He insists. Now he wants to more than ever.

Guido followed the gray slats of the house across the driveway up to the eaves, the gutters, the gray overcast above.

"So let him get married. It's his life."

"But she's as old as he is! What would they have together?"

"Don't sell them short, Lisa. They could be stronger than we are.

"He's dying, Guido! Don't you understand?"

"Maybe she'll help him. She'll keep him busy."

"But she's not one of us! It's disgraceful! She's not even religious. I don't know what she is. Some flavor of Protestant. How could she fit in with us?"

"She'll change. Papa will insist."

"How do you know? You haven't even met her."

"Is she coming for Papa's birthday?

"Bruno, Frankie, and Little Tom have gone with Papa to try to persuade her to come. I don't know if she will be here."

"Well, if she's here, I'll talk to her when I get a chance. Does she know about Papa?"

"I think so, but I'm not sure. I hear them on the phone. He keeps begging her and she keeps saying no. What for, I'm not sure."

"Papa? Beg!"

"Well, it's not exactly begging. But he keeps asking her over and over to become part of the family. You should hear. He's like a boy younger

244

than Frankie. He talks to her I don't know for how long. It seems like hours."

"Don't listen. It's none of your business."

"It *is* my business. He's my father. He's an old man. And he's dying. We have to take care of him. He never seems to care for himself."

"That's just the way he is, Lisa. You know that. Let him be. Love him. Help him. But do it quietly."

"You sound just like the priest."

"Me? Come on now! I'd never make a good priest.

His mood changed suddenly to meet her petulance as it reached its zenith. He reached for her, drew her up out of her chair, and swept her up in his arms.

"You really think I'd make a good priest?" he teased.

"You're terrible!" she scolded.

He waltzed her around the checkered tile floor. "Just think what understanding I'd have."

"Guido!" she cried. "Stop it, please! We have to think."

He stopped and studied her. "Try not to worry, Sweet. We'll do what we can. But don't make his life miserable. Not at the end. Love him. Be with him. And if he wants to marry, let her do whatever she can if she accepts him. Maybe she'll help."

"How can you stand there and talk like that? He's your father! You can't just let it go like that!"

"Well, what am I suppose to do? he shouted. Her insistence was beginning to make him angry. "I will do what I can! We'll get him the best treatment and care we can! We'll love him! What else is there?"

"Quiet down, Guido. Maria will hear. And she'll tell Papa."

"Maybe she should hear. Maybe someone should tell Papa. Then he'd know what his daughter has been up to."

"But I have to do something!"

"Get married yourself," Guido said abruptly, startling her. She searched his face. "I'm not joking," he said. "Find a man of your own to take his place."

She stared at him stunned by his blunt words. Then he touched her arm and turned from her. He left going for his coat by the door at the other side of the house.

"I'll be back!" he called over his shoulder.

Lisa heard the closing door as he left her alone with her worry and grief.

"Look who's here!" Tomaso yelled as he entered leading the way followed shyly by Margaret. Little Tom clung to Margaret's hand, Frankie and Bruno came up behind. Maria came to greet them, but Lisa remained in the kitchen.

"I'm so glad you decided to come," Maria offered. She came forward to embrace Margaret in welcome.

"Well," Margaret said. "They made me an offer I could not refuse," she joked. Maria laughed touching Margaret's arm. Frankie and Bruno chuckled politely. Tomaso beamed.

"Little Tom was the one who won her over." Bruno said.

"We all helped." Frankie added.

"How could I refuse such a charming little boy?" Margaret confessed. "And also the kind invitation by your brother and husband?" she added.

"Little Tom takes after his uncle Guido," Bruno said. The comment sailed by Margaret, but Frankie nodded in agreement, and Little Tom smiled self-consciously.

Then Tomaso helped Margaret out of her coat; the others took off theirs. Frankie collected them and hung them in the closet by the front door while the others paraded into the kitchen.

"Look who's here." Tomaso announced.

Lisa stood at the sink preparing a salad. She set down the knife, wiped her hands on her apron, and turned, a weak smile on her tight lips.

"This is Margaret," Tomaso said. "Margaret, my daughter Lisa."

Lisa moved forward offering her hand in greeting. Margaret moved to meet her taking Lisa's hand in both her hands then softly embraced Lisa surprising her, stepping back holding onto Lisa's arms.

"I am so glad now that we are finally met." Margaret said smiling, her eyes bright behind her wire-frame glasses.

Lisa felt on display with everyone watching. "Welcome to my home," she offered glancing at her father to see his response.

Tomaso ignored Lisa's remark about 'my home'. Instead his face displayed his delight watching the two women greet each other.

"So you're finally here," Tomaso said. "Come. Have a seat."

"How about some wine." Bruno added.

"A small glass maybe. That would be nice."

"We ought to have champagne," Tomaso said.

The others were surprised but enjoyed Tomaso's excitement.

"For your birthday you always have champagne?" Margaret asked. She searched the faces of the others standing around where she sat at the table.

"No, not for my birthday." Tomaso said. "To celebrate our coming marriage."

"You still going to get married!" Bruno exclaimed. Then he realized what he had asked when Maria nudged him. But Margaret appeared not to have understood his remark.

"Sure, why not?" Tomaso asked. Then he pulled up a chair close to Margaret. "So when will we marry?" he asked quietly taking her hand.

"Such a surprise," she said. "With all your family here? What must they think?" She searched the display of mixed expressions on those witnessing the exchange.

Little Tom was the first to voice his approval: "Then you can come live with us!"

Margaret reached for him to hug him. "Such a sweet boy." she said.

Maria, Bruno, and Frankie just nodded their acceptance. Lisa stood silent.

"But first we celebrate your birthday," Margaret suggested. Then we must talk again soon about marrying."

Even before they sat to eat, everyone decided that the celebration of Tomaso's birthday would be one of the best they ever had. Tomaso was pleased. Everyone praised Lisa's preparations as the food was delivered to the table. Margaret especially exclaimed her admiration.

"Maria helped. She always does," Lisa insisted.

"Just wait until the wedding!" he promised. "You'll see what Lisa can do!"

But Lisa protested. "I can't do all that! There's just too much to do! You can't expect me to do all that!"

"No! No!" Tomaso said. He was pleased that she at least seemed to have resigned herself to her father marrying. "We'll hire people to do the work of course. You will just make sure that everything is right. No skimping on anything!"

Lisa appeared relieved. "Well, we should eat. Everything's ready."

"Where's Guido? Tomaso asked. "He said he would be here."

"Guido was here but went out earlier," Lisa explained. "He might have had a performance this afternoon. But when he left he said he'd be back."

"Maybe we should wait for Guido."

"Let's have more wine. Come, Margaret. Sit by me."

Tomaso directed her toward the chair at the end of the table next to his at the end where Lisa always sat. Margaret sat, and Bruno, Frankie, and Maria studied Lisa for her response. Lisa turned toward the sink to finish the salad. Maria joined her to help prepare the food. The others stood waiting not sure how Margaret's displacement of Lisa would affect their seating.

"Sit!" Tomaso ordered.

But before they could maneuver around each other. They heard the front door open.

Guido entered shaking himself from his coat while handing a large paper bag to Bruno. "Here. You can open this." Guido said.

"Champagne!

"For Papa's birthday!"

"No." Tomaso said. "For our marrying! Quick! Get the glasses!"

And everyone laughed.

Tomaso introduced Margaret to Guido who went to her taking her hand.

"So this is the lovely lady who's stealing our Papa's affections."

"Who's stealing?" Tomaso protested. I give her my love gladly. And there's plenty left for the rest of you because my heart is big."

"Sure, Papa." Guido turned back to Margaret still holding her hand then drew her up from her chair and embraced her leading her out to the checkered floor of the kitchen and twirling her in a slow dance delighting her.

"You should have warned her about him!" Bruno quipped.

"Guido!" Tomaso commanded. "Behave yourself! Come! We're now ready to eat.

Guido guided Margaret back to her chair. "You can't always have her for yourself, Papa, now that she'll soon be one of us." Then he bowed to her and went to the end of the table opposite Tomaso. "Where's the champagne?" he asked.

Maria brought glasses. Bruno poured for everyone. Even Little Tom was given a small amount. He was wide-eyed impressed at being considered old enough to have a share.

Guido raised his glass. "Let's drink to Margaret and Papa for their union and for the long and happy life that they will share."

And everyone, even Lisa, joined Guido in his blessing.

Then they sorted out the new seating arrangement. Maria helped. Margaret would move to the other side of the table by the window next to Tomaso. Lisa would regain her usual place allowing her freedom of movement to the stove and sink and cupboard. Maria would sit next to Lisa. Little Tom would sit next to Maria. Guido moved from his place to sit beside Margaret allowing Bruno to regain his usual place at the end opposite Tomaso next to Little Tom. Frankie would sit beside Guido. So now that they were ordered they sipped their champagne, and as Lisa and Maria brought more platters and dishes of food to the table placing them in the center within easy reach of all, they began. Tomaso took up the platter of pasta and held it for Margaret.

"We always start with pasta," Tomaso explained. He helped her with her plate.

"Just a little, please. So much food there is that I'm not used to." Margaret said.

Tomaso passed the platter to Guido who served himself then passed the platter down the table. So they began and so they continued until their plates were full, joined finally by Lisa and Maria who settled into their chairs and filled their plates. Then they all paused.

"Margaret?" Lisa asked. "Would you please lead us in giving thanks?"

Tomaso studied his daughter but was silent.

"If you would like." Margaret said. "I would be pleased."

Then she offered her thanks for being here with such kind and loving people and for so much food. And she asked for health and happiness for all those in this home filled with so much love.

She sat silent while the others signed themselves. She waited until the others began to eat. Then she joined them.

When they finished their meal Maria went to prepare coffee while Lisa went to bring the cake that she had made with Maria's help.

Margaret exclaimed her admiration of the cake. Bruno and Frankie agreed with her remark. Little Tom was overwhelmed by the size.

"But what about candles?" Little Tom asked. "We ought to have candles! It's not a birthday cake if it doesn't have candles!"

"We decided to limit candles to one for each decade." Maria said as she began placing candles on the cake.

"*Bene!*" Tomaso exclaimed. "That should be enough. We don't want to burn down the house."

Everyone laughed.

When the doorbell chimed and Margaret went to answer the door, on opening it she was pleased to see the young woman who stood at her doorstep in a long black coat and black shawl to ward off the spring chill.

"Lisa!" Margaret cried in delight. "How nice to see you. Come in, come in why don't you? Welcome.

Lisa smiled at Margaret's cheerful greeting noting again how Margaret always pronounced her "w's" as "v's," sounds that lingered from her first language.

Margaret turned aside allowing the young woman to enter.

"Thank you," Lisa said as she passed Margaret who held the door. Lisa shook off her shawl letting her long black hair fall free.

"Would you like coffee perhaps?" Margaret asked. She searched the thin pale features still young most likely reflecting those of Tomaso's first wife. "I've just brewed a fresh pot."

"Thank you," Lisa said. "I would enjoy that. The air still has a chill."

Margaret turned and led Lisa into the kitchen. "Yes. But with spring finally comes nice weather. Let me have your coat, Lisa."

Lisa shook herself from her coat then handed it to Margaret who took it into the front room and placed it over the back of a chair. Then she returned to the kitchen. Lisa had draped the shawl over her shoulders.

"Please," Margaret said, motioning for Lisa to sit. Then as Lisa sat at the table, Margaret took two heavy fireware mugs from the cupboard and placed them on the counter next to the sink. She took up the pot sitting on the stove and filled the cups with coffee that was steaming and fresh and pungent. She brought the cups to the table and set one before Lisa.

"Thank you," Lisa said. She lifted the cup to her lips and sipped the hot brew then set in on the table. "That's good," she said. "Papa has mentioned your coffee and how good it always tastes."

Margaret just smiled. "I've been doing that for a long time," she said.

"Papa has been drinking coffee for a long time."

"Yes, he has. And we've shared many cups since we met."

"You could share your coffee with all of us."

"You are all welcome to come visit anytime."

"Yes, we know. That's why I came. Especially after my behavior at Papa's birthday."

"What behavior? I noticed nothing. You welcomed me. You were very gracious to me in your home. I had a very pleasant time. And you have such a nice house and such a nice family. But you came for something else."

"Yes."

"About your Papa wanting us to marry."

"Yes."

"He's told you that I think that our marrying would not now be so good?"

"He's told me that you thought you both were too old to marry. And we know what we learned from the examination you both had for the license. Is that perhaps what has changed your mind about marrying Papa?"

"Yes. But I have not said to him anything about the examination."

Lisa studied Margaret's face behind her wire-rimmed glasses. She sipped her coffee. "Then he hasn't told you anything?"

"What should he have told me?" Margaret asked.

"Better he tell you himself. But he's said that he did not want to burden you because of what you have experienced in your previous marriages. Why would he not want to burden you?"

"Perhaps because my life before was not always so happy as now with your father."

"What happened? Please, if you can, help me understand."

Then Lisa listened while Margaret recalled for her what Margaret had told Tomaso about her former life. After Margaret finished, Lisa sat quiet. She sipped her coffee. "I'm sorry for you," she said.

"No need for you to feel sorry for me. All that's past. All that was part of living. Now with your father, I have had a good life. But with both of us so old and other things such as the examination."

"But Papa needs you," Lisa said.

"He has you and the rest of his family. Why now he needs me?"

"He wants you near him now."

"I'm always here. I will always be his friend. He can see me whenever he wants. He now sees me every day. We can still do things together as we do now."

"But he wants more."

"I know."

"What can he do? What can *we* do to help you reconsider?"

"Nothing. You've done so much by coming. It shows me how much you love your papa even though I know you really don't want us to marry."

"Perhaps you're uneasy about coming to live in our house."

"No. It will always be your house. I've lived in such places before. And even if your papa and I should marry and something should happen to your papa, it will still be your house, and I would of course find other arrangements.

"Perhaps you don't like the idea of having to be confirmed in our faith to marry Papa.

"No. I wouldn't mind. There are not so many differences. And what I see the times when I have gone with your father to what you call Mass are mostly in the way people are supposed to respond such as in signing or other things during the services. But that's just the way you do things. Our services have some of the same things."

Lisa finished her coffee and set her cup on the table. "Well, thank you for listening. Thank you again for the good coffee."

"You would perhaps like more?"

"No, I better go. Papa's probably wondering where I've gone."

"Thank you for coming. It's nice seeing you again and nice to have visitors. You are a good daughter. Does your papa know that you came here today?"

"No. He told us all not to bother you. That we should respect your decision."

"I expect that he would do that."

"But what could we do to change your mind?"

Margaret just slowly shook her head.

"So has he told you that he's made arrangements?"

"Arrangements?"

"That he will go somewhere he will be cared for so none us suffer? He especially mentions you because of what you told him."

Margaret studied Lisa's face. "No." she said. "He has said nothing to me about such arrangements."

"So he hasn't told you?"

"What should he have told me?"

"The results of the examination?"

"No. He has not yet told me about any results.

They fell silent. They searched each other's eyes.

Lisa's eyes and face revealed her sudden worry. "I better go." Lisa said. "I think I've said something I shouldn't have."

"Perhaps its best that you did. But please. You come again soon anytime. I would like you to visit and to come to know you better."

"I will. If Papa doesn't find out I've been here and have told you something I shouldn't have. And I won't bother you again about Papa." Then she added, "But we could visit all the time if you were with us."

Margaret reached to cover Lisa's hand. "I would like that very much. But would you really want me in your house?"

"If that's what Papa wants and will make him happy—especially now. And it's not exactly my house."

"Yes. I suppose. But it will always be yours no matter what your father and I decide.

Lisa rose. "Thank you."

Then Margaret went for Lisa's coat and helped her into it. Lisa covered her hair with the black shawl. Then she turned and hugged Margaret and Margaret returned her embrace. Margaret followed her to the door.

"Soon it will be warm."

Lisa nodded. "And I am so ready for spring!"

"Yes. Auf Wiedersehen, Lisa!"

"Ciao, Margaret!"

Lisa went out and Margaret stood watching as Lisa went down the steps and out to the sidewalk where she turned toward home.

What a nice young woman, Margaret thought watching Lisa move up the street. Such a good daughter everyone should have. Then she thought of Tomaso. And then she thought for a very long time of what Lisa had told her.

Tomaso returned angry from a visit to Margaret. He, in fact, was more than angry. He was furious. He stormed through the front door then through the dining room searching for his daughter.

"Lisa! he screamed. He found her in the kitchen with Maria and Bruno.

He stood in the doorway in his coat his face livid with rage.

"What's wrong Papa!"

"What's wrong? You should know what's wrong. How could you?"

"What is it? Why are you so angry?"

"Why am I angry? What you did. What you told Margaret.

"I'm sorry, Papa. It was an accident."

"An accident! How could it be an accident?"

"I thought you had told her. I mentioned to her that you had made arrangements. I wanted to help her not have to worry about you."

"How could that have been a help?"

"I thought that if she didn't have to worry, she would agree to what you want."

"Well, now she certainly doesn't want any part of what I want, thanks to you."

"I'm sorry, Papa."

"Sorry isn't enough. Perhaps you better think of making your own arrangements?

Lisa eyes filled with tears when she understood what her father was suggesting. She looked at Maria and Bruno for support.

"Arrangements?" Bruno asked finally able to break into the confrontation. "What arrangements?"

"I want her out of my sight."

"Oh, Papa!" Maria cried. "She's your daughter! How can you even think that!"

"After what she's done!"

"She said it was an accident," Bruno insisted. "You can't throw you own daughter out of her house for an honest mistake."

"An honest mistake! And it's not her house! It's mine, and it would have been Margaret's if this one had not made what you consider an honest mistake!"

"Enough, Papa!" Maria ordered.

Tomaso stood in the doorway fuming while Maria went to embrace Lisa who wept in her sister's arms. Then Tomaso turned and went back through the house and out the door heading for the steps that would lead him down to the river.

When Tomaso returned home, his anger finally calmed after his walk that had led him again to the yellow shack with its chimney billowing black smoke into the bright spring air, he was met with a surprise:

Margaret sat at the kitchen table across from Lisa and Maria and Bruno, all three with grim faces above their steaming cups of coffee.

"Margaret! Why are you here?"

"Lisa asked me to come."

"And so did we." Maria added. Bruno nodded in agreement.

"So you came. Why?"

"Because what they told me you said to Lisa."

"What I said I said in anger. Now I know what I said was wrong. I'm sorry Lisa." He went to his daughter where she sat. She rose to meet his embrace. "Please forgive you Papa who is not so young anymore and sometimes doesn't act his age."

"I'm sorry for you anger, Papa. I didn't know you hadn't told Margaret about what the doctor found."

"And you must know Tomaso that she really didn't tell me directly. She just mentioned arrangements she said you had made."

"Yes. I understand." Tomaso said.

"Well, I have something to tell you about the examination.

"Yes?"

"Perhaps we should go someplace where we can talk."

"If you were part of the family we would expect you to share with all of us what you might tell me." Tomaso said arguing his persistent theme.

"And you are almost part of the family now," Lisa observed.

Maria and Bruno agreed.

"So," Margaret said, reaching into her purse sitting on her lap. "I, too, had a phone call from my doctor. This is what they gave me after I went to see them. I asked them to write down for me what you will read." She withdrew from her purse a long white envelope with an official looking return address. She opened the envelope and withdrew a folded sheet then unfolded the sheet with an equally official looking letterhead. She handed the sheet to Tomaso.

"Read for yourself," she ordered quietly.

Tomaso read the letter. Then he handed it to Margaret while looking steadily into her eyes. Margaret passed the sheet to Lisa.

"Maybe I shouldn't read it." Lisa offered.

"Please." Margaret said. "If I'm as you say already part of the family. Let Maria and Bruno also read."

Lisa read the sheet then passed it to Maria who read and handed it Bruno. Lisa bent to hold Margaret. Maria and Bruno exchanged expressions.

"I'm sorry." Lisa said.

"Well, such again is part of living. Perhaps we should have champagne."

No one spoke.

"Perhaps I should go." Margaret offered. "We have all had enough feelings for today."

"You should stay for dinner?" Lisa suggested.

"Yes, "Tomaso agreed. Maria and Bruno both echoed his response.

"But we only have wine." Bruno added. "And I think we could use some right now." He rose and went for the always-handy jug of blood-red wine.

Tomaso removed his coat, went to his bedroom to hang the coat in its place; then he returned to offer his hand to Margaret, drawing her up into his arms. "I too am sorry for you. I am also for me. But now, please, since we are the same, for God's sake—and mine—will you please be my wife?"

Margaret studied him. Then she looked at the others who waited.

"For as long as I can be," Margaret said finally.

Tomaso hugged her hard then offered his lips that she readily accepted. The others exclaimed their delight. And each in turn embraced Margaret then Tomaso.

"Where's Guido?" Tomaso shouted. "Where's the champagne!"

And at last everyone laughed.

When Margaret and Tomaso were finally married, Margaret's son and some of her other kin came to see her given away, her son doing the honors. He looked even larger bringing his heavy Protestant body into the foreign church to walk her down the aisle and to hear the Mass being said for his mother in words he could not understand. She, of course, had willingly changed faiths for Tomaso. And the son had finally accepted this change after he accepted the idea of her marriage to Tomaso. Yet, embarrassed, unsure of himself, he had entered the dim ghostly light of the strange church. He came, sat still, straight, and uncomfortable watching the Mass, the delicate movements of the priest, the kneeling people, and the staring icons along the walls. Hearing the mysterious tongue, seeing the confusing movements troubled him. So he was much relieved when everyone followed Margaret and Tomaso out beneath the shower of rice, down the church stairs, into the mild spring light.

They celebrated the marriage late in the day seated at long dark wood tables covered with crisp white cloth. They ate endless quantities of food; they quaffed quantities of wine and beer from a limitless supply. They ate and drank until the music started. Then they danced late into the mild spring night until they were wrung with sweat and parched with thirst so that they drank again and danced again and laughed again as they clapped their hands in rhythm keeping time to see Tomaso with his curious hop dancing on and on and on with his new and smiling bride.

A Cool, Closed Room Within a Summer Night

"My God, you people work fast," the priest said. He started into the room. Surprised, the three of them moved aside, Blondie and the blond girl to the cart and Claude to the window.

The priest had come to give the man last rites, to bless the man and to absolve him of his faults. But the priest had been too late. So when he came through the door, he stopped. He searched the room as if wondering what to do now that he was late.

The priest stood looking at the brightly lit room probably seeing what Claude had seen on first entering from the dark corridor of the ward: the garish light off the jumbled array of old discarded equipment, the metal urinals reflecting the overhead bank of lights, chipped beds, worn and stained mattresses, and then the space thrust in among the rubble—the metal gurney and the long wrapped package bound with paper tape, the two figures by the gurney dressed all in white, and Claude also in white beside the window.

Claude studied the priest's young face, a contradiction above the black medieval robe. He saw the lines across the brow, the gray thinning hair, but the gray eyes, so lively, were questioning. Claude at first thought the priest appeared frightened. He wondered why. Why should a priest be afraid of beholding death? He reflected then on the studied calm and

258

nonchalance, the gay banter of the two, the blond girl, the young man Blondie, as they had flung the crackling paper across the face, across the naked limbs and loins, across the chest as Claude had entered. What were they hiding by that nonchalant fling? And why was he bracing himself as he had entered. He thought then of the long walk with the gurney carrying the wrapped body through the maze of halls. He thought of his dropping in the elevator with the gurney through the deep shaft to the hollow concrete passage in the basement.

Claude became alert as the priest stepped into the room and came to the end of the gurney. Claude moved closer to the window to let the priest by.

"You want him unwrapped? Blondie asked with apparent disgust.

The priest reached into his pocket; he uncoiled the white band of silk then ducked his head through the loop.

"Maybe if you just unwrap the face," the priest said. His voice seemed apologetic.

With a studied air, Blondie ripped open the flap that covered the man's face. Claude recognized the man from earlier in his shift. What difference was there now? None, so he thought at first. He saw again the growth of peppery beard, the sallow yellow tinged face, the sharp cheek bones, but then he saw the lowered eyelids—so different now from when he had seen them open, the eyes studying him as Claude had come upon the man on the gurney in the hallway at Admissions. The white shroud of paper around the head, now that difference, too, was striking.

The priest began intoning in a voice that they could almost not hear uttering strange phrases that they could not clearly understand. With two thin fingers the priest signed a cross over the man's face, sealed each eyelid with his thumb, then sealed the cooling lips.

The two stood back from the end of the gurney. No sign, no show of emotion, they waited. Claude also waiting stood long-armed with hands uncrossed watching while the priest droned his low incantation.

Quiet. The room was quiet. Now even the light reflected off the instruments, the bright fixtures seemed quiet. All seemed quiet: the steady murmur of the priest, the slow movements of his long hands, his thin fingers, his bowed narrow head with ratty hair.

Quiet. The world was quiet. The open window let in the summer night. The warm calm air eased in and brought the darkness and the silent throb of colored lights from dark buildings, their windows gleaming in the pulsing light. The summer breeze brought in the quiet glow of yellow houselights, the brighter glow of fluorescent streetlamps on stirring summer leaves.

Now as he stood in that quiet, Claude thought about the man that lay upon the cart; and as he recalled how they had met earlier that hot quiet summer night, he had trouble remembering the man's name. He could readily recall the man's face. He could close his eyes and still see how the man had looked earlier, but he couldn't recall the man's name. He guessed that he never had bothered learning it. Why should he have? He had only seen the man a short time before bringing him up to the ward. But Claude remembered Bealmer. He had seen Bealmer three times before he had carted Bealmer off to a ward. No, come to think of it, he had seen Bealmer only twice. The third time Bealmer hadn't actually been there, just Bealmer's things. How many days ago had that been? Claude couldn't determine.

Yet how easily now while the priest droned on Claude recalled the incidentals that had bothered him earlier this evening: How reluctantly he had come to work tonight, almost as if he sensed that something might happen. How reluctantly he had risen from sleep—heavy, groggy, tired within the heat. How reluctantly the car had started. How he had worried about being late because of the car.

He had waited then tried again. The engine had caught, had held, had gathered to a roar. He had revved the engine, unsprung the handbrake, pulled out from the curb around the parked new car that gleamed beneath the bright glow of the streetlamp.

Then he had reached the side street that lay in humid darkness broken by the sweep of headlights softened by the yellow lamps from silent houses, varied by the staggered spray of streetlights on the branches of heavy summer trees.

Starting up the hill the car had labored against the steep grade allowing him to glance through open windows at the dark wood interiors, the beamed ceilings above the unlit brick fireplace, the occasional dark figure before the window, dark shapes that surprised him by returning his gaze making him turn away. Then he crested the hill and started down the long gradual slope that led toward colored lights, through sounds of loud music and the nervous press of late night crowds.

But parking had been easy tonight. Yet there were still the few dark blocks to the hospital. He had read about recent beatings, robberies for a pittance. Such a death seemed more like sacrifice, such a waste. Was there no more than this: A lonely cry upon some darkened street? A living soul sacrificed—for what? To satisfy some being mostly beast? He remembered having thought that.

So the darkness had troubled him. What could he do? He had started past parked cars beneath dark buildings rife with yellow lamps in small dark rooms. Then the darkness in between the buildings, the narrow car-thick side street beneath the heavy trees had splayed onto a concrete avenue filled with light.

The night bound building where he worked loomed thick and dark and massive above the street. Up along the side, the single strand of lights from stairwells climbed up the side but left the top in darkness. Then he saw high upon the roof the slow pulse of the red beacon. He watched the beacon as he approached. The building rose above him growing in bulk and mass as if it were a living thing. He had wondered what he was up against tonight. Had he really wondered that? Or was he now simply thinking of the man whose name he couldn't remember lying wrapped in paper on the cart while the priest droned on in what seemed like endless pleading.

Tonight was different for Claude. He had always worked the dayshift before. He thought of the bright sun-washed streets. He recalled the unfelt reassuring language of traffic, the noisy intermingling rush of people. Tonight he had heard the quiet muffled voices; he had seen the shadows of lone figures at the darkened wooden bus stop. Then the empty trackless trolley, a yellow hollow within, hummed to a stop, hissed open, closed, slowly swung around the corner then glided down the hill toward the bright maze of city lights below and the distant speeding cars along the freeway, the throb of neon from downtown buildings. He had turned between the iron railings around the small lawn and reached the door and the worn brass handle. The door to his surprise had opened with a yank. No one challenged him. During the day a security guard always stood near. Where was that security tonight?

He had started down the concrete stairs to the basement. The hollow yellow walls sent back the hollow sound of his feet descending. From somewhere above a door jarred open. He heard words captured briefly in the hollow of the stairwell. "Clearly what I would do in this case . . ." The footsteps carried the voices upward. Another door jarred open and then jarred closed. He again heard the sound of his feet descending in the hollow stairwell.

He reached the basement stifling from the lingering daytime heat and the overhead pipes. He entered the empty locker room. He sidled through the gray wooden benches and gray steel lockers until he reached his. His keys jangled on the ring, the locker key scraping in the lock. The locker door rattled open. Then the noisy keys and coins teetered with the bench as he emptied his pockets.

Blondie arrived while he was changing. Startled at first, Claude had moved aside. As usual, Blondie eased past not offering a greeting as most others would even if they didn't know him. Claude thought that Blondie was obviously impressed with himself for reasons Claude could only guess: youth, blond hair, handsome features, trim body. Claude often saw Blondie during the dayshift. Blondie would pass Claude's table in the cafeteria looking straight ahead, looking at nothing or no one, apparently aware that people might be watching as he passed, most likely hoping that they were.

Tonight Blondie wore a turtle-necked jersey that appeared odd for a warm summer night and blue soft pants that appeared somewhat snug. He held a smoking cigarette between his teeth until he began changing; then he set the cigarette on the edge of the bench and finished changing into a fresh starched uniform. Once changed, now completely in white, he replaced the cigarette between his teeth and worked a comb in long limp strokes through his fine hair. Then Blondie left without a word to Claude.

As Claude remained lingering in the locker room reluctant to start his shift, the heavy stillness surrounded him: the running water of the urinals, the rasp of cloth from his starched uniform as he forced his bare legs through flat stiff pants, forced his arms through flat stiff sleeves. Then he slammed the metal locker door, the sound thunderous; he forced keys and coins into starched pockets and glanced toward the dark screened windows above the lockers.

He recalled the dim memory of a car he now imagined. He knew the owner. He always saw her in the hallways and at her desk. He had studied her as she passed only briefly noting his gaze; he had watched her behind her counter as he moved around the ward: her fine delicate features; her bright eyes, swelling bosom and hips, fine firm legs with slim ankles. Then as he watched her walk away straight and determined moving to her desk, her work, and the clattering keys of her machine, he wondered about the secrets of her life, those rituals of her day, her morning preparations: the combing and painting, the sheathing of smooth softness on her body. He thought about her life at night of comfort among cool sheets that warmed and grew scented with her flesh. He thought about her in stirring darkness. Then his throbbing pulse would wake him from his dream, and off he'd go down corridors limp-limbed and slow until the blood and his purpose returned and he would hurry to his neglected tasks.

One of those times hurrying back as he had passed Radiology, he had seen Bealmer there as big as life lying on the gurney, a slight smile of resignation on his sunken face. Bealmer had raised a limp boney arm as Claude passed. Claude had stopped.

"How are you, friend?" Claude asked.

Bealmer just swayed a free hand.

"When they going to let you out?"

The man's eyes watched him then changed as if he had turned them in toward some personal sorrow.

"It's about time they get you out to here, isn't it?"

The man smiled wryly. He tried to shake his head then gave up.

"It'll be soon. You'll be out of here in no time."

But the man didn't' try to respond. He turned his head away from the light of the hallway.

"Believe me!" Claude insisted.

But when the man had closed his eyes, Claude had hurried on leaving Bealmer waiting for the negative images of his radiated bowels.

Passing on along the corridor that time he had seen Bealmer, Claude had thought again about the woman he had studied while he worked, and he recalled another time when he had watched her through the screens above the gray steel lockers while he had changed into street clothes. He couldn't help watching her he told himself again. His quickening pulse, the silence, and her unsuspecting innocence had compelled him.

So he had watched as she stood beside the car unaware of his gaze. He had viewed the slender legs, the dimpled swells behind the knees, the white milky flesh above—all had stabbed his loins while she unlocked the car, sung wide the door, and dipped into the seat. He had flushed with splendid bitter pain to see the light skirt gaping, the bent spread legs, the firm thighs, and then the soft swelling and the dark whorls beneath the silky white fabric. She had straightened and lifted to settle her skirt; she had slammed the door and sat listening to the engine.

Then she had noticed him through the screen gazing up at her. Her eyes had held an expression that had startled him: Part stare, a flicker of fear, then of indignation, and she had turned away so fast he had little time to realize that she had seen him. Backing her car, she had turned it forward and drove away. After that brief encounter, each time he passed her in the hallways and searched her face, she kept her eyes straight and cold without any sign that she had ever seen him.

Tonight, as he had stood between the lockers looking through the screened windows into the darkness remembering the brightness of that day he had reconsidered the event and wondered if he had really seen her that time. Perhaps he had looked and only seen the parked car, or perhaps he only had imagined all that he had seen when he had thought of her after he had passed Bealmer waiting in Radiology.

He had left the locker room; he had slowly climbed the stairs. Early before his shift, he had been glad he had time for coffee. He needed coffee. But he had been bothered when he found the cafeteria closed. Here, again, was something different. Yet he had seen the coffee shop open, so he had turned in at the door that always had barred him during the day because of it being closed. No one was at the counter, so he took a seat there. He glanced around at the interior.

Blondie and the blond girl and a few doctors whom he recognized were sitting in the large booths opposite the counter. From time to time he often had seen Blondie with the same girl. He had often seen them in the cafeteria as they sat with other aides and orderlies. Everyone in the group seemed the same: the women somewhat plain, slightly heavy, but coiffured and smiling. The blond one always with Blondie squinted behind plastic-rimmed glasses.

They always seemed to be joking and laughing. Claude wondered what they had to laugh about, but they appeared to laugh at everything. They laughed while eating and sipping iced water from scratched glasses, smiling and nodding while they chewed their food. All their laughter thrown back from the pale green walls joined the clash of droning voices, the ring of metal forks and knives and spoons, the scrape of plates and dishes.

They hadn't been alone. For everyone else seemed to laugh as well, talking gaily, unconcerned, ignorant, ignoring the neglect of the dark lonely suffering beyond the pale green walls, the high ceiling of the large room in which they sat and laughed.

Claude tried to be fair. Why should they worry? Should they suffer as others did? How could they? Should they stop living because other lives had ceased and always would? No one else seemed to care. Did he? Why should they?

He thought again of Bealmer, that gaunt lonely man lost within himself. Lately, he thought he might have become like Bealmer almost as if thinking about the man had changed him into the man himself. His own reflection showed similar prominences and protuberances of skull. Yet, he would never really be Bealmer no matter how long he thought about the man.

He recalled their first meeting. What had attracted his attention? The man's thinness? His quiet acceptance of his condition? Bealmer hadn't demanded attention as so many others had. In contrast, Bealmer had seemed to appreciate the little attention he received. He appeared to show a sense of joy over even being noticed. He had always remained quiet when someone stopped to talk to him.

"How you doing, fella? How come you're here?

"They don't want me anymore," Bealmer had said matter-of-factly.

"Who doesn't want you?" Oh, no, here was another complainer. "Oh, come on! You're only making that up."

Yet as he had continued to talk to the man, Claude came to accept the man's story, perhaps because he had witnessed the family and their dealing with Bealmer and his condition. He recalled the impeccably dressed woman not young anymore but not old who spoke to Bealmer as he waited for examination and admission. She had stood vigil with a stern tight-lipped countenance that suggested she was annoyed at being there. She had also appeared impatient with everything, especially with Bealmer's insistence that he wanted to be home.

"Don't ever get old," Bealmer suggested. "You get sick. They'll get rid of you. Ship you off. Lock you up. You wait. You'll see."

"Now, Dear, this is the best for you," the woman had said admonishing Bealmer. Claude had wondered to whom the appellation "Dear" could have been applied since it might be applied to anyone—spouse or father. So Claude couldn't be sure as to their exact relationship, although in the end he decided the connection didn't really matter.

"We want you to get well," the woman had said straightening the light cover Bealmer had continually fretted off. His boney hand again had worried the faded blanket from his thin chest that appeared lost within the threadbare gown.

So Bealmer hadn't really told him much. The woman's attitude had revealed more as she stood vigil, and Bealmer's sad resignation as well said as much once he accepted the reality that his protests and his desires would be ignored convincing Claude of Bealmer's situation. Then the woman had left followed by a fleshy anonymous man both leaving Bealmer on his own, and Claude had carted Bealmer off on the gurney, had stood beside him as they had admitted him, had taken him up to the floor depositing him with gaily indifferent personnel, and then had returned to his other chores. He had forgotten about Bealmer until that other time he had come across Bealmer waiting in the hallway beside the dark room filled with captured images of ghostly bones.

Claude had been roused from his reverie as he waited self-consciously sitting alone at the counter of the coffee shop when a large heavy woman—enormous really—came from an end booth where she had been chatting with staff. He ordered. He waited. He sat back as she placed his order. He paid. He watched her move away. Her legs and ankles surprised him: her legs were knotted and veined, but her ankles were thin. Her ankles made him aware of her huge frame above them, aware of her heavy arms that strained her sleeves, of her fat fingers, her sweaty hanging jowls. He saw, too, her short black hair streaked with gray, her wire-framed glasses.

The enormous woman behind the counter had made him think of other women whom he had helped, their hearts or kidneys having grown tired of bearing all the weight. He recalled the tired sad look, the resignation, and the strange sense of peace those women seemed to have as he had helped them standing at the end of the gurney pulling at their arms to raise them while the intern thumped their back and probed their loose age-worn bellies. He watched the woman behind the counter. Her thin-rimmed glasses, her netted hair, her red shining face made him wonder about the condition of her heart. Then he had finished his coffee and had started down the hallway towards his station. That's when he first saw the man whose name he couldn't remember waiting for him.

No one else apparently had been there to take him to the floor perhaps because of the change in shifts when those finished fled and those coming on duty were busy reviewing charts.

Claude could not have missed him. The gurney sat in the narrow passage leading to the ER. Claude had squeezed between the pale green wall and cold metal edge of the gurney. He had paused looking down at the man wondering why the man was there in the hallway. Then Claude had sensed something wrong.

The man lay under a light blanket that had slipped to his waist leaving his chest and belly naked. The man shuddered. His hand that lay upon the blanket at his waist quivered, grasping for some unseen thing, something he wanted but couldn't have.

"D.T.'s" Claude decided. Then he had wondered if perhaps the man was only cold. Claude pulled up the light blanket so that it covered the man to his neck. Then for some reason, inexplicable even when he later recalled, he had looked into the man's eyes reflecting the ceiling lights, reflecting his own image peering into the man's eyes. Would he ever forget the man's face? The man's jowls were wrinkled, his beard grizzled, his hair peppered, more gray than black. The man's face around his eyes and around his neck were spotted and scabbed. Here was one that Claude didn't have to de-bug. Yes, he recalled thinking that. Well, he had grown tired of cleaning dirty, bug-infested people! Why not? How much could one person abide? After all, he, too, had limitations!

Yet he had felt guilty then. He had checked the level of liquid in the intravenous bottle hanging from a metal pole above the man's head. He also checked the plastic tubing running from the bottle to the man's arm. He checked the catheter held by a piece of tape upon an area of clean yellow leg surrounded by grime and matted dirty hair and bug bites. Then he finally noticed the man watching him.

"How you doin', friend?" Claude asked uneasy.

The man's eyes moved then stared. The man quivered, strained for air, strained toward Claude. The man's hands grasped again reaching. Claude had again settled the covers around the man's neck, and then had left him. Claude had passed Admissions.

"Evening," he said. The young dark-haired girl had looked up and smiled raising her eyebrows. Claude had worked for some time before he had been able to get her to do even that. She went on typing. Her machine clattered. "What's happening to the man on the gurney at the end of the hallway?" he had asked.

"He's waiting to go up," she answered without looking up from her work.

"Where's his papers?"

"I think the intern took them to the floor. That man's a Stat."

"And he's sitting in the hallway?"

She shrugged and clattered the keys of her machine.

"I'll take him up," Claude had said. She hadn't bother answering. "Tell the ward nurse, will you?"

"Sure," she had said. She had continued typing.

He had gone back down the hallway to the man on the gurney. Then he had carefully steered the gurney through the passageway to the elevator.

At the floor, he used the door hook to leave the elevator stand open. He started down the hallway hurrying, steering the gurney before him trying to keep it from the walls. The I.V. bottle clinked against the metal pole; the man's eyes wheeled and caught the ceiling light. The gurney wheels thrummed; and as Claude and the man approached, the nurses at the station had looked up, looked dismayed, bored, each in her own way. One had started toward him reaching for the gurney as he neared.

"Who's this?" she asked.

"No idea," he said. "You're supposed to have the papers."

"Oh!' she said. "He's the one we've been looking for."

She had looked down at the man on the gurney, her smile all toothpaste white, all-rouged lips smile. "Hi!" she had said. "Where you been?"

She had taken him then, gently wheeling the gurney away toward the end of the ward hallway.

Claude had turned, creeping back toward the shadows, listening to the murmuring echoes of the nurse's soothing voice as she babbled to the man on the gurney. Claude had thought again of Bealmer. As he had passed the dark rooms, he saw the white shadowy forms hulked upon the rows of perpetual beds. Where was Bealmer? Perhaps he was in one of those rooms asleep, or muttering to himself, or perhaps complaining about the injustice in his life, some slight, real or imagined that he exclaimed in his dreams, the re-runs of his fleeting days. Had his people come for him? Had they finally found him? Had they finally satisfied his petulant desire to be at home? Claude had wondered as he reached the darkness. Why should he have thought of Bealmer then? What was that man to him. Out of all those he had attended, why conjure him? Claude recalled the room of lighted bones, the image of the wasted man upon the gurney receding from him now, whirled away as he had reached the elevator, released the door hook. He had gone back down to ER.

Now that he considered the event, Claude remarked how quickly he had forgotten the man on the gurney he had just taken up to the ward, the man whose name Claude couldn't remember. Yet, he told himself, there were always others to attend, other tasks to do. So he had busied himself checking oxygen tanks, making up gurneys, transforming them from purple-brown, bloodstained rubber mats upon shiny metal carts that suddenly became white, sterile looking beds. All he needed was a white sheet and a fresh, ironed pillowcase. He was amazed at how much such white could cover. Then he got the call.

"A Unit Three on Four," someone had called.

He had expected that call in a way. He had started for the Morgue. "I'll be at Unit Three," he had said to the nurse behind the desk. She had nodded and continued studying her newspaper. He had gone on along the corridor slapping the morgue book against his leg.

The corridor had been empty. The X-ray technician sat hunched under lamplight. Claude had seen the light skin, the fiery hair, the cold stern face. She hadn't bothered looking up as he passed. He hadn't expected her to. He had tried to be friendly with her once, but she had chilled him. So he ignored her. Then he had caught a glimpse of lighted bones: a ghostly brightly illuminated skull with blind sockets, the dark shadows of living brain upon the negative.

He had reached the freight elevator.

Unlike during the day, no one was on duty. The carriage cage was dark except for the red light that showed him the motor was turned on. He flipped the switches. Dull yellow light exposed worn brass, the chipped and scored woodwork of the cage. At the bottom of the well, the motor whined to life. He closed the cage then spun the control.

They climbed, the cage and he: the carriage swayed as they rose: the floors appeared, passed; a number painted on the doorway of the floor appeared and passed, then another slab of concrete, another doorway with the floor number until the Fourth. He released the control. The carriage slowed then passed the floor then settled back. The motor whirred in the deep shaft. The cage door rattled open collapsing upon itself against the carriage wall. The heavy wall door slid open. He hooked the elevator door and started down the dimly lit hallway.

The rooms he had passed were dark. The hallways were dark except for the light at the nurses' station. Here the nurses had sat lounging. They had turned as he approached from out of the dark hallway into the light of their station. They had noted the book he held against his leg.

"Down at the end of the hallway," one had directed. He had nodded passing. They had turned back to their shared joking banter.

He had to admit now a sense of apprehension as he had reached the end of the dark hallway, not because he was attending to some event that was new to him, this handling of the dead. But this time, tonight, the dim quiet of the hallway and the maze he knew lay ahead after he retrieved the wrapped body had for some reason slightly unnerved him. He surmised that he had really expected this sometime, especially when they told him that sometimes he'd be working the nightshift. He had ignored considering that possibility, deciding to face the situation when it finally arrived. Well, now that possibility had become real: He had imagined the long basement corridor, the bare twisting pipes, the hot dark passageway, the dark locked rooms with identifying labels, the last door blank—the Morgue—and what it hid.

During the day, he had never really been alone: another orderly, a mortuary director, the coroner's assistant—someone always had been with him. He had helped as they left following them into the sunlight brilliant after the dark interior, he looking after as they drove away. Yet when he had turned back, he had always felt uneasy. He had tried to reason out his apprehension, successful, he supposed, eventually until he guessed that he had almost developed a sense of curiosity. Then sometimes he had deliberately remained behind in the cool, closed room. He had read the name cards to see who was new, who was now there whom he had perhaps attended. Or, as part of his job, he would clean up the red and watery gore from the cold trays while glancing into the chilling darkness to see the other shrouded shapes reposed.

But now, tonight, the newness of the situation, the fact that he would be going alone at night made him uneasy. So he had prepared himself. What might he encounter? What had he been expecting? He recalled passing the dark rooms on the wards, he thought of the dull round nightlight that made the broken night within the room seem darker. He recalled the stir of white bulked shapes beneath the covers. He had heard again the mutterings. Was death in there? That room? What room? In what darkness did it lurk?

The end room. He had turned in expecting it to be alone, as he had always found them. But what he had found surprised him. He had found light. He had found brightness. He had found people. More than he expected—almost too many—too many lights; too many people. And piles of junk: discarded equipment, gleaming metal fixtures, tubes, trays, bottles. Among all this rubble, the man whose name he couldn't remember was being wrapped.

The man lay naked upon the sheet upon the gurney. The young blond woman ripening toward later heaviness and pain helped Blondie fold the paper flat across the seedless loins. She smiled while working, not looking, just chatting with Blondie.

The two worked and talked. Both smiled. Their teeth seemed much too white; their hair, much too combed. He was surprised to see Blondie there. The man always had appeared so clean before, always had appeared so delicate. Claude suddenly objected to the turtle-necked jersey that now definitely seemed out of season and out of place.

Blondie flung the flap of paper over the face. They worked in the corners of the coarse absorbent paper sheet. Claude saw the stubble beneath the nose, around the chin.

"Almost done, I see," he had said as he entered the room.

"Just about." Blondie said.

Claude had placed the red morgue book on one of the discarded tables. He had helped tape while they lifted. First, he wrapped the head, winding tape around the neck. He felt the sharp hard edge of skull. He taped around the shoulders, then the waist, then the thighs. They held the feet while he wrapped the ankles. All the while he taped, he could feel the man through the coarse dry paper. The body still felt firm and warm, the flesh still like living flesh.

"Tags on?" he had asked too late.

"Sure," Blondie had said.

"I guess we can go." He had meant the man and he. He had felt himself begin to hold on to himself, bracing himself for what was ahead.

But then as he was about to leave, as he had grasped the gurney, suddenly from behind him coming silent, coming quick and large, a dark shape had loomed within the doorway. And Claude had turned in fear.

271

The droning voice stopped. They rustled from their spots.

"You people certainly work fast," the priest said again. He looked at each of them searching their faces. Then he turned, treaded toward the doorway dipping his head again to remove the loop of silk, folding it as he left. Then he was gone.

Blondie rewrapped the face.

"All set, I guess."

Claude again grabbed the gurney end shoving the morgue book under the wrapped sack. Blondie slipped his thin arms through the starched white jacket. He grabbed the other end of the gurney.

"As long as you've come up, I guess I can help you," Blondie said.

Claude was surprised. Then he felt relieved.

They moved to take it down, to take it through the dim halls, to take it from yellow light that reached along the walls until it edged into darkness. They took it past black rooms lit only by the glow of nightlight, hushed rooms that stirred with mutterings as they passed. And as he journeyed, Claude could image himself as Bealmer looking out at the passing figures in the dim light seeing the white clothed forms, the healthy fleshy look above the humped inert shape on the wung-wheeled cart.

Then they descended toward the morgue, the center of the maze of pale green hallways and concrete corridors. And as they sank, he imagined the cable that held them. Suspended, they dangled by a thin wire, a thread of utter hope and startling belief as they hurtled downward toward the cool, closed room, dim even in the day, lighted only by a skylight open toward the sun the man upon the cart would never see again.

They slowed then stopped. The carriage settled, the shaft door, cage door opened. The scraping hook held the door. They wheeled the cart into the corridor—what stifling darkness. They reached the blank door. Claude unlocked it. They pushed the cart into the cool room. Blondie flipped the switch dazzling them in the sudden blaze of overhead light. The latched, unlatched, unlocking locker door startled them. They reached in and withdrew the rasping, gleaming metal tray that held a bitter chill.

They used the yellow hoist in lifting it, sliding the cold thin band beneath, looping it, attaching it to the sharp black claw at the end of the thick chain. Then Claude groped for the ganglia of controls, found the button, the nerve, and pressed.

The motor woke the silence but not the dead. He felt the pliant flesh still warm, watched the white wrapped form bow as it rose. Then they slid the limp and sagging heap upon the metal tray. He felt it shake before it settled. Blondie moved back. The locker door shot to; the loud latch caught. They turned. Blondie took the empty cart and fled. The door snapped and locked from the outside leaving Claude alone.

He braced himself even though he knew he could escape. The stillness returned. His flesh crawled. Alone, he studied the heap of plasma-stained sheets that someone had flung against a wall. He went to snatch them up to stuff them in the crowded bag of others. Then he paused; he turned to go but saw the triple rows of dark enameled doors. He saw the white crooked cards with penciled markings shoved into metal frames on the doors almost as if in haste as someone had fled.

He moved along the rows of cards to straighten them. He read the names of those he never had known until he stopped before the locker of the man whose name he couldn't remember. There in the metal frame of the locker door above the locker with the man whose name Claude couldn't remember was the name of someone else.

Bealmer! He was there! Claude suddenly felt weak. His head spun. And suddenly the image of that man came up at him, struck at him, and made him blanche in fear and reel in sorrow. He snatched the locker handle yanking it. The door broke back releasing chill like some escaping breath. Then, instead of bulk, instead of white shroud, instead of sallow feet with horny nails, he saw the empty polished tray steeped in gore. He saw the other reposing shapes.

He slammed the door. He studied the card with Bealmer's name that someone should have carried along. Why hadn't they taken it? Then he used the card, reversing it to etch in ink the name he hadn't been able to remember. He carefully placed the card in the metal frame of the locker below. He turned, went to the door, went out into the corridor allowing the door to latch by itself. He made his way upward toward the light and the warming heat of summer.

The night was calm after that. The quiet dawn came before he expected it. He found time to watch it come. He witnessed it from the hill: the gathering yellow and rose-colored light on the windows of staggered buildings, the dark water of the Sound brightening. He saw the slowly moving lines of cars along the freeway below.

And with the dawn came his relief: red-haired, freckled, young, smiling, eyelids puffy with sleep. Claude passed the keys, gave his report, and dragged his weariness toward the hot basement where he moved between the rows of gray lockers. He heard the quiet trickling urinals. He watched the dazzling light flame through the screened windows above his head. Then as he left, as he passed the dark corridor that stopped against the blank door, he thought of them both, while he continued on his tired way toward morning sunlight and a slow ride to the hill's edge where god-like he saw the vast sparkling lake, the thick carpeting of pine and hemlock, the distant purple mountains before he dipped, then dropped toward sun-washed streets that led him toward home and quiet dreamless sleep.

The Subterranean

On the eve of his twenty-fifth anniversary as Bleiber ended work, he knew that it was time to quit. In the past twenty-five years changes in the sound of traffic on the pavement overhead helped him determine the time. And sometimes in certain seasons of the year the shadows and softened rays of sunlight off the wet walls and dark water of the sewer told him he could stop now. Whatever the cause, Bleiber suddenly became aware that he had numbed himself throughout the day to endure the mindless tasks that he was required to do. He began each day wishing it were already over, but he quickly accepted that the day's work had just begun. So as he worked throughout the morning, he gradually lost his awareness of his immediate surroundings. Then he never thought beyond the moment, and even in that moment he had nothing more than a vague interest in what he did—except perhaps for the possibility of alligators. So he worked until the sound of footfalls above his head, the changing rumble of traffic made him aware of where he was and that it was time to quit.

Then Bleiber roused himself from his haze and pulled his large heavy frame up the iron rungs set in the concrete wall. He trudged long-armed up the metal stairs, the heavy rubber boots of his waders sounding in the hollow of the walls until he reached the heavy metal door and went through. The door struck closed behind him shutting out the possibility of alligators and sending echoes that were lost in the final darkness of the maze he had left behind.

Yet in the fading light, as Bleiber cleaned his boots and equipment, showered, changed into street clothes, and said good evening to his men, he hoped that tomorrow would be no different than any other in the last twenty-five years. He recalled the first day that was still vivid for him. Sometimes the shadows falling just right, sometimes the sunlight off the walls with a patina of green mold or streaming through dark silted water reminded him of that first day. Then he sensed his age. He felt the difference. He saw himself as that young man whom he had left behind. What had happened to that person who at that time was still more of a boy? Where had that boy been lost along what dark tube, what reptilian corridor? That first day he had been excited about starting although nothing out of the ordinary had occurred. Tomorrow, he thought, his latest should pass like any other. He just wanted to be left alone to sink into his quiet private thoughts.

When he went to clock out, he couldn't help but note the slip of paper attached to his timecard. He at first thought he knew what it was about: some notification, some new appeal to have more contributions deducted from the amount he already felt had grown too small. He gave his share and his blood at regular intervals. Let others pay, he decided, as he took his card. Then he reconsidered. Could it be that perhaps someone had noted that tomorrow was his twenty-fifth anniversary? So what? Little matter. He expected the usual—a scroll and medal he would lose in the back of some drawer at home. He had seen others get them. And now he was quite aware that he had earned one of those tokens himself. Twenty-five good ones gone, he mused. What had he to show for all that time? Maybe they would give him a raise. That would be welcomed but most unlikely, he conceded, given the reports and complaints about the company for which he worked having difficulties that were never clearly or explicitly explained.

Reconsidering, he read the memo quickly at first, not really comprehending what he saw. They had noticed. Twenty-five years—the place was part of him. He discovered how much a part when he reread the memo.

Bleiber read the statement a third time. Yes, that's what it said. At first, he thought he might have misunderstood. But no, the words were the same the second and third time as they had been the first. Now he simply saw the words he had overlooked. The meaning had been there all along.

He laughed quietly to himself, except that as he clocked out, as he placed his timecard in its proper slot and folded the memo tucking it into his shirt pocket as he left, he wondered how he would tell Emma? He knew he would have to keep what he had read in the memo from the Old Man? Of one thing Bleiber was certain. Here on the eve of his twenty-fifth anniversary, his wife would have something for him; surely she would offer him something, and she was sure to help him celebrate. Now he had something for her.

He came out of the building into the late mild afternoon, paused for a moment to watch the people passing, to view the traffic, and study the overcast that appeared as if it might release rain. But he breathed deeply of the mild fresh air and turned for home.

He reached his street. He waved to Balistrari standing behind the counter within the small store with its green wooden front, its large window reflecting the fading sunlight and the dark buildings and the dark round-shouldered figure of Bleiber as he passed waving before Bleiber turned up the stairs to his flat. Here Bleiber stopped. Before, he had always climbed quickly glad to be home. Now he paused. How would he tell her, especially when she had suggested that finally they would recognize his dedication.

"You'll see," she had said. "They'll give you something."

Now as he gathered for the climb, Bleiber smiled to himself.

Oh, they indeed had given him a gift.

He solved his dilemma easily enough. He simply placed the memo before her on the table at which she sat. She displayed her understanding by her silence. He was grateful for her consideration. She, in turn, appeared grateful that he didn't mock her former suggestion.

"What will you do now?" she asked.

He shrugged. "What's there to do? I'm tired. It's time to rest. I can use the rest."

"Yes," she said. "You have earned it."

"Maybe," he said.

She remained quiet and reached for his hand to touch him.

Then Bleiber ate a quiet meal while dear heavy Emma moved quietly around the kitchen gathering his food to the table then sitting while

Bleiber ate in brooding silence made heavier by a car horn, the sudden cry of children, the echoing ghostly voices throughout the building. And then he suddenly thought of alligators.

After eating, Bleiber rose and kissed Emma on the forehead thanking her for the meal, a special treat of his favorite food to mark the eve of his anniversary. Then he went into the front room to the overstuffed chair in the corner by the window. He turned on the lamp, then settled himself to read by hooking the gold wires of his glasses behind his ears, opening the book to where he had marked his place.

Then he heard the rap he had somewhat anticipated. Yet he tensed suspecting who might be the caller since the sound seemed to come from wood striking wood. Bleiber rose and moved across the faded carpet.

Opening the door, he stood there, an aging man before an older image of himself. His father teetered just beyond the threshold waving the cane he had used on the door inviting Bleiber to come celebrate. Bleiber was a bit surprised that his father had remembered the cause for celebration. But he noted the slight sarcasm in his father's voice. He knew that his father had imbibed too much. Bleiber slowly shook his head. Perhaps he should keep from the old man the memo he had received. For he knew that he would have to control himself in response to whatever his father had to offer.

"I don't think that's a good idea, Papa," he said. Still using the same old title, the same relationship between father and son since Bleiber was a child, he wondered if it would ever end even with his father's demise. Then Bleiber noted that the barren plaster walls of the hallway, the square hollow of the stairwell carried his father's voice behind the dark closed doors.

Bleiber waved his father across the threshold. He turned, moved to the center of the living room, turned back, waiting while his father, always seemingly prepared, hunched and shook himself from his light rain coat. Then his father folded it, took the matching light tweed cap, much like Bleiber's, exposing his gray thinning hair, and placed it on the pile. He handed the coat and cap to Bleiber but kept the cane he used as much for show as for support. He held it as he smoothed his thinning hair.

Bleiber went to the bedroom to deposit the garments on the bed. Emma looked at him as he passed through the kitchen. Bleiber rolled his eyes to the ceiling. He went on through to the bedroom while Emma padded to the front room to greet the old man. Then after a polite exchange, she excused herself and left the flat closing the door quietly behind her. She crept down the stairs listening and looking until the door was lost from sight behind the turn of stairs and carpeting and the spaces between the banisters.

Bleiber placed the pile of clothing on the neat bedspread then went back to the living room. His father was standing at the window looking out at the city. The sight of the old man standing there relaxed and lost in thought made Bleiber more certain in accepting now that his father had come.

"Would you like something to drink?" he asked hoping that perhaps his father might ask for coffee that he could well use given his condition.

His father turned from the window, his eyes scanning Bleiber's face questioning. "That would be fitting," he said. "What do you have to offer?"

Bleiber noted the hardness in the old man's voice. He felt suddenly weary, as if somehow he had been in a fight he was too tired to continue.

"I have wine. You can have that," Bleiber said finally.

"That will do. I thought perhaps it might me beer."

Bleiber briefly flared, then sighed and checked his urge to lash back. But he had trained himself over the years, just as his father had taught him to argue.

"I have wine," he offered again, softer this time. "You can have that."

The father sensing his son's mood simply nodded. Yet when Bleiber turned and moved into the kitchen, the old man's perennial disappointment flared.

"What vintage is it?" he called. But Bleiber either did not hear or ignored the wattled cry, and the call half died in the old man's throat.

Bleiber came back with a half-empty gallon of table wine swinging from his finger. He scissored two goblets in his other hand.

The old man smiled wryly. "Splendid," he said. "Splendid." Then he waited apparently resigning himself as he seldom did.

Bleiber sensed his father's changing mood. He, too, now held his bitterness in check. He filled the glasses then handed one to the old man. His father raised his goblet. "What should we drink to?" The memory of your mother? If she were only here." The old man's eyes became glazed as if he were looking a long way off at something invisible. Bleiber as always felt shut out from the old man's world.

"Where will it end, Father?" he asked, his voice hushed and subdued.

"End? Why should it end? End what?"

"We've been over this. Don't start again. I wanted my own life."

The old man drained his glass and went to the table by Bleiber's reading chair. He set the glass on the table. The sight of the closed marked book made him fume." "And you still read!"

"Why not? I enjoy it."

"You work all day in waste and filth and then come home to read."

Bleiber shrugged and went to the widow. Children played in the street avoiding cars. "What does it matter now? he said to himself. But his father caught the remark.

"What's that?" He came to Bleiber at the window. He searched his son's face. "What do you mean?"

"Twenty-five years. That's a long time."

"So it is. I don't understand."

"Forget it, Papa. It's nothing."

"Don't tell me that! Why mention it? What's wrong?"

"I'm tired. I've had a long day. I have to get up early. I can't sleep like other people."

"I'm an old man," Bleiber's father admitted. "I'm allowed to sleep longer now. You wait. You'll see. You'll be allowed to sleep longer too someday."

Bleiber knew he had diverted the old man's thought. Yet, now Bleiber fought the urge to tell the old man about the memo he had received at work. He would blurt out what the memo had said. Then he would add: "Now I can sleep longer too!" There it would be, just like that. Doing so would be so easy. He thought that somehow the revelation would help him.

"More wine, Papa?" He reached for the old man's goblet, but his father declined.

"No. I've had enough. I'll leave now." He handed Bleiber the goblet. "Thank you," he said. "It was good enough."

"Sure, Papa. I buy what I can afford."

"You could have had more," the old man persisted.

"It's over now, Papa."

"Over? I suppose. Someday you'll come to your senses."

Someday? Come to his senses? About what—his working for twenty-five years at a job that his father had always disapproved?

Bleiber thought that the old man's mind was wandering. Age? The wine on top of whatever his father had before? And who knew how much the old man had been drinking before he came? Bleiber felt again his fatigue. Now he wished his father gone so that he could rest. Tomorrow, the last day, at least he would finish right.

"It's late, Papa. I have to work tomorrow."

His father nodded. "Late. Too late."

Again, his father had misunderstood. "It's been all right," Bleiber said.

"I can't see how you've done it," the old man said. "All those years. And you still read." His father studied Bleiber's face waiting for an answer.

"Would you like more wine?" Bleiber asked instead.

His father waved him off. "I must go. I've stayed too long. I have a busy day tomorrow of conferences with clients. Why I came, I don't know. It's hopeless."

His gaze dropped to the faded carpet then rose again to study Bleiber who waited patiently watching the old man's face. How dark it seemed, so often inscrutable with thought. He wanted to do something to ease his father's doubt. But, then, what could he do for the old man? What could he do for himself especially now with tomorrow his last day? "I'll be all right, Papa," he said finally.

The old man looked again at the carpet and slowly shook his head.

Bleiber went to get his father's coat and cap. He helped his father into the coat and followed him to the door then watched him move to the stairs. The old man paused at the top of the stairway to look back once more at Bleiber standing at the open door.

Bleiber stood at the door watching his father slowly move down the stairs. The old man looked town at the carpeting, one hand sliding down the rail along the wall, the other holding the cane for support. Bleiber watched until his father disappeared behind the turn of the stairs. Then as Bleiber turned back into the room, he heard the voices of his wife and father as they passed each other on the stairs. Bleiber turned into the room allowing the door to remain open.

He moved to pick up the empty goblet his father had left on the table by the window and paused to watch the old man on the street below look both ways before slowly crossing. Bleiber stood at the window as the double image of the old man using his cane moved up the street along the windows of the storefronts. Then Bleiber turned and took the goblets and the jug of wine and set the goblets in the sink. He set the jug on the sideboard and watched the swirl of wine within the jug catch the slanting light before settling to a quivering stillness. He heard the front door close then Emma's quiet solid step.

She came to stand in the doorway of the kitchen. She watched as he moved about the room returning the jug to the cupboard. Then she followed him into the living room.

"You're lucky you weren't here," Bleiber said. He moved to the chair in the corner by the window. He settled again noticing the rings from the goblet on the table beside the chair. Then he began to read but stopped to search for his glasses, put them on, and turned on the lamp against the gathering darkness.

Bleiber rose at his usual time, even though he had received the memo. Then after eating the same light breakfast of plain dark bread with black coffee, he stood at his window high above the city street and watched the expectant light at the horizon behind the dark buildings. Bleiber liked to rise a little earlier than he had to. Then he could watch the growing dawn. He liked the strange comfort, the strange small joy of morning alone relaxing from the stiffness of the night watching the light, his head thick with thought waiting for the day recalling his father's visit of the night before. He wondered about the day ahead, this day, of course, somewhat special. Then while recalling his father's visit he wondered, what, indeed, might he have become had he followed his father's way? But he decided that there was little use in wondering now since doing so was a little late for that.

So Bleiber stood at his morning window sipping the steaming coffee, wiping away the brown beads from his gray full mustache, watching the morning light until it began to thin. He drank, turned, set the cup in the sink, stretched, and gathered for the day.

His cap hung in its place behind the kitchen door. He remembered the first one his father had given him when Bleiber was a boy. He set the cap firmly on his head and picked up his lunch pail. Then he went through the flat to the dark bedroom to kiss Emma warm under covers. The fragrance of her warm body from the flowering of last night's too seldom lovemaking sent a dull stir through his loins. Bleiber turned toward the door, toward the day, toward the dim light waiting for him beneath the pavement. Bleiber went down the dark stairway then the dark hallway to the street noticing on the way the worn and faded carpeting that he could still recall as new. Then as he entered the street still in darkness between the buildings the sky above the street silver blue, Bleiber placed his morning cigarette, paused to light it and puff, then plodded up the empty street.

Balistrari, the green grocer, had set out his fruits and vegetables, his magazines and newspapers. Now he was hosing down the walk in front of his store when he saw Bleiber coming up the street. The sight of Bleiber with the old tweed cap pulled low over his head, the cigarette dangling beneath the mustache, the sight of the large stooped shoulders, the black lunch pail dangling from thick fingers made Balistrari want to turn to seek the safe dimness of his store. Yet how many years—Balistrari couldn't say—had Bleiber lumbered up the street toward him wearing that same cap, carrying that lunch pail with crackling paint? And Balistrari sensed, not really knowing why, that somehow his day would be incomplete without seeing Bleiber moving toward him as he had all the other days before.

For even on Sundays Bleiber would pad in his slippers over the hosed down pavement, the pavement dark and fresh smelling, as Bleiber came during the week, sleeping a little later perhaps, coming to buy his cigarettes and his Sunday paper. Sometimes Balistrari when especially tired felt like shouting "Bleiber, straighten up! Take off that silly cap!" Instead, Balistrari always continued to hose off the walk in front of his store until Bleiber reached him.

"Morning," Bleiber said softly. The water from the hose hissed on the pavement in the quiet of the street.

"Morning," Balistrari replied.

"I need some cigarettes when you have time."

"Balistrari nodded." O.K.," he said. "Be right with you."

"Sure," Bleiber said.

Bleiber watched while Balistrari turned off the water, undid, then curled the hose. Bleiber followed Balistrari into the store then waited while Balistrari put the hose away in the back room. Balistrari came forward behind the counter as Bleiber went to the fruit bins under the storefront window, carefully chose a large apple, came back inside, and paid Balistrari for the apple and cigarettes.

"You ought to buy your cigarettes by the carton. It's cheaper," Balistrari said as he had now and then for as many years as he had known Bleiber.

"Sure, you're right. One of these days I'll do that."

Then Bleiber went off down the street. Balistrari stood on the drying walkway before his store and watched Bleiber, shoulders stooped, cap pulled down over his gray hair, black crackled paint lunch pail dangling from his fingers, disappear around the corner moving toward the hole that would hide him for the last day.

Bleiber walked the rest of the way to work and entered the building where he changed into his work suit that still carried the dank stench of the sewers from the day before. He pulled on the long rubber boots that reached about his waist. Then he scuffled with the rest of the men down the iron stairs. The sound of their heavy rubber boots echoed against the concrete walls as they descended.

They worked through most of the morning using shovels and even their own bodies formed into chains to break loose the waste and debris that had settled into a thick mass. Bleiber followed along with a large broom to make sure that at least for that day there would be no more blockages. Thus they wandered through the sewers, their feet splashing. They watched for alligators. Their first discovery of one had surprised them since they had heard that the reports of such creatures that had been abandoned down toilets surviving in sewers had been more myth than fact. Then on sighting the first one, Bleiber couldn't quite believe what he saw, the large yellow eyes staring at him. Startled, Bleiber's reaction had been to strike at it with a shovel, but the blade only rang against the tough hide, and the critter, more disgruntled than angry, had slithered off into the dark caves filled with muck. After that, they hadn't seen any since that first encounter except for one time that a crew member claimed to have been attacked when he had come upon one suddenly, but when no one else had seen the creature, they all dismissed the report of the attack as a bad joke.

Halfway through morning, they stopped for a negotiated break climbing up over iron rungs set in concrete walls, climbing out from the darkness through a doorway at the bottom of the subway, squinting against the sunlight, ignoring the curious stares of people descending. The others went before him leaving him to climb alone. They scuffled ahead to a blue and white-striped corner food stand. They stood near the stand sipping coffee from cardboard cups, changing hands to cool their scalded fingers but enjoying the heat from the cups after the chill of the sewers. They stepped apart to let him through. He bought coffee and left them. They closed together to talk and joke among themselves.

Bleiber set his coffee beside him on a bench and lit his second cigarette of the day. Then he stretched his legs so he could sit more comfortably in the high stiff rubber boots. Stone, a younger man, thinner, and a bit taller than Bleiber came to sit by him. Bleiber recalled the first day that Stone had started work. Bleiber had shown Stone what to do because the other men had mostly ignored the new man. They had shaken Stone's hand, had nodded to him acknowledging the introduction. Stone had been smiling and open, but Bleiber had seen that the others resented Stone fearful of Stone's newness. Bleiber had shown the young man what to do.

"Hey, Bleiber!" Stone exclaimed sitting on the bench. "What you going to do this weekend?" Bleiber winced at Stone's intrusion. Yet he accepted the man, grateful in a grudging way for the man's attention. Out of all those he had worked with over the years, Stone was the only one who seemed to really try to approach Bleiber.

"Nothing much," Bleiber said. "Maybe go to the park"

"The park? I've been thinking about doing that. Probably go see my nephew. Maybe take him to the zoo. Maybe show him the alligators."

"Really?" Bleiber asked. He sipped his coffee.

"He's been wanting to see them." He fumbled beneath his waders for a watch.

"There's still time," Bleiber said.

"Not much. These breaks never seem long enough. Hey! Wouldn't it be great never have to go back! Just stay here. Watch the people, especially all the women."

"You'd get tired of that, too, after a while."

"Not me! Be better than having to wade through that crap!"

"You forget after a while," Bleiber said.

"You been here a long time, huh?"

"Too long."

"Hey! Remember the first day I started?"

Bleiber nodded and lit a cigarette off the stub of the old.

"Hey, Otto? How long you been on this lousy job?"

Bleiber pondered whether he should tell.

"Twenty-five years—today," he revealed finally.

"Twenty-five! Today! Really?"

Bleiber nodded.

"Hey! We ought to celebrate!"

"What's to celebrate? A job, that's all. Too many days."

"Hey! I know," Stone said. "How about a beer? Yeah! Let me buy you one after work."

Bleiber looked at the man next to him on the bench. Bleiber had always walked home immediately after work and always alone. Sometimes, Stone would walk part way with him but not far and not for long, and Bleiber would always walk on home by himself.

"There's nothing to celebrate," Bleiber said again after a while.

"Hey! What you mean? Stone argued. "Twenty-five years? That's nothing? That's hell!"

"Not anymore," Bleiber said.

"Huh? What you talkin' about?"

Bleiber with some reluctance and not sure of why groped for the memo he had found the day before. He handed the slip to Stone who read it then handed it back. Bleiber returned the slip to his shirt pocket.

"So what? Let's have that beer anyway."

Then Stone pushed himself from the bench and looked at his watch.

"I'll buy. I'll wait for you." He started back toward the dark opening that led beneath the pavement. He turned back. "Remember!" Stone said.

Bleiber watched him go noticing how Stone picked up the other men, stopping by them, gathering them, then leading them. Bleiber finished his coffee and dropped his cigarette into the empty cup. He followed Stone while crushing the cup in his hands then tossing it into a nearby sewer.

As he worked throughout the rest of the morning, Bleiber thought about his first day twenty-five years ago. How happy he had been to find work but fearful and anxious because he was new, because he did not know what he should be doing, and because no one would show him. So he had learned by watching the others and following what they did. His mother had been fearful too. He would be working beneath the street. That crust of asphalt above his head could collapse on him for any reason and crush him, just like that. Bleiber also had the problem of his father's response to Bleiber's decision to take the job offered him. His father had fought with him from the very beginning, and for some reason Bleiber couldn't fathom, fought with him still just as he had done the evening before.

But Bleiber had met Emma. He had courted her in his own quiet way, and she in her own quiet way had received his attention. Then he quietly had proposed marriage, and she quietly had accepted. His father following his typical manner had howled. He had screamed abuse on Bleiber, on Emma, on Bleiber's mother who had borne it all. His father had set out in his typical fashion following the methods of his profession the several key reasons why Bleiber shouldn't marry, ignoring, of course, or dismissing out of hand Emma who stood silent beside Bleiber who took all the condemnation trying to shield her.

"They're too young! What's the hurry? Look at the economy! He doesn't have a steady job! What does he do now? Day labor! Cutting lawns! Hauling trash! Loading and unloading trucks! What kind of opportunities will he have doing that? He ought to be in school learning for a noble profession—a doctor, perhaps!

"Or lawyer?" Bleiber asked.

"Yes! Why not? All you need to do is try! Such work has done all right by me."

"But we've struggled too," Bleiber's mother had added. "Where would he get the money for school?"

"I struggled just to make it through technical school," Bleiber added.

"Where will he get enough money to support a wife and then children if they should come."

"We'll manage," Bleiber said. Then he, finally having had enough of his father's rant, took Emma quietly by the hand and led her away.

He and Emma were married when Bleiber's mother signed for the license. And, of course, as his father had so wisely predicted, Bleiber and Emma had struggled. She had found that she had conceived. Bleiber was thrilled but suddenly loaded with the burden of responsibility. They told Bleiber's mother who was equally excited, but they followed her advice and avoided Bleiber's father. Then they were crushed by Emma's miscarriage.

Why had Bleiber wanted Emma for his wife? How could Bleiber explain since he wasn't sure himself? But he knew that his father's way of life—what his father called a noble profession—repelled him. Bleiber could never decide on a reason why he didn't want to follow his father's lead except that he knew from his previous struggle with schooling that he just didn't have the ability. He simply didn't want it. He wanted Emma. How could he with such limited learning explain the nebulous emotions, the vague stirrings, the amorphous desires that he had just thinking of her and then seemed to fill him when he saw her. Her soft beauty, her flowing warmth, her bouquet of fragrances—all these were real. They were immediate. He wanted them now. He wanted her love and her warmth. And Bleiber decided that he would do something on his own of his own choosing. That sense of freedom seemed to give him direction and drive. So he had looked. So he finally had found the job. So they had married. So they gathered bills, especially because of Emma's miscarriage. But after that no children came. Now Bleiber was glad that it was too late. And at work nothing had happened. Nothing had ever happened—except for that one alligator. The foreman had introduced him to the crew then had just left him with the others. Bleiber had learned the job on his own.

Bleiber worked the rest of the morning remembering events of the last twenty-five years. The job had always allowed him his thoughts and reveries. And quite often he pondered what he had read the night before. He often read the newspaper that he referred to as "the poor man's encyclopedia," or he read a news magazine. But mostly he read the works of great authors. He had been reading *The Canterbury Tales* in translation the previous night before his father had arrived. No surprise why his father had exploded at the discovery. Bleiber felt fortunate that his father did not know of Bleiber's aspiration to read the same works in the original English of the Fourteenth Century. Wouldn't his father be appalled? But Bleiber on reading a few passages of the original had become fascinated, yet he had admitted his limitations and resigned to reading what he could.

Just after his break he received a direct message from the superintendent. Bleiber had sloshed through the water to the iron steps; then he had climbed, the long rubber waders dripping, heavy and awkward to walk in. He had hung the boots and coveralls in his locker

"You better go," Stone had urged. "Take your time."

Bleiber was curious that Stone should be advising him, but he said nothing and took Stone's advice. So feeling lighter from his loss of waders, he went to the office to see the superintendent.

He watched a young woman with pale lips and dark hair hold her breath as he stood before her telling her that the superintendant had called him. He then followed her rhythmic movements as she went to the glassed-in office at the rear. She came back to tell Bleiber to wait and that Mr. Haskell would see him in a few moments. Bleiber thanked her and turned to the bulletin board. He surveyed the notices and posters so that the young woman could breathe.

"Otto!" a voice chimed. Bleiber turned to see the clean man in neat dark suit, white shirt, and solid colored tie.

Bleiber nodded. "Yes. You wanted to see me."

"Yes, Otto. Why don't you just come in? Just come right through here." The man in the suit, white shirt, and tie held open the gate. Bleiber entered and stood waiting for the man to move. Then the man started up the aisle turning to usher Bleiber along. "I'm Superintendent Haskell. I don't believe we've ever met." The man offered his hand. Bleiber took it, met the man's challenge, then let the hand drop.

"No we haven't," Bleiber said. "But I've seen you around."

"Yes, of course. That's part of my job description. I make the rounds to keep in touch, to see if everything is going O.K."

Superintendent Haskell turned and headed for the glassed-in office. Bleiber followed glancing at the women with their soft neat clothes and hair, their painted nails and rouged lips. He glanced at the smooth sheathed legs ending at a fleshy knee then disappearing beneath a dress or skirt. Bleiber slouched along the aisle between the desks.

The fashionably dressed women paused at their machines looking up as Bleiber passed, exchanged looks on observing him slouch by, then dropped their eyes to their suspended work.

Bleiber stopped just inside the door of the glassed-in office. Bleiber looked back along the row of women at their desks. Then he glanced around at the darkly stained shelves and furnishings. Superintendent Haskell went around behind the dark massive desk and sat down in the large high-backed genuine leather chair. He opened a folder on the desk and looked up at Bleiber. He saw Bleiber standing just inside the door.

"Oh, I'm sorry!" Haskell said. "Maybe you'd like to sit down."

"Sure. Thank you," Bleiber said. He eased himself into the chair arranged before the desk. He sat at the edge of the seat, his hands between his knees.

"Well, Otto, I've had a call from Senior Vice President Jacobs in the downtown office."

"I see," Bleiber said although he really didn't.

"I guess you already know about the problems we've been having?"

"Problems? Who doesn't? We all have problems."

"The company's. You know. Money, of course."

"Bleiber knew. He nodded. "That's why I've lost my job."

"Well, you didn't exactly lose it. We—they . . ."

"The company."

"Yes. We're simply asking you to consider the possibility of retirement."

"No one asked me anything."

"Oh, but that's what the call from Senior Vice President was about."

Bleiber nodded. Then he remembered his cap. He took it off. He held it in his hands between his knees.

Superintendent Haskell sat back in his large high-backed chair of genuine leather. "You've been with us a long time."

"Long enough," Bleiber admitted

"I hope you've been happy working for us."

"Happy? It's been steady work. I've tried to do my job and not screw up. It's fed me, fed my wife, gave us a place to lay our heads. Happy? I never thought of it like that."

Haskell rocked forward in his chair.

"Oh," Haskell said. "I see."

What did he see? Bleiber wondered. "Something wrong?" Bleiber asked.

Haskell sat back in his chair. "Well, you've been with us a long time."

Bleiber shrugged. Why the big deal about how long he's worked? He knew how long he had been on the job. What difference did it make now? After lunch, only a half-day left. Bleiber suddenly felt his hunger.

"If you had been satisfied, well, perhaps it might be easier for you."

"Satisfied? Now that's another story. No, I can't say I've been satisfied. Are any of us satisfied? Are we supposed to be? Are you?"

Haskell shifted in his chair.

"Satisfied." Bleiber continued. No, not exactly. Like I said. It's been all right. It's been steady. I've tried to do my job."

"Yes, you have. I can see that from your file. And Vice President Jacobs mentioned that in our phone conversation.

Who was this Jacobs guy anyway? Bleiber wondered. How many vice presidents did the company have if one of them was a Senior Vice President?

"It'd be a shame to give that up now."

What was Haskell getting at? Give up what?

"You're not really ready to retire, are you?"

"I got a few good years left in me."

"That's what we mean."

"I don't understand."

"You get laid off now, you lose those years. No job. No retirement. You ever consider that? You'll lose your benefits."

Bleiber considered. "No. I guess I never thought of that. I've always thought that retirement is for old men."

"Well, maybe you should have thought differently, Otto. Maybe you better reconsider."

"I'm not old enough to retire. I might look it, but I'm not."

"I didn't mean that, Otto. I meant your age would be a problem. You retire early you wouldn't get the benefits because you're not old enough."

"I couldn't, could I?"

"No, you couldn't."

"So if I could keep on working, I guess I'd be better off."

"Yes."

"But I don't have a job. I got this yesterday." Bleiber groped for the piece of paper.

"I know all about that, Otto. That's why I called to ask you to come see me."

"Vice President Jacobs?"

"Right, Otto. He wanted me to talk to you. He wanted me to see what you had in mind. What you might have planned doing."

"Plan? I hadn't planned anything. I just got this memo yesterday. Believe me. I didn't expect it. I could have used some warning."

"You've never considered the possibility? You've known about the problems. Everybody knows. We're short of funds. No money anywhere.

We've had to lay people off in other sections. You should have seen the possibility."

"But I've been here so long," Bleiber said dismayed.

"No one's safe, Otto. Not in times like these."

"What you going to do when they come after you? Wouldn't they gain more by cutting some of those with big paychecks? Maybe the company has too many vice presidents."

Superintendent Haskell jacked himself up in his genuine leather chair. "That's not for you and me to decide, Otto. Maybe we'd better talk about you. What can we do to help you?"

"Well, you can give me back my job!"

"Right! You have it!" Haskell declared.

"What!"

"Sure, it's yours."

"You mean I'm not being laid off? That's great! Wait till I tell my wife!"

Haskell laughed at Bleiber's excitement. The women looked up from their machines. One swiveled in her chair. "Hold on, Otto," Haskell said. He glanced along the line of women at their desks. Their eyes dropped to their work. The one who had swiveled in her chair swiveled back. "It's not as easy as that."

Bleiber squelched his excitement. "What you mean?"

"Well, there are complications."

"Huh? Complications. What complications? Do I keep my job or don't I?"

"Well, you see, we've already given your position to someone else."

"Who?"

"Stone."

"Jerry!" He's foreman now! I don't believe it!"

"Well, he is."

"I'll be damned!" Bleiber said to himself; so that's what all that giving advice was about and the way he had handled the men during the break.

"So we can't very well take it back now and let you remain as foreman. Think of the trouble that might cause. And we still have the problem of money. Someone has to go."

"Then how can you say I still got a job? I got no job. Where's the job?"

"The stockroom."

"The what?"

"The stockman's retiring next month. You'll take his place. We'll carry you until then. You'll work with him learning your new job. That is if you want it. He's old enough. He's too old, really. He should have been gone long ago."

"Me? A stock boy!"

"Stockman, Otto. It's work. You'll be your own boss. You'll be able to work until retirement when you'll get your pension and other benefits. You get laid off now, what do you get?"

"Don't I get paid severance? You'll have to pay me plenty. I'm foreman."

"You were foreman, Otto," Haskell corrected.

"O.K. I was," he pondered. "Stock boy! How about that?" he asked himself.

"Your severance pay wouldn't last forever."

"You're right. But I got savings. The company's supposed to pay me something on my savings plan. Half again what I save. Over twenty-five years I got plenty saved."

"Not if you get laid off. You lose that bonus. You only get what you've saved. What did you save for? Retirement, I bet. You see? You lose that too. Then what?"

"I don't know. I'm too old! Nobody'd want me. Besides, I'm nothing. Just a laborer. What could I do? Who'd hire me?"

"Seems silly for you to be looking for a job when you already have one."

"Maybe I'll just lay around. Take it easy for a change. I could use it. I earned it."

Haskell seemed upset by this sudden turn in their exchange. "You're young, Otto. You got many good years left."

"As stock boy?"

"Stockman, Otto. You'll be your own boss. And it's work, Otto."

"I don't know. I never thought of me as a stock boy."

"O.K.," Superintendent Haskell sighed. He leaned forward to rest his forearms on his dark massive desk. "Why don't you consider the offer? You're probably hungry anyway. It's almost time for your lunch break, and I've taken up too much of your time. Why don't you run along, eat, and think about it. I'll come to see you after lunch. Maybe you'll know better then once you've had something to eat.

"Yeah, sure. Why not? Bleiber said. He rose then turned and slouched back the aisle along the row of clean fragrant women. He left the office and made his way toward the basement locker room and his languishing lunch pail.

Superintendent Haskell watched the gray-haired man with stooping shoulders slouching through the aisle. The women glanced as he passed. Haskell closed the folder on his desk; then he reached for a tissue in his desk drawer and blew his nose hard.

Bleiber ate his lunch from the crackled pail sitting on a bench in the locker room with his back against the green steel lockers listening to the other men play cards. He never played himself. At various times earlier in the twenty-five years he had wanted to join them, but no one had ever asked. Then finally one day when Stone had suggested to the others that Bleiber sit in, Bleiber had refused shaking his head excusing himself because he had never learned to play. Now he finished his apple and lit a cigarette. He thought of Balistrari in his small green store. Bleiber leaned his head against the locker, closed his yes, and listened to the quiet droning voices of the men at cards at the same time he watched Balistrari move around his store in among cramped aisles, behind the enameled case chopping meat, behind the counter helping customers, mostly old heavy women who swayed in from the street beneath the green and yellow striped awning lowered now against the bright sunlight. Bleiber pushed his cap forward over his eyes to shut out more of the light. He smoked slowly drawing on his cigarette thinking about the women he had seen in the office. Then he thought of Emma and how he had left her in the morning, and then he noticed that he no longer heard the voices of the card players. He rocked forward away from the locker pushing back his cap and opening his eyes. The men were quietly studying their cards. Stone looked at Bleiber then glanced toward the door. Bleiber turned. Superintendent Haskell stood at the door in his dark suit, white shirt, and tie then came forward smiling.

"Here's Otto now," he said

Bleiber rose. He snuffed out his cigarette in the ashtray on the bench. The other men watched from the end of the locker room.

"Well, now, Otto. What do you think? What's it going to be?"

"I don't know," Bleiber said. "I haven't decided."

"But I asked you to, Otto," Haskell said.

Bleiber shrugged.

"It's important for you to decide. You want to throw everything away? After all those years, Otto, what about your family? Maybe you need to consider them. What will they think if they know you had a chance and threw it away?"

"All I got is a wife to worry about. We'd make out all right."

"Don't be foolish, Otto. Think about it."

Bleiber thought.

"Maybe you haven't had enough time to consider our offer. Maybe you should take the rest of the day off. You can have the afternoon to decide as a token of your anniversary. Consider too that we don't do what we're doing for everyone. But you've been with us a long time and we want to repay you for your loyalty and dedication."

Bleiber stared at the man. Loyalty? Dedication? Who was he talking about? What was he talking about?

"Yes," Haskell said. "Take it. You're free to go whenever you want."

"I don't need the afternoon off."

"You've earned it Otto. Use it. Think about what we've offered you. Decide for yourself. You need the free time to think. We know you don't want to make a snap decision."

"Who needs the afternoon off?"

"There's no hurry. I'll ask you tomorrow. Enjoy your free time."

Then Haskell left the locker room breathing deeply sucking in fresh air. Bleiber stood watching Haskell go. Stone came forward while the others still hung back gathering up their cards and preparing for their return to the sewers.

"Hey! Aren't you lucky, though! The rest of the day off! Did you hear?"

Bleiber stared at Stone searching his face.

"You better take it, Otto," Stone said. "They don't do this very often."

Bleiber turned to get out of his work clothes. The other men started out of the locker room toward the iron stairs that led beneath the pavement. Stone stayed behind. He leaned against the lockers watching Bleiber remove his work clothes. "Already he's playing boss," Bleiber thought.

"Where you going to go with all your free time?"

Bleiber shrugged. "I don't know. I didn't think I'd have the rest of the day off. Go home probably."

"You're lucky."

"Maybe."

"No maybe. I think you really are. You get the day off. You get to keep your job if you want it."

"It's not the same job."

"What you want? You'll be working. You won't have to do a lot. You won't have to be the boss."

"No. You'll be that, huh?"

Stone watched him. "Sure. You're right. I will," he said. "But you'll have it easy."

"Maybe," Bleiber said. He paused reflecting. "What'd you do in my place?" he asked.

"Me? I'd take it."

"You would."

"Sure, why not? At least you'll have something. You'll be clean all day every day. You'll be better off."

"Maybe," Bleiber said. "That's what Haskell keeps saying. But you know what they're trying to pull, don't you?"

"What?"

"I get laid off, they have to pay me severance. I take the job, maybe I'll quit, or they fire me for whatever. Either way they save money."

"Maybe you're right."

"I know I'm right. I've heard of it before. Wait. You'll see."

"You wouldn't quit. I know you."

"Maybe not. But they won't hesitate to fire me if they want. Maybe I won't even take it. I get quite a hunk if they lay me off."

"It won't last. Besides, you'd get tired just laying around. You're not that kind. You're a worker. I've seen you."

"Maybe," Bleiber said. He studied the man.

Then the stillness of the locker room, the running water made Stone grope for words. "Look, what about our beer? he said finally.

Bleiber grabbed a towel and wrapped it around his waist. "I better shower," he said. "You better go after your men." He searched the other man's face. Bleiber saw in those dark eyes the look he had seen years ago when Stone had been a kid. Stone was still a kid, Bleiber thought.

"Maybe some other time then." Stone started toward the door.

"Good luck," Bleiber called. Stone stopped, turned back.

Bleiber kept silent. He looked at Stone until Stone turned again and hurried after the other men for whom he was now responsible.

Bleiber went to clean himself of the day's work. Showering by himself, he noticed the hiss of the streaming water against the concrete floor, the suck of water swirling down the drain. Then as he dried himself he listened to the gurgle of the toilet tanks. He went back to his locker to dress in his street clothes. He heard the sound of his locker door slamming shut, his footsteps echoing as he deposited his towel in the empty sack at the door. He left the locker room. He headed for the open air.

Bleiber stood gaping at the nearly empty street. A lone car passed him hitting the manhole cover. He had always hated that. He knew that some people did it deliberately. Bleiber winced and watched the car until it was lost from sight. A man passed him looking him over turning his head to keep Bleiber in his sight as he passed. Bleiber felt odd, felt awkward, felt out of place. What was he doing here? He didn't belong here at this time of day. He sure must seem that way to others. Look how they seemed to gawk at him.

Bleiber started for home. He knew that place at least was a haven even with Emma not there attending to her volunteer work at the daycare. Then he saw the mute sign dim in early afternoon sunlight. He stopped. He considered. How often had he ever had a chance like this before? Now he had the luxury of time.

He turned beneath the sign that somehow appeared strange. He walked into the darkness of the bar. He waited for his eyes to adjust. A short man with black combed back hair came forward behind the bar as Bleiber eased himself onto the soft high cushion of the bar stool. Bleiber felt good just to sit, but the man stood before him waiting. Bleiber saw the glowing beer sign, so he ordered beer, sat back, and relaxed while the man snatched a glass for a stack of glasses behind the bar and filled the glass beneath a tap. Bleiber paid and sat looking at the mirror behind the bar. He felt strange. Half conscious of the image of himself in the mirror here in the nearly empty bar at this time of day he appeared different. He thought of the men he worked with; he could imagine where they were at this time of day and what they were doing.

Then Bleiber noticed the man and woman at the end of the bar. They seemed to be avoiding the windows and the brightness of the street; that they were and why, Bleiber wasn't sure, but that was his first thought on noticing them, perhaps something about their attitude and how they seemed to cling to each other and how they eyed Bleiber where he sat at the other end of the bar near the door and the bright street. The man leaned on his elbows above the drink before him on the bar. The woman watched Bleiber while taking slow drags from a cigarette. Then the woman snuffed out the cigarette in the ashtray before her on the bar. She slid from the stool lightly resting her hand on the bar to help her. Bleiber eyed the skirt slide up the thigh, stop, then fall as the woman reached the floor. Then the woman swayed to the door of the restroom. She glanced at Bleiber as she disappeared behind the closing door. Then the man came off his stool quickly starting toward Bleiber and appeared angry. Bleiber gulped his beer and left.

Bleiber reached the sidewalk followed by the loud muttering from the man behind him in the bar. Then he slowed. Safe now, he stopped. He squinted against the light. Were those the kind that peopled this time of day? He felt full and a bit heady from the beer, and he stood in the bright sun noticing again the differences in light. Seldom had he seen the street like this. He often had come this way before, but now the difference in light gave everything new appearances: the line of quiet cars along both sides of the street, the windows of the storefronts reflecting the parked cars, the few strolling forms that moved along the line of stores and along the stoops of old brick buildings.

Well, what should he do now? He should do something different now that he had time. He should think. He should decide. That's why he was here now, why they had given him the rest of the day off. His freedom was costing them money that they claimed they didn't have enough of. Well, too damn bad, he decided. They had insisted he take the time. Besides, they could afford it with what little they paid him. And his decision would save them plenty.

So he ambled enjoying the sunlight, the differences in the street, the quiet, the freedom from the constraints of time and from the darkness he knew was there beneath his feet.

Bleiber thought then of his father. Wouldn't the Old Man be surprised! His father from time to time had urged his son to come visit him during the day to see what his work was really like. But Bleiber always had resisted by finding some compelling obligation for his not visiting. Most times the obligation was his job. Bleiber understood, of course, what his father really wanted was to show Bleiber what he possibly had been missing all these years. Before, Bleiber had begged off. He had to work for a living, so he had told his father. And when his vacation time came, he was ready to take full advantage of the time he had away from work. By then, the old man had followed the direction of his own obligations and interests, and Bleiber always had managed to escape.

Now he reconsidered—he thought—he seemed to be doing a lot of that lately. And he found himself without excuses. Yet he fought himself. Let it go! He told himself. Then he recalled his father's visit of the night before. Maybe his going to see the his father would help them both. He could even ask his father for advise. That might make the Old Man feel better—and mostly likely even more superior. His father was getting old. Bleiber wasn't getting any younger. Perhaps the time had arrived to declare peace—or at least a truce.

Bleiber used the subway to get to the complex of buildings in which his father had his office. Waiting for the train, Bleiber saw the door he used so often to get from the sewers to the street above during his rest breaks. Then he thought, wouldn't it be something if they came now? They would see him, be surprised, and he would off-handedly report to them the reason for his being there and for his taking the train. He thrilled with delight. He might even go with them for coffee. Wouldn't that be something? They'd grow purple when they had to go back and he could remain.

No. Too early for them to break. He'd have to wait too long. Besides, they probably wouldn't care anyway. But if he got laid off, he could do it. He could do whatever he liked. He could go to the park that would also be quiet this time of day with hardly any people there. Then he could sit. He would study the buildings that rose above the trees. He could wonder about the people in those buildings, wonder what they were like. He would watch the women come from offices. He would watch them spread papers or napkins or whatever on the benches then unfold their lunches from paper bags. He would watch them eat. He would see the rich people emerge from towering apartment buildings that rose above the summer leaves already yellowing. He would watch those leaves fall, watch them pile. He would walk on them, hear them crunch beneath his feet, watch kids stack them and dive in them and fling them. He would see the long gleaming cars glide and stop, discharge their passengers, then glide again. He would observe the slow sure movements of the wealthy entering plush lobbies and rising unseen to some unimaginable height above his bench, above the trees, above the park where Bleiber sat in foreign sunlight, heavy with dreams.

The subway train arrived waking him. He scrambled with the crowd then braced himself against the gleaming pole while the train took him to the stop from which he could go to where his father had his office. Bleiber asked someone for help. Then he started off in the direction the person had pointed. But when he found the building and entered the lobby and saw the corridors leading off in several directions, he felt lost. A security guard asked if he needed help.

Yes, he certainly did. But even after being offered directions, once beyond the lobby, Bleiber felt lost again. The corridors seemed a maze. And what he observed surprised him—he had expected something else, something newer, something modern: Instead, the twists and turns of the dull dirty yellow plaster walls, the drab brown tile that led him past the dark closed doors with little squares of rippled frosted glass that dimmed the light behind to a lime green glow distorting dark shadows flitting back and forth across the blind windows reminded him too much of sewers.

He also was startled by the expressions on the faces in the rooms with open doors. The sunlight from the windows behind the people hunched behind desks made the rooms appear dim like caves or narrow cells.

He unexpectedly came upon his father emerging from his office into the hallway. Bleiber again was startled, this time by his father's countenance. The old man seemed fresher, somehow appeared younger, and he didn't have his cane. Most of all his father's manner—his initial surprise quickly controlled—made Bleiber have second thoughts on his having come.

"So, you're finally here!" his father exclaimed.

But Bleiber hadn't come to have his father gloat. Bleiber again thought of his father's visit the previous night. What a difference! Now his father seemed haughty and condescending in contrast to last night's abject bitterness and disappointment. Maybe it had been the booze.

"Come in! Come in!" his father said. His father ushered Bleiber in toward the desk piled with papers, in among the many shelves of thick colored books that lined all the walls. "Sit down!" his father ordered. Bleiber sat in the chair before the desk, the second time today. They studied each other in silence. "Why are you here at this time of day?" his father asked. "Has something happened?"

"They gave me the afternoon off," Bleiber explained. "After twenty-five years, an afternoon off!"

"And you came here?"

"You said I should, Papa. More than once. You've always said, 'Come see how the other half works.' So now I came."

"So now you see," his father said. He waved his arms indicating the piles of paper on the desk and the walls of books.

"It's different," Bleiber admitted.

"Different! That's all you can say? Come! I'll show you around. Then you'll see. We'll have coffee. I'll introduce you to colleagues. You'll hear what I do from others."

Bleiber cringed as the thought of this threatened exposure. He understood now that his visit was being transformed into his father's triumph. Yet when his father rose and came from around his desk and started for the door, Bleiber followed. His father negotiated for him the puzzle of the corridors Bleiber had floundered through by himself.

Bleiber again thought about his own job, or, more exactly, his former job. If he could take his father there, Bleiber would have to be the one to lead; his father would be the one as lost as he was now. Yet, now both places seemed about the same. Why was that, Bleiber wondered? The similarity puzzled him at first. Then he noticed the large offices or sections, the banks of desks, the rows of women almost identical to those he had seen before lunch in the superintendent's office. And he was reminded of the reason for his being here where he found himself.

Then they reached the café. They took a seat next to a well-dressed man his father obviously knew. Bleiber was introduced. "You have a son?" the man said in surprise. "You never told us you had a son!"

"Of course I have," the old man said glancing uneasily at Bleiber. "I'm sure I've mentioned him to you several times."

"Oh, now I remember," the man said looking Bleiber over.

"He's a laborer," Bleiber's father said. Bleiber wasn't sure how he should take his father's tone of voice. "He works with his hands, not like us. He serves society as a public servant," the old man added.

Bleiber was reminded of his dilemma. "Not anymore," he corrected.

"What's that?" his father asked. "So there was something more to that funny business last night."

Bleiber thought his father hadn't noticed. He dug in his shirt pocket, brought out the slip, handed it to his father. His father studied the memo, his face changing as he read.

"You see now what happens?" the old man gloated. "No vision! You should have planned! You should have . . . ."

Bleiber fled back through the dim maze to the bright freedom of the open sky.

Bleiber turned through the park. He headed down a path between green shrubs and bushes beneath trees still in full leaf. He went along the path to the lake. He strolled the path that circled both sides to where the path led outside the park. Around the lake along the path old men on benches warmed themselves in the afternoon sun. Bleiber passed them as they nodded in the changing light. He noted the thread worn tweeds, the gray bristles on the wrinkled flesh, the spittle at the corners of the mouths, the quick startled jerks as the heads dropped when they sank deeper into slumber. Then they came awake with blank eyes, blinking against the bright sun before they settled back to sleep.

Bleiber thought about his visit to his father. What a disaster! His visit had been taken as a pilgrimage. Yet, Bleiber had nothing to repent. Let that old man lose himself in his books. Let him thrill to his way of life, to a world that appeared conjured in dreams. Let him lie. Bleiber only asked for the same.

Bleiber scuffed around the lake to where the path broke out of the park. There he stopped. He gazed into the water at the deep sky and the high clouds that traveled over the face of the water. He felt the warmth of the sun on his clothes. He raised his eyes toward the old men on benches scattered around the lake. He turned and went down the path and out of the park.

As Bleiber passed, Balistrari, the grocer, peered out from the dim interior of his store. Bleiber saw the startled expression as Balistrari glanced up from serving a customer. Even the customer fluttered in her exhortation to Balistrari as she watched Bleiber hold up a hand in quick salute to Balistrari as Bleiber passed.

Bleiber swung around the railing of the porch stairs and started up toward his flat. He was glad now to be home. He knew now he should have come here right away in the first place. He understood that now, and he felt joy at his discovery. But Emma wasn't there when he arrived, as he knew she wouldn't be.

Bleiber walked through the quiet apartment to the bedroom. He studied the neatly made bed with sunlight falling on the ribbed spread. "Chenille," Bleiber thought to himself.

He walked back through the rooms to the kitchen. He hung his hat in its place behind the door. Then he turned to the refrigerator. He took out a beer. He opened it. He drank deeply. He thought this beer better than the one he had quaffed in the bar. Then he thought of the woman on the barstool. He thought of the women he had seen in offices. He heard a cough from somewhere in the building. He listened to the vague hushed traffic on the street below that was becoming busier in the late afternoon. Bleiber sniffed, the sound loud. He went to sit in the stuffed chair by the window in the living room. Before he sat, he saw the large windows of the stores along the street below. He tried to settle into reading but couldn't and gave it up when he found himself reading the same paragraph more than once. He thought of his father. He thought of old men on benches in the park around the lake.

Bleiber drank his beer and listened for footsteps on the stairs. When they finally came, Bleiber felt warm again inside. He went to the door to wait when the footsteps reached the landing. Then the footsteps passed on, and Bleiber stood watching the door. He thought of men in glassed-in offices. He thought of fragrant women. He thought of men in locker rooms. He saw the expressions on their faces as they talked while removing work clothes then using a towel to cover themselves while treading to the showers then returning to their lockers to dress in their street clothes. He followed them as they left.

Bleiber heard a noise below. Someone started up from the street. He listened again while the footsteps came nearer. Then he heard the deep heavy breathing from the climb. But this time, too, the footsteps passed by, and Bleiber stood looking at the door waiting.

The day following his twenty-fifth anniversary Bleiber went to work and worked the whole day.

Period of Adjustment— Heads, I Win

"What you gunna do when you get out?" Peterson asked.

Claude Giles sat back in the lawn chair, his weapon resting across his legs. He searched the low hills that made the country seem a maze. A "demilitarized" zone, a no man's land, no one was supposed to be there. His job was to keep them out. He watched for movement.

"Who says I'm ever gunna get out?"

"Come on, man, you're not a twenty-year dude!" He joined Giles in his search.

"Who knows what might happen," Giles said. "You know why I'm here. I got it once. I could get it again. Next time they'll put me in a bag—free trip home."

"Not here, man. We're safe here."

"No one's ever safe—anywhere. Specially not here. Too easy. Look at us! Lounging around in lawn chairs. You'd think we were on a picnic. We don't watch out, we'll get it when we've let down. That's when it happens."

"Not here, man." Peterson insisted. "This time is different. This one's a turkey shoot, man!"

"Some turkey shoot," Giles said. "Those birds got weapons too. Don't ever forget that. Look what happened before. Ambush—that's it—game's all over. Demilitarized Zone! Baloney! Look at this!" Giles insisted, offering Peterson his rifle.

"Forget it, man! I've got one!" He took a drag off the joint then passed it over to Giles. "Relax, man! You're too uptight!"

"Friggen A, dude! I've got good reason!"

"Yeah? So what's so different about you? You're no special case. Lots of guys get it."

"I'm different all right," Giles insisted. "I've been here a long time. Longer than anyone, I suppose. And look at me! I'm a mess." He raised the bottle from between his legs and held it to his lips, tipping back his head while still managing to survey the terrain. "I drink too much," he said, lowering the bottle and passing it to Peterson. He took a toke of the joint. "I smoke too much of this shit!"

Peterson drank from the bottle and waited for the joint. "So does everyone, man! What's so different! You got to do something, man. Otherwise you'd go nuts!"

"Yeah, that's what I am!" Giles insisted. "And you know why?"

I lost my nerve. Me—the big patriot, the big war hero, comin' here to fight for my country, fight for my flag, defend it to the death. And then, Pow! I get it! No more of that hero crap for me, mother! They just try to send me back to my old outfit, I freak. I start goin' ape, smashing stuff, putting my fist through walls!"

"Well, you're set now, man!" Peterson assured him. "You'll make it. No sweat!"

"They gave me a medal," Giles said. "They shipped me here. And you know why? Because I'm still good. Better than I ever was. They know I'll do my job. And I do it. And you know why? Because that's what it is—a job. No Big Patriot stuff for me, man. I just do what I'm supposed to do. That's it. And absolutely nothing gets out of my sight alive. Easy life, all right. Better than that patrol crap. I never knew what hit me."

"Lighten up, man!" Peterson soothed. He returned the bottle. "You'll make it. You're tour is almost up. You'll get back home, you'll forget you were even here."

"Only way I'll forget is when I'm dead. And who says I'll go home. What for? Nothin' there."

"So what then, man?"

"What you mean?"

"When you get out, man. What you gunna do?"

"Travel probably."

"Travel! You ain't had enough!"

"Not like this! No slop or muck. My own country. Open spaces. Not this. Sun. Sky. Wind devils that billow dust. The coolest, weathered barns, old gray shacks collapsing with years—all spider webs and moss—it's great. Farmland. Clean earth. That's where it's at."

"You'll get it, man," Peterson said. "Just hang on. Don't lose it."

Giles looked at him, quieting "Oh, believe it!" he said. "I will do it. Don't you worry!"

Giles turned back to the maze of hills stretching endlessly below him and far away. He caught a flicker of movement. He hunched forward in his chair. Peterson joined him in his search.

"See anything?"

"Over there. Check it out."

Peterson raised the field glasses, adjusting them. He nodded.

"Whose turn?" Giles asked.

He sighted through the scope, sure now of what he had within his sights. His finger tightened on the trigger.

"Mine, I guess," Peterson conceded.

"Take it, then," Giles offered. He sat back in his chair, took a drink from the bottle, then looked out across the endless range of hills enjoying the brightening sun that warmed his back and melted the infernal, chilling haze.

Peterson—a crack shot—did his job.

Period of Adjustment2:
Tails, You Lose

Someone had a bottle. We passed it around keeping it low. We knew that as long as no one saw it, we'd be all right; we wouldn't be bugged. But let someone see it, we'd all catch hell. They'd worry our butts. We could be shipped. How would we like that? I could see the top sarge's ugly face right now. "Back to the mud!" he'd threaten. No more this good life, plenty of eats, dry bunks, clothing always clean, starched even, cared for by the locals, our "housekeepers," young women, little more than girls who did more for us than just "keep house." So we kept the bottle low, passing it around, following it with a toke of local weed.

The Zone was deadly quiet. Large winged, hooked-nosed birds soared high then dropped. We let them go. They were no sport. They didn't bother us, so we didn't bother them. We watched them glide, soar, then plummet toward the scrubby growth, almost a game reserve, where no man was allowed. The wildlife flourished. But let us see anyone there, our job was to zap them. So we sat and drank and toked and watched for movement.

Most guys took it for sport, at least at first. They always came here from the lines after just having gotten it themselves. Then they seemed to want to get even, zapping everything—at least those in the Zone who shouldn't be there.

I got here the same way. Up to that time, I had played the hero. Fresh from The States, I was doing my bit, defending my country—that sort of thing. Then one day coming back from patrol, while we were sauntering along, we got it—the whole bunch.

I guess we had asked for it. We had been warned. But we thought we were all so cool—you know—seasoned warriors. One time, goofing off as usual, some of our own guys had leaped from the trees.

"Bang! Bang! You're all dead! Everybody laughed. Big joke.

One of them, a real serious dude, always buckin' for rank, had tried to sober us.

"Think we're kidding, huh? We heard you guys for miles! What if we had been gooks? You'd all be zapped!

"Go on! Get lost! Our guys yelled, laughing, strung out on grass. They found the whole scene funny.

Later, when we all did get it for real, there wasn't a sound. One minute we were walking along, goofing off on our way back to camp, the next thing I know, the guy in front of me collapses, just like a limp sack. I guess I was lucky. I thought at first I was dead. But we were close enough to camp, so they got to me fast. After I healed, I got the heebies. So they shipped me here.

Now as we lounged around on watch, I got the bottle. I took a long pull. By now, for me, the stuff was cool. It didn't burn even when I chugged it straight without a brew for a wash. It was good stuff. But then we always got the best, even the weed. They practically gave it to us. Only thing, we weren't suppose to drink while on duty. Get caught—bad scene—"international repercussions!" they'd yell at us. "Bad for civilian morale at home!" "Our image, you know!" That kind of canned baloney. So we kept it low, and we were cool.

I kept the bottle, holding it between my legs. My weapon lay across the arms of my chair. No kiddin'! we had lawn chairs!—all the comforts of home. I watched the Zone, looking out over the sea of low hills that flowed away toward the north. The sun warmed the valleys, flaring the haze that rose from between the hills. The sun through the early morning ground fog made it hard to sight anything. But soon the sun would scatter the haze giving us a clear shot if anything moved. I took another pull from the bottle.

"Come on!" Peterson complained. "Keep it moving! You think you got a lease on that jug?"

I passed the bottle. "I'm going to miss this stuff when they ship me out."

"You can buy it," Gomez suggested.

"Not this cheap!"

"Sure, but there's something better that won't be so easy to get."

Gomez dug in his jacket pocket, brought out the stash then rolled the joint. He lit and sucked. Then he passed it on so that it followed the jug. "Good shit!" he said.

Soon we were stoned. For a while, we forgot why we were here. It just felt good to sit in the sun. We watched the birds sail on the updrafts from the hills. I thought it would be nice to be like that.

"Like what?"

I hadn't realized that I had uttered my thoughts out loud. "Like those birds—they're so free—soaring like that."

"You're flying now, hombre! What for you want to be like some bird. Besides, they're killers, man!"

"Get out of here!"

"You think I'm shitin' you, hombre? Those dudes are hunters. They're fightin' for their lives. Same as us."

"Not me. Right now—with this good shit in me—I don't have a fightin' bone in my body—not even between my legs!"

It felt good to just sit and float and not have to think about why we were here. The few times I first had something in my sights, I had felt a kind of thrill, a surge of power, just like I had felt when I had gone hunting with my father. But here the feeling—at first—had been stronger, more fierce, almost evil when I reminded myself what I had in my sights. Then I had seen the round hit home, the flesh and blood and bone, and it was if I had been hit myself. Yet, later, with the help of booze and weed, I had cultivated a practiced indifference.

"Yeah, but someday you're going miss all this," Gomez offered.

"You will." Peterson agreed.

"Miss what? This? Not me!"

"You've been here too long, man," Peterson soothed.

"You got that right! I'm ready anytime they say go!"

"It's only a job," Gomez offered. "Why sweat it? It's not our war. We didn't start it. The Big Honchos. They always start it!"

"Yeah, man, but look who's got to fight it!"

"Fight? You call this fighting?" Peterson raised the bottle in a toast. "All wars should be like this, man!"

"Keep the bottle down, hombre! You get us all busted!"

"All wars have been the same. You should hear my old man talk."

"The problem with you is you think too much. Look! What would you do? You resist like some guys, you get tossed in the can. They treat you like scum, man, knock you around, break your bones. After you get out, no one will touch you. They treat you like you're some kind of freak or something. This way. You do your tour. You come out a hero, man. They give you benefits. Shit like that."

"Sometimes they ship you out in a bag."

"There you go again! So that's the breaks. That's war. That's life. We all got to go sometime, man. We all got our own war. It's all the same. If you make it, you've got more possibilities that you would have without. Like everything else, it's a gamble, man."

"Possibilities?" What you mean, possibilities?"

"Training . . ."

"Training! For what? For this?" I offered him my weapon. He waved me off.

"Like I said. Benefits, man. You can get a place of you own for practically nothing. How could I get something like that on my own. That's why I joined, man. You think I enjoy this? You can go to school, get an education, get a degree, get yourself a good job, make lots of coins. You see? They make it up to you, if you can hack it."

"They can never make it up to this dude. You're never the same. You come out something you thought you'd never be. And those years are gone!"

"They go no matter what. What would you do instead? Get a crummy job that you soon hate. Run around in some suped-up bomb you owe your life to. Meet some chicita, probably, get in her pants, knock her up, get tied down. That's what you would have done."

"This will stay with you all your life."

"Like my old man," Peterson agreed. "He's still fighting the last one."

"It's the same one," I said.

"He still thinks he's a hero. That's all he's got, man."

"I want something more," I said.

"Don't we all! What makes you so special? That's your problem. You always think you're so cool."

"I'm special, all right! Want me to show you?"

"Cool it, dudes!" Gomez cautioned. "You're being watched. Have a drink."

I didn't want it, but I took the bottle anyway. I pulled on it, but on top of the joint, the booze made me gag. I passed it on. "I've had it," I said. I scanned the Zone. Then I raised the glasses.

"Got something?" Peterson asked.

"Check that out," I said. I passed him the glasses.

"Old eagle eye." he said.

"Just like those birds."

"Whose turn?" I asked.

"Yours," Peterson said.

"Like hell! You can't get off that easy. I had it last time. It's yours, baby. Take it."

"Don't want it," Peterson said.

"Someone's turn. Whose?" Gomez asked.

"Flip a coin," Peterson suggested.

"Heads I win, tails you lose," Gomez joked.

"Cut it out! Someone's got to," I said.

"What for?" Gomez demanded.

"It's our job. Here's your war, baby. Take it."

"Up yours!" Gomez yelled.

"Knock it off!" Peterson said through his teeth. "You'll get us all busted."

We followed his glance toward the command post. Brass and stripes ambled in and out of the tents enjoying the sun. One or two had stopped. They seemed to be watching us. We turned back, quieting, keeping the bottle low. Then Peterson flipped a coin. "Call it!" he demanded.

"Heads!" I cried.

The Fun House

He wandered into the Hall of Mirrors. He entered as easily as he had found the carnival: Driving along the road, coming upon the tents, the plumed banners, the litter, the people, he had stopped. He wandered first among the ambling crowds, between the tents, though noise and rich aromas of food, past strong odors. Then he found the Fun House. Perhaps the blaring loudspeaker, the laughter of the mechanical fat woman, her stiff movements had attracted him. Why? He couldn't say. Then he turned his back to the crowds and noises, the thick aromas and odors and colored lights.

At first, as he moved into what would become a maze, he saw the carnival reflected in the mirrors. He noticed the deep reflection of the sky and clouds. Then the carnival and clouds became disturbed, became a jumble of lights, a confusion moving over the imperfect surface of the mirror at the entrance, until finally he lost himself among the mirrors. As he moved in farther, the laughter of the fat woman faded but remained; the few scattered people who passed him as he stood looking at his own distorted image disappeared slithering around a silvered corner. He was left alone with the distorted image of himself, the quiet murmur of his heart, the loud sound of his own thoughts.

He felt good in a way to be alone. Here, where the noises of the carnival were softened but still could be heard, he could study himself. Continuously distorted in one way or another in one mirror after another he moved slowly down one corner then down another moving without concern, moving with amusement as he saw his image splay then thin, dissipate, diffuse, then be restored.

Here in this maze, his image distorted, he could focus on his life. A short time ago he had been thundering along the expressway toward the distant city where he lived. Before that, he had been at the cabin on the lake packing for his return. He saw the open suitcase, the folded underwear. He reflected on his idle weekend, the leisurely breakfasts while he read, the lounging on the sun-warmed wooden pier beside the placid lake, the drifting boat, the moving rings of skimming water insects. Before the weekend, his life, his work, his days trailed out behind him.

Now, here among the black, plowed fields, the green woods, he had found the carnival. Even now as he wandered the maze he could see in his mind the rush of traffic along the wide road that swept incessantly through blasted trees, through hills of strata, across alluvial plains ripe with stagnant water. Even now he could imagine the city itself: the distant towers, the streets below the towers, his home, his life suspended. He would be there soon; he would take up his life again; he would move again toward some unknown, uncertain future. He would have been there sooner. But he had stopped.

The weekend. Yes. That had been pleasant. He had enjoyed the quiet, the lazy warmth of lounging in bed with rolls and coffee he had made for himself, had served himself, returning to the bed to prop himself and eat, to relax and hold himself within the comfort of his pleasure. He had enjoyed the heavy summer nights beside the lake and the yellow light that had circled him in the stirring darkness of the cabin as he read. Yes, the weekend and this diversion, this spontaneous act were part of the whole. All had restored him.

Perhaps he shouldn't have gone alone. She might have come along had he only asked. They had enjoyed some pleasant times before. Why had he thought they couldn't now. Her involvement, her friends, her activities, her own work had held him off. He guessed that both of them had grown quite used to the idea of doing things apart. So when he thought of the weekend he only thought that he would go alone. She probably wouldn't have gone anyway, he told himself. But perhaps he should have asked.

He decided then that they would have only quarreled throughout the weekend destroying any chance of the serenity he had experienced. They had been doing so much quarreling lately. Apart so much of the time pursuing their individual goals, when they came together they only fought. Perhaps the weekend might have changed all that and might have brought them together again—If they could only keep still, if they could only stop talking. He should try himself, he realized. He should do something. He would, indeed, he decided, if he could just find the exit to this place. He thought then of her, warmed to the thought of her, thrilling at the thought of his new sense of purpose, at the thought of seeing her again.

Something at the entrance had been uttered about a door, something that had been slurred out of the corner of the mechanical mouth of the fat woman as he had entered. Where was that door? He wondered. He should go now, the pleasure of his indiscretion having jaded. He had been amused at first to see his image so distorted. But now he knew he should leave.

He moved through the corridors of mirrors following his receding image that marched away toward an infinite point where his image disappeared. He sought the door that he had heard mentioned confident that he would find that exist and then find himself outside in the cool night air ready to continue his return home. He understood at once that the corridors he wandered through appeared longer because of the mirrors. And he had been in these places before. He never really had much difficulty before. One simply followed the inside wall of the maze; eventually that wall would lead out. But here now something seemed unusual. Here each time he turned a corner expecting to find the exit he only saw another endless corridor. Yet he knew it must end somewhere sometime.

He had heard of others being lost for hours in such a place. He suddenly felt uneasy. He must leave now really. He shouldn't have stopped in the first place. Now he would be late in arriving home. True, he still had the evening, but he always looked forward to relaxing before the start of a new week. Suppose, then, that he had, indeed, become lost. Did they ever keep track of those who came in? Did they ever search if someone didn't reappear after a reasonable time? What would he do if he really were lost? He would be late now in arriving home; that was certain. He examined his watch. It was running. Yes. He held it to his ear and heard the reassuring counterweight; he saw the sweep of the minute hand. He wound it—it mustn't stop—then he checked his winding. Getting the mainspring too tight would ruin the works. Keep calm, he told himself, keep calm.

Who was that staring? The image seemed younger. Could these mirrors do that too—make him seem younger? He looked barely twenty. Those thin pale features that had thickened seemed thinner. The hair seemed fuller. What had he been like then: What had he wanted then? Really truly wanted?

His first real job had been on a fishing boat. He recalled the cold early mornings on the inland sea. He would rise in darkness then make his way through barren streets to the dock, to the yellow warmth, the muffled voices of the coffee shack. How good the first cigarette and coffee had always tasted. Then they would leave easing along the slip between the other boats bobbing in their passing wake. And as they had reached the open water, the light had grayed, and they had moved through early morning fog that seeped upon the quiet water. Then as they worked paying out the nets, the engine a dull comforting throb, the sun would slowly dissipate the fog and steep the bitter early morning chill from his bones.

He had enjoyed that work because of the early morning quiet. Yes, he had even enjoyed the loneliness of his morning thoughts. He had found a mystery in the dawn, a magic that he never had again. Somehow, that magic had escaped him with the dawn and dissipating fog that had brought the day. He recalled now that all the while he had that job he had stunk of fish. So eventually he had moved on to other jobs and other disasters.

He moved now again searching the walls always looking at his image in the mirrors. Turning corners, he always saw the long corridors of his image disappearing far away. Sometimes he heard voices, phantoms that encouraged him. Apparently there was hope after all. So once or twice he had called out, but the voices never emulsified into solid forms. The voices always drifted off and died. He admitted finally that he was lost. Calling to the fading voices moving somewhere in the maze he heard his anxious cries returned by laughter. He resigned to groping through the long corridors.

He slowly forgot about he time. He checked his watch. The watch had stopped. Time had stopped. His life, his work had stopped. He thought about the door. He thought about the carnival beyond. So much time had passed he had difficulty remembering the sounds of the carnival, the sights and aromas and odors, the appearance of the sky that now must be dark. He wondered from time to time why no one came to find him. From time to time he stopped; he listened. Silence. He groped on.

Finally after so much looking at his image, seeing himself so often that he wondered where he began and the mirrors ended, all he really knew was the sound of his throbbing heart against the hollow of his skull. After so much time he turned a corner fully expecting to see another corridor exactly like the others he had always seen. Then one time when he turned a corner, the long corridor raced away to meet the tiny image of a door.

He hurried then choking on his joy. Beside him he saw the following image on the walls along the corridor. He hurried stumbling, afraid the door would be lost, afraid to believe the door was real and was really there. But the image grew, and once again the details of his whole life raced before him. He anticipated their return: his home, his daily drive to work that he had come to dread and that he did in resignation. He thought of the tedium of the work itself, and he thrilled to think that these would be his again: the comfort of that empty desk at work, the intrusions, and the irritations. How he would welcome them once released from this endless corridor of mirrors forever throwing back his distorted image. He thrilled with joy at the dream of his freedom and the thought of blue sky once reflected in the sterile shimmering silver of his mirrors.

He reached the door. He grasped the handle yanking at the handle several times before the door came open. He cried out in despair. Then he set off down the corridor of mirrors that continued beyond the door.

It would never end. When was the last time any voices had floated in his mind echoing off the walls? Why did it never end? He groped, trying to remember but finally despairing. The sounds of voices, the sounds of the carnival, the rich thick aromas and odors: Those had never really been, he decided. He had only imagined them. He was only imagining all this. This was only a terrible dream. He could wake himself if he tried. He tried. He saw his own image staring. Life was not a dream.

He stumbled on crashing against the walls when the corridor ended. Once he fell. He turned the corner crawling while his mind and heart throbbed until he thought they would burst. Then he saw the other door.

He crawled along the corridor of mirrors until finally instead of always inching away before him the image of the door increased. It filled his whole mind. He could see the grains of the wood in the door, the board paneling, and the doorknob. He pulled himself to his feet at the door hanging onto the doorknob suffering to his feet leaning against the door gasping for breath to calm his aching heart, his throbbing brain.

Then he backed away from the door and stood for a long time with his arms hanging at his sides, his head hung forward. His thinning hair fell in his eyes. He stood that way remembering the carnival. He recalled the sounds of voices, the sounds of laughter, sounds of joy, shrieks of fear. He remembered the hills, the woods, the fields in fallow dirt, the smell of new rain on warm earth, the sunrise on the far hills, the birdsong midmorning, the glow of the Wanderer at twilight.

At times his hand reached for the door. But he stood looking at the door dreaming of the green hills far away, dreaming of the possibility of a life beyond the door beyond those green hills, dreaming of his work waiting for him there. He thought of her there. Then he recalled the other door and his disappointment. His fingers slipped from the doorknob. His arms dropped heavily to his sides. He sunk to his knees looking at the door. He sat back against the silvered walls and watched the door. Then after a time he slumped against the wall with his head upon his chest, his gaze upon the door.

They found him there. The door he lay before banged in letting in the rush of sounds, the blare of music, the shrieks from rides, the incessant laughter of the fat mechanical woman bending in derision, her laughter echoing away along the mirrored corridors. The whirling lights swept along the silvered walls. The walls threw back the rainbow light, the color of the deepening sky, the high white clouds that caught the setting sun, the deep green richness of the darkening hills beyond the door.

Ready Witness

This was one race he knew he would win. So as he drove the snaking mountain road to the top, he glanced through openings in the forest on either side. He swept along roaring on the straight ways, squealing on the curves. The dark trees towered and thrust their green boughs into a clear sky. Between the trees, the gorge opened to the valley below, and the valley stretched away to cobalt blue mountains distant and beckoning. At the bottom, he saw the broad and swiftly moving stream now appearing as a rivulet.

He climbed, the wheel steady in his hands, the power beneath his foot reassuring; and as he saw the stream, he recalled the morning swim that still refreshed him. The day began in heat, and the quiet clarity of the water, the school of fish among the mossy rocks beneath the surface had made him seek the pure depths. He felt again the icy shock on his naked flesh, the sharp pain in his testicles. The memory made him shiver as he saw again the stream between the trees.

Then the gorge was closed from view. He turned back to the road. He stomped on the gas pedal. The rear wheels grabbed; the car lurched; he held on; and the straight road raced beneath the car until it snaked again, and he shifted down, took the curve, then suddenly saw the finish: the lodge at the top set at the mountain edge. As he neared, black moving figures became people, the lodge developed balconies and windows with painted shutters. A crowd lined the railings. But it ignored

318

him. Instead, the tourists gazed out across the chasm and the valley to the mountains beyond.

Quieted, brought back to himself, he parked the car between the proper white lines on the asphalt, locked his wallet inside, then walked through the lodge to the railing at the edge of the gorge. He studied the scene: the trees and the mountains, the faces of the cliffs, his eyes dazzled by the sun off the blue-gray rock. He caught tiny movements. His eyes swept the sheared mountains. Again, he caught a glint. Then he had them. He watched the struggle of the gnat-like men on the sharp wall across the gorge.

He envied their endurance. They hung there. One, recovering, moved, groped a quarter of an inch, then stopped. The others, reviving, followed: first one, then the other, then the third inched and stopped, groped and stopped, then hung exhausted. But they persisted beyond exhaustion; they endured; they continued; they dangled from crumbling rock. And all that struggle was simply to get to the next ledge, to get to the top. He had gotten there more easily. Once there, all that he had to look forward to was the long weary ride down. Unless, of course, something happened: a pylon easing from the rock; someone losing grip. He could see them all twisting, twirling silently downward to the thick green plush below.

He grew tired from watching their struggle. Below the balcony, squirrels sat on haunches begging for the food people had learned to offer them. He watched the people feeding them; then he searched again for the climbers across the gorge. He gave up, then turned and left the crowd, the squirrels, the climbers on the cliff, and he walked up the path to the edge of the mountain.

He stood alone; he leaned over the lip; he looked down to the bottom of the vast gorge. The river was a brown streak through green felt, the highway a black stripe. He watched the moving speck of vehicle. He looked again across to the climbers.

The last time he had stood here, he had nearly fallen. Standing at the edge that dropped away into nothing, he had wondered what it would be like to fall so far. He had watched himself descend. Recalling the time diving from a high bridge when he was a child, he remembered how it had seemed so long before he had hit the water at one point in his descent, suspended, he had become afraid.

The last time he had stood here, he had let his imagination extend the dive from the bridge in his youth, and he had seen himself endlessly falling, until leaning forward, he had teetered at the brink. But that time someone had been there. A voice had cried out, and he had seen the valley break away below. He had grown afraid, had backed away from the edge. He had turned. The man had searched his face.

"That was close," the man had said.

"Yes. Thank you," he had lied." I was dazzled by the height."

He had tried to remain calm. He had felt the man watching as he had turned. He had made his way back along the trail to the car. Yet, that one witness, that one voice crying out had helped, had called him, and he had suddenly seen the mountains and the deep gorge. In contrast, his life, his trouble seemed almost petty. His problem was no problem. Why should one dead man matter so much? He was exaggerating again. Dwelled on enough some slight by someone, his smallest failure reflected back upon himself, destroyed him. Realizing his absurdity, he had driven slowly back along the snaking road to the bottom of the gorge.

There on solid ground he was safe. Or so he thought for a while, at least, the vision of himself upon the mountain, his gnat-like figure against the vast sky had carried him, giving him reassurance. Yet even in his acceptance, in his sense of new perspective lay the possibility of a more profound despair. For when the brute facts came back at him, they caught him up then pressed him with their persistent crush, and he had felt again how he had failed.

Now as he stood here, he saw the clash and chaos of his daily life that had sent him here again to prove something, prove that he could come here again after being so afraid. Below, at the bottom of the gorge, remembering, his fear had grown so great he had been plagued with dreams from which he bolted with a cry. The quiet night sounds had steadied him, and he had lain awake thinking, convincing himself how easy, how interesting, perhaps, it might be to travel here again.

Then morning sounds would bring back his world. The low declaring voice raised in strident song outside his window; the insistent blatant car horn coming every day, starting at the street end, then rising in one continuous intensity as the car approached. Jarred from stirring, sensuous dreams, he would lie there in the early morning listening to the exchange of thick voices, he involved unwillingly in their world, unwillingly brought back to himself again to the silent stirring shadows on the sunlit shade and later to the image of a full bodied woman with rich moist lips within the radiant sunlight who turned away from his long gaze.

Here, too, was sunlight. Here, too, the radiance and scattered shadows exposing soul and accusing him for one man's death, his father's, a suicide that had haunted him always. He, the only witness to a sudden, individual act, witness to a choice with infinite consequences, to the violence of and the denial of life and to a denial of him, he, the son powerless to halt the savage sound, that fierce explosion beside his bed waking him with splattering flesh, the ripe, thick taste and feel of blood, and then the crushing burden of his father's full, dead weight.

Each day, grown to an image of his father's former self, he had made his heavy way: A stop for breakfast: the same cafe, the same silent, sleep-thick, chewing people absorbed in satisfying news. He, a witness, watched through curling, morning smoke the same bustling waitress who kept them all alive, who offered him his usual morning toast, already cold. Each day, he ate, he paid, he left, turning up the street toward night, toward muted streetlamps, his room, his recurring dream in which he always dropped his keys.

He grabbed for them, then gave them up and having lost them, dove.

He stretched his arms and fingers toward the cliff across the way, then hung there for a moment before the weight of his world pulled him down toward the brown streak, the green felt of trees, the moving speck of life along the black strip of highway. He went down with one last look at the private struggle of the men across the gorge.

Then he was falling; he knew he was falling; and for the first time, he realized what he had done. He was surprised, but he was calm; he was falling. He felt suspended, just as before, just as in his dream from which he would soon awaken. How easily he could forget about the actuality of what he had done. How easily he might forget about the consequences, the inevitability. He wanted to roll over on his back and watch the billowing clouds and hovering birds, those circling, soaring forms slowly rising above him, receding from him as he went down. He forced himself to think, to remember where he was, what he had done, his only real act, and suddenly he was afraid.

This was no dream. He knew his helplessness: nothing he could possibly do would wake him now. Terrified, he screamed, as if somehow that scream would release him from his commitment, as if that sound could free him from his act. Then moments passed and finally even his scream became absurd. He knew its uselessness; and he accepted, he surrendered; he spread his arms and fingers to embrace the wind that ripped his face, his clothes,. He gave himself to the force that pressed against his thighs, his arms, his loins. Finally, he was nothing, and suddenly he felt released. Freed from himself, he submitted; he felt the surge from his loins and he surrendered himself, surging deeper, longer than any time he could remember.

And with that surge, his throbbing pulse blinded him to the ripe earth that rushed to take him so that he did not see the green plush breaking into hills and trees. He did not see the trees spread into boughs. He did not see the grass beneath the trees.

He felt a shock, so great and hard, it felt like ice.

CPSIA information can be obtained at www.ICGtesting.com
Printed in the USA
LVOW13*1653280114

371326LV00012B/798/P